Cod in Devon!

Sandy Fish

Lyra

Granny and I were in the gift shop
in Hartland Quay in Devon and I saw
this book.

I thought it would be a really great
read for a lovely young girl I knew,
and that was you!

Hope you like it.

Lots of love from

Grandad and

Granny

xxx &
xxx

Cod in Devon!

by

Sandy Fish

Blue Poppy Publishing 2020

Cover design by Paul Humphreys inkycovers.com

Published by Blue Poppy Publishing, Devon

ISBN – 97-1-911438-67-0

First edition.

To

My Mum for the Inspiration

and

Mrs B for the Patience

CHAPTER 1

"I'm sorry, Howard, but there really isn't anywhere else, it won't be for long."

Jan inched through the door into the cool shade of a gigantic information board on the lookout for its next victim. Only the foolish ignore a font large enough to read from Pluto, so she looked and instantly wished that she hadn't.

'We are not responsible for any loss or damage, howsoever caused'.

All she wanted to do was park for a few minutes, not stand in front of a pompous proclamation that sought to sidestep all responsibility for these ridiculously miniscule parking bays. But her feet refused to budge, a sense of foreboding had them glued to the tarmac. She wavered at this chilling message of authority. To park or not to park? Was the question that bounced around her anxiety annex until she realised that cameras were on the lookout for chancers who hadn't paid.

How much? Is the next question as she took off towards the meter fully expecting to find a 'pay what you think it's worth' button; she returned two minutes later and five pounds lighter.

Any other day she would have driven into the leafy car park half a mile up the road but that isn't an option when you're already ten minutes late and Jan didn't do late.

Her restless fingers danced across the bonnet. The details of two oversized family cars that threatened Howards paint work were noted in case a claim for damage became necessary in this already contentious domain. Then, she drew breath from deep beneath her Vibram soles and bolted to the station uncomfortably flawed and fashionably anxious.

The short ramp at Tiverton Parkway offered only the briefest moment for composure; she checked her watch and hoped for a miracle. But time did not stand still. As she pushed the door, ten minutes had been lost for ever.

A compact ticket hall provided the perfect arena for Hayley to occupy centre stage. Unmistakably an Elliot child she stood bronzed and radiating amid the casual commuters. Even at fifty-five and slightly overweight, she exuded youth and mischief.

"G'day, Sis," she boomed confidently.

Moving forward at pace, Jan reduced the gap between them in an effort to close down the spectacle that might make loud reference to lateness. Her sister expects, older sisters do or at least she used to.

"How was your journey?"

Hayley ignored the question and grabbed her sister for an affectionate heart stopping hug.

"It's been terrible, sat up in Bristol for eight hours I won't get back. Shared a wooden bench with a no-hoper on one side and a doughboy squeezed on the other. Couldn't even catch a bit of shuteye between the whingeing and the snoring. But hey look at you, still a skinny and shy little thing aren't yah? Thought that police force would have toughened you up a bit."

"I could have collected you from Bristol if you'd let me know."

"What? not complete me journey when I've paid for a ticket? No, I'm getting me money's worth."

Jan freed herself from the warm embrace that had caused a minor meltdown and tried to shift the focus elsewhere with vague compliments regarding Hayley's healthy complexion. But when that awkwardly petered out, she took hold of the lone suitcase and directed her sister to the splendour of a June morning, presently obscured by the frenzy of taxis and their choking cloud of diesel fumes.

The case with a mind of its own bounced with random glee across the car park whilst Jan's mind was being reprimanded over the ten-minute issue. For all her planning, she had failed to make sufficient allowance for unforeseen events, events that had led to this wholly avoidable crack in her ice shelf. It was the yoghurt pot in the cupboard incident. It can't have been there long, she'd had some for breakfast. But it spoke of absent-minded chaos that Jan was not about to subscribe to. Consequently, the cupboards had to be emptied and checked before she could even think about leaving the house.

"Must say, even though you're late, you did bring some weather with you. Pretty nice for England, although with it being winter back home, it feels quite normal."

Jan loaded the suitcase onto a protective sheet in her forensically vacuumed boot alongside a cooler bag, a wrapped hospital-style blanket and her mandatory emergency overnight kit. The word normal had temporarily pushed lateness aside. *Normal,* she thought, taking note of what it felt like at 07:03 in the morning.

With military efficiency, Howard's paintwork was scrutinised for dents, scuffs or signs of interference. Only then did she invite Hayley to take a seat. She then carefully closed the door, took a few slow deep breaths and walked to the driver's side hoping the clumsy cloud of difficulty would soon disperse.

"Like I say, I'm surprised you were late. I mean you police can drive at any speed you like, can't you?"

"No, no that isn't true and besides, I'm not in the job anymore. My last day yesterday, so as of now, I'm just a normal person."

Jan stopped herself from going on, realising it didn't sound right but she didn't know how else to say it. It had been thirty years, more than half of her life in uniform upholding law and order. Now with barely seven hours under her belt she had entered an unfamiliar world without back-up or intelligence.

With her estranged sister strapped into the passenger seat, the journey to the motorway had all the qualities of a driving test; fear, apprehension and cripplingly sensitive peripheral vision that tried to anticipate the emergency stop signal whilst nerves unravelled in the footwell.

"Long overdue this little reunion, beauty of an idea you had there I reckon." Hayley's words poured with approval.

"Well, I know you had the furthest to travel but I'm glad you could find the time to come. It's easier for me now that I'm retired." Jan took a moment to let her words sink onto a soft pillow, amused by the enormity of this word that she had always associated with the elderly, not a fifty-year-old. She breathed slowly and deeply and as quiet as she could manage before her next attempt at relaxed conversation.

"Have you heard anything from Mike?"

"Well, there's a story right there, he's really difficult to get hold of, he's more mysterious than you are."

"I'm not mysterious. I just don't need a big fanfare; I like to quietly get on with things."

"Yeah so long as those *things* aren't people," she laughed playfully and pushed Jan's arm. "Honestly how did I end up with a brother and sister who find it so hard to speak to anyone?"

"Well, I don't do social media, it's too public and out there."

"It's supposed to be flaming public, that's how normal people communicate these days."

It was a point well-made but didn't sit comfortably with Jan and her newly appointed internal tug-of-war team. They were ready to contest the issue, make a case for her to opt out and still call herself *normal.*

At the M5 she headed south, assuming that south would be the right direction. The last time she'd heard from Mike was seventeen years ago when he rang to say he couldn't go to aunt Ethel's funeral. He'd mentioned 'Cornwall' and 'committed' in the same breath and rang off shortly afterwards. She would have noted his number, but it was withheld. He always sent a card at Christmas and occasionally for her birthday. And, although he never offered his address, over the years when the ink wasn't overly smudged, she had gleaned St Austell as the postal sorting office.

"I'm assuming we're heading for Cornwall; is that right?"

"Yeah, just head for Cornwall, lives by the sea I reckon, why wouldn't you? I mean look at the size of Straya, no one in their right mind lives in the centre."

"Somebody must live in the centre."

"Like I say, no one in their *right* mind lives in the centre. We're bang on Airlie Beach, it's ace. Looking out across the water, listening to the ocean, feeling the warm breeze as you wake up to the excitement of the day. What drongo wants to go inland and live in the dusty fields with all that racket from the cane toads?"

"Well, yes, you have a point," said Jan trying to imagine Airlie Beach. "But you might be surprised to learn that the centre of Cornwall *is* occupied and it's quite dense in places."

Jan's grip on the steering wheel intensified as the scant detail of their destination enveloped her. Expansive breaths plumbed the familiar depths of her lungs as she tried, discreetly, to conceal her inability to do vague.

"Anyway, I'd have thought you'd have a big folder on Mike; spill all the dirt with me. You know, with your police computer, get his address, phone number, offending history, job, library number all that sort of stuff."

"Hayley, that's not allowed, it's an offence, there is no way I would even dream of doing that. I know no more about Mike than he's already let on and that's pretty much nothing."

"Wasted opportunity I'd say; I hope you're not going to be all stiff upper lip on this trip. It's time to shake loose, live dangerously."

"That won't include breaking the law or doing anything remotely dishonest, it's not who I am."

"Well, you haven't lived in the real world yet, that's all I'm saying."

Hayley had the wisdom of a mother long before she became one. And it was true, it was early days, early hours to be precise, not exactly a full picture of reality. Nevertheless, Jan had every confidence in the protection offered by her integrity armbands.

"Okay look, I'll Facebook him and get the details, it might take our entire journey to get a response, like I said, you two are mysterious." Hayley unlocked her phone and set about an elaborate sequence of taps and swipes that eventually made a connection with her social media world.

Jan ignored this latest attack against the person she had become and instead, returned to the unknown destination problem that splashed around, uninvited, in her stomach acid. Putting discomfort aside, this problem had spawned a further raft of concerns primarily; whether she could find a safe place to park Howard and where she could get fuel. A full tank wouldn't last long after three speculative laps of the Cornish coastline looking for who knew where.

With no estimation available for their time of arrival, Jan fell back on familiar practises. Start with what you know, she thought, her mind staring into a jumbled basket of litter. 07:26, the time was always a good place to start. So, if she drove directly to the Cornish border, that would take them to approximately 09:00. It would be unrealistic to drive past a brew stop, particularly with the way things seemed to be going. So, adding an extra hour would see them at the border by 10:00. Jan took a calming breath, with the next couple of hours planned out, there was no need to worry just yet.

Hayley, meanwhile, had buried her face into Facebook and momentarily disconnected from the real world. This provided much needed respite for Jan who could now relax her shoulders and cruise along the nearside lane unchallenged. Her thoughts turned to Mike and his life and how he had turned out. As a boy he'd been obsessed with trains and anything mechanical. She marvelled at his ability to occupy himself for hours in the total solitude of his imagination. He was five years younger and she envied him for being so absorbed and clever. What was it like for a young boy in a house full of women? How did he identify? Was he okay? Why had they not kept in touch?

The memory of childhood turned its attention to the front seat, the sister who went away just when Jan craved company and affirmation. Hayley had grown up fast, stayed out late and eventually, or as soon as she could in fact, left them behind. Overwhelmed with feelings she didn't understand, Jan took up residence in Hayley's bed and mourned her departure. It was aunt Ethel who eventually coaxed the timid creature back to the light with a piano and books and kindness.

Hayley's phone was now making its way to her bag and it appeared she was about to re-enter Earth's orbit and dock with reality. So, to avoid any potential atmosphere, or further accusations of awkwardness, Jan headed up the homecoming.

"Like I said, I'm glad we're all getting together. I think no matter how difficult it might be, it's important that we all catch up, I mean we're all we've got."

"You speak for yourself; I've got my Len, and the boys – of course, fully fledged and left me nest. The boys I mean, I've still got Len, the lummox, going through his mid-life crisis. Anyway, I think after all this time it would be rude not to catch up with your siblings. Though I'm already concerned about you being out here in the big wilderness, now you've quit that police job."

"I didn't quit, I retired, there's a whole world of difference."

"Exactly, a whole different world."

"Well, that's fine," said Jan. "I've spent enough time with the liars and the cheats and the aggressive nobodies, it's time to live differently, as far away from the criminal world as I can get."

"Jeez, good luck with finding your dream-like utopia, what about the real people? You'll miss them you know."

"I don't think so. I refuse to share my retirement space with anyone who skates rough shod over my values."

There was a finality to Jan's minor outburst, but Hayley didn't seem to be on that page.

"Well, get you, Sis," she said as if preparing for a declaration of her own. "I'm still not entirely certain how you managed to get into the police force looking at your track record."

"Honesty and integrity, it's what the police stand for, it defines you, it drives your every thought and action and I'm proud of that." Jan smiled in a private way, comfortable on familiar ground. "My track record, as you put it, is without blemish."

Hayley was looking out of the passenger window and not, it appeared, at the view. She'd covered her eyes and nose to stifle her response but was exposed by jiggling shoulders that conveniently gave her away.

Jan was adamant that she wouldn't be drawn into her sister's juvenile attempt to undermine and trivialise important values but nonetheless, it had to be addressed.

"What now? What's so funny about who I am?"

"How quickly you forget. If honesty and integrity are what you stand for tell me, did you mention anywhere on your application form the small matter of shoplifting?"

Jan's eyes flashed from the road to Hayley's face in the briefest of moments, eager to understand the nature of this accusation.

"What shoplifting?"

"So, miss honesty and integrity, you have told a lie, your whole career built on sand." The laughter grew louder and a whole universe more irritating.

"Hayley, this is not funny in any way. I'm going to stop at the services. I think some coffee is in order." Hayley continued to snort as Jan wrestled with her mad idea to put a family reunion at the top of the 'Must Do' list.

Had this been a day out with an assumed friend, Jan would be looking for the earliest opportunity to terminate the excursion, make some excuse to remove herself from this unnecessary discomfort.

This is my time, my life, my way, she thought turning onto the slip road. But in so many ways it wasn't. After all, she had been late, not Hayley and above any other difficulty, they were sisters and they had to carry on. Cod ham it, if only I'd been on time, I'd have been waiting on the platform, showing her how important this is, the years would have fallen away and I would not be standing on my back foot. Not that I have a back foot, what a stupid thing to say, Janet Elliot.

At a safe and courteous speed Jan directed Howard to a quiet area of the car park just as the jury returned their verdict.

"So, officer, guilty as charged, a blemish on your character, a criminal record." Hayley bellowed with mock judicial superiority before she fell about laughing again.

Away from the oasis of plenty, the engine fell silent; Jan gulped for breath and turned to face her sister.

"If you're referring to the time that I entered a shop, selected an item and left without offering payment then yes, in that respect I have a blemish on my character that I have had to live with. It hasn't been easy, I immediately regretted it, the consequences were more impactive than you ever imagine they could be at the time. It shaped and guided my entire career and I have been a better person for it."

Hayley wasn't done with this topic and clearly saw further mileage in her exposé.

"So, did you lie on your application?"

"I did not lie; I was six years old and I took a Fruit Salad or a Black Jack, whatever they were called, from the corner shop, total cost one old penny."

"I knew it, I was right, all police are corrupt!" Hayley folded her arms and gloated in a manner that would not have been acceptable in an English court of law. She seemed determined to rinse every last ounce of pain from this nugget of information. "Oh yes, and whilst we're on the subject, what about your respect for race and diversity? You can't call a sweet a Black Jack."

Jan found herself swimming in an imaginary whirlpool of doom with a distinct lack of her buoyancy aids but, with measured care, she presented her summary.

"Firstly, I did not name the sweet and secondly, I was below the age of criminal responsibility, a customer."

"None paying. That doesn't exactly make you a customer does it?"

"Look, we were kids if you care to remember, learning the ropes, the tough lessons that stay with you. You were only eleven years old yourself, I thought you had more important issues to think about."

"Yes, like how to *spend* my pocket money."

"Like I said, it shaped my whole life, I had guilt you shouldn't have at that age and no idea how to make it go away. I liked Mr Morley; he was just one of those lovely people. He was kind, well known and he had a sweet shop. Everything a kid could want but, because of that one stupid act, I felt that he hated me, that everyone would be looking at me and talking about what I'd done. I never went into the shop again, it was awful. I wished for that moment again and again so that I could pay and feel normal."

"So *that's* why you had loads of money when we went on holiday. Where did you hide that? I spent a good deal of wasted time looking for it whilst you were in the bath."

Some incidents never leave you, no matter how much counselling or therapy, they are etched into your history and shudder through your whole body any time it suits them. So vivid, like yesterday, her heart drummed that familiar rhythm of angst.

Today was my clean slate, my new beginning, fifty years bundled and cut loose until my sister arrived, she thought, struggling to keep her head above the waterline.

Without full consideration, Jan leaked further detail.

"It bothered me, hurt me if you must know. I was glad when we moved away, although I had trained myself out of a sweet craving by then. The guilt crippled me, I was determined to be the model of honesty, to challenge wrongdoing and to ensure that the rest of my formative years were within the law."

A silence lay across the car like a blanket of snow on a windless morning. Jan shivered and took a long steady breath.

"We've all got secrets, Sis," said Hayley opening her window to allow the beautiful June air to waft in. "Did you mention it though, the old one penny shoplifting?"

Jan gathered herself for what she hoped was the final round of questioning before this topic could finally be put to rest. Then, quietly, she delivered her closing statement.

"Yes, if you must know. I purged myself at the interview, I had to get it out there, lay myself bare. But actually, I felt stupid, this tiny morsel of information was swept away without interest or scrutiny. It left me exposed, but unburdened and free to pursue the only career that could indemnify my actions."

Hayley rested her arm through the window as her mouth broadened for the curtain call. "You really are a fruitcake; I can't believe you haven't let that go. Anyway, more importantly, what's for brekky?"

CHAPTER 2

"Aunt Eth used to take us for picnics, didn't she?" said Hayley peeling back a slice of the rough-cut granary. I thought you might have grown out of it by now, but hey I don't dislike a cut lunch or whatever you want to call this. Mind you, I didn't know we were in the grips of a ham ration."

"Do you take sugar?" asked Jan in an effort to divert attention away from the catering; she carefully poured two half cups of coffee into the deep reusable mugs.

"Yeah, I'll have one please. Well, will you look at that Thermos, haven't seen one in years. Back home we just have the Esky except, we're trying to keep everything flippin' cool."

Jan spooned the sugar with chemistry precision and stirred gently. With mugs secure in the holders, she arranged a small pile of paper serviettes on the dashboard and placed one across her lap before carefully unwrapping a sandwich. She reflected on the practical picnic habit that had stayed with her, the connection not credited in any great way to aunt Ethel until now.

"Yes, she was fond of taking us out into the countryside or down to the beach or wherever the bus was going that day. Do you remember her chequered bag with plastic handles and a zip across the top? I always looked forward to the surprise of lunch when she finally pulled it open."

"Yeah it was nice, but you must have been at that age where you hung on to it. I reckon I was moving more towards proper food at a café, not that she could afford it."

"She was good to us; well she was good to me. I think Mike was happy but it was always hard to tell. It can't have been easy for a single woman to have three kids dumped on her doorstep. Cod knows how I would feel if that happened to me now."

"Were you the only one at the funeral?" asked Hayley still playing with the bread, "it was too far for me you know and costs a fortune to get here."

"It was a pretty quiet affair. There was a small group from the Salvation Army, a neighbour, some colleagues from the library and a couple of chaps from the Institute of Advanced Motorists."

"But she didn't drive, did she? Well, we didn't have a car at our disposal that's for sure."

"I don't know if she had a licence, it didn't occur to me at the time."

"You know, Sis, I'm beginning to see some huge missed opportunities, all this information you could have found out about our family. I don't know what you did in your police world, but like I say, you did have the opportunity."

"I did not have the desire to lose my job in the frivolous pursuit of a family tree fact find. Aunt Ethel had her whole life plan rudely interrupted; I wouldn't blame her if she only told us what we needed to know. I was just grateful she took on the burden. She certainly helped me turn out okay. It's Mike I worry about."

"If you worried about him so much, why didn't you stay in touch?"

Jan couldn't answer that, she could blame her career perhaps, maybe the job had made her cynical and hard hearted although she didn't believe she was, particularly.

"It's been difficult, I threw myself into my career."

"I blame aunt Ethel for everything," said Hayley rising up the mischief scale.

Jan instantly stopped chewing. "But you're okay, aren't you? Nothing happened did it? I mean you could have said something."

"No, my little Lamington, I mean you and Mikey, the troubled twins." Hayley laughed and rattled Jan's arm then patted it. "You're still easy to wind up, I'm so glad I came, we're going to have some fun."

With a mouth full of sandwich and a mind full of memories, Jan tried to make sense of her head. Hayley and I seem okay, at least two of us have survived with our morals more or less intact. She took a few long, quiet breaths and trundled in the direction of her happy place where she could observe her sister in detail from the safe outpost.

The Elliot's are a good-looking bunch, she thought, noting the thick straight eyebrows and deep dark eyes that they both possessed. A gift from their handsome father and stunning mother who never got to grow old. They weren't there to guide and care for each child in turn and weren't able to help her as she struggled with Mike.

Grey marched between the healthy brown waves of Jan's short tidy hair. As it would have done through Hayley's had it not been suffocated at the roots, by her stylish surfer-chick blonde treatment. Even so they were unmistakably related, sisters joined on a level that needed little scrutiny or reference. Each family, unique and special, sharing behaviours, attributes, DNA and glue. This, often-underrated, truth that connected one person to another began to ooze like expandable foam into the long-neglected void around Jan's heart. She was so absorbed by the reality of sitting next to an actual relative that Hayley's casual disregard for crumb catching went unnoticed.

"What you smiling at?" said Hayley picking up her coffee.

"I can't explain it; it's just that it's quite amazing to be with someone who shares family quirks. I mean look how you hold your mug between your thumb and middle finger; I thought that was just me."

"Well, Sis, I think you'll find that I started that. I mean look at our long straight chip-like fingers, Elliot specials they are. We had a fascination with hands if my memory serves me right. No one had hands like we did. Even little Mikey had pretty big shovels. Now, the mug thing came about because we were looking at our special hands and deciding what job each finger should have. Do you remember? The pinkie finger was for being posh, drinking tea when aunt Eth's friends came around. But we had to take it too far, walking about with our pinkie sticking out all through polite conversation. Jeez I'd forgotten that me self. That was a funny thing. Then your ring finger, well Robert as we called him, that was for scratching. Thumb and middle for tumblers and small items and the pointy finger for pointing!"

Jan held out her hands and went through the actions like an animated child eager to be involved. She remembered Mike barely in control of his faculties, learning the Elliot code and causing fits of laughter as he acted out their secretive sign language.

It was now 08:18 and the *late* incident began to evaporate from her memory as an improving picture danced into view along the horizon. She'd glimpsed their strange youthfulness held within the archives of long matured bodies.

This is inexplicably amazing, almost spiritual, thought Jan floating in her private happy world. I'm sharing a space with a proper relative.

The Elliot bond had emerged like a butterfly from a chrysalis, colours became vibrant, wings strong, all senses focused, a beautiful maiden flight just moments away. Her face radiated from a smouldering pile of ash, a closed pit of emptiness, for decades a place of neglect. Now, free running along a giddy teenage path, carefree and exposed, in a whirlwind of unfamiliar elation.

Slow, slow, don't get carried away, there is a lot to achieve today, she thought. Highs get dealt a devastating low blow sooner or later, don't be that person. Jan dragged herself back into the moment and having discounted crisps as too messy and chocolate definitely off the menu, she asked Hayley if she'd like an apple.

"No, I'm good thanks, I'll carry on with this sanger, I like a challenge," she said fixing her gaze on Jan. "Look at us, the Elliot girls, picking up where we left off, except I hope we don't have to share a bedroom on this trip; jeez I'm done with that. Where's me privacy eh?"

In all the planning and research that Jan had attempted to overlay on this journey, she hadn't actually booked accommodation. There were options of course, the best possible outcome would be Mike turning out absolutely fine, all was forgiven, lives in a big house, insists they stay. Or possibly, Mike lives just over the border, mission accomplished he doesn't have room so they drive back to Jan's. Or a combination of the two; Mike lives further down towards the pointy end in which case she had a handful of hotels to try should it get late in the day. Thankfully, the peak season on the peninsula was still a few weeks away which left the option of a last-minute room firmly on the planning table. At the back of her mind though lingered another option; what if he's hostile, resentful and unforgiving?

"It was tough for me too having to share a room you know. You put on me something rotten. The cutlery, cheese grater, the box of Sugar Puffs and a trail of toothpaste that all mysteriously turned up in my bed. Items of school uniform going missing, your very loud and repetitive playing of Rod Stewart songs into the evening when I was trying to sleep. I'm surprised I'm not a nervous wreck."

"Too late," laughed Hayley.

On the crest of this warm and fuzzy cascade, Jan wanted to share more with her sister, it felt natural and possible, but something held her back. She couldn't take it for granted, these feelings couldn't be guaranteed. Instead, she took another sandwich in an attempt to soak up the spicy internal soup that was trying to bubble.

In a clearing, two rows ahead, a blue Mini Clubman drew her attention. It contained a large dog barking and bouncing across the rear suspension.

"Do you remember the old Mini Clubman? It was about half the size of that one. Mum used to run us to school in it although I can't ever remember sitting in the front."

"Well you wouldn't my, little Sis, would you? that was my seat. Older sisters get these perks."

"That was hardly fair, with me in the back hanging on to Mike. You try holding a solid lump of a baby when you're only a kid yourself. Thank cod there was seat belt legislation by the time I joined the police. I could educate the irresponsible parents who didn't secure their children properly. Unless they were in the back of course, made so much sense allowing kids to roll around on the back seat until 1991."

"Do you keep saying cod?" asked Hayley picking up a serviette.

"Yes, and it's not a big issue thank you. There's no call for swearing, or being sworn at or mixing in company where a sentence can't reach the full stop without the F word."

Hayley slowly wiped her fingers, looking as if she had reached a verdict on the subject, but instead moved on to another matter.

"Do you think mum and dad died because they weren't wearing seat belts?"

The unexpected reference to the premature demise of their parents flummoxed Jan who, until now, had always assumed that her search for answers was a one-woman crusade. She had trawled over the incident countless times. Looking for vital information, the facts that might put her mind at rest. Apart from a short report from the coroner's office citing 'Accidental Death', there was nothing that could satisfy the curious mind.

"I really don't know. I was hoping that being in the job, might help but it didn't. At first, I bombarded my sergeant endlessly, where could I go, who could I ask? But, like I said, the information held by police isn't something to be used for your own private research and I wasn't about to jeopardise my career. I did write to a couple of government departments though, you know like anyone can, but if they did know anything, they were unwilling to share it with me. It's haunting really to think that some official might have prevented information, if there is any, from coming through to the next of kin."

"Exciting though eh? I mean, they weren't just our mum and dad, they were... I don't know celebrities maybe, people up there, doing stuff. What if they were training to be the first husband and wife astronauts?"

"It doesn't matter, Hays, I'm really sorry but it exhausts me, I've spent years dwelling on the subject. I just wish they were still here, our mum and dad."

Like a disused railway line, Jan had felt abandoned, left to make a new life for herself, an unshared history. And now she wondered how different life might have been if, perhaps, their parents had been running ten minutes late.

"Sorry, Sis, it was on me mind on the plane, coming back to England and all, it brings things home. So many questions."

The Mini Clubman had their full silent attention, each with their own thoughts until Hayley decided to share.

"Now, what I really want to know is why you haven't been snapped up. Surely when you're thrust together with all those police people somebody must catch your eye?"

"Career, that's what it is. Back when I joined in the eighties there were strict rules and an undercurrent that moved you downstream if you even thought about having a child. That was just about career over. Had a few relationships if you must know but nothing serious. The job was more important to me and now, having spent more than half my life in uniform it feels odd to be just wandering around in my own clothes."

"Yeah, I can see your point, but don't worry; I can always take you shopping, get you spruced up."

"I'm being serious thank you. It's just odd, I don't expect you to understand that."

"I do, Sis, I think. Anyway, it's a good job I've arrived to help you find your feet." Hayley rattled Jan's arm again with an affection that Jan had started to relish.

"Now, I'm going to take me self over to the dunny and freshen me self up, shouldn't be too long. Are you coming?"

"No. I won't just yet," replied Jan. "I'm going to have an apple and wait, otherwise I'll have to pack this lot away from sight."

"Relax, Sis. Let go of the job; who'd want to steal our sangers? You're supposed to have retired from all that stuff."

"Yes, I have and as I said, I fully intend to step away from distrust, lies, suspicion and double dealing and live a normal life in the community, blissfully unaware of the existence of crime."

"Well, it doesn't much sound like you've started yet."

"Look, one thing is certain even as a civilian it should be obvious to anyone that thieves will steal whatever they can if it's on display in a vehicle."

"Even five-day-old ham hidden in a sandwich loaf?"

"It isn't five days old and anyway they don't know that do they?"

"What? that the ham's out of date?"

"No, Hays. One thing leads to assumptions, they only need a tiny hint of a possession left on display and they wonder what else you've got."

"Crisps or a satsuma?"

"I'm not prepared to take the risk; I'll wait here for you."

"Okay, Marple. I'll leave you to adjust to retirement whilst I mingle with the normal people." She climbed out of the car and slammed the door a bit too heavily mouthing "sorry" through the glass as she headed off to the facilities.

The ham's not that bad, thought Jan rearranging her cooler bag. She took a serviette and brushed crumbs from the front passenger seat into her hand and lowered the window to scatter them for the birds. A disorderly platoon had been gathering and flew forward to reap the meagre offering.

The Mini Clubman kennel continued to frustrate the unruly dog. Might be an Alsatian, she thought, repulsed by the Turkish bath of steam it had panted across the windows. She decided it looked like high maintenance and wouldn't be featuring anywhere on the 'Must Do' list of her new world. Maybe a cat? Although they can smuggle a fur coat full of debris into a house, padding their muddy feet over sofas and seats. Maybe nothing would be best she concluded while checking for crumbs around the handbrake and settling into her apple.

Jan had always felt the most affected by the death of her parents; she was the sensitive ten-year-old middle child. Constantly looking for ways to demonstrate her worth and justify her place in the family, she was the squirrel, active and productive looking for ways to make her parents proud. Her school achievements would fly hot off the press to be thrust into their hands before the headmaster's signature was even dry.

Hayley on the other hand at fifteen saw herself on level terms with their parents, growing up fast and not paying too much attention to academic work. Her interests lay in fashion, music and boys.

Mike was just five and outwardly made a seamless transition from the family home to his aunt's house. With his box of Lego to play with, all that had changed was the carpet he sat upon. If a five-year-old could feel indifference, then maybe that was it. He was a quiet, self-contained boy creating detailed structures from the depths of his imagination without even the slightest connection to a dark or damaged origin.

Children and death had been enduring events throughout Jan's career. All too often she was the officer on the doorstep holding the crying child in cosy pyjamas. A favourite coat, a small bag of possessions and a life changed forever.

Inadvertently she became a specialist in the 'death message'. The sombre faced officer in uniform opening and closing the garden gate in a slow, deliberate manner. The arrival at the front door, removal of the hat. Her words at first superfluous, she could only defend her position from the rapid fire of questions: 'Who? Which one? Where?' A volley that would inevitably lead to 'How? When? Can I see them?' Followed by the outpouring of grief and anger and the final question; 'Why?'.

Sometimes, when a person is one hundred and six years old, the 'Why?' is easy. But a child or young father, a brother on his gap year, here the 'Why?' was tough. The reply needed tact and care; qualities that she often struggled with.

Quite simply the answer is; his heart stopped beating. Although flippancy has no place when dealing with grieving relatives, Jan constantly wrestled with the theory of a soft truth, a concept that lived uncomfortably close to the corral labelled 'white lies' which in her view kicked a ball around with dishonesty.

Occupying a protected parallel world came with the training; Jan was skilled in the art of disassociation and sometimes appeared cold and immune to the trauma. She would silently focus on her own relationships which didn't take long, there had been so few and no one had come close to the dusty space reserved for 'significant other'.

She knew how important it was to appreciate those around you whilst they still had breath, it was blatantly obvious. But, when it came to family who were hidden or miles away, the appreciation of them became more of a longing, an idealisation that could paint over the gaps with false memories.

Her sister wasn't a disappointment so far, more of a shock, an acquired taste. They were bound to have grown apart; it was inevitable and natural and yet, there were glimpses of the undeniable warmth and mischief that ran throughout their childhood. As Jan dropped her ravished apple core into a small compost pot in the cooler bag she was overcome by the idea of 'family'.

We're getting on just fine. I'm someone's sister, it's a funny feeling being with a relative. My whole police career, I'm PC Elliot but now, I'm a *sister*.

As the realisation washed over her, the spicy soup bubbled again. Warm affection pulsed through dormant areas of belonging and raked across embers of a long-lost civilisation that had bordered on extinction.

She glanced at her watch and wondered how long Hayley had been and then dismissed the thought. What does it matter if it's 08:45 or 09:45 or whatever? I will no longer be a time slave, I can be late, it isn't a crime. But it is disrespectful, it's arrogant and I shouldn't have done it.

As much as she tried to ignore the issue, the argument continued to bob about on a tranquil sea with the outright winner still refusing to declare. She puffed noisily but nothing would budge except time itself which continued to sail effortlessly through her day.

The subject was temporarily set aside when, upon opening the boot, she was greeted by a more pressing matter; that of the unacceptable incursion of a suitcase into 'Jan's territory'. But this unfortunate reshuffle was about to be usurped by the chaotic scene developing across the car park. The Alsatian keeper had returned to the Mini and foolishly opened the door whilst balancing her bag of fast food on the cup holder alongside a carton of flat latte expensive mocha or similar.

Bring a flask, thought Jan watching the scene unfold, it's all about thinking ahead, planning your journey.

And there it was, the lack of planning in the picnic office had now led to an immediate lack of foresight in the car door logistics department.

What was she thinking? What am I thinking? Perhaps it's the Hayley effect? Jan smiled through a slight sense of guilt as she watched the impulse picnic cascade to the tarmac. The Alsatian pushed out from its confined quarters and lapped up the latte before devouring whatever the upended bag contained, followed by the bag.

"That's really not funny," said Jan looking around to determine how many others might have witnessed this unkind entertainment. She looked again at the casually dressed woman. "Female white, five foot five, small build…stop it Jan, it's a member of the public in distress."

With a sense of duty still strapped firmly about her person, Jan turned this compulsion into something more practical and set off across the car park to offer support. But she was stopped in her tracks by 'The First Cut is the Deepest' which flowed from the side pocket of her cargo trousers.

The text was short:

Help.

Keeping an eye on the Mini situation, Jan replied:

Have you run out of loo roll?

No, there's a hold up. Replied Hayley in double quick time.

Well you'll just have to wait.

Resisting the temptation to add important detail about the British way of life Jan took another step towards the Mini only to be stopped again:

No listen, Marple, there are masked men!

Masked men? Typed Jan, eventually.

Hayley didn't reply, her communication preference had shifted and she pressed into life 'I Don't Want to Talk About It'.

It had always been a talking point amongst her colleagues that Jan, *of all people*, should entertain the irony of such a ringtone. It was her one guilty act of frivolity and had served her well. Except the time when she'd found a distressed male on a bridge parapet. Rod's heartfelt words had drifted through the night air and almost certainly would have pushed Jan into the inspector's office had she lost her man. But fortunately, it prompted a conversation that broke the stalemate and lightened a dark place with no harm done.

Now, as she stood in a very bright and sunny place, Jan considered the possibility of a hidden message contained within the texts as she waited for an appropriate moment to interrupt Rod.

"What are you talking about?"

"There's a flaming hold up. I told you two minutes ago and unless I'm mistaken, you still haven't turned up!"

CHAPTER 3

Hayley's tireless creative invention had well and truly risen to the surface. This outstanding jolly jape designed no doubt to make her sister look foolish appeared to be gathering momentum. But, having suffered already, Jan was not prepared to venture along that particular road, preferring instead to see how far Hayley would go.

I don't have to do this, she thought feeling somewhat exposed between the Mini and her Golf. So, she decided to offer some practical advice.

"Well, why don't you go out of the fire door?"

"I can't."

"Why not?" Jan scanned the immediate surroundings trying to catch sight of her sister, who would, undoubtedly be enjoying the spectacle.

"I'm stuck in the cleaner's cupboard."

"Where?" said Jan masking agitation with deliberate Pythonesque steps back towards Howard.

"The cleaner's cupboard; mops, buckets, loo rolls."

The key fob glistened in her hand, she was only one click away from her comfortable safe place so, Jan decided to play along.

"What possessed you to go in there?"

"To hide from the mad men, it seemed like a good idea at the time. Look, are you going to do something or what?"

She's getting desperate now, this will soon be over thought Jan; no longer feeling the need to shelter.

"We need urgent help in here."

"I thought you were alone?" said Jan scratching her stomach as she scanned the car park for a second time.

"No, I didn't say that. It seems a number of other people thought this was a good idea too. There's Ann Wilkins and her eight-year-old Sarah, Mrs Marshall with her shopping trolley and Marble the Italian greyhound and then there's Clint who is rather tall but thankfully a stick of a youth. Said he was a goth by the way just in case you need to know that in the rescue plan. Oh, and I nearly forgot Brian, the toilet cleaner."

"Brian?" She knew this wasn't the right response, but this was too clever for Hayley. Surely, she hasn't roped a group of strangers into her joke and created a role call scenario? Maybe this is the Australian way, thought Jan blowing a few steady breaths away from the phone.

"Yes Brian, don't get all uppity it is *his* cupboard."

Torn between being made a fool of again and the crippling sense of duty, Jan scrutinised every corner of the car park, hoping to clock evidence that would prove or otherwise that this was just a silly game.

"Are you sure?"

"Course I'm flaming sure; said he'd worked here for a few years. Look, enough about my people, are you going to help or not?"

In a blur of mind and motion Jan had paced twice around her car before she even realised what she was doing. Returning abruptly to the moment she commanded her limbs to get a grip as she pulled up to stand firm, well, as firm as she could manage with her heart beating a wobbly rhythm.

This is exactly why you shouldn't use a mobile phone whilst driving, she thought, you just don't know what the rest of you is doing. As the precipice of embarrassing doom edged closer, Jan couldn't quite ignore the possibility that there was some truth emanating from her sisters pleading predicament.

"What's happening outside of the cupboard? What can you see?"

"Well, there's a lot of shouting coming from over by the shop, I've lost sight of the two men for the moment."

The morning of temporary angst that had been slowly evaporating, had now been replaced by an iceberg. How can one person create so many extreme phenomena? thought Jan as she battled to draw breath and buy herself some uncomfortable time.

A varied career on the front line had regularly thrown unexpected challenges her way but this was different. It was beginning to feel every bit like a training exercise except she didn't have the scenario sheet which outlined the first objective, she didn't have a colleague to bounce ideas off and she didn't have a plan. Instead, never failing to appear in her hour of need, she had anxiety her closest friend who could always be relied upon to make things worse.

"It's no good heavy breathing at me, *do* something," shouted Hayley her voice more strident and Australian than Jan had, up to now, been familiar with.

"Look, you need to call the police, you don't know what you're dealing with." Said Jan, desperately clinging to the hope that a colleague would materialise.

"I have called you; you *are* the police; my people are relying on you. I've told them you will sort this out."

"Hayley, why did you do that? Honestly, I don't believe this." Jan scratched for words just before breath rationing was reinstated. She grabbed her wrist, looking for comfort in the time. 09:10 which, she realised was absolutely no help at all, it was an irrelevance, a distraction. "Cod ham it," she whispered.

"There's no need to swear, we are listening you know, and Marble is really shivering. Oh, and Mrs Marshall would like to sit down very soon if you could just consider that for a moment. Also, Clint has an exam in a few hours to see if he's got a Mensa brain and he doesn't want to be late. Will you please get on with the rescue, jeez I think even I could have done something by now if it was you stuck in here."

"I'm thinking," said Jan rubbing her forehead with the heel of her sticky palm. Why hadn't she shouted 'Gotcha Janet Elliot'? How long can she keep this up?

Hayley broke into Jan's thoughts. "Hey, look I can just about see them through the door grille. Two of them like I said and they're wearing black balaclavas and yeah, I thought so, one of them has a gun or a Taser or something, waving it about all over the place."

"What colour?" Asked Jan realising that it might be time to make a decision.

"Black."

"Is it real?"

"How do I chuffing know? Look, you have everything a normal detective would need to solve the case so will you please just get on with it."

Jan disengaged the phone from her reddened ear and hung it loosely by her side, longing for a luxurious moment to compose herself. But the pause gave voice to unhelpful thoughts.

How can this not be my fault? First, I'm late and then, instead of chilling out and going to the toilets with my sister, I sat here more concerned with my global security and now look what's happened.

The plan for the day had been buried or maybe even gifted to someone else who was likely having a rather nice time. I did not fail to plan she wailed at her internal supervisor hoping to reacquaint herself with the day she should be having. If I'd just been on time, I wouldn't be in this dungeon with dilemma.

Jan paced the length of her car, now consciously aware of her position as she returned to the scenario and checked the facts.

What do I understand to be the situation? What type of situation is it? Do I need back-up? YES! Jan screamed internally hoping the supervisor was paying attention.

While she considered that Hayley was outspoken and appeared to be a friend of drama, she couldn't discount the fact that her sister might be a reliable witness who wouldn't dream of exaggerating the points and gravity just to secure a police response.

"Cod ham it," shouted Jan banging her first on the roof as she brought the phone back to her ear to formally terminate the call.

"We are still here when you've finished using bad language in front of an eight-year-old."

"I'll call you back." Jan ended the call and quickly checked her roof for signs of damage. Her eyes danced on the tide of adrenalin that had taken control of the moment. She took a long, balanced breath from her pelvis to her shoulders and attempted to harness the surge. This called for action, it was a 999 call. Consumed by procedure, she began to process the incident, the correct response when racing to a scene. Ordinarily, the radio operator would supply highly researched information including warning signs, suspect profiles, proximity of armed officers; who would be making towards, and a negotiator; already deployed.

Everything you need to make a safe assessment, thought Jan trying to rein in the galloping adrenalin. Except... I'm on my own. This isn't how you go to a job; this is madness.

Her feet, however, ignored this overinflated trivia, they were skipping on an altogether different path. Up on her toes, light and agile she looked towards the oasis of plenty. People were now running from the building, those less able shuffled, some screamed as the band of disorganised helpers pushed them further away. They took cover behind cars, any car and lit cigarettes to save their lives.

This is real, my sister really is in danger. "Come on, Jan, it's time to act," she commanded. Then flying like a ferret on a fun run, she made her move while a mantra played over in her mind. 'Gather Information, Assess Threat, Powers and Policy, Tactical Options, Take Action, Review'. All spinning around in a vat of sticky treacle called the Human Rights Act.

But this mantra, held briefly in a whirling firkin of formality and emotion, began to sink like a blob in a lava lamp. As all powers bestowed upon a police officer had in fact evaporated at the stroke of midnight leaving her with only the pointless powers of a citizen. But in this dynamic call to arms, she ignored that minor detail.

With cheeks radiating red from her fifty-metre dash, Jan arrived within the personal space of the Mini. Dancing from side to side, drenched in an alarming amount of sweat, she tried to maintain some distance between her and the slobbering dog. In any ordinary police day, she would probably have called for back-up to a person such as herself at this moment in time. The Alsatian keeper, understandably, stepped back and pulled the dog squarely between them.

"Hi," said Jan holding her chest trying to push a discomfort back into place. "I know this must appear odd and please don't be afraid. Look, I'm PC3485 Jan Elliot – retired." She panted and dripped like the dog between them. "There's an incident over there, it's pretty serious I think." She held the woman's gaze and saw it soften. "Your dog looks strong and capable, I just wondered if he was trained in anything?"

"Apart from theft and ASB?" she replied. "Why do you ask?"

"Well, he just looks like the sort of animal that should be a police dog."

"He is, or rather was, he's been retired." She rubbed his ears affectionately as a trail of drool dribbled down her trousers.

"Don't I know that feeling. Being retired I mean, not the ear rubbing and definitely not the drooling." Jan became conscious of the heat that burned across her face as she wiped her mouth but there was no time to back away from her mission, she had to push on. "Will he chase things?"

"Yes, when I say he was retired, he didn't actually make the grade. He's a bit wilful; he would chase anything and everything and he's pretty fond of black. Unfortunately, he sank his teeth into one officer too many. The head of the dog unit thought it was just a training issue but after he too was bitten, Sabre was retired the same day. Shelley by the way, housewife, failed academic, soft touch for the Alsatian rescue group." She raised her hand in acknowledgment and smiled.

"May I borrow him?" Amazed by her own bold ingenuity, Jan took on the stance of a super hero with arms crossed high as she surveyed the dog; an alien, abhorrent, hairy, filthy beast.

"Well, why not? I thought something was going on when I saw the odds and sods spew out into the car park and huddle over there. I was a bit busy sharing my lunch to take too much notice. What do you intend to do?"

"I think it would be helpful if he caused a bit of a distraction, maybe chased a few people, I just have a feeling that his presence might help the situation."

"It can't do any harm, as long as they're in black," she smiled again. "Let me get his working harness."

Pleased that she didn't have time to consider the habits of her new colleague, Jan slapped her thighs, not so much like the principal boy in a panto, but like an athlete getting ready to run the race of their life.

"I'd better come with you just in case he runs amok and you need help." Sabre barked excitedly as the harness was secured. "You could do with using up some excess energy, couldn't you my panting prince?" She passed the tightened lead to Jan. "Looks like you're going on an adventure."

Unsure who the comment was meant for, Jan held the lead with uneasy determination and leant back to counter his strength. She soon discovered that not only was Sabre loud and mucky, he was also very fast.

He was a dog ready, ready for action and reward although technically he had already had a reward before starting this task but such is a dog's brain. He bounded enthusiastically towards the doors a snarling frothing mess of hair and strapping. Curious faces peeped around cars and campervans as the dog and two obviously mad women were dragged on towards danger. Sabre made a number of unscheduled stops along the way, cocking his leg at two posts and the unmanned Costa trailer. He was getting in the zone; he knew this game and he knew how to play it.

In the calm of these three-legged moments, 'I Don't Want to Talk About It' rang from Jan's thigh. Hayley gave the update that staff were being shouted at and two shoppers and a charity worker were being forced to lie down.

Sabre had dispensed with his pre-fight checks and lunged towards the doors just as Jan managed to get both hands back on the lead. But the dynamic approach was abruptly halted by the unhurried swishing of the double doors. Sabre planted his face squarely onto the glass wiping a huge swathe of slobber as it dragged his elongated pink tongue out of his mouth. Once in the inner chamber and now clearly angry he lurched forwards again and made exactly the same mistake. The inner wall of glass brushed the fur between his eyes before releasing him into the action. He filled the cavernous hall with an echoey slobbering noise and instantly elevated himself to leader of some imaginary pack.

With the highly buffed floor working against her, Jan lost her footing and landed effortlessly onto her bottom behind the low wall that embraced the McDonald's seating. Ingrained dog and detritus oozed from the lead onto her white knuckled fingers as she fought to keep control of her wild animal.

On course for a collision with the crammed information stand, she was forced to take further immediate action. She stretched her legs forward and leant back as far as she dared as her rubber heels stuttered across the vinyl. With lungs puffed into booming bellows she shouted a command high into the rafters.

"Put down your weapons or I'll send in the dogs!"

Whether this was heard by those that needed to hear it and whether indeed it was the correct terminology she was not entirely certain but she could hardly shout 'Police!' as both her and the dog were now retired.

In any case, Sabre had no truck with lawful commands, he had heard enough and with a final yank on his harness he bounded forward leaving Jan spinning like an upended turtle. He was free at last to pursue the level of fun he had enjoyed at police training school before he had been taken out of service for officer safety reasons. He was a predator, shaggy and low, galloping with Exocet eyes towards the target.

"Quick! Down!" shouted Jan bundling Shelley behind the waist height territory wall. They clung to each other, trembling with excitement and anxiety. Comrades in arms thrust together a few moments ago by a bad-mannered dog.

What have I done? thought Jan in a panic. Dog out of control in a public place. No briefing or objective. Just a reckless disregard for the safety of others. I just let him go. My cod I'm going to get a criminal record, thirty years unblemished career. Day one of retirement a criminal. No, no, no, she wailed to herself holding tighter to Shelley's arm.

"You okay?" she asked, her gentle voice struggling to compete against the backdrop of chaos that zoomed overhead from the battlefield.

"What have we done?" cried Jan, realising her actions had been ill-conceived and foolish.

Before Shelley could offer a comforting reply a loud authoritative voice echoed through the air space.

"Don't move!"

Sabre, who had made a solid first impression as regards his delightful behaviour, predictably didn't take any notice of the order. The slobbering snarls and excited barks seamlessly continued.

Tentatively Shelley put her head above the parapet then turned to Jan holding her firmly by the shoulders.

"Don't worry," she smiled. "I think it might be okay."

Buoyed by this news, Jan got to her feet and stared into the distance, still not quite able to see or determine what had just happened.

"It sounds like he's playing now," said Shelley with a hint of pride in her voice.

Jan followed the curve of the wall as anxiety morphed effortlessly into something entirely more pleasant.

"That's a relief, come on we'd better get a clearer view of the action." She led off at a slow jog along the green walkway that seductively guided the unwary towards an ambush of cash guzzling outlets.

Like a fawn on an icy lake she danced across the highly polished floor which she soon discovered was part of a crime prevention strategy. Ensuring that any would-be criminal trying to leave at speed would instantly find themselves conspicuously prone.

Red and yellow warning signs at frequent intervals caught the eye and frowned advice regarding the 'Hazards of Hasty'. Underwritten with the tired excuse that the management would accept no responsibility for injuries howsoever caused by those that exceeded the advised speed limit for their walkway.

Speed tiptoeing, suited Shelley who was making good progress. "He'll need his reward now, dogs are totally driven by the need to chew on their cuddly toy after they have pleased you," she said rummaging in her bag.

With a flourish, only understood by dog keepers, she proudly produced an unrecognisable black furred animal held grubbily together by dried slobber.

As they passed the phone shop and swerved around the donut display, Jan finally had a clear view of the scene some thirty metres ahead.

"Oh no, Shelley, quick, grab Sabre!"

CHAPTER 4

Jan and her new best friend arrived on scene to fading applause and laughter at the unexpected incident outside WHSmith. Hayley bounced forward and grabbed Jan.

"Did you see that, Sis? it was truly bonkers. The great hairy hound ran at the boys in black and frightened the flippin' life out of them, they fell backwards over a book display and landed upended in this week's best sellers. He then pounced on the charity table, grabbed the giant stuffed sun bear and started ripping it to shreds."

Shelley picked up the trailing lead and made a manful effort to pull Sabre, who was barking mad, away from the regrettable pile of fur fabric and stuffing.

"Then Brian," continued Hayley, "you know, Brian the cleaner I met in the cupboard? Well, he is just a hero, exploded on to the floor with two mops and a roll of black bags and whoosh, bang, crash he had them guys totally beat. On the deck, all tied up going nowhere. You'd have seen it if you'd got here a bit quicker."

"We had a mini briefing as it were." Jan sighed with more relief than she knew what to do with. She was on the brink of tears, the kind of tears that prompt a tetchy parent to dismissively ask 'What are you crying for?'. The truth was, that at this moment in time, she really didn't know. Could it be sheer relief that all appeared to be well, no offences forthcoming, reputation intact? Was it the guilt from doubting Hayley's word? Or was it something that had caught her completely off guard; the sudden all-consuming sense of concern for her sister's safety? In an effort to distract herself, Jan returned to her extended duty where she would claim her damp face was nothing more than perspiration.

"So," she said checking the time at 09:35, "Sabre caused a commotion, distracted everyone, the suspects were detained and then he eats the sun bear? Well, that's different."

"He clearly had a unique way of working that wasn't truly appreciated by his colleagues in the force," added Shelley beaming at her fluff covered companion.

As the small group talked in loud tones of wild excitement Jan became aware of the lingering smell of dog and lathered leather on her tacky hands and the dust and detritus of a public floor embedded into the fabric of her freshly laundered clothing. She liked dogs at a distance but found them too high on the maintenance scale as this incident had proven and, it confirmed her decision that the acquisition of a dog would definitely *not* feature on the 'Must Do' list.

She stood silently in the hubbub observing human kind and sometimes not so kind. Like rats on a raft, these strangers had been joined by fate and bonded forever by service area glue. United by a careless disregard for their onward journeys, they intended to stick around for the conclusion of this exceptional event.

A ragged queue had formed behind the book stand. It seemed everyone, except Mrs Marshall, wanted to have a selfie with Brian and the suspects before the police arrived. It went without saying that this kind of behaviour would be frowned upon by Devon and Cornwall's finest once they had taken charge.

Disrespecting the suspects and trampling all over the scene is wrong, thought Jan burying her hands deep into her pockets. She stared beyond the scene trying to make it go away but it persisted. Like microwaved minestrone burning her tongue, Jan was forced to open her mouth and say something. I have to, she thought, I have the experience to advise, it's down to me. She imagined in that moment, that the crowd knew she was a police officer, that they'd be expecting her to act and muttering because she wasn't.

What if the amateur paparazzi are standing proud with a foot resting on the chest of a suspect, desperately clamouring to be the first to post a heroic photo across social media? It was more than she could bear. Without further hesitation, fuelled by a burning hot soup, she marched behind the stand and mustered an unimpressive trembly voice.

"This is a scene you know, it's important that it's preserved for the investigation." With her heart thumping out of her chest she dearly wished she had not embarked on this course of action. But instinctively, here she stood looking every ounce like a middle-aged busybody. It didn't help that her forthright sister was in the naughty crowd.

"What's it to you?" chimed a young man in the uniform of the shop. "My boss won't be too pleased with all this mess, will he? I'm just putting it out there, showing the bigwigs what I have to put up with."

"I, I'm not sure the police will agree with you on that," she said tentatively stepping backwards in an effort to extract herself from the confrontation.

"Well," he continued, "if they're so bothered, they should have got here sooner, you can't freeze frame your life waiting for a police response."

Undeniably he was making perfect sense, thought Jan, of course he was I mean his badge stated he was the manager, Brad Ford, no nonsense youth of today. She walked back across to

Shelley and Sabre realising that her normal life had arrived at a different platform and her train had already departed.

"I can see why Sabre is finding it so hard to retire," she said, "things don't appear to abide by the same rules, it's like another world."

"Oh, I don't know, I think it's the same old world really, it's just how you deal with it," said Shelley pulling the fluff from his coat. "I think the best way is to just hold onto your values and go along for the ride. That's what Sabre seems to do and look at his happy face."

In a moment of absent-minded carelessness, Jan was on the brink of twirling Sabre's shaggy coat through her fingers but sense arrived just in time. With mind and body splashed from within by the hot fat of a pig roast that slowly rotated around her spine, Jan had found comfort in the warm soft bun of a stranger called Shelley. A connection worthy of further scrutiny.

An alliance that had made Jan feel immeasurably safe and supported, just like her colleagues in the collectively and affectionately termed 'police family'. A group of people recruited, vetted and trained to a uniformed standard where, irrespective of age or experience within the ranks, there was a common truth that beat through the honest heart of the organisation.

Now, as a civilian, Jan had instantly recognised that same standard of honesty and humanity in Shelley, part of the wider police family, except that she *wasn't* exactly; the family connection was Sabre. Nonetheless, Jan couldn't dismiss the fact that, in a necessary instant, she had put her trust in a stranger.

Before she could pursue this eddy of emotion any further, a diminutive individual stepped out from behind the charity table and was heading in their direction.

Tanned from birth with the stature of a small teenager, he bore the face of a wise man in simple clothing with sandals that exposed his brown, bony feet.

"What are we going to do about my sun bear?" He said quietly to no one in particular but perhaps meant for Shelley as she had hold of the destructive creature with fur all around his face.

"Ah yes, the sun bear," said Shelley surveying the mountain of fluff swirling gently across the vinyl.

"In my country they are endangered," he said picking up the separated head whilst hopelessly trying to push stuffing back into the ripped nose and ears.

"Well," said Hayley emerging from the photo shoot, "looks like the sun bear is just as endangered in this country." She smiled into the unreceptive audience.

Shelley again pulled Sabre away from ragging every scrap of black fabric he could get his teeth into and tried unsuccessfully to push him behind her legs.

The weight of responsibility lies squarely with me, thought Jan trying to deal with an uncomfortable constriction to her vocal cords. Robbed of speech she wanted to do something, touch him, pat him in some way.

Oh, this is ridiculous, yet another embarrassing mess, what am I thinking that I should be going anywhere near police business? She revisited an old regret. If I'd just gone to the loo at the same time as my sister, the dog wouldn't be on the scene and the sun bear would still be recognisable. Why am I so stupid?

If that was me, she thought looking at the crestfallen saviour, I'd be crying right now. She imagined how alone he must feel, not just because he was without his life-sized companion or that he was courageously campaigning far away from home but because he was a very public victim in a crowd of unfeeling, evidence gathering, social media bystanders.

As the spotlight shone down on her decision-making Jan concluded that at 09:45 the errors were now ahead of the triumphs in her first day of freedom in this new normal world. The tiny ripples from her decision had rolled into the distant community and barged unhelpfully into their lives. She inhaled deeply and held it whilst she thought of a solution. As time ticked slowly in a peaceful zone far away, her mind skipped like a flower flitting bee before she exhaled loudly on a drift of inconclusive air.

I am a member of the public; how hard can it be? An incident happens, you call the police, they deal with it, and you get on with your life. Beginning to feel helpless as well as useless, she had to do something but found herself wanting to say what many in the small crowd were already muttering.

"Where are the police? What's taking them so long?"

She moved away from Shelley and her sister who were engrossed in retelling the event from entirely different viewpoints and cautiously approached Brian. Brian the calm conquering hero who had charmed the captives into a docile state of surrender. The photo queue had disappeared leaving only Brad and his assistant looking on.

Condemned before she could speak, in the face of youthful hostility, she drew breath – make it a large one, and summoned a voice that she believed would convey the right tone and attitude. It was a voice she'd used on the bin men when she'd asked for a replacement recycling bag. The immense sense of relief and triumph hard to contain as she bounced back to her front door.

"Do you have a spare black bag please?" Her enquiry was met with a friendly Welsh voice, efficient and capable and wholly receptive to her needs.

"Yes, of course, you'll have to rip one off yourself like, I'm a bit committed at the moment with these two."

Jan noted a firearm tucked into the belt of his navy work trousers and even at these close quarters, she couldn't determine if it was real or imitation. A shiver rattled down her spine touching every rib along the way before something akin to a giant sink plunger thumped her in the stomach at the realisation that Brian was totally unsupported. The crowd were enjoying the show from the side-lines, but there was no help forthcoming. Brian occupied that lonely outpost of expectation, he had taken the lead, shown himself in a different league and thereby walked into isolation.

"Are you okay by the way?"

"Yeah, I'm alright, long as the police get here soon or my leg might go to sleep."

Here he is operating on his own, no colleagues, no backup, no plan. He instinctively got this under control, a good decision, thought Jan, this is how normal people help out. A role model for normal life in a far from normal situation.

As she ripped a bag from the roll, she noted that the suspects were unmistakably female and that Brian appeared to be using the appropriate restraint techniques to take account of their size and gender. He had beautifully improvised with the black bags and cleaning equipment. This was a member of the public getting a job done, no accountability or scrutiny from the police, no training certificates or approved techniques, this was just doing what was needed. Although how long Brian could detain these two suspects legally and defensibly was something that troubled her.

How do you deal with criminals when you're no longer in the job? thought Jan walking back with her bag. This was new territory and not territory that she felt qualified to deal with. Retirement was to be a world without criminals. Full of nice people, kindness and joy, peace and tranquillity.

As the sound of sirens approached, a splintered wedge was driven between dreams and reality and forced Jan to focus on the task in hand.

"Let me help you gather up these pieces," she said to the bear keeper.

"Thank you," he replied with the quiet manners of a faraway culture.

This would have to be completed in full, totally and utterly, if she was committing to the task, then these were the terms and conditions. Every scrap of fibre would need to be gathered into this bag; all pieces of fabric obsessively reunited with all of the other elements that collectively could rebuild a life-size sun bear. It's the way it had to be, her duty to the bear, a commitment that she had mentally made with 'Sulung', the name on his ID badge.

In a short window of flat calm, Jan relaxed into the positive feelings of her good deed on the back of her not so positive good deed; letting go of the dog. The swirling fluff replaced the whirl of mush that oozed inside her head as she tried to find her place on the other side of the enforcement fence. The do's and don'ts in civilian street were more complicated than she had ever imagined. How do people live like this? she thought.

And still, the police were not on scene, which didn't now surprise Jan. She could imagine the silver commander pawing over the site plan and then briefing personnel thoroughly with regards the possible scenarios and the correspondingly desired outcomes.

Now confident that every last strand of bear had been collected, Jan was overtaken by an unexpected surge of heat that rushed from her stomach and rippled into a prickly discomfort across her scalp. No, no, no Jan, you idiot. Her gaze centred on the contents of the bag in a forlorn effort to divert attention from her face. The theoretical score card now confirmed that 'errors' were comfortably ahead of a small lame horse misnamed 'Triumph'.

She glanced at Sulung, realising from her pit of shame that in her effort to comfort and support him in his hour of need, she too had destroyed part of the crime scene. She clutched the bag tightly, briefly contemplating emptying the contents into a heap at her feet until the modern wisdom of Brad Ford played over in her mind. 'You can't freeze frame your life waiting for the police'.

She wrestled with the wisdom of youth, a topic she knew so little about, and the police policies and procedures manual, which she ought to know a good deal about. And concluded, on this occasion, that an unfamiliar grey area might exist as she began to appreciate that waiting for a police response isn't always convenient.

Preparing a defiant mental speech seemed a tad disrespectful but the words flowed surprisingly freely at the moment around Jan's head. Because, now in the position of a customer, she did not feel that the police were providing a particularly good service. She was entitled to an opinion as a protected member of the public and besides, she thought, not every scene is going to be how you'd like to find it; we are just people making mistakes and getting on with life; how can that be wrong? But she knew it was wrong, quite wrong, she was supposed to know better. Working out this clumsy mistake needed time, she closed her eyes and rubbed her forehead with one hand while gripping tightly to the black bag with the other. Hoping against hope that she could channel a stitching elf to perform some miracle with the bear.

"Everything okay in there?" asked Shelley.

"Yeah, just be glad when this is all over to be honest." Jan immediately chastised herself for voicing a phrase she had long since despised. I really am losing a grip on my life and my values she thought, closing her eyes in the hope of activating a reset button. What is going on? Why do people say 'To be honest'? I hate that expression. What is the point? I mean if you have to qualify or preface something with 'To be honest', it can only imply that unless you've thrown in the verbal truth card, everything else you say is a pack of lies.

As she made yet another attempt to dock in the real-world Jan shook her head and absentmindedly buried her hand into Sabre's dense fur before speaking.

"Sorry, yes, fine, just a lot to think about. A lot has happened hasn't it?"

Shelley pulled Sabre back from the black bag of bear pieces.

"Look, me and the farting failure are going to step outside, I need to put him back in the car, he's had far too much excitement."

"Of course," said Jan momentarily regaining some composure. "Thanks for your help and just going with it, very public spirited I think."

"Wouldn't have missed it," smiled Shelley holding tightly to her over-excited companion as he dragged her away.

Like a child handing scruffy, overdue homework to the geography teacher, Jan offered Sulung his disassembled bear. She tried to apologise but it seemed inadequate under the circumstances. Instead, she smiled sympathetically and gently touched his arm in the hope it would convey the correct message in his culture.

Only a few moments ago Sabre had been fading nicely into the distance but now, at the top of his vocal range and re-energized, he announced his arrival at the entrance.

Beyond the barking, Jan could just make out the unmistakable sound of a highly trained police unit. Confident loud commands peppered with the occasional untrained scream.

"Get that dog under control, madam!" Shouted a male voice in the distance operating, one might assume, a few octaves above his normal range.

A response reflex, that hadn't yet been disabled, pushed Jan to high alert and primed her to face the developing incident. She glanced towards brave Brian and his audience who were devoid of community gumption.

Is this the rank and file that I'm supposed to join? She held that thought as her shoes took off at a safe speed, leaving the normal people to stand around waiting, it seemed, for act two.

At the entrance, the four armed-officers clearly hadn't judged Shelley or her dog to be a threat as they entered the gap between the two sets of doors. But Sabre had his own mind and the men in black appeared as a gift in his world. He launched forward and pulled Shelley to the floor as he grabbed the holster strapped to the first officer's leg. He tussled with the prize and caused the officer to respond with an involuntary jig.

The sight of the Glock 17 pistol bouncing freely on the lanyard caused the three standing officers to also spring into a merry dance. Their screams magnified within the confines of the small glass cell.

Aware that, under the circumstances, she could not assist and should take cover, Jan crouched once again behind the McDonald's wall. This time on the side of the seating, safe in the knowledge that it offered about as much protection from a 9mm round as a Double Cheeseburger.

The former highly organised unit had disintegrated into a dancing quartet. With naked arms held high above their heads, they hopped and kicked out in an impromptu display of traditional ceilidh steps.

Shelley, now on her feet, tugged at the lead as she steadied herself against the wall.

"Madam! Control this dog!" screamed the officer wearing the important chevrons.

It could have developed into a long drawn out incident featuring a negligent discharge, injury, paperwork, writer's cramp but more pressing for the service area, a further delay in an appropriate police response. So, it was fortuitous that Sabre now had a pressing need for an excitable pee which greatly surpassed his fun with the screaming officer.

Leaving a warm trail of gloopy dog spit, he released the holster and thus the officer attached to it and with reckless predictability he charged at the closed door.

"It's all over," said Shelley stating a fact.

"Yes, it is, madam," shouted the important officer. "That dog is out of control in a public place and should be muzzled!"

"No," said Shelley who appeared to have more to say.

"Yes, madam, you are interfering with a reported armed robbery and I cannot stress how serious this is to public safety. Now, step away and get that dog out of here."

Shelley looked smug as the door opened for her companion. "Come on, Sabre."

"Sabre!" Shouted the officer again.

"Yes, retired police dog," she smiled holding tightly to his harness.

"I knew it," cried the bitten officer rearranging his Glock. "He's had my leg before and not when I'd had a gun strapped to it. He shouldn't be allowed in public areas, or anywhere in fact where there are members of the public."

"Isn't that the same thing?" asked Shelley screwing up her nose as she exited the building at the breakneck speed of a desperate dog.

"Buffoon," said the senior officer reorganising his team. "Good job he's gone, imagine the chaos he would have caused."

Taking a moment, they regrouped and fluffed themselves up in an effort to regain control and portray an appropriate image; that of the highly trained, invincible armed unit that they were supposed to be.

In the gripping silence that followed, Jan huddled against the wall, unable to decide whether to stand up and risk being shot or stay where she was and risk being shot. The swish of the glass door announced the second coming of the excitable officers headed by the sergeant shouting in a loud officious voice.

"Report...Clear...Down...Hostiles at fifty metres. On my command!" And other nonsense as it sounds to civilian ears.

The patter of force issued combat boots squeaked towards Jan as she sat tight becoming increasingly aware of the fast food detritus around her trousers. She stared at her scuffed shoes, trying not to breathe as thistle infused blood scratched through her body.

Why didn't I stand up? What brainless decision was this in your catalogue of stupid decisions Janet Elliot? She wanted to kick herself, thump her head with a heel strike, go back to bed and start again. But these are not the options available to a cowering fifty-year-old woman who arrived late at Tiverton Parkway.

Gripped by her own doomed imagination and tormented by what sounded like a giant spider running around in squeaky footwear, Jan held herself tightly and screwed up her eyes hoping for a miracle.

"Stand up, put your hands where I can see them!" boomed a voice from overhead.

She moved slowly and carefully like she had something to hide feeling every bit like a criminal instead of Jan, who would very much like to move normally. She resisted the urge to brush debris from her trousers and held her hands at shoulder height before turning, tentatively, to face the full weight of the law.

Letting out a sound not recognised in Jan's vocabulary, her eyes widened. With shoulders rubbing the lobes of her ears, a normal breath was out of the question.

"Are you okay, madam?" enquired the sergeant moving tight into the wall.

"Urgh, urgh, urgh," panted Jan, "urgh, yes thank you."

"Have you been threatened?"

"No, no, I was with Sabre," Jan managed. Desperate to stop shaking, she leaned into a chair.

"Are you injured? We can get you some help. That bloody dog."

"No, no, he was good, amazing actually." Jan diverted her eyes away from the armoury and towards the small crowd in the direction of WHSmith. "You need to be over there really."

"Right, stay here, we've got this now, you're perfectly safe." He pointed towards the chair and indicated for Jan to sit before the elite team pressed on towards their objective.

With the incident all but over, the public felt exhilarated and safe. So, all that remained was for a small input of organised common sense to guide their lives back to normality. However, with the arrival of four bumptious boys bearing weapons and attitude, it appeared that the end no longer seemed nigh. The end seemed to be disappearing over the horizon unwilling to surrender to this outlandish use of verbal force.

The former relaxed and jovial group began to huddle together. They watched and waited; protective arms clutched across their bodies. With the exception of Mrs Marshall, who was either fearless or partially deaf.

With a common objective, the team pushed on towards the hostile crowd, officers took cover at various points. They knelt momentarily behind flimsy chairs, they tucked in behind the large donut cabinet as they assessed the threat that lay before them. Then, only ten metres from the scene, the striped leader shouted.

"Armed police! Get down, stay down. Put down your weapons! Put your hands where I can see them."

Mrs Marshall, who quite obviously dwelled in a different era of courtesy, obedience and respect, tried hard to conform with the rapid-fire instruction. Her efforts woefully out of time with the orders, she had only managed to repeat a few set moves. Hands onto shoulders, down to hips, she touched her ears, then shoulders and hips and after two circuits she appeared to have forgotten what the order had been and why she was waving her arms about. Whatever she was supposed to be doing she was definitely unable to perform the 'Get down' bit. Although, inevitably, 'Stay down' would be easy, should she ever find herself there.

With strength returning to her legs and an overwhelming desire to be with Hayley, Jan followed in the footsteps of the officers, fairly confident that the scene would probably still be how it was left five minutes ago.

Brian the hero had clearly anticipated this moment. Having secured his prisoners sufficiently so that he could stand, he slowly raised his arms with one hand gripping a novelty Welsh flag that had earlier cascaded onto the floor from a plastic pot near the best sellers. He waved it slowly above his head as he spoke.

"I don't think you should shoot us, mate, we're not the enemy. Not being funny or nothing but the pair you want to get your hands on are contained down here. They're quite safe, not about to hurt you."

"You! Keep your hands where I can see them. What's your name, sir?" Demanded the team leader in a harsh tone that echoed across the quiet retail cavern.

"24008090 guardsman Jones, retired, sir!" shouted Brian pulling himself awkwardly to attention with arms and flag still aloft.

The officer didn't have a clear view of Brian and all he could realistically assume from this retired guardsman was that he appeared to be in his late fifties, spoke with a Welsh accent, had short greying hair and was wearing a pale blue shirt and for some reason had thought it appropriate to wave a novelty national flag. Understandably suspicious, it was clear that the officer still had no idea what they were dealing with.

"Right, guardsman, you stay exactly where you are, hands where I can see them and put that flag down."

The leader, followed by one of his team, moved with painstaking caution towards Brian. The other two officers kept the group under control with a few well-placed looks and the silent threat of firepower at their fingertips.

The crowd were beside themselves with eager anticipation as the two officers rounded the book stand. Mrs Marshall may also have been beside herself, but she wasn't sure.

Presented with their first sight of the glossy black bags and bodies assembled at Brian's feet, there seemed to follow a mostly improvised panic scenario. The team leader, hoping to impress with his mental arithmetic, determined that they faced at least two potential suspects lying on the floor and Brian, an unknown quantity with apparent military training. Plus, the underlying threat from a crowd of smiling assassins, although not Mrs Marshall of course, her threatening days were probably over but he didn't seem entirely certain of that.

"Back-up, we need back-up!" Shouted the flustered officer into his radio.

CHAPTER 5

The audience took their instruction and obediently filed into the makeshift waiting area, amid a growing hubbub of objectionable chatter.

"I can't quite believe I'm back in this flaming toilet block again, I don't even want to go, but your friends in blue seem to think I do."

I do, thought Jan trying to wiggle more room for the expanding bladder held in the confined space of her misnamed cargo trousers.

"No different at home, flaming police turn up and make it all look so complicated. Didn't you have a let's cut to the chase button, an override that meant you could get it solved and sorted within the hour?"

"No, this is real life."

"Still life more like," said Hayley leaning herself against the row of washbasins. "It feels like we're the criminals, I mean what right do they have to march us all into this draughty dunny? It's a makeshift cell block."

"It has to be done like this, it's all about safety of the officers and the public; containing the situation and bringing it to a safe conclusion. Coupled of course with evidence gathering so they can determine who might be responsible for the offences, if there are any. A very long list in fact of things that have to be done in a certain way. There's little point in having all that training if officers just make it up to suit the impatient members of the public at the scene."

"Well sometimes the impatient members of the public have a valid point. Anyway, why don't you tell the prison guards you're a police officer?"

"Retired."

"Less than twenty-four hours retired. Surely you're still believable and honest and wouldn't make stuff up?"

"Of course I'm still honest, like we believe Brian to be, but these are just words if you can't prove your point or demonstrate some integrity."

"I suppose you're right about that, I mean they've taken poor old Brian prisoner…"

"He's helping with enquiries."

Drawing on decades of experience with this type of incident, Jan had confidence in the system. The knowledge that this would, eventually, get resolved and a decision would be reached. Suspects on one side, witnesses the other, process complete, the court can decide. But now, outside of the loop, not privy to the flow of information, she found herself wandering in a strange wilderness. She grabbed the neck of her loose-fitting grandad shirt making a subtle effort to waft out an uncomfortable cloud of warm air while her head tried to process all that had happened by 10:10 on day one of the rest of her peaceful life.

It's not my day. Why do people say that? No, it really *isn't* my day. This is not *my* day. The thought of such injustice dragged like a lost anchor across her chest as Jan succumbed to what she believed to be the prattle of a stir-crazy mind. It's not my day, because it is

NOT my day. This is someone else's day which, frankly, they can have right back. This is the day of Jan who was ten minutes late, it is not where I should be. This day belongs to the person who is lagging behind, I want my day back now, I need and I want to get out of here. I shouldn't even be in here; this is a nightmare in someone else's world. She could've gone on but her sister had some rather important information.

"Anyway, about proof. I did record the whole incident on my phone you know, it's brilliant. Well, it serves a purpose, could earn me a few bucks, about time old Hayley had a bit of good luck don't you reckon?"

"Hayley, why didn't you say?" whispered Jan.

"What, that I needed a bit of good luck? Or that I could earn a few bucks?"

"Neither, why didn't you say you had some proof?"

"Well I don't know about you, but I haven't noticed the Feds being very chatty up to now. No, it's awesome, it clears Brian, shows them dumb blokes up as a right pair of drongos and all the while that mad dingo can be heard in the background ripping the sun bear to bits."

With a discrete snatched glance towards Sulung, Jan gently grabbed Hayley's arm hoping it might turn down the volume.

"Look, anyway, great witness you are. The two suspects are women if you care to look closely at your evidence."

"How am I supposed to know that when they're all dressed in black? It's a minor detail. Anyway, if they'd just been bothered to ask for my help in the first place, we wouldn't all be kindled up in a toilet block."

"Kettled, the expression is kettled," Jan corrected with a degree of finality.

Hayley rolled her eyes and let out the sigh of a horse with loose velvet lips. Which was followed by the voice of an elderly female with loose lips in cubicle three.

"I wouldn't mind the kettle going on, dear, I'm a bit parched."

Hayley took a few steps forward to identify the frailty emanating from the open cubicle. "Hello, Mrs Marshall," she said in a long-lost pal tone. "I see you've found somewhere to sit, how's Marble?"

"Look, he's shivering, he's really cold, I had to take his coat off when we got off the bus so he could have a little wee."

"Well, why don't you put his coat back on, Mrs Marshall? I'm sure we won't be kept much longer," declared Hayley with not much confidence.

"Oh, I can't do that, dear, I put his coat in my shopping trolley."

"Okay, well let's find your trolley and sort out that little problem."

"Have you got my trolley, dear?"

"Err, no. Do you know where it is?"

"Is it in the shop, dear? Is it alright? Can you fetch it for me?"

By the time Mrs Marshall had come to the end of her suggestions, she had undoubtedly forgotten the question. She cuddled the trembling dog affectionately jangling the thin lead that attached to an oversized, leather cummerbund of a collar.

"At least you've got Marble with you, that's the most important thing, don't you reckon?"

"Has there been a hold up? There was this young man with a gun you see, told us to put our hands up. Has the bank been robbed? I have to pay my mortgage today."

"Actually, Mrs Marshall, that isn't quite what happened. Well, I don't reckon so anyway."

"Are you having trouble remembering, dear?"

"There's deffo, sorry I mean definitely something upsetting me. I tell you what, you just sit yourself there, and it'll all be sorted before you know it okay?" Hayley retreated back to the washbasins like a cartoon cat feeling the ground behind it with each fat probing toe.

She leant into Jan and whispered her concerns.

"Jeez, that's hard work isn't it?"

"She might have dementia or something," replied Jan quietly.

Often called 'the conductor', Jan had located many of her high-risk vulnerable adults on the circular shopping bus. They would travel in comfort all day long with not the faintest idea how many times they might have reached their destination.

Taken home and introduced to what should be familiar they embark on long looped conversations featuring; 'Whose house is this? Where am I? Who are you? Where's Jeffery?' Long lost in their own minds and losing a grasp on reality, these fragile souls slip further from independence into the arms of state control.

A stranger, the uniformed authority briefly stepping in before passing the baton of responsibility to a battle scarred relative or another agency in the often-misplaced belief that the process could somehow make it right.

The lack of elderly relatives in her own life and the benefits they bring, was a sadness that touched Jan deeply. Their constant guiding light, the practical common sense and an unfathomed layer of wisdom. Although, arguably, with the pace of change racing through the 21st century their views and beliefs were more likely to be dismissed as antiquated or obsolete.

Jan moved forward, pushed once again by her strong sense of civic duty.

"I'll ask the officers, see if we can't get the shopping trolley back for her."

Sometimes it's the little things, a connection, she thought on her way towards the entrance. But as she prepared her request with a slow deep breath, Jan made an uncomfortable observation. She was no longer part of the team, she was adrift, she'd dallied on the high seas of freedom and realised she was completely lost.

Tongue-tied and tiny she had put herself at the forefront, volunteering for an interaction without basic training. Which was a surprise after thirty years that had seen every aspect of police life tested, refreshed and requalified throughout the entire calendar year. Even the lesser known 'How to' courses. Like; 'How to address an officer of higher rank', 'How to keep marked police cars in a clean and tidy condition', and 'How to create a nutritious hot meal during a night shift', had made it onto the schedule.

"Excuse me," she said, the words rapidly evaporating upon contact with the air. "The elderly lady in the toilet there," she quickly turned from the attentive gaze of the officer and pointed towards cubicle three. "Well," said Jan her eyes now resting no higher than his radio. "She has left her shopping trolley outside and I wondered if she could possibly have it back?"

The officer appeared to be well versed in cordon conversation and stock answers. So too was Jan, it was an aspect of the job that served to limit time wasting questions and protected the public from what they don't yet need to know. But she knew, as soon as he began to speak, that her words had already been confined to an unimportant waste bin.

"We can't disturb the scene at the moment, if you could just sit tight for a little longer, madam." He replied in that familiar authoritative tone that encapsulated everything you needed to know about where you both stood.

Training in courtesy and respect invariably involved the use of appropriate titles. 'Sir' or 'Madam' are the go-to addresses when the name or status of a person were not yet determined. No one seemed to argue with these terms in the classroom, there appeared to be little doubt as to their appropriateness. Unless, that is, you are on the receiving end as Jan had just found out.

She pictured herself standing in the doorway of a brothel or sulking like a naughty child, chastised by her displeased mother. 'Madam' did not conjure courtesy and respect, it felt patronized and closed. Too distracted and insulted by this word, Jan immediately felt like a lowly member of the public a MOP in police acronyms and the police were very fond of an acronym. She could barely remember the answer to the shopping trolley issue and she didn't much care – now that she had been called a 'Madam'. A woman of ill repute, an ordinary person in the community held back from crossing the thin blue line by a single weighted word – 'Madam'.

She knew her place now, it was a shock, a bellowing put down. The hurtful realisation that she stood not firm, but excluded; the other side of the drawbridge where, in that moment, it seemed to matter.

Her body tingled from head to wobbly legs as she retreated back to Hayley, feeling every bit like a proper little madam.

Conscious she had raised the temperature in the toilet block with the heat from her exposed face, Jan contemplated using a cubicle to relieve her other issue. But, not being a fan of the now unisex toilets, due, in part, to the unhygienic practices of the male species, she decided against it.

Time moved slowly in civilian land. Just being able to listen in on the police radio helped most jobs tick along quite nicely, being aware of the hold ups or further developments. Just hearing the various pieces of the job come together, things the public weren't privy to. Being on the cordon, keeping quiet when pressed by a passer-by or witness. It was fun, she knew she missed it already particularly in her current predicament amongst the crowd. Yes, you could ask a policeman for the time all day long and you'd get an honest answer but, ask about an inconvenient delay and you mine a rich seam of stock answers; 'I'm afraid I don't know', 'I can't tell you', or 'It might take some time'.

A cold front plummeted through her central core and extinguished the blue lamp that had yesterday burned with belonging and friendship. Regret rippled relentlessly, rising then falling and sweeping away the only family she had ever truly known.

The first twenty-four hours of this new beginning, eleven hours to be accurate, most of that spent trying to sleep, had been fraught. Her body and mind restless with emotions that churned painfully, into a rancid butter. With the itinerary planned in great detail and timed to perfection things should have gone well but they hadn't. Nothing was going to plan at all, whatsoever.

She screamed, loudly, inside her jumbled head, trying to hear herself think above the noisy babble of the restless inmates. With eyes focused on a small square of floor she let out a long continuous breath, inhaling deeply several times; wrestling for control as she summarised this gross inconvenience.

Freedom, day one. Held in a toilet block due to lateness at station to collect loud destabilising sister who has already been stuck in this very toilet block whilst a robbery occurs in front of her eyes. I commandeer a dog, under what civilian powers I have no idea, but said land shark destroys a prop belonging to a diminutive Asian gentleman who I hope isn't an overstayer. I then allow immature witnesses including aforementioned sister to dance over the scene taking selfies. Aargh! She let out several more trademark long blows holding her chest and dreaming of six o'clock this morning, when she still had a grip on her destiny.

"You okay, Sis? Looking a bit hot if you don't mind me saying. Why don't you spend a bit of time in a cubicle? I bet you'll feel a whole pile better."

"No, I'm okay, really," said Jan, slightly mortified by her sister's loud observation.

Stilted chatter puffed up from the loose gathering, who had settled onto reality TV as a topic of conversation. More than one voice had mentioned hidden cameras which prompted elaborate preening and posturing from a select few who were, presumably, hoping to demonstrate their obvious and loveable character traits.

Dismissing the notion out of hand Jan entertained a survival scenario. *What if these people are the people that I have to work with to escape? What if we find ourselves fighting over plans and jostling for leadership? What if we had to complete an emergency speed icebreaker in order to bond? What if these people are my team?*

Fortunately, common sense prevailed before she could suggest the 'Two Truths and one Lie' game. Back in the moment, which was slightly depressing, Jan decided to use this nebulous confinement to build upon her bond with Hayley, who would surely be her closest ally.

"Not the best start to our get-together is it? I mean we could do with a bit of a rewind, catch up with ourselves. I'm not sure how to begin really." Positioning herself effortlessly as the younger sibling and bowing to the certain wisdom of her sister, Jan managed to elicit an acceptable response.

"Too right, feels a bit like a spin dryer, all tangled together and longing for the ironing table."

The faintest of relaxed smiles toyed with Jan's face, she felt the warmth again, a tepid glow that surrounded their attachment. *This is my sister, my only sister. The one who I am connected to above any other female on the planet, how absurd,* she thought.

Thirty years apart, three hours united. Jan marvelled at the invisible unbroken thread that still held them together. She might bang and crash all over the place spouting an unfamiliar language from down under but underneath, somewhere in there, is my sister of old.

She sidled along the washbasins careful not to sit on a damp patch or touch anything vaguely germ ridden, then gently bumped into Hayley.

"Look I'm sorry I was late. Things seemed to conspire against me and once that clock has ticked on, you really can't get it back to where you want it to be. The chance has gone, the moment passed."

Hayley studied her little sister for a moment, as though she were stalling over the appropriate reply.

"I'm a bit tetchy too, what with all that's going on, it's a heap to deal with, there's a lot on me mind, things you wouldn't believe."

She's my sister, thought Jan offering a reassuring smile, my amazing sister so, surely, we can sort out these small areas of spikiness. I can salvage this day I know I can, once we get out of here.

Her thoughts were interrupted by a tiny voice belonging to Ann Wilkins who directed a question towards Hayley in an apparent misguided assumption that she was in charge of Mrs Marshall.

"Do you erm…think this would erm…help Marble?" Came the tinny breathless sound. "It's…It's a snood. My, my daughter Sarah who you met in the erm… erm… in the cupboard." She gave a short giggle, her face flushed and the knitted purple and grey snood that draped limply across her tiny fingers, was proffered towards the temporary lodgings of Mrs Marshall.

"Well," said Hayley ushering her into view. "Let's ask her, shall we?"

Ann Wilkins glowed a sheepish amber at the cubicle door as she searched for a safe place to fix her eyes. But she needn't have worried, Mrs Marshall was fully dressed sitting next to Marble who was fully undressed below the toilet roll holder.

"Sarah erm…doesn't need it she's erm…she's a bit hot now and we've been erm…been inside for some time."

Why would a child need a snood in June? thought Jan glancing in the direction of Sarah some twelve toilets away. I bet the poor kid's glad to get rid of it.

Chapter 5

Sarah was engrossed in some fantasy world. Pink earplugs trailing overlong wires to the tightly gripped mobile device as dextrous thumbs brushed decisively across its face.

Is this the future of mankind? Is this what I have to look forward to? An impersonal fantasy world where my brother and sister exist in some virtual dimension? Where real relationships are cast aside, nothing more than complicated clumsy distractions? I won't let that happen.

Overwhelming thoughts left her drained, Jan found herself once again riding the roller-coaster of doom, it could be going up or coming down it mattered not, the discomfort would be the same. She steadied her galloping heart to walking pace, setting it free on the sand of her safe place as she determined to be the antithesis of this cold modernity. Every effort must be made to get the best from our reunion once we're back on the road.

Ann Wilkins was still engaged in her own tortured world of the unfolding snood saga, holding it so delicately in her outstretched hand that it almost fell from her grasp.

The toilet team began to take notice of this welcome distraction as the babble faded to silence.

Hayley stepped sideways into the cramped space and helpfully caught hold of the garment before it could tumble to the floor. Like an alien trying to understand the human form, Hayley gazed briefly at Ann Wilkins as though she too were from another planet, the one beginning with 'V' perhaps.

"Well, that's kind don't you think, Mrs Marshall?" Hayley held up the snood for inspection.

"I think it will keep my little poppet warm thank you." She stroked the soft wool with her frail fingers lost in another moment. Marble placed his shivering head on her lap as if to prompt Mrs Marshall into action. "Yes, this is for you," she said gathering up the material. But, before he could lodge his head into the makeshift coat, she had gone off in another direction and plunged a hand deep into the pocket of her vintage swing-style coat. "I might have a mint imperial at the bottom here if your daughter would like it – as a thank you." She continued to rummage in the cavernous pocket, pulling out a handkerchief, some hair grips, a florin from years gone by and a small, well reduced pencil before her fingers eventually settled on the gift in question.

"Yes," she said, "I've got hold of one." She dusted the dull off-white naked mint and slowly proffered it towards Ann Wilkins.

Again, Hayley assisted in the transaction of goods, holding the mint between thumb and middle finger as she turned towards the mortified recipient.

With the first flush still upon her, Ann Wilkins was near to melt down as she took custody. An item she had neither expected nor wanted but found herself holding under the watchful eyes of every member of the toilet team, except for Sarah who was too engrossed in another world to appreciate the conflict occurring in the real one.

As the blanket of tension wrapped the toilets of woe, the team were definitely feeling it. Jan glanced at the confident and defiant looking child who would shortly be approached by her mother, the complete opposite, who had possession of the mint with a destiny.

The sensitive soul couldn't even accept graciously and then once out of sight find the nearest bin. No, the team knew this was going all the way. Ann Wilkins may have been hoping for the ground to open or for the kind Venusians to pay a visit and whisk her away to a happy place but, in their absence, she continued.

Through the heat of her burning head and neck Ann Wilkins commanded her mouth to speak.

"Thank you, thank you erm… very much, it is so lovely of you, I know my daughter erm… she likes mints." The nervous giggle was followed by the final words that by any standard could be deemed as the 'she's gone too far' statement.

"She'll really like this mint erm… I know she'll enjoy it, so much. But you really erm… really shouldn't have erm… we didn't give to receive … we just wanted to help."

It was an award-winning effort of over the top, unnecessary airtime. Ann Wilkins bowed her head and pressed her hands and the mint to her chest. She had clearly expended too much emotional energy; inadvertently placed herself centre stage. Concentrating on her breath, she looked down as if to prepare herself for the next round of embarrassment.

The toilet block was still, save for a gentle flow from the automatic tap that wouldn't switch off. The audience, on the verge of applause, were mesmerised by the unfolding action. The officers guarding the exit point had moved into an observational position, earpieces removed.

Walking in small totting steps Ann Wilkins made her final descent towards Sarah, who was still far away in some other life or death reality of her own. She moved in close.

"Sarah, that nice Mrs Marshall is very grateful for your kindness," she whispered at the pink earplug.

"Well I didn't have much choice, did I?" came the reply, wrapped in all the defiance of a teenager trapped in the body of an eight-year-old.

"Well erm… darling, she has sent you this erm… thank you gift."

As Ann Wilkins began the painful uncurling of her fingers, the team held their breath, every face turned, every ear strained. Everyone except Mrs Marshall who seemed oblivious to any excitement other than the trendy snood that now stretched around her much loved pet.

Too afraid to witness what she couldn't prevent, Jan closed her eyes, every muscle in her face crumpled like a screwed up crisp packet as she waited for the inevitable, excruciating disaster.

A few feet from the action, watching the scene unfold was Clint, the self-professed goth. He too was clearly troubled by what was about to happen and, in a perfectly timed move, stepped forward to save the day.

"Say, what's the game?" he asked as he bounced in that trendy fashion towards a girl less than half his age.

With the perfect etiquette of the modern child she replied without taking her eyes or thumbs away from the task in hand. "Holy Kitty."

"Great, what level you at?"

"Three, highest I've ever been," came the engrossed excitement from a girl who still had no idea who she was talking to.

"Yeah it can be tough unless you know all the tricks."

She didn't reply, perhaps she felt undermined by someone who claimed to know something about her game world.

"If you like I can show you how to move up easier," he said with a kindness often lacking in the youth of today. "You won't lose where you're at, we can freeze that while I show you."

Ann Wilkins nervously seized the opportunity to wrap the mint in an old tissue and bury it deep into the self-conscious contents of her bag. Like a professional shoplifter, she focused on a total discrete concealment of the object. Then, cooling slightly, she turned her attention to this young man. It should be obvious to anyone that her concerns would now switch to the strange male making conversation with her daughter in the ladies' toilets.

Sarah plucked her eyes from the screen and quickly thrust her device at Clint noticing this black clad tech wizard for the first time.

"You were in the cupboard, weren't you?"

"Sure was," he replied quickly freezing the game before tilting the screen back towards her. "Now, look, if you press the screen here and then select 'level', it opens a portal giving you access to the route required in order to complete that phase see?"

Sarah awoke from her mobile phone trance and surprised her mother by engaging in a conversation with another human being. The assembled crowd from an older generation now felt that they were witnessing something no less monumental.

"Wow! that's brilliant," she said. "I haven't had anyone to help me, Mum doesn't know anything about what I do."

"Oh, I bet she does," said Clint offering a glance of warmth and maturity towards Ann Wilkins who coyly responded with a pink face.

With the screen unfrozen, Clint passed the device back to the eager thumbs of Sarah and watched from a comfortable distance to ensure she had mastered her new skill. It was never in doubt, children could nail IT whilst most parents were still searching for the shed key, never mind the nails.

No longer required to spring into action, Jan found herself once again contemplating the normal world. Ordinary people doing extraordinary things, she thought, realising this was a strap line for the special constabulary. A slogan that had fluttered into the overburdened knowledge basket of policing had reformed as some spoof recruitment drive, with Clint up there as the new poster boy.

I suppose that's a benefit to come out of being late this morning, she thought, I mean I wouldn't have seen Clint in action, wouldn't have had my faith in the youth of today moderately restored.

The dexterity and knowledge of this young man hadn't been wasted on Hayley either. She had the antennae of a battle worn mother who had learnt the art of knowing what her children were doing, even from the other side of the house. She knew when to get involved and when to back off and at this moment her curiosity was aroused.

Above the renewed chatter of the captured comrades, Hayley made herself heard.

"Hey Clint, you're a bit of a computer bod, are you? What about mobile phones? See, I've just come over to England," she said walking and talking and waving her phone towards him. "I've got this odd problem with me access. For some reason I have to keep inputting my details every time I make a call or check me social stuff, flaming annoying. Wasn't like this at home, I reckon it's ever since I left Singapore it's been crook."

"Crook?" he said clearly amused by this colourful intrusion.

"Blimey, we do speak the same language you know. Crook, sick? broken? that kind of thing, anyway, can you help me?" She waggled the phone in front of his dark brown perfectly balanced eyes.

Will I ever have my sister's confidence, move normally through the world and have meaningful conversations? Pondered Jan as she methodically washed her hands and tried to erase the unthinkable germs and disease that cling during a prolonged confinement in public toilets. Of course, this is all totally wrong, she thought, a loo was supposed to be used briefly and privately, it was not a place for conversation and IT repairs.

A more detailed survey of the collective group was now required in case she really did have to rely on them in some spontaneous call for action. Based on the most recent events, she redrew her fantasy team by asking the primary question: what skills do they bring? She would definitely have Clint; he was clever and considerate. Brian would be in of course, if he was released, he had demonstrated bravery and combat skills. Mrs Marshall though, wasn't being considered, not even as a dog handler. Then there was Hayley, rubbish with identification but might talk us out of trouble. She pondered her own role as the hand dryer wafted the heat of a blow torch across her fingers.

Uncomfortably hot and still overwhelmed by the enormity of her new life she was once again lured towards the entrance, this time by a gentle cool draft. She stopped short of the two officers who had resumed their containment duty, to consider her next move. With Hayley still talking loudly against the background of noise bouncing around the clinically tiled walls, Jan braced herself and stepped forward.

"Do you think we'll be held for much longer?" She found herself foolishly whispering.

"I couldn't say, madam."

Jan absorbed the crushing blow of that word again and probed the fresh-faced officer who didn't look a day over sixteen.

"I'll see what I can find out for you, madam."

Is he saying that deliberately? Does he not know how irritating that word is? She forced a gracious smile and said nothing.

He stepped away and spoke with confidence into his radio. Marginally out of earshot he could have been ordering his lunch for all she knew and all she would ever know now that she was a freshly pensioned civilian.

"My sister captured the event on her mobile phone apparently." Jan had an idea that if she offered this nugget of important information, maybe the invisible line between them would dissolve and she could perhaps, for a moment, gain access to her old life.

The second officer, a man mountain with muscles bulging obscenely from his short-sleeved wicking T-shirt, responded.

"We'll get to that in good time, we just have to secure the scene and the suspects. Shouldn't be too much longer," he said, firmly dismissing the spokeswoman.

Futile and pointless, thought Jan, might as well be their names. No wonder the public get annoyed.

She was the impatient fool with a breathing problem floundering like a fish in a shallow puddle, exposed and uncomfortable with eyes that bulged unattractively. Jan should have known better than to risk all this exposure at 10:45 in the morning on day one. She cupped her hands and rubbed each thumb slowly and deliberately over the other which looked, for all the world, as if a genie was expected to appear with a coffee table A-Z of being normal.

Hayley, in full animated flow near the fire door, called out.

"Hey Sis, come and meet Clint," she hailed, commanding the room once more. "Fair dinkum phone wiz aren't you, mate? and here was me blaming Singapore." She prodded him on the arm with warmly received affection.

"Oh, hi, I'm Clint," he said faltering slightly. He offered a hand and shook Jan's with little more substance than an ostrich feather.

"Yeah, Clint mate, my sister's one of them," she said raising her eyebrows and nodding towards the door.

This unexpected public announcement wasn't necessarily the reason that Jan was cowering in a dark hole. It was more the shock that her own mind was falling over itself to deny that she'd had any connection to the police force whatsoever.

Trapped in a narrow corridor of grimy doors and grubby sinks, she turned from the crowd, which was nigh on impossible.

"Hayley please, I'm retired," she whispered from behind a clammy hand. She looked at the floor and longed, like people do, for a distraction.

"So you keep saying, but you did charge in here with that donkey of a dog and save us all before the damned uniforms got here. Come on, let's hear it for my sister." Hayley turned to the crowd who were once again on the edge of their seats; well, Mrs Marshall was.

Jan sidestepped into an empty cubicle, catching her arm on the flimsy partition. Cod, cod, cod she shouted at no one but herself, why are these places so small?

It's a claustrophobic mess that's what this is, a complete and utter disaster, this is not how I live my life. Her face smudged like a badly drawn line portrait as she screwed her eyes into another dimension.

Outside, the mixed voice hip-hip-hoorah built to its third rousing crescendo prompting Hayley to push the door against Jan's other arm and drag her out into full public view.

"Come on, Sis, take a bow, the crowd love yah."

Jan held up her hand, which looked for all the world as though she were in court about to swear an oath. Then, before Hayley could organise a party or demand a speech, Jan ducked into the cubicle and quietly locked the door. Absolutely desperate for a pee, she took a deep breath, blocked out the world around her and hovered in hope.

CHAPTER 6

The sun set on the longest day and then rose to reveal the tattered team who had suffered and survived without food or water in the face of this interminable incarceration. Such harsh conditions would be deemed unsuitable even for the resilient police support unit – the PSU, that hardy bunch of souls who could sleep anywhere as long as food wasn't in short supply.

But it was stuff of fancy, for Jan had slipped from reality and put her mind in the hands of an autopilot who was happy to accommodate her darkest fears. Thankfully, these unhelpful thoughts were intercepted by the arrival of a visitor. It was the familiar face of the sergeant aka Carl Cooper who appeared to have calmed down a little.

"The area is now safe, nothing for you to worry about, thank you for your patience. Due to the skill of my highly trained officers, we have got to the bottom of this. Persons have been detained and removed, they no longer present a danger to the public and therefore, I should soon be able to get you on your way."

"Has Brian been arrested?" shouted Hayley moving herself forward. "He's innocent, he's a hero."

"All I can say, madam, is that Mr Jones is helping us with our enquiries, I am not at liberty to say more. Regarding your position, I have a team of officers from our investigation department who will be along shortly to take statements where appropriate. At the very least we will need to obtain your contact details. We will also address any welfare concerns in connection with what you may have witnessed. In the meantime, I have negotiated with McDonald's who will be providing complimentary refreshments while you wait."

"How long's that going to take?" said Hayley now almost at the front of the loosely formed queue.

Ignoring the heckler, Sgt Cooper continued. "My officers here will escort you over to the seating area where I would ask you all to remain until we've spoken to you individually. As I say, as soon as we've completed our enquiries, we'll have you on your way."

Now fully under his nose, Hayley unleashed her mind. "Bet you were surprised that Brian the cleaner was an army commando? Who would have thought it? You don't know people, do you?"

Like a relaxed cat waiting to swipe the brave and foolish mouse, Sgt Cooper kept half an eye on this minor irritation.

"Anyway, if you want evidence, I recorded the whole thing on me mobile. Look, if I just show you what I've got this'll all be done a lot quicker and me and me new mates will be able to get on with what we want to do instead of doing your work."

The distant hand dryer fell silent, Jan winced, fully aware that her sister was pressing all the wrong buttons.

It took Sgt Cooper little over a minute to view the footage and determine that it was important evidence. He thanked Hayley and before she could utter the words: 'I told you so' or similar, he deftly produced, from his impressive assortment of pockets, a small evidence bag into which he dropped the item.

"Oi mate, what are you doing? You can't keep me flaming phone, I've just got it fixed. My whole life is on there, you can't just keep it."

"I'll need the PIN code too please," he continued with his firm unblinking tone.

"What? I can't tell you that, it's confidential. I shan't flaming tell you, why should I? I've just been robbed."

"May I remind you, madam, that obstructing an investigation is an offence for which you may be prosecuted."

It was a fruitless stand-off; it had the potential to escalate and Jan knew the consequences. They could end up spending even more wasted time at these services or worse in these toilets or worse still, at the police station.

"Jiminy cricket! I was just being helpful, doing my bit to help poor Brian and now it's me who's turned out the flaming victim."

"You will get it back," offered Sgt Cooper routinely.

"When?"

"At the end of the investigation."

"Well, how long is that going to take?"

"I can't say, but the sooner we get a statement from you…"

"You want a statement too? Jeez. Look, I need my phone – family reunion, meeting my brother Mikey. If I don't have my phone how am I supposed to contact him?"

"I'm sorry," he said closing the door on her wasted protest. "If you could just follow my officers to the seating area, we can start organising those statements." He then turned, with the unhurried purpose of a policeman in uniform and walked away.

Like the fly in the pitcher plant, every slippery word pushed her further from the phone. But, with determined futility, she followed the bagged mobile out of the toilets until Sgt Cooper disappeared to leave her bereft and bewildered.

"I thought you did well, not to get too angry, I mean it could have messed up our day. We really could have been in trouble there." Jan studied the distressed face across the salt speckled table.

"Aargh!" cried Hayley. "That's the last time I'm helping the flaming police. I've been robbed and stranded on the other side of the world."

They sat, each in their own space as if too drained from the events of the morning to utter any more thoughts. The bubble of silence that fell between them had been wrapped in the lingering smell of fast food that choked the sweet air of freedom.

Hayley, like a kestrel looking for prey, had her eyes locked onto the last position she had clocked Sgt Cooper, she wasn't giving up easily, if at all.

Perhaps she didn't understand the investigative practices of the British police force thought Jan who had drifted into a moment of calm and collided with something strange. This wasn't her happy place or her safe place, it was somewhere else entirely which, as yet, lacked a place name. Not that she approved of place names, such terms did not sit comfortably. Where she chose to go and what she wished to call it, was her own business and didn't need some overpaid mind doctor to define it with a label.

This reflective moment was cheerily interrupted by the arrival of complimentary coffee served with pizzazz by the exuberant McDonald's manager. Earlier he'd released eight terrified staff through the fire door before he stood firm behind the McFlurry machine refusing to *dessert* his post. Overcome with pride and excitement, he handed out beverages with all the flair and commitment of a silver service waiter.

Clint and Sarah were drinking milkshakes, laughing and joking like sister and older brother under the nervous watchful eye of Mrs Wilkins who sipped a cup of tea.

"Look at those two," said Hayley trying to calm herself with the heavily sugared coffee. "A little bit of magic going on there I reckon, and as I'm in possession of the number for me new mate Clint, I may as well send him a text or two just to embarrass him."

"Hayley please."

"Don't get excited, only pulling your tail. Still, it'll be useful to call him if me phone settings go walkabout again."

"I'm not sure Clint can help you with the current problem."

"Damn," she said, jumping up to scan for Sgt Cooper and the important plastic bag.

Jan checked her watch, 11:25 and the lessons in being normal were hitting her thick and fast. Of course, it was right to offer the phone evidence, she reasoned, everyone has a civic duty to help police officers prevent crime and catch offenders. But it appeared that this confiscation would have a significant impact on Hayley and for a moment Jan wrestled her conscience; should she have kept quiet? She banged her coffee cup onto the table; no, that would be morally wrong. Of course it would, why was she even thinking like that? Yesterday, it wouldn't even have entered my head, it's ridiculous. Note to self; don't let standards slip from sight, these challenging moral dilemmas could lurk anywhere.

"You okay in there, Sis?" said Hayley taking a break from Sgt Cooper to resume her admiration of Clint and Sarah. "Do you think that'll be us when we finally catch up with Mikey? We'll just click and the years will melt away?"

"I can't imagine it somehow, seems a big ask after all this time. We've got history, inside information about each other, that's quite different to two strangers meeting and hitting it off without all the baggage."

"Yeah, but look at us? I know all your little secrets and we're doing alright I reckon."

Jan had to agree things had improved over the last few hours and the lateness incident felt like a distant domino that lay low.

"I just wish it was the day that I'd hoped for," she said sipping the fluffy coffee.

"Look, Sis, you were late, I'm surprised at that. I was, and still am in fact, jet-lagged and quite a bit has battered us this morning.

Whilst I didn't imagine you'd turn up in a print dress with a Victoria sponge in a biscuit tin, I did think we might have taken a moment to have a good look at each other and find our common path. We could have checked out more of our little traits and battle scars. Filled in the gaps and found the glue, you know, Sis, that bond that makes us family."

Hayley's brief assessment sent a shiver of warmth across a long-forgotten seat marked 'Middle Child'. Jan thought she'd lost this *place,* grown out of it, that this sense of being had gone forever but, it had not. It was her destiny, the connection, the realisation that you only know your true *place* in life when you're among family.

"Well, I agree with that, it was a bit rushed, but hopefully we'll soon be on our way again and back on track. It is nice to see you, you know. You forget, don't you?" Jan smiled as she spoke from the protective wrapping of her recently uncovered family seat.

Middle child frustration hadn't always been easy to bear. She'd watched and whinged as the older sister stayed out late, ignored her younger siblings and lorded it over them with the privilege of older status. Sometimes, frustrated by the comfortable middle, Jan had nurtured her own ideas for brood management.

When Hayley packed and departed for her adult adventures, Jan was wallowing in the painful uncertainty of her first teenage year. The euphoria of finally being the eldest in the nest was a short-lived blur. One side of her boat was leaking through the hole in her starboard side as she realised that things under the old regime hadn't been all that bad.

Thrust into the top spot with a leak and no rudder, Jan had an unspoken responsibility to guide and protect the next, and indeed only, one down. Overwhelmed by her own issues and insecurities she felt an everyday failure in her duties towards Mike. She withdrew, like teenagers do, longing for her irritating big sister to reappear in the bed opposite. But it was never going to happen. Hayley had been carried off like a bubble in the wind and burst onto a different continent far from view.

"I really don't know how Mike will be. I haven't spoken to him for at least seventeen years and then it was just to let him know the date for aunt Ethel's funeral. But he, like you, never came."

"It was ten thousand miles. It's a long way to come to sing a hymn and watch a curtain draw around a box containing who knows who."

"That's true; it didn't seem much more than that. It's funny to think that for all we are or do or become, we still only get a half-hour slot, with a few people singing an unfamiliar tune before the coffin conveyor tips you into the fiery furnace."

"Don't get all sad on me, Sis. We're not dead yet you know."

"Well, I wasn't really in the mood when it happened."

"Jeez, I didn't know you had to be in a certain mood before people could die on yah."

"No, it was just that I'd had one of those years when I seemed to be dealing with sudden death after sudden death. I was getting a bit of a reputation. A rumour did the rounds that I was having an affair with the coroner, but he was old enough to be my grandad I imagine. He's dead now anyway."

"Killed him off too eh? Listen, you single girls shouldn't be so fussy."

"Do you mind, I have standards."

"I think they're a bit too high, Sis, if you ask me. You know, if you want to share your life you have to look at the options on offer, focus and adapt."

"Well, anyway, death focuses you. Focuses you on how precious life is and how it can be gone in just an instant. I suppose I was feeling quite alone and vulnerable."

"My point exactly; alone, vulnerable. You need to listen to yourself before you find you're going down the death slide with no one to hold your hand."

"I don't need my hand holding. I've been surviving quite nicely thank you."

"Like I say, you need to listen to yourself. You could have called me, told me all about your lonely old life with the dead people. I mean you haven't exactly been the big communicator over the years. Thought you police people would be good at all that stuff."

"Well, I have kept all of your emails updating me on the boys and the business and life in the sun. I replied to all of them, I know I did."

"It'd be a lot easier if you weren't such a dinosaur and got yourself set up on social media. You'd be in my circle, be able to see all the photos and videos, get yourself with it."

"Yes, I know, but I don't want to get dragged into all that looking at your phone every few minutes business, wondering who's doing what. I'm starting a new life away from the public gaze. Well, that's what I'm hoping for once this incident is behind us."

"Me own sister not wanting to look at me photos, how did this happen to you? Is it the police? Have they made you into a hermit dinosaur? You should try and get some compo; they should have prepared you a bit better for the outside world."

Treading an unfamiliar path can fill you with doubts the moment you realise you've left your shoes at home especially if you don't have a plan. But Jan *did* have a plan; the problem was, they were running several hours behind schedule.

Hayley appeared to live in an exciting social whirl that Jan struggled to imagine, without any point of reference, how that must feel. Her sister had effortlessly taken to her new family position and subsequent motherhood. A different role on a different continent far away from Jan's world.

"I hear what you're saying, I do but that's not my life, I'm doing okay my way. I suppose I've got used to Mike not being in my life, just as you've had to get used to it."

"Yeah, but like I say, I am the other side of the world. You live one English county apart; what's your excuse?"

Jan thought carefully, not intending for a dramatic pause but it was too late, the moment had been crossed through with a blue highlighter.

"Oh, Sis, you really are a lemon pavlova. You're priceless. You wait 'til I put this out on Facebook."

"No, please don't do that," pleaded Jan, scorched by a rash of prickly heat that smothered her body and bubbled her eyes with salty emulsion. Winded by the blow of a pending public humiliation, her hands snapped across her face with elbows firmly planted to the table

"You alright in there?" Hayley took hold of her sister's elbows and squeezed gently. "I'm only joking with you, Sis; like I say you're still very easy to wind up."

Like a limpet at low tide, Jan's hands remained clamped to her face as Hayley firmed her grip and valiantly rocked the immovable arm pillars.

"Come on, baby Sis, I know you're in there."

"Go away," said Jan in a childlike tone.

Hayley slid her fingers to the forearm pressure points and pressed mercilessly until both hands sprung from Jan's smiling face.

"See how you've missed me? It's a good job I've come over to sort out this little Elliot reunion."

"It was my idea."

"Yes, but everyone needs a party planner, don't they?"

The responsibility of policing had swamped Jan's entire working life to the exclusion of all else except for one weighty issue. Mike was her elephant in the room, the darkening shadow that had developed into a cloud of storm proportions. She was his eldest sister for the purposes of his childhood, he relied on her as much as Jan had relied on Hayley, except Jan wasn't Hayley, she was terrified.

"I hope he made it okay."

"Made it?" said Hayley collecting up the coffee cartons.

"Yes, you were our rock, my rock, I don't think you realised that. I couldn't look after him like you did."

The burden never strayed far from Jan's mind and she knew it would have to be reconciled before she could comfortably claim her destiny.

"Come on, Sis, I had a life to live had to go out there and grab it. Then I met Leonard and the rest is written in dreamtime I expect. Look, I haven't kept in touch with Mikey as much as I should have, I think you must have coached him in your reclusive ways. I wait for days sometimes for a reply on Facebook but at least he's on it and uses it, eventually. Anyway, it's not him or you that's delaying this reunion, it's the extraordinary length of time you have to wait for a policeman around here."

Jan smiled and found herself relaxing once again into the safe company of her sister. All her vital signs appeared to be reading normal and a calm anticipation filled the air.

"Do you think they'd mind if we had another coffee?" asked Hayley getting to her feet.

"I shouldn't think so, but take this." Jan extracted a ten-pound note from her wallet and placed her order. "I wouldn't want you getting into another scene."

"What do you mean by that, Sis? Well, anyway, what's the harm seeing if we can get free refills? There's no need to be all bashful, this is the real world, it's okay to be a freeloader now and again."

The freedom Jan had wanted from retirement was still playing hide and seek somewhere in the middle distance but, despite all that had happened, she began to focus on the good bits. She had survived an encounter with a dog, the incident with a suspected firearm and the embarrassment of peeing in a mixed public toilet. She had also reconnected with her sister who seemed exactly the same except for her age, her looks and her accent. In spite of all that, they had picked up their unbreakable thread and seemed capable of skipping along nicely.

Hayley placed two coffee cartons between them and passed the folded ten-pound note back to Jan.

"I'm sure that guy thinks I'm a drongo asking for latte with sprinkles, why don't you just have a cappuccino?"

"It's not the same," replied Jan gazing across at Mrs Marshall. "She looks a bit lost, doesn't she?"

Without pausing to discuss the matter, Hayley picked up her coffee and moved tables.

"Hello, Mrs Marshall."

Jan arrived a few beats later sipping her sprinkled latte and listening as Mrs Marshall promptly evacuated her mind.

"I get on the bus every Thursday to do my shopping but the shops have all changed; have they been moved, dear? They aren't where I left them last week. The Midland Bank was there, look." She pointed a crooked finger towards the sparkly phone accessories unit. "I buy my pick and mix from Woollies as well but I can't find that either. I always have pick and mix for the bus, dear."

"Oh, dear. I say," whispered Hayley. "First she lost her trolley and now it appears to be her marbles too."

"SSHHH! she's very mixed up," replied Jan hiding her mouth behind the cup.

"You're not kidding, even I know the Midland Bank went years ago."

"Stop it, she's very vulnerable and needs help." Jan attempted to take control of the situation and started by quizzing her sister.

"Was there anyone else with her when you all met up in the cupboard?"

"There was no room for anyone else; didn't you see the tiny space we were crammed into?"

"Yes, but was there anyone she may have been separated from?"

"What kind of crazy question is that? I hope this wasn't a style of questioning you used when you were parading around in that uniform. We didn't have time for all that 'Hello how do you do, who are you travelling with today?', it was about survival. Squish in the cupboard, introduce yourself later."

"Is this what I've got to look forward to? Life in a community with a total lack of observational skills, no awareness of surroundings, no evidence gathering?"

"Whoa, whoa, whoa! hang on a minute who was it that gave you a running commentary through the door grille? Who was it that filmed the robbers and will, as a result of my 'Free Brian' campaign, be given a citizen's award for my services to British policing?"

"Okay, okay I agree you did do quite well, showed a lot of initiative, just need to work on your identification skills."

"Yeah, good, see it isn't just you highly trained current or ex or retired or whatever you are police, with initiative and I'm not even getting paid, am I? Which reminds me, I've had a thought about that phone footage, what do you think they'll pay me for it? You know all about this stuff, what's the going rate a thousand? Ten thousand? I don't mind if they pay me in Aussie dollars."

"You'll be lucky to get it back anytime soon; it has been seized as evidence remember. I'd be surprised if you could claim the bus fare to collect it."

Avoiding further distraction, Jan turned her attention back to the immediate issue of a confused elderly dog walker.

"Mrs Marshall?"

"Hello, dear."

"Hello, Mrs Marshall, I'm Jan from the toilets remember?"

"Are you my neighbour?"

Undeterred, Jan pressed on with her enquiries. "Where do you live?"

"Well, next door to you of course. Are you being silly, dear? Your cat keeps coming into my house which is very naughty because Marble doesn't like cats." She paused and her eyes fell heavily towards the table between them until they were lifted again by her next thought. "Could you help me?" she said quietly before her eyes returned to the table.

Somewhat relieved, Jan acknowledged this small breakthrough, it seemed the real Mrs Marshall still had her hand firmly on the self-preservation button. She was calling time on all this confusion and asking for some real assistance to transport her back to the world she knew.

I just need to find her address, thought Jan confidently.

Of course, Mrs Marshall was not on the same page, or chapter, she was still in her unfamiliar world far away from the clutch of a passing do-gooder.

"I need the Midland Bank," she said. "I have to pay my mortgage; I do on a Thursday."

Jan shuffled in her seat, winded by her own quick-fix mindlessness and lack of progress. More questions needed to be asked and more answers needed to be dismissed.

"How did you get here?"

"I got off the bus, dear. How else do you think I got here? Young people haven't got the slightest grasp." Mrs Marshall trailed back to her table gaze as the pointless inquisition continued.

"This isn't a bus stop; you're not supposed to get off here." Jan winced at her own voice, harsh and unfamiliar. Her palm rubbed against her forehead willing for compassion to be restored.

"You have to get off the bus to get to the shops, dear," continued Mrs Marshall. "Why are you trying to confuse me?"

"No, Mrs Marshall, I'm just trying to get things straight, you see you won't find the Midland Bank here and today is Monday."

"Is it? oh dear, I haven't paid my mortgage. Will they take my house away? I can't have Marble living on the streets. I don't want to live on the streets, the postman won't know where I am. I haven't packed my things."

As if to make her own mental amends Jan reached out across the table and gently held the frail hands.

"It's okay," said Jan with a tenderness that she was pleased to find at this moment. "We'll sort it out."

"Oh no dear, you can't pay my mortgage."

"Look, what we'll do is ask the police to help you sort it out."

No longer a responsibility that Jan had to bear, she would hand this over to her former colleagues to carry out the appropriate house and welfare checks. With a gentle squeeze to the hands Jan released Mrs Marshall.

"Oh no, I don't want to be arrested. Can they do that, dear? Arrest you for not paying your mortgage?" She sat as a deflated, defeated soul might, lost and alone in a world of confusion. A world where she occupied a corner seat frightened by the events that played out in front of her with tricks and flicks that made no sense and never would again. She pulled Marble close to her knees and rubbed his delicate ears until he sank to the floor out of reach.

"Don't worry, we'll get you home soon. Let me get you another coffee while you wait."

"Chocolate. I'd like hot chocolate please, dear."

Hayley followed Jan to the counter.

"Jeez, talk about kangaroos loose in the top paddock."

"That's unfair. Imagine how you'd feel, shut away in some strange place where you didn't recognise anyone and you were frightened of everything that was going on around you."

"I do know how I'd feel, are you forgetting why we're here? I don't think you fully appreciate the distressing ordeal I endured in that cupboard."

"Entirely inappropriate," said Jan as she watched the manager whip up the fluffy beverage.

"Only joking with you, Sis. Will we have to take her home?"

Jan cupped her hands around the fresh hot chocolate and imagined the frail hands that would take her place. She'd met many Mrs Marshalls in her time they were a sadness that resonated like a soft Japanese wind chime deep in her stomach. Lovely people who'd been snatched from in front of our eyes to live in a world we cannot see.

"So, is that a yes or a no?" said Hayley following the hot chocolate to its destiny.

"It's not my responsibility anymore, finally there's an advantage to being a civilian. It will rest with the next sensible officer I speak to."

CHAPTER 7

Armed with paperwork, three plain-clothed officers looked set to bring an end to this inconvenience that Jan had thus far endured on her first day away from police work.

Two of the officers carried well-worn document cases crammed with the necessary paraphernalia for their evidence gathering task. The third held a clipboard decorated unprofessionally with an assortment of stickers that included one from a company dealing with banana imports and a garish two for one supermarket offer in red.

I couldn't work with that officer, thought Jan shaking her head and feeling embarrassed on behalf of the Chief Constable. Surely this is not the image he would want officers to portray in the public domain? Still, it is of no consequence to me anymore.

She fiddled with the durable digital watch that had kept her life in order as a timepiece should.

12:05, we must be at least two hours, maybe more behind where we should be in my day, the day that has been hijacked. If only time didn't matter, if it passed without consequence, but it doesn't. Time is brief, moments lost forever with regret occupying a bigger pile every day and, for all my planning, today is no exception. We could have caught up with Mike by now and it could all be over with.

Soon tabletops were spread with statement paper and notebooks. Jan lived in hope that the boys in blue, or rather civvies, would be fast and efficient in their work. After which, she would be free to return to the new normal, yet to be defined, world.

As a key witness Hayley was scooped up first along with Brad the manager from WHSmith and Sulung the charity worker who was still handling the black bag containing his bear bits.

Thankfully, not everyone needed to provide a statement and it wasn't long before Jan swapped places with Sulung. Struck once again by the withering sense of guilt and responsibility at his predicament, she made a mental note to explore how she could best support his charity.

As an experienced statement writer, Jan was succinct, no deviation, no embroidery just chronological facts relayed with her usual brevity. With the matter drawing to a close, she swivelled from the plastic seat just as Hayley started shouting across the tables.

"Jan, Jan, I gave them my Aussie address but they need a contact number in England and they've got me phone, haven't they? Can I give them yours?"

Jan left her statement in the podgy hands of the sticker book king and moved across to join Hayley and her substantially smarter officer.

"Hello," she said holding her phone so he could copy from the screen.

"My sister is a retired police officer you know," beamed Hayley looking pleased by her latest attempt at embarrassment.

"Really?" said the officer in a dry manner, "enjoying it?"

"Not yet, it's like I'm still there. I'm trying to get away from this sort of thing; criminals, crimes, dishonesty."

"Yeah, that would be nice wouldn't it?" he said remaining entirely focused on his task. "Just a few signatures, if you're happy with what you've said?"

"Sure, jeez mate, you're making me doubt me self."

He pointed to the places that, once signed, would turn this ordinary piece of paper into an official legal document.

"Right," he said retrieving his pen from Hayley, "if you wouldn't mind waiting here, there're a few things I need to check; shouldn't be too long."

"What checks?" asked Hayley as the officer gathered his things. "Look, we need to be on our way and you need to sort out poor old Mrs Marshall, she's a lot more important than little old me."

"I'll be as quick as I can." He disappeared to the temporary operational command post behind a flimsy wall of advertising paraphernalia and some wholly resistible merchandise.

Sensing a slight change in the atmosphere Jan plunged into action.

"What's going on here? What did you say to him?"

"How do you mean?" she said folding her arms and swaying slightly pulling at her elbows.

"You're edgy, look at you, I know the signs. Since you've been sat with that officer, something isn't right. Did he say something to you?"

"No. Now give me a flaming break, I told you it's me jet lag and that painful train journey."

"Are you sure? Are you sure you're okay?"

"Look, I just didn't expect to encounter the finest police force in the world quite so soon in me trip. It's very intimidating, we all know how good they are."

"Are you being sarcastic?" Jan eyed her sister with concerned suspicion.

"Well, maybe just a little. Let's face it they did turn up a bit late didn't they? Got their faults like the rest of us."

Their conversation was broken by Detective Sergeant Paul Plummer. He shook hands, introduced himself and then purposefully sat opposite Hayley while Jan struggled for breath such had been the firmness of his grip.

DS Plummer was, without doubt, the smartest officer Jan had met so far today. A fine example of an officer who wore his own clothes to work. He had standards that she approved of. Neatly ironed shirt, appropriate choice of tie, suitably smart working trousers and shiny shoes. Not too shiny, he wasn't causing concern in that regard but overall, he was reassuringly well presented. He opened his black leather document case and produced the evidence bag containing Hayley's mobile phone and placed it in full view on the table.

Distracted by the sight of her must have (back) possession, Hayley sat forward attentively.

"Oh good, can I have it back now?" She smiled, pulling herself up straight like a child trying to behave for a few minutes.

"Well, yes you can." DS Plummer delivered his words carefully and monitored her reaction.

Hundreds of planned interviews had taught Jan the benefit of this measured approach, there was an agenda; DS Plummer was laying a trail but what for? Jan should wait to see where this would lead but, on a wave of broken babble, she launched a surprise attack.

"What? Give it back? It's evidence, surely? You can't give it back just like that?"

Hayley pushed Jan's arm. "Here, whose side are you on?"

Undeterred, Jan sat forward and steadied herself, frantically trying to order the strands of information that bounced around her overexcited head. And as soon as she had them all pieced together, she would show the DS the error of his ways and thus retain the integrity of evidence held by Devon and Cornwall Police.

But, standing opposed to this procedural knowledge that battled for a voice, was a lump of expandable foam that wanted to supress all this nonsense and fill her head with bubbly softness. This interjection by the moral standards committee that had caused Jan to flounder for a moment must be dismissed after all, she reasoned, the issue should rest with DS Plummer, the rightful owner.

This brief connection with a fluffy pillow had created a space for Jan to relax and straighten her thoughts. It's history, unnecessary clutter, let it go, you're a member of the public now, you have to trust this officer.

Feeling as though an hour of internal debate had just concluded, Jan sat back and concentrated on quality breathing as DS Plummer resumed.

"Yes, it is. You're quite right. This phone is important evidence."

Jan found it hard to read his face and had gathered nothing from his tone so, she fixed her eyes on him and waited.

"But there is something more important that I need to discuss. Are you two travelling together?"

"Yes," said Jan still unsure of *his* direction of travel.

"We're meeting up with our brother Mikey for a reunion," added Hayley as she relaxed in her seat.

He held a silver Parker pen motionless between his hands and then continued.

"Where does Mike live?"

"Not exactly sure," Hayley shrugged. "Somewhere in Cornwall, that's about all I know. We're heading that way and hopefully he'll get back to me with an address before we fall off the end, you know Land's End? Of course, it isn't Jan's usual way of doing things. She likes trips all planned out with a Thermos and cut lunch."

"That is totally unnecessary information, Hayley. So, sergeant, what is this all about?"

"You can call me Paul if you'd prefer," he said opening a buff folder. "Let me just establish a few things first, if I may. You are Hayley Allblack, you live at Engles, Ocean View Drive, Airlie Beach, Queensland and you flew from Cairns via Sydney and Singapore arriving into Heathrow on June 13th?"

"Yes, and I can explain."

"As I understand it," continued DS Paul Plummer sticking to his train of thought. "You have a brother, Michael Elliot forty-five years old living in Cornwall."

Hayley stared longingly at her phone and dismissed his accurate summary.

"You really are on the ball today."

"Hayley," said Jan falling instinctively into the role of second interview officer with the need to chastise her sister. A sister who had all the hallmarks of a guilty person. But what has she been doing and why are the police interested in her travel itinerary? As she reflected on their morning so far and the mess they currently found themselves in, Jan was now anything but relaxed. She looked intently at her new colleague imploring him to speak, to bring her up to speed with the case and reveal the extent of Hayley's crime.

"Ah, yes and you," he said making relaxed eye contact with Jan, "you are the other sister?"

Her mouth fell open, slightly, as she sifted through the nonsense that poured uninvited into her head. What? Come on, Paul mate, I'm on your side, you can't turn on your colleague like this. What possible reason could the police have to scrutinise me? I definitely returned all my kit, well, except for the torch but the guy in stores said that was personal issue and I could keep it. It can't be that surely? And I closed my email accounts; no one could send a rude message to the chief, not in my name anyway. Maybe someone has complained? Yes, that could be it, someone didn't like my handling of their case, their life took a terrible turn and it was because of a decision I made. Oh no, who could it be?

She took several deep breaths, rescue breaths; any breath at all would be useful as she floundered back into the moment in her civilian seat.

"Yes, Janet Elliot PC3485 retired as of yesterday but I can't say as I'd noticed yet."

"Okay, well I'll be blunt, the thing is Michael Elliot is wanted."

"What?" Jan had risen and then fallen back into her plastic chair before blurting out all the usual questions expected of a distressed relative. "Wanted for what? How do you mean? My brother Mike? Are you sure? Why?"

"I am sure, Jan, I'm sorry if that came as a shock. Did you really have no idea?"

"Of course not, are you absolutely sure it's the same Mike Elliot?"

"Yes, there is no doubt. I have to say, it's a big plus for the security services that you didn't know. That's how it should be, it's just that you being ex job, it was a risk that, well that you might have found out something."

"I *am* not, *was* not, that sort of officer. I can't believe we are even having that conversation."

"I know you're not, we had to do some checks."

"Were you monitoring me at work?"

"Well. *I* wasn't but you know how it is, we're all being watched, it's part of the job."

"Questioning my integrity?"

"You don't want to be questioning that, Paul, my sister is very sensitive about that sort of thing." Hayley turned away, tittering triumphantly.

"Are you making this up? Is this some kind of joke? Is this because I didn't want a drunken leaving do? Are my team behind this? Because it's not funny anymore, in fact it wasn't funny to start with." Jan dug her sister in the ribs. "You can be quiet as well."

"Jan, this isn't a joke. I don't have any information on your leaving do or lack of," offered DS Plummer.

"Then give me some more, convince me. What is he wanted for?"

"I can't disclose very much – you should appreciate that; this is an intelligence led operation and we're working with very little."

"I had noticed that," giggled Hayley bouncing around with renewed excitement.

"It's a highly sensitive operation, I don't have the right clearance for the full briefing but, in a nutshell, Michael Elliot is involved in a security risk. It's imperative that we locate him."

Hayley resumed her posture of the expectant school child and sat up to the table.

"Whoa, whoa, whoa, hold it right there, mate." Hayley turned to face him. "Are we talking about *our* Mikey? Our Mikey who sat on the lounge floor building Lego fire stations and painting model aeroplanes as soon as he got home from school?"

"Yes," added Jan feeling the need to clarify the identity of this man she hardly knew but nonetheless was her brother and, in her opinion, couldn't possibly be the same man they were getting all excited about. "Our Mike who went to technical college, did something techy and then disappeared from my life?"

"Not a bit of intel I am in possession of, but essentially yes, your brother Michael Elliot." DS Plummer continued to weave what little he did know into an engaging tale in the hope that he would fulfil his own important brief. "There is another element which poses equal concern, a little-known terror group called *Voleur Payé* who are also looking for your brother."

"Who are *Voleur Payé?*" asked Jan trying to remember something useful from the 'How to deal with a Terrorist Threat' mandatory training module.

"It translates as Paid Thief so we could assume they want to take something. That isn't in the intel package that I have been given by the way, but it might be relevant. This slightly complicates things as the operational objective is to secure both Michael and *Voleur Payé* at the location."

"What location?" asked Jan desperately wishing for a pocket notebook to hand.

"His location, where you are meeting him presumably."

Hayley looked at Jan who might have shrugged if she hadn't been in shock.

"But we don't know his location, I'm fairly certain we did mention that minor detail to you, Paul the policeman."

"You did; however, an assumption has been made that you weren't intending to drive aimlessly around Cornwall for the rest of the day and that you would eventually procure an address."

"Is that so?" said Jan fixing her eyes on Hayley.

"You also need to know that *Voleur Payé* have installed some software on this phone. Have you any idea when this could have happened?"

"Flaming drongos; is nothing safe in the world? Course I don't know when that happened, I only use the phone, I don't have the first idea how it works do I?"

"Okay, that's understandable; *Voleur Payé* appear to be quite a sophisticated organisation, but we just don't know. The certainty is that they pose an imminent threat to national and international security, it is imperative that it is neutralised as quickly as possible. The order has come from the top. I haven't seen that order myself but I am acting on *my* orders which are to secure your cooperation in this critical matter. We cannot risk a security breach of this potential magnitude."

"Steady on there, mate, you're putting the wind up me and besides, like I said, we don't know where he is, I'm still waiting for news, which could be in that mobile phone. But you might know that if you did your investigation properly." She reshaped her coffee cup with restless fingers that loitered near the evidence bag ready to grab it just as soon as DS Plummer gave the nod.

"This is amazing. Mikey, our brother involved in something that could be on the news any minute now. Wait till I tell the boys that their uncle is an international criminal."

"Not on the news, this mustn't get out, it goes no further." Making the tiniest adjustment in posture, DS Plummer delivered the statement with an authority he had so far disguised well.

He was an officer that Jan could imagine working with over a couple of shifts, doing things properly and professionally. An officer who would expect the same from all those he had dealings with. She felt an allegiance to her new colleague and wanted to be utterly straight with him. Hayley was a spirited reinvented Antipodean live wire and Jan felt the absolute necessity to state the obvious to the trusting DS.

"Perhaps, you shouldn't have told my sister then, sarge." She expected Hayley to dive in and defend herself at any moment or perhaps for the DS to repeat his warning but, neither was forthcoming. Jan was left to dangle in still air which gave her time to talk things through.

"I mean she, well *we* actually are just civilians, aren't we? You have shared some pretty sensitive material and we are not bound by an oath of allegiance or any other code of conduct, we are free to go

about our business and speak to whomever we like. At least that's
what I understood retirement from the force to be."

DS Plummer chose his words. "It is true to some extent."

Jan pressed her cheeks firmly wondering why it was an
unwritten certainty that if you held a bunch of balloons you would
always attract an idiot with a pin. Not that she regarded DS Plummer
as an idiot, far from it, but he seemed to be pushing in a pincer
movement, extracting air from his prey before they shuddered to
death.

"To some extent? What do you mean to some extent? I *am* a
civilian, I am not part of this investigation, no, let me clarify, I do not
want to be part of this investigation. You can't just bowl into
someone's private day and expect them to drop their plans and do a
bit of police work. I'm sorry to be outspoken and maybe a little
disrespectful, but I'm done with all this. Today is mine to do with
what I want; the freedom to do as I please."

"We are offering protection during the operation. Specialist
resources will be monitoring your every move. You will be kept safe;
you have my word."

"What about lunch? you know, a girl needs some lunch."

"Not lunch. Look, I know this isn't what you were expecting
and you're probably not very happy with me right now, but I am
only acting on orders. Undoubtedly, we could jeopardise the
operation by telling you this, but as I said it is imperative that we
secure Michael and the information he is in possession of. Whether
you like it or not, you are already involved. This phone, your phone,
Hayley, has been tracked by agencies working on the other side of
the world and your arrival in the UK has been seen as a breakthrough
moment."

"You've been spying on me? Wow, I hope I haven't been
rude on my messages." Hayley covered her mouth and giggled
before her eyes popped over her hand with the alarmed expression
of a cat caught stealing your salmon. Then, with a sharp intake of

breath through radiating cheeks, she stifled a heartfelt, "NOOO! Did you see the text I sent to Gail about Leonard? Oh, please say that you didn't, I'm not ready to go public on that."

"I didn't, but then I wouldn't as I say I only have clearance at a fairly low level."

"Oh my god. Jeez, I'm going to be thinking about that all day now. Can you arrest people for what they say in a text?"

Aware that he still hadn't secured an agreement DS Plummer sort to dismiss this line of questioning.

"I shouldn't worry too much; as I said this is a much bigger and far more important operation and that's all the security services are interested in."

In an unexpected moment to herself, Jan had been thinking. Not only about the emotional curve her sister had just travelled around but the equally pressing matter in hand. She assumed an unfamiliar persona, one that she hoped reflected the new normal as she delivered a well-considered speech.

"Let me make one thing very clear. At the risk of repeating myself, I retired yesterday, this is my time, this is where I discover me in a peaceful spa setting far away from the criminal underworld. This is where I choose my friends carefully after I have mentally vetted them as far as a civilian can vet another civilian. I am to surround myself with honesty and integrity wrapped up in happiness. I did not retire to get involved as a *civilian* in some secretive plot to undermine something we are not sure of that could have international ramifications and let's not forget risk. Potential risk to our own personal security, our lives and futures."

There was an attentive silence so she continued.

"I'm sorry, DS Plummer, I know you're doing your job as I would have done, but we are not interested. Besides, if my brother is a criminal, I have no desire to meet up with him and play happy families when, as you've shockingly alluded to, there has been a breach of trust. I will choose my friends but obviously I am unable to choose my family. Naturally, that comes as a huge shock and disappointment but I am not now inclined to meet up with Mike. I have no appetite to sit in conversation or appear to condone his actions or conveniently ignore what my brother appears to be doing. I am not going to break my retirement vows to myself within the first twenty-four hours or, more to the point, EVER."

"Hang on, Sis, don't I get a say in this? I mean, I *am* here for the reunion, travelled miles for this and I reckon I'd like to see Mikey whatever he's done, he's still family. No, Sis, I think we should go, help the British and international authorities, get some answers, ride the excitement. You know up to now I never really understood the police and with my sister being one of you, Paul, it had kind of diluted the magic for me. I mean my kid sister doesn't exactly do excitement. But hey, we've already foiled a robbery today and now we're being offered another task, it's because we're good, Sis, don't you see?" She tussled at Jan's arm. "We could be like an ace team, trendy clothes, blue light for the roof, driving at speed…"

"No," came the firm duet from Jan and the DS. A word that spread like a blanket over the bird cage and rendered the excitable kookaburra silent.

DS Plummer dropped his head and slowly fiddled with his pen. Jan was mesmerised by this hypnotic action as it smoothly twizzled through fingers in the fascinating mirror of a left-hander.

A few moments later Jan was lifted from her trance when the DS stopped. He held up his pen like a baton and conducted his carefully chosen words with emphasis and importance.

"You are both in potential danger if you don't go," he declared, his words landing heavily on the reluctant recruits. "If you don't continue your intended journey, lead us to Michael…" he faltered in his search for the appropriate phrase for this audience. "Look, *Voleur Payé* are desperate, whatever they are chasing they are determined and will, undoubtedly, be ruthless."

"What?" gulped Hayley, crushing her newly remodelled coffee cup.

Jan was helplessly attached to the now motionless pen held in the strong steady hand.

"As I said, I have only limited information at my level. But, if you look at the size of the operation supporting this, I think we can surmise that this is considered a top-grade threat to UK security. Your cooperation is imperative."

Hayley wriggled free from her temporary stupor and seemed to have arrived at her rare senses.

"Hang on a minute, mate, surely the best police force in the world with all that intelligence you keep going on about can find out the zip code for me little brother Mikey and whilst you're about it, you could pass it on to us, save us the bother of guessing." She relaxed back into her seat beaming as if she'd won points in a televised slanging match.

"I cannot compromise the operation regarding what we know and what we need to know. But, Jan, you must be aware that often a situation needs to play out in order to secure the evidence required. It may be that *Voleur Payé* are incompetent and misguided and they've inflated their own importance. On the other hand, it is coincidental to me that their interest in your brother has sparked this big budget operation with a large team that formed up in a very short space of time."

Big budget in the West Country? thought Jan. Where have all these extra resources come from? Something had to be going on but she couldn't grasp the apparent connection to Mike or even more pressing, what role she was expected to play.

With arms folded she ventured forward trying to squeeze air across withered vocal cords.

"Look, DS Plummer."

"Paul, please."

"Right, yes, Paul, as I was saying, I may appear a bit dense and uncooperative but I really don't understand why Hayley and I can't just carry on with our day, without having to be concerned by some special operations team that log our every move, our every loo or brew stop and note what flavour ice cream we have."

"I know this must have come as a shock and it's fortunate that we had this incident as cover, it's enabled us to talk to you both without suspicion."

"How do you mean, Paul mate?" Hayley took the lead from her sister and leant like a shadow across the table.

"It has created a sterile area, police everywhere, place cordoned off, nothing out of the ordinary. It's highly probable that there are members of *Voleur Payé* sat in a car out there getting very impatient and concerned at this delay."

"How do we know they're not in here eating burgers and chatting with us?" Hayley lowered her voice before she continued. "I mean what about my little mate Clint over there?" She turned, slightly, and waved.

"You're safe, everyone in here has been thoroughly checked, or we wouldn't be having this conversation."

Fighting against an unwelcome surge of prickliness, Jan fluffed herself up and stared directly at the DS.

"Has this whole incident been staged? Was this just some elaborate, poorly conceived heist?"

"No, you have my word, we just got lucky, I can assure you of that," he smiled.

"Not very lucky for the sun bear or Sulung or poor Mrs Marshall who you still have to take care of." Jan pressed home a few points of her own. "So, if these terrorists are in the car park, you must know their vehicle, their names, details?"

"If I knew and if it would help the operation to tell you, then I would, but I don't and it wouldn't help either."

"Jeez mate, she was one of you yesterday, surely she can still be told the secret stuff?"

"I'm sorry but you know these things are on a need to know basis and it isn't considered that you need to know."

Jan grasped Hayley's wrist firmly and pinned it to the table hoping to deflect a potential outburst.

"I'm still uncertain about what you expect Hayley and me to be doing? What if we don't agree? I mean you can't endanger civilians in some police operation just because they're related to a Cornish criminal mastermind."

"It's true but, I'm sure I don't need to point out potential offences that you may commit, offences I'm sure you'd be familiar with; assisting an offender, obstructing a constable and without doubt there would be other lesser used offences that the Crown Prosecution Service might eagerly support. If only to win the monthly sweepstake regarding an archaic offence brought to court and charged before the holidays."

The atmosphere of informative bonhomie began to slip from view. The cuddly bull terrier had begun to growl, he'd forced them onto a prickly path towards a thicket of summer gorse.

She pondered his words and simmered. Good luck getting home on any of those offences, DS Plummer. Her face crinkled and contorted; he might not be bluffing; she wasn't ready to take the risk. For cod's hake! What is going on? She swung her legs sideways, elbows propped between the table and the seat back as her heart raced down a bumpy track, a last skip to freedom before the cell door closed.

"I can see you're angry, Jan. As I said, I can promise you full support and back-up."

"What does a perfect day look like, Paul? Is there ever a time when an officer can just retire and leave it all behind? Surely this isn't what other people have to endure in their normal lives?"

She turned back to the table and Hayley who seemed to be highly amused by this public display of emotion. 13:10, over halfway through a gloriously awful day. She didn't feel that her expectations were too high, no fame or fortune required, nothing impossible except it appeared to be exactly that. A tangled, awkward unexpected angst, dripping annoyingly into her leaky tent.

Jan knew that at present the DS had very little that could stick, he was being professionally heavy handed, he obviously needed to secure cooperation; that had been his role from the start. But could criminal charges be brought? Was this so important that threats and security breaches would be neutralised without a second thought and there would be consequences? Consequences that Jan had no wish to discover. No, indeed, DS Plummer had effectively hit the panic button and brought Jan to her knees from where she clutched at one final and slightly obvious straw.

"Reading between the lines, if Hayley's phone is being tracked, why don't you keep it? Monitor it yourselves, cut us out of the loop? Let Mike give you the clues direct?"

"It's a good point, but we can't take the risk. Mike is clever, he will be feeding you information. It would only need an odd erroneous word or phrase from us for Mike to realise you've been intercepted. We need him to lead you to the location, taking *Voleur Payé* with you. Operation SOUWEST has been set up to capture and secure this sensitive information, like I said, a lot of units are involved."

"How many units?" asked Jan.

"I can't say, but teams, you know specialist teams, experts in tracking and surveillance."

"Is that why it's unimaginatively called SOUWEST? Special Operations Unit West I presume?"

"You want Jan and me in the team, adding our expertise?" said Hayley who appeared keen to have a good role in this important sounding police job.

Almost resigned to the direction this day had taken, Jan sort further clarification.

"What about *Voleur Payé?* What might they do if we don't cooperate?"

"I can't speak for them we don't know enough about their operation. They possibly have a cell on British soil, they are mobile, there are at least two of them but maybe more assigned to this task. Level of violence unknown. Methodology? Ideology? bit sketchy."

"So, you've got nothing. There are two mad French thieves who desperately want to meet my brother because he is a bad man with a secret and you want to engage the services of retired Jan and Hayley the holidaymaker to lead you all to a lovely reunion somewhere in Cornwall?"

"Yes."

"No."

"Why not yes?" questioned the excitable Hayley. "We'd be like Cagney and Lacey or Starsky and Hutch or Turner and Hooch."

"Hooch was a dog."

"Yeah well, anyway, I could be in the team that solved an English crime whilst on my travels. Imagine me social media status, I'd be recognised in the streets back home. I'll be a legend, a woman in my own rights, a hero or…"

"Dead," added Jan trying to stop her sister from dissolving any further.

DS Plummer appealed in a tone that Jan was only too familiar with. When there's an urgent need for cooperation but you don't want to sound too desperate, you fall back on flattery.

"Jan, come on, you have all the skills, you know how this works. They may even take you back."

"I don't want to go back, Paul, I'm retired! I do not need to impress anyone at the board, I am not looking for a job."

"I'm sorry, that was the wrong thing to say." He softened again. "I've given you everything I know. It's a lot to get your head around. I accept that you're retired and I know you don't have to, but just put yourself in my shoes, no not *my* shoes, *your* shoes when you were dealing with the criminal underworld that pervade our streets. Information that we carry and keep in confidence to protect lives. The long game where you submit intel but can never be told whether it was you that managed to find the last piece of the puzzle that could bring down a criminal mastermind. Our informants, our own eyes and ears, the cooperation of the public, these are the sticky glue we need to prevent the threat that normal people are blissfully unaware of. If this operation could run a different way, you know it would. Involving you, well not so much you, Jan, but certainly Hayley, who is largely an unknown quantity and greater risk, wouldn't be on the table if there was another way."

"I'm no flaming risk. Don't forget I recorded the last incident and gave me sister a running commentary. I think I've made up for anything else you might have got your hands on." Hayley still seemed desperate to display the qualities needed to secure a job on the back of this informal interview.

"Yes, I appreciate your evidential cooperation today," he said. "Can I count on you both now?"

Jan quietly digested his words and those from her sister the potential liability. After a short deliberation, she outlined some important requirements.

"There are a couple of things you need to be aware of first, DS Plummer, Paul. Firstly, Sulung over there needs a new sun bear. Secondly, there's a welfare concern, already mentioned. Mrs Marshall with her dog Marvel or Mangle or something appears to me to have dementia."

"The dog's got dementia?"

"No, Paul, Mrs Marshall doesn't know where she is and doesn't seem to know where she lives or how she got here other than on some bus – a Greyhound for all we know. I think you should extend your important operation to include the repatriation of Mrs Marshall before she becomes a missing person or worse."

Faltering slightly, he responded.

"That's not really my field."

"You're a policeman at the end of the day, Paul. You have a duty to prevent and detect crime, bring offenders to justice, all of which has been happening in bucket loads this morning I agree, but don't forget in addition to that, you have an undeniable duty to protect the vulnerable."

He sighed, Jan was right and now that she had passed the hot potato to him, he could hardly ignore it.

"I'll run some checks, find out where she lives but only whilst you give serious consideration to what I've just told you."

Jan tried to back-calculate where ten minutes earlier might have placed her, a world far away from these events, a preferable day, one from which she had now been excluded.

CHAPTER 8

"The Humpy is such an unusual address isn't it? And 'What-a-view' well, that's such a tremendous house name, Mrs Marshall. How long have you lived there?"

Mrs Marshall didn't respond, she gazed out of the window a world away from June 2015.

Jan screwed up her face and cast an eye to the rear-view mirror which told her everything she didn't need to know.

Why didn't you prepare for this unexpected passenger and her dog Janet Elliot? A dog sat on the seat, why? Why? Why didn't I bring an extra cover, a tarpaulin, anything to spread under an elderly person who may have medical needs or might be leaking? What if the dog's leaking? Why can't it sit on the floor? She breathed, rather too obviously.

Job cars had a kit box containing useful things, providing that the previous driver had replenished stocks. There would be a wealth of items that the practical outdoor officer may need at their disposal. Like a throwing line that could assist in the rescue of a conscious person wishing to get out of the open water. It could also be used to lead a stray animal back to a secure field and to lash an unseated aluminium greenhouse to a lamp post during high winds.

Cod how I miss those waterproof seat covers, thought Jan taking a series of purposeful breaths intended to distract from the unexpected items in her seating area.

Of course, on a positive note, she did have a cover to shield her boot from the antique shopping trolley and its unknown contents. But then again, the smell of dog wee that oozed from the fabric had no regard for a boot cover. Her sterile zone had been compromised and the sheet would be going in the bin.

At least DS Plummer had worked one tiny miracle, he had managed to persuade WHSmith to foot the sun bear bill, arguing that it was this distraction that had saved their staff from potential harm.

With a huge lump of guilt brushed from her shoulders, Jan should have been celebrating the importance of that closure. But instead, she was being driven to despair by the distance they still had to travel, according to the satnav.

In the front passenger seat, Hayley was developing her character nicely and had taken on the persona of a well-seasoned officer who had earnt the right to moan.

"I can't believe he couldn't find the resources. I mean this is putting on the public a bit. No wonder he's keen to get our help with this operation, they've clearly run out of proper police officers."

"Are you having an operation, dear? I had an operation last week. Oh, what was it for? Let me think, it'll come to me. I don't like the beds, all that flaky paint on the bedstead. I said to matron, this needs a lick of paint."

"No, we are going to be the new Cagney and Lacey, Mrs Marshall, we have an assignment to travel to Cornwall, meet our brother Mikey who has been a bit naughty whilst being chased by some French terrorists calling themselves Paid Thief.

"Hayley!" whispered Jan. "Careless talk costs lives."

"Jeez, Sis, what century are you in? That's all that world war talk, you are a bit excitable at times. I think we'll be all right." She shook her head in mild amusement and turned to the back-seat occupants. "How's Marble doing back there?"

"Edith Piaf," said Mrs Marshall still gazing out of the window.

"What was that?" said Hayley.

"Edith Piaf – Paid Thief," came the reply.

Steadying herself with the steering wheel, Jan turned this information over in her mind. There was something curiously surreal about this journey. Am I dreaming? she thought shuffling the letters of Paid Thief around to spell Edith Piaf. It was true and what of that?

Mrs Marshall had stopped staring and pulled Marble close as she stroked the fine bone china of his velvety head.

"Where are you taking me?" she demanded in a frail and tearful voice. "Who are you?"

"It's okay, Mrs Marshall," said Jan acutely aware that this half-hour journey might prove distressing to more than one person in the car. "Edith Piaf; that was very quick, can you make any other words?"

"Edith Piaf," she repeated and then continued from some faraway place. "It was during the war you know, women had to work. The country had no choice, I was one of the youngest code breakers, lovely girls I worked with. It was long hours but you didn't mind, just got on with it. Lives depended on those messages. We were appreciated though. Oh yes, Winston Churchill himself came down. Do you know what he said? 'You are the birds that laid the golden egg but never cackled'. Oh, that was such a boost for morale, we loved that. He looked tired you know, had a lot on his mind, poor love. It was hard work but we did have some laughs. Mary, she was the funny one always telling us a story. Well, it was rationing and food was short but she knew this American airman, gave her all sorts of things she said, cheered her up no end. They were lovely times really, if there hadn't been a war on of course, the dancing, the music, lovely."

"Flaming Nora," cried Hayley. "Is this some kind of a joke? You two reminiscing had me going there, I'm a bit out of touch with English humour."

"Only a quarter of a mile and we'll have you back at home, Mrs Marshall," said Jan slightly concerned by the narrow country lanes.

Doubting the satnav, as anyone with a shred of common sense should, Jan paused in the mouth of a dubious entrance.

"It's not very wide, the Humpy, is it?" she said proceeding at caterpillar speed through potholes and loose gravel as large tufts of unkempt grass brushed the exhaust pipe.

"No dear, not in a car, you should walk more."

"Were you at Bletchley Park?" asked Jan making an effort to zone out from the stressful lane.

"No dear, not today, I don't think so, you're confusing me. Has the milkman been?"

The tired 1930s bungalow occupied the centre of a generous sloping plot and showed evidence of a long-forgotten structured garden now overgrown with apathy and the absence of a good hedge trimmer.

"Shall I take hold of Marble whilst you get out? I bet he loves this garden." Said Hayley her eyes glued to the panoramic view that stretched down to the sea below.

Armed with the shopping trolley, Jan walked up the small stone stairway leading to a part glazed original front door and tried the twisty door handle. Unlocked, it creaked open and gently swept aside a small hillock of junk mail. In a room somewhere in this modest sized house she could hear the noise from a radio or TV and an argumentative male voice shouting and swearing nearby.

With her senses on high alert, Jan bristled and whispered to Mrs Marshall.

"There's someone in the house."

"Yes dear, that's Stewart, he says he's my great-nephew, have I got a great-nephew?"

Jan didn't have the confidence to rely on Mrs Marshall's suggestion and with a potential intruder somewhere in the house, it would be totally inappropriate to leave without checking first. With a snatched breath, she cast her voice into the din.

"Hello? Hello? We've just brought Mrs Marshall home. Hello?"

There was no reply, no break in the raucous commentary from the male or the loud TV.

Why am I even doing this? she thought as the spikey familiar whoosh of adrenalin pushed her forward to the wooden door on the opposite side of a rather spacious hallway. She opened it as wide as possible and then stepped over the threshold.

It appeared to be the lounge; heavy curtains were drawn against the light from a south facing window as a veil of heavy smoke hung like a mucous cloud at eye level. At first, she could only see the bright glare from a screen but then, out of the darkness, she saw him.

"Who the farting fruitcake are you? Get out of my house!"

A male in his early forties, unshaven and unkempt, leapt from his chair and stood before her behind his precariously overweight torso balanced in an unsavoury manner on the waistband of his shapeless joggers.

"I've told you, get out or I'll call the police."

"She *is* the police, *we* are the police in fact," said Hayley who had bowled in behind her slightly shorter sister.

"Hayley, be quiet. We have brought your aunt home; she was lost at the... at the shops. We found her, drove her home, just wanted to make sure she was safe and had someone to look after her."

"I look after her, she does alright with me. Did you get my baccy? I hope you haven't come back without that else you'll just have to get these *police officers* to take you shopping again and some beers would be nice too."

"Now, look here," said Jan in her occasionally authoritative police officer voice, "we are not running Mrs Marshall around the countryside doing your bidding. She needs to rest; she needs a cup of tea and a bit of consideration."

"Don't get all hoity-toity with me you old dishcloth do-gooders, you've brought her home now clear off back to your knitting group and let me finish my game, I'm only four frogs away from the next level."

"You're not kidding there, mate," said Hayley marching towards the window. She drew back the heavy curtains to reveal the sun-drenched patio and lost cottage garden beyond.

"Don't open those curtains, I can't see my screen, this is crucial, you stupid bird."

"I suggest, Stewart, that you take yourself off to another part of the house, we are going to drink tea and let Mrs Marshall recover." Hayley unplugged the computer with the deftness of a mother's hand.

"What you do that for?! You've effing gone and done it now." Bouncing his rotund nakedness into the light, Stewart raised a fist full of tattoos as he pushed Hayley towards the window. With the instinct of an outfielder running for the big catch, Jan flew between them, creating space for her defensive stance.

Stewart relaxed his fist, quite probably overwhelmed by the sight of two uninvited and apparently unhinged women in some dramatic frieze before him. The timely ring of the hall phone gave him an excuse to duck out manfully.

"That'll be me bookie, he'd better have some good news."

"Are you alright, Hayley? You really shouldn't pretend to be a police officer, not only is it an offence, it might also provoke a reaction that we can't deal with."

"Rubbish, Sis, he didn't for one minute believe us; he's just a lazy oaf and besides I can pretend to be one if I like. Surely, it's only wrong if I impersonate one? Anyway, thanks for stepping in there, partner, with your cool little moves. Of course, I had it covered you know, but thanks all the same."

"Shall I put the kettle on?" said Mrs Marshall making her way through an adjoining door into a large cluttered space that used to be a fully functioning kitchen.

Jan followed, keen to ensure that she had sufficient food in the cupboards and could demonstrate some level of competence to look after herself. Failing that, she must be left with a person capable of providing that care. If Stewart proved incapable, Jan would have a duty to remain until she could firmly wedge the baton into someone else's hand.

The room was dominated by an out of place industrial cooking unit camouflaged by a thick film of slime that dripped in brown tones down the door fronts. An extravagant assortment of utensils had been knitted together with brown cobwebbing and hung from hooks and rails to complete the greasy aluminium grotto.

Mrs Marshall set a large black kettle on the gas which required a two-handed effort to wobble it across from the creaky tap. This was followed by a slow game of hunt the mugs, presumably, as doors were opened and closed as if she were doing semaphore.

Hayley sat herself at the long pine table stained with food and drink dating back to the dark ages in a room long neglected.

A pile of brown faded newspapers stood like a trig point near the picture window next to an antique dresser that displayed four rows of fine china plates under a thick veil of damp dust. Opened and unopened post and piles of junk mail weighed heavily on a dull, dark upright piano.

"Jeez, this takes me back," said Hayley. "I reckon this place has got more history than the whole of Straya."

Marble had settled into his basket near the piano to recover from his ordeal. He still wore the snood donated in his hour of need and one could only wonder how long he would have to endure this embarrassment.

During her service and on the odd occasions when Jan had volunteered for plain clothed duties, she had been meticulous in creating her wardrobe. Clothes for work and leisure fiercely separated by her version of the Berlin Wall. Equally, within the home, outdoor clothes and indoor clothes were carefully zoned to prevent avoidable contamination of her furnishings.

It wasn't, therefore, a surprise to Jan that her eyes were blurred by red flags that flapped in every direction. All she could think of, looking around this neglected real-life museum, was the state of Howard. Grease, detritus and personal germs from the clothing of Mrs Marshall and her dog in a snood, all liberally smeared across the back seat. She wanted to leave now, clean it thoroughly, take a lovely hot shower and change her clothes. But it couldn't happen, free-will had imploded under a sagging shroud of care in the community orders and police work.

"Are we going to do it then? Carry on to Cornwall find our Mikey and solve a great crime?" asked Hayley, who had been having thoughts of her own.

"I'm not sure. This isn't what I wanted or expected of retirement day one. This was my new beginning; I feel like I've been mis-sold my pension." Jan toyed with the idea of sitting down on a frighteningly unkempt seat, fully aware that it might just finish her off.

Keeping half an eye on Mrs Marshall she decided to air another concern.

"Aren't you just a bit disappointed to discover Mike is a criminal? I know I am."

"Hey Sis, don't be so quick to judge, he might be doing something against his will, forced into it. Our Mikey might be weak and pathetic, in need of our help. It might be up to us to rescue him."

"Or catch him," mumbled Jan.

DS Plummer's untimely suggestion that Mike was connected to the criminal underworld had weighed heavily and shovelled more damp coal on her fading embers.

How could this not be her fault? She screwed her eyes towards the picture window, struggling to see through the veil of cloying yellow. I have created a monster, all because I didn't make an effort with him, we barely spoke. On the very day that she'd planned to spring-clean her world and make peace with Mike, she'd been comprehensively derailed in mind, body and clothing.

Movement from the lounge, returned Jan to a state of high alert, she was reminded of Stewart, the unknown male. Whether the bookie had brought joy or otherwise, the shouting and swearing had resumed above the pings, dings and croaks of some amphibious computer game in the smoky living den next door.

The broken china plate clock on the kitchen wall displayed a solitary second hand pointlessly resting at nine, the house forever in a quarter to something state. At 14:15, in a state of her own, an idea, a vague line of enquiry was floating to the surface as Jan picked her way towards the piano.

With forensic care she cleared the lid of mail and glossy flyers and the velvet topped stool of magazines and a dog bone. It was only a theory, but it had to be tested, how else could she be certain?

Non, je ne regrette rien immersed the room in Parisian nostalgia which brought an end to Mrs Marshall's door banging. She began to sway gently as the music infiltrated a tiny corner of her mind that held lost fragments of a time gone by.

"Edith Piaf; how beautiful." Mrs Marshall steadied herself towards the moment. Soft in pitch and tone her voice filled the neglected gloom with joy and romance through the evocative rendition that she knew so well.

"'No Regrets', it was her big song, long after the war, but the French were so exciting and passionate, they fired our hearts. This was our song, Stanley and I, when things had settled down and we were finally able to get married. It was a lovely time."

With Mrs Marshall so near and yet, quite evidently, so far away, Jan delved deeper. At the end of the piece, she turned up the tempo and belted out the toe tapping Glenn Miller classic 'In the Mood'.

In a moment of unsteady madness, Mrs Marshall closed her eyes. It was clear she had found herself in a bustling dance hall, where music and friends went hand in hand with dancing and uniforms. She smiled and drifted, attempting to twirl in her swing coat and dip down on her dodgy knees.

Jan lightened her touch and pressed softly for answers.

"What did you do at Bletchley Park?"

"Code breakers, lovely times, Dotty was the only civilian in our group you know, but we treated her just the same, we all just had to get on with it."

She couldn't make it up, surely? It's in her, she's living it, thought Jan.

The music that served to lift Mrs Marshall, swirled Jan into the grip of a down draft as she made last minute adjustments to her preconceived idea. How had she come to live like this, neglected and trapped in this dust pit? She should be revered, thanked, waited on and loved.

She was a wonderful person, a lady who had made sacrifices and written history, the history that affects us all. She had helped to save our civilisation which, as Jan appreciated, had enabled her to sit here freely and play this piano. This was undeniably freedom, a little inconvenienced but nonetheless freedom. For all her grumblings, Jan knew that she was lucky and that she was free.

Sometimes, the symbolism represented in a simple circle can be a bit overwhelming. History dictates the future, we share the journey, largely unconnected and yet in every way imaginable, our actions cause a ripple. Some ripples are big and splashy, the headline grabbing bow waves, others barely detectable.

As a small flood of grateful souls waved at her raft, Jan knew that her legacy would be swamped by failure. Failure to prevent crime because the reality all day long was that flouting the law seemed far too natural to a certain sector of society. Then, like an incident in the night, Mike flashed through her mind. The young boy she'd neglected with the ripples from her own anxiety.

With the impromptu concert drawing to a close, Jan's attention returned to the matter of Mrs Marshall and her life as it radiated across the pond. One ripple in particular had undeniably travelled in living history and bumped into Jan. Right from her teenage years, there was little doubt in Jan's mind, that the reason she could play the piano so well, was because of her aunt Ethel. But now she began to appreciate that this too was down to this one simple truth; aunt Ethel was free to teach her and that had *everything* to do with Mrs Marshall.

Even more spellbinding, within the theatre of this circle, was the irony that Jan was playing a piano that belonged to this exceptional woman from history. A woman whose hard work and altruistic dedication to the war effort had made this brief entertainment possible and absolutely deserved.

Of course, you could overthink things. So much for planning, she thought. But how curious, how dabbed odd that Mrs Marshall could look at this terror group and make an educated connection. Was there anything in it? She considered whether their call for assistance could now, responsibly, be ignored. Like Buckaroo, the choice was clear; either kick away this knowledge, scatter the pieces far and wide, or carefully hang them all together, solve the puzzle and tame the mule.

As she closed the lid across the keys that had brought Mrs Marshall to life, Jan was consumed by her own world of nostalgia as she dreamed of a giant Buckaroo and the pony she never had. How vivid it all was, she could clearly hear Buckaroo kicking fiercely amid the pitter-patter of approaching hooves. And then in that instant, Hayley turned towards the lounge.

"Jeez! What the…?"

But, before the recently concocted pseudo police unit could discuss tactics, Stewart was forced to respond.

"NOOO!"

Then, from the shabby gloom that enveloped this forgotten world, an impatient male voice shouted.

"*Arrêtez! Arrêtez! Arrêtez!*"

CHAPTER 9

With ears pressed firmly against the painted door, Jan and her new probationer listened intently to the partly dynamic action that was unfolding in the adjoining room.

"Yuk, what's this?" said Hayley wiping the side of her face.

"SSHHH!" whispered Jan.

"It's flaming marmalade, it's all over me cheek."

"Welcome to the glamorous world of policing," said Jan maintaining her post.

As her heart beat a rhythm against the door, Jan was in danger of giving away their position before she had fully considered her options with the National Decision Model.

"Argh zee English are so fat, is zis how zee brains of Britain dress? *Alors*, my little Fabergé egg. *Donne moi ton secret maintenant, et je te tue*," shouted the feisty French intruder failing at English for infants as he pranced in the gloom behind superfluous sunglasses. His stylish Poldark hair flopped to the beat of every word from its lofty position just below the compact ceiling.

"Give me your secret now and I kill you," came the staccato translation from his shorter accomplice in the ill-fitting purple shirt. He knelt behind Stewart who lay beached on the floor unsure of the best way to roll.

"I, I, I'm just playing me bloody game, what an afternoon this is, first the do-gooders turn up and now some raving loonies. Look, mate, I have no idea what you're on about, I'm just two frogs away from another level."

"Don't be getting zee funny with me. Stupide English and zee pathetic joking's. We have no utilisation for the ugly sisters *avec du thé dans la cuisine. Relinquish des secret*, you greasy tin of sardines."

Followed by the unemotional translation, "We have no use for the ugly sisters drinking tea in the kitchen."

Jan had heard enough to know that there was an urgent need for action, whatever that might look like. She flung open the door and pushed forward with Hayley firmly at her shoulder. "This is NOT Mike, this is not who you want, this is Stewart, we only met him today, he is not intelligent."

"You cheeky cow, you all just barge into my house and insult me and expect me to sit here and take it? An Englishman's home is his castle and I will not have an invasion by the French or the Women's Institute while my flag's up the flagpole! Now get out the lot of you!"

The startled invaders spoke hurriedly in their native language punctuated by Gallic shrugs and a short exchange of theatrical slaps. Upon realising their mistake, they thundered as much as you can thunder in lightweight continental footwear, back through the front door.

Jan made a quick check of the ashen faces that peered out of the gloom and then, as if jabbed by an EpiPen of instinct and folly, gave chase. At the front door, she cleared the stone steps in one leap and got to the lane just as the smart black van had carelessly reversed away up the Humpy.

With every bone in her body trying to shake free from its neighbour, she waited for some desperately needed breath.

"What am I doing? Have you completely lost your mind, Janet Elliot?" Giving herself the slow once-over reconfirmed what she already knew, that she possessed a total lack of police kit and protection. In the diesel smoked air, at odds with the wildflower surroundings, she evaluated the threat. The terrorists that had materialised at this hidden address. Their demands for a secret in exchange for death, which she felt was rather poor bargaining, and their quite apparent urgency to find Mike.

She walked towards the bungalow at the only speed available to a body pumped full of adrenalin. It wasn't unreasonable to assume that at this rate she would be too tired to wrestle with the Mike issue if they should ever find him. As her heart slowed to a comfortable beat, she noted the simple schoolboy error; the getaway van was facing the wrong way.

Back in the lounge, Hayley had once again opened the curtains wide enough to allow sunlight to illuminate the yellow bands of dust and dismay that strung out across the room. Like a mother to all things she tried to offer Stewart some comfort without actually touching him.

"Look, that was a bit full on, a mistake obviously, think of it as a bad dream. You were brave fair dinkum, but you might want to change your trackie daks, mate."

He looked forlornly at his favourite slob trousers.

"I thought I was going to die; do you know how that feels?"

"Not yet, no."

As Jan entered the room, her face battled like a prune against the additional odour that had poured into this sour house of depression. Her clothes would have to be burnt; it was the only option she could entertain.

"You know what this means don't you? They *are* following us."

"And they're going to kill us all?" offered Stewart.

"Well, not you, Stewart. I think you'll be okay," she said still struggling to breathe.

"Yeah," added Hayley, "we'll be leaving you now and you can catch your frogs and we'll deal with ours." She turned to Jan, "is that right?"

But before anyone could decide, there was a further assault on the weary front door. An enormous crash introduced a parade of sturdy boots that pounded across the hallway to the lounge where they stopped cleanly. Four faces perched on square shouldered officers filled the space like a living breathing door as the loud verbal commands rang out.

"POLICE! Stay where you are!"

"Timed to perfection," said Hayley. "It's all over, the kettle's on and up turn the plod."

Stewart collapsed to the floor again. "Oh god, can't anybody see my flagpole!"

"Where are they?" shouted the lead officer.

"If you mean the French tourists, they left," said Jan. "Surprised you didn't pass them on the lane."

"Right okay, we'll just do a search of this place, make sure it's all clear."

"Be my guest," said Stewart resigned to the relentless invasion of his castle. "I just want to say though, I'm nothing to do with this. Where's Aunty? I need a cup of tea to calm me blooming nerves." He shuffled off to the kitchen holding his trousers with gravity doing its best to expose his dimpled white cheeks.

Jan noted that the professional DS Paul Plummer had applied vapour rub to his top lip and entered the room without an outward trace of discomfort from the sickening stench.

"Are you two okay?" he enquired.

"Yes," said Jan. Hayley nodded as she struggled with the window latch. "Yes, bit of an afternoon but we're okay. So, were they *Voleur Payé?*"

"That's right, they are following the sophisticated software on your phone, Hayley, we're not sure exactly what its capabilities are. It's fortunate we didn't run into them; we have to maintain cover if this is going to work."

"Fortunate for who?" added Hayley, her head hanging out of the window. "Besides they could have tailed us to this address, I don't class that as being all that sophisticated."

"Point noted, but we are here now, right with you. This is exactly why we need you two in the hot seat. You won't be taking this journey alone. Can we count on you?"

As her mind raced and her retirement plans receded, Jan knew that Operation SOUWEST wouldn't stop until they'd reached their objective. She moved to the open window and drew a scented breath from the summer blooms that pushed through the undergrowth. How dare these jumped up continental conmen intimidate my sister, who's done nothing wrong? Well, not much wrong, it was only a throwaway line claiming she was a police officer. Threats to kill? Intimidation? They can't do that.

These real and hugely concerning facts were in stark contrast to the other wafting element of unfathomed concern that would shadow this journey. An element called Hayley, the inexperienced crewmate, essential but unknown and unskilled. Although it was true to say, on the plus side, that Hayley had shown courage and maturity in this most recent event. She'd also made the selection for the fantasy toilet team following her positive interaction with a youth. Law and procedure make up only a small part of policing. Largely it's about confidence and interpersonal skills which Hayley possessed by the bucket load alongside her banter which was coming along nicely. All things considered, it appeared that Hayley was more qualified than Jan to hold the Office of Constable.

Maybe she won't be that much of a liability, perhaps this could work and as my sister we are at least on the same side, want the same thing. What's the worst that could happen?

She quickly dismissed that thought and turned to her infinitely qualified partner.

"We need to sort out this mess; retirement starts tomorrow." They exchanged a smile, apprehension, nerves, excitement? Who knew? Jan addressed DS Paul Plummer to deliver her verdict.

"I don't see that we have much choice, this is clearly a big operation and in addition to that, they have annoyed me with their threats and arrogance."

"Yes," said Hayley, "and I heard them say that the English were fat. But, then again, I am almost Australian so that rules me out."

DS Plummer subconsciously pulled in his developing donut belly.

"Good, thank you, I promise we'll look after you."

Resigned to another day of police work, Jan assumed the role.

"I have a brief description of the men and their vehicle is a black Mercedes van, Vito or Sprinter perhaps. But with all the dust they kicked up in the lane I was unable to get the registration number, I think it had foreign plates."

"Okay that's helpful but, as I stated earlier, we wouldn't look to intercept them at this stage."

"They are quick though, Paul, look how quickly they got here."

"Yeah," added Hayley, "I'm more interested by how quickly you got here. I hope you're going to tightened up your act a bit, officer. We need proper back-up. If they say I'm going to kill you, I don't want the envy of the world's police force turning up as I'm being measured for me coffin."

Jan knew this was true but dismissed the observation.

"Hayley, that's not helpful."

"Well maybe not but neither is being flown home on Qantas in the hold rather than a comfy recliner."

"14:42," said DS Plummer. 'The cheese is on the board'. He made an entry into his pocket notebook.

"What's that? Your shout for lunch, Paul?"

"No, I'm afraid not, Hayley. Look we'd better make a move. We'll be right with you, remember? Do you want me to put their minds at rest?" He nodded towards the kitchen.

"No, we can do that," said Jan. "I can handle it."

CHAPTER 10

"Blimey, Sis, the stench in this car is unbelievable, you must have used an entire pack of wet wipes. What is that? Dingo's Delight?"

"Jasmine and juniper actually, shame I can't use it on my clothes, I feel so mucky it's horrible." She tried to relax, but it was impossible. "I mean Stewart was the last straw really, I'm not used to that sort of encounter in my personal life."

To his credit, Stewart had found some manners by the time they'd departed. Realising perhaps that they were not the enemy and, all things considered, he had it pretty good. Hayley had located the washing powder and patiently showed Stewart how to operate the machine before sending him off to have a shower. Mrs Marshall eventually found a mug and made herself tea before instructing Jan to remove whatever it was that looked to be strangling poor Marble. He was then rewarded with a small bone shaped treat which he crunched politely in his basket.

Satisfied that the trio weren't likely to cause each other immediate harm, Jan was able to release herself from the welfare responsibility and concentrate on their next unscheduled task.

The scenic route that would put them back onto the A38 wasn't wasted on Hayley as she feasted her eyes on the abundant variety of ancient trees and greenery that this part of Devon had to offer.

"Fair makes you want to move back when you see all this; it's unreal. I'd forgotten what it was like. You're very lucky, Sis, and by the way, when did you get to be a concert pianist?"

"I'm not a concert pianist, I just love playing and I played a lot after you'd gone. It was tough, I don't think you realise."

"So, you replaced me with a large wooden instrument; are you saying I was big boned?"

"Look if you must know, you did leave a big hole when you packed up and went. You may have been having fun on your freedom travels but I was a bit lonely. If it hadn't been for aunt Ethel getting me interested in something, who knows what might have happened?"

"Hey you mean my little sis might have gone off the rails?"

"No, I don't think so; I just might not have tried so hard at school I suppose. It gave me a focus and a point to everything. It's amazing really, once you get into it, enabled me to disappear into another world. Aunt Ethel took the classics to a whole new level, she was very talented, I just wanted to do the same, she came alive when she played."

"I think you came alive too, Sis, back there. Did Mikey play?"

"No, I think he was wired up differently, used his hands in a different way I suppose."

Clearly Mike was wired up very differently, thought Jan, to the extent that a team from Operation SOUWEST needed to secure him and whatever it was that threatened national security. A rush of acrid gloop began to burn through her body as she battled to hold it together and focus on the narrow lanes.

"You've gone a bit of a funny colour, you feeling crook, Sis? Not sure this car is big enough for any more odours if you don't mind."

Jan stopped in a snug passing place as two horses and eight cars trundled by. In her fragile mind, another page had turned in the *Guilt* chapter, why didn't I teach him the piano? Why didn't I spend more time with him? I'm just so stupid and now look, he's in a complete mess.

"What do you think he's mixed up with? Got any ideas? said Hayley. "What if he's built a rocket for the first space launch in Cornwall? Or what if he's found a way to make gold, tons of the stuff? If he's got any sense, he'll stash that before he gets caught."

Hundreds of ideas had already been bounced around the walls of Jan's head without the need for Hayley's imaginative suggestions. A burning ball of speculation was one thing but what they really needed were the facts to support this glaring headline. The headline grabbing news that her brother appeared to have progressed from practical child prodigy to grown up 'Mr Big'.

They joined the dual carriageway where Jan tried to relax into the hands of the satnav, which would give her time to devise a plan for this unorthodox investigation. Contrary to her normal style of policing, she did not intend to sit and wait for orders and decisions to trickle through several levels of authorisation before any action could be taken. She had to control her destiny, get the whole sorry incident wrapped up without getting unduly side-tracked.

If standing at the top of a cliff takes your breath away, standing naked in the same place without back-up or structure will really put the wind up you. And Jan did feel naked but now, curiously excited at the prospect of free thinking.

"What do you think to Edith Piaf?"

"I thought you played that beautifully, Mrs Marshall was well away, crooned like a quivering canary."

"No, I mean the connection, the link, do you think there's anything in what she said?"

"Seemed a bit dotty to me," said Hayley. "I mean I could have come up with Edith Piaf if I'd thought about it."

"That's just it, she didn't think about it, the link was there; it was intelligence and that's what we need; an intelligent ally."

"What, like Mrs Dotty Marshall?"

"It's Mildred actually, I saw it on some of the post. No not Mrs Marshall, we need Clint, Clint the whizz-kid who's trying to join Mensa."

"Hey, you get your own contact." Hayley smiled before quietly whistling a few bars from 'Stranger in Paradise'.

"You remembered? I can't believe it, wow that takes me back." Jan peeled her eyes from the road. "I was right there, took me straight to the house, the three of us up to no good or something that we considered to be naughty."

"Jeez it's funny to think that such a simple little tune could make us stop what we were doing to find whoever it was that had put out the call. You forget how powerful that was. Bonded us I reckon, something that connected three crazy kids and made us feel safe."

"I'll never forget hearing that as I stood in the playground, my first day at senior school, I don't mind admitting I was petrified. I thought you'd gone so it was an enormous comfort to hear you whistling, it put me right into our safe place somehow."

"Yeah well, couldn't miss me little sister's first day, I was on the way to catch the bus to me new life but, I had a few minutes to spare so, thought I'd better drop by first."

If there was any truth in the saying that time dragged when you watched the clock, then equally, it had to be true that time and its speed was relative to the company you kept.

Thirty-seven years of separation had just been evaporated by this short, significant whistle that bridged the huge passage of time and glued their lives back together. The bubbly warm jacuzzi, that was her sister, wrapped Jan in a Witney blanket of effervescent comfort, pulling her close in a way that only families can manage. A feeling that Jan had forgotten and yet, it was a feeling she had missed most of her adult life. Droplets were dispersed from her eyes before they had chance to fully form and get in the way of more important issues like – the Cornish border and their distinct lack of a forwarding address.

Hayley picked up her phone and might have been on the same page until she said what was on her mind.

"This is quite serious isn't it? Is this what you did every day? This kind of stuff where it's all tense and dangerous?"

"Well, no, not every day was like this, pretty varied though, bit edgy at times."

"Who would have thought it, my little sis? I did think, before today, that you were quite boring doing thirty years in the same job being ordered around and then taking it out on the public. I mean the way I see it is the police just seem to be party poopers. They stop people from doing things, tell them off, then the next minute they start locking you up. Live and let live that's me, have fun, get down to the beach as soon as you get the chance."

"Innocent people have nothing to fear, is the guide I've used throughout my whole service, it's only the guilty who might fear justice."

"Still, you know what? I was pretty surprised when you had the guts to step in to protect me from Stewart, not that I couldn't have handled him, I mean I had it all under control of course. But hey, me little kid sister prepared to put herself in harm's way. It's always been very much the other way around."

"That was several decades ago when we were kids and you were bigger than me, I'm quite capable now."

"Yeah maybe, but I am still bigger than you all the same. Anyway, stop making this difficult, I just wanted to say thanks again, okay?"

"Okay, well that's okay." Thrust into the unfamiliar role of temporary guardian to her sister, Jan couldn't determine whether she should mourn the passing of childhood or embrace the notion of a more equal family billing. But this dilemma would have to wait, due to a further concern that troubled the front seat passenger.

"Do you think we'll die?"

"What?" Confronted by a thought she'd hoped not to air, Jan dampened down as best she could. "No, we just have to follow a few simple rules and then we'll be okay, stick to the plan, you know all the usual advice."

"And what are the rules? What plan? What's the flippin' usual advice? I need to know these things."

Not wishing to see her sister puddle into a vast emotional pond, Jan pulled together a far from ideal improvised training plan. "First thing to do is stay vigilant, look out for each other. We have to stay ahead of the criminals, which looks a bit difficult when we are likely to end up in the middle. In addition, we have to obtain and use any intelligence with utmost consideration, particularly where it could affect the safety of ourselves and others. We have to operate within the law and use appropriate powers. Give it our best shot and above all, we must work as a team and even further above that, we have to trust each other."

"All right, don't overload me, I'm new to all this, go easy on the rookie."

"Fair point. But, it would help enormously if we knew where we were going. So, I think it's time you contacted Mike for an address."

Lost for words for once, Hayley concentrated on her phone.

"What shall I say? 'Where are you, you big time criminal?'."

"No, you can't say that, we mustn't let him know there's a pincer movement going on."

"This is pretty full on, Sis. I think I need the next lesson in your policey ways, get me up to speed. Perhaps the next bit will be more interesting, come on, I need to be clued up in me new job." Hayley looked at Jan with the excitement of a person much younger as she listened obediently for instruction.

"Just say something like; 'We're on our way. Where to?'"

"Nope, can't do that, he'll know that isn't me talking. No, it's okay, I've got the idea, let me do it in the language of Hays."

Slightly concerned by the rejection of lesson two, Jan drove on towards the border; it was mid-afternoon, or 15:28 to be precise.

The language of Hays spilled through her fingers until she paused, deleted and began the whole process again before she was struck by a more pressing concern.

"What did Paul the plod mean back there about the cheese being on the board? I hope he wasn't talking about you and me, cos I think that sounded a bit rude."

"Probably just code for how the operation is coming together." Jan had skated over his comment, allowing her poor fatigued brain some protection after thirty years of jargon overload.

"Well, he'd better have been talking about those French boys, they're more fromage than we are."

As the senior member of the team, Jan decided to make a brief stop in the lay-by. "I have to pursue an idea."

"Oh, how utterly exciting," beamed Hayley as she managed to shave yet more years off her true age. "At last, the security sisters have a plan of action. There, I've sent that by the way. He doesn't reply very quick, not sure why, something to do with his work he said. Jeez, that's funny, his work, if you can call it that, Mikey."

"What did you say?"

"Something to do with his work."

"No, what have you put on Facebook?"

"What you said but my way."

"What way is that?"

"Honestly, I'm not the criminal here. I put, if you must know; 'Hi Kid, Bonnie and Clyde are on their way to get this solved, where can we find you? Let's get it over with'."

"I hope that's a joke, Hayley, your phone is being monitored you know, what if the French boys think you're passing on coded information? What if they think you're trying to let Mike know he's in potential danger? And what if Mike then realises that we are part of a trap to find him and he decides to go on the run? If he disappears and stops communicating that would make us dispensable. Cod in Devon! all my life I thought you were the sensible one."

"I need more training," offered Hayley realising her error.

The lay-by was noisy; Jan was rattled and began to compare Hayley to a newly sworn Special Constable. Very often they were over awed by the uniform, their powers and the flash of the blue lights. The difference being, Specials wanted to learn, wanted to help, needed to go home feeling amazing. With all the kit and a radio at their disposal, errors were points of learning, donuts at most, risk could be managed through their development. But here, Jan was out on a limb, without kit or communication. A flash of doubt had illuminated the actions of her sister and colleague. Was newly appointed civilian officer Allblack up to the task? she really did hope so.

Propelled along in a line of traffic in the outside lane, Jan noticed a dusty black Mercedes van with a purple shirted passenger pointing frantically through the window.

"We're still being followed or rather, they still know where we are Hayley, we have to be careful. Now, I need Clint's number."

"No worries."

With the engine switched off Jan picked up her phone and made the call and before nerves or anxiety could intercept the line, someone answered.

"Clint? Clint is that you? ...It's Jan, you know the service area where we met Sarah and then you fixed my sister's phone?... that's right, Hayley and you gave her your number."

Clint engaged in the conversation whilst Hayley tried hard to listen in.

"Yes, that was quite inspired I thought... what is it that you do, Clint, if you don't mind me asking?...

"Are you? Well that is highly commendable and I'm not at all surprised. Look, I was just wondering if you might be able or willing to help us solve a bit of a riddle that's come up?...

"Okay, well what it is, in a nutshell is, there are these two French men who are calling themselves *Voleur Payé*...

"Yes, that's right Paid Thief, well someone did an anagram and came up with Edith Piaf. These French men seem quite determined to travel to an unknown location in order to steal something sensitive or secretive or of high importance let's say, from another person...

"It is a bit of a puzzle, but I have a feeling that there's a connection somehow. I wondered if you might care to, well you know, have a think about it if you wouldn't mind. Obviously in your own time but if I could just stress there is an urgency to it...

"What? Me? yes, I am a retired police officer... No, my sister wasn't joking... Yes, it was all a bit embarrassing... I know I wish she wouldn't as well... Do you? That's interesting...

"Anyway, is that okay? Oh, and how did the exam go?... Oh good, yeah that's brilliant thanks, mate...Yeah, don't call Hayley's phone, use my number."

The contorted heap on the passenger seat could contain herself no longer.

"What did he say?"

"Well," said Jan, pleased that she'd found someone intelligent to explain their predicament to, "he is currently a special needs carer."

"No flaming use then given that Edith Piaf is most probably dead."

"Let me finish, he is also studying part time at college – computer sciences with a view to join the police or some security service, he also thinks the exam went well too."

"What did he say about me?"

"Let's just say he sussed you out as someone keen to tell everyone I was a police officer, but at least that added a bit of credibility to my enquiry."

"Bonza! I knew I was an equal in this team, if it hadn't been for me moving amongst the people and finding Clint, where would we be? I'm adding the excitement here; I'm laying trails, planting ideas…"

"Planting your feet more like, what must Mike be thinking now he's got that cryptic message? I'll be surprised if we ever find him, this is serious business, Hayley, this is my world, it's not a place to mess around in."

"Yeah well, don't go underestimating your teammate, I just had a little set back. On the job learning this is, you have to allow for that." With a look of defeat, she played with her phone like a sulky child until she took off in a different direction. "I wish my boys were as clever as Clint."

"How are the boys?" said Jan slipping back onto the dual carriageway.

"Well, they're all grown up, off doing their own thing, I hardly see them. They're both big and strong and flew me little nest with barely a second glance at their mother. If I wasn't in their Facebook group, I'd never know what they were doing." Back on safe ground Hayley spoke freely.

"Carl, my big little man, he's twenty-four now. Works on the prawn trawlers up in the north, spends months out at sea and when he comes back, he slots into his life up in Cairns. Girlfriends, drinking friends, prawn friends, who knows?

"My baby boy Johnny, he had his twenty-first this year. He lives mostly on Hamilton Island working on the Whitsunday Island ferry service, seems to enjoy it. Tanned like beef hide and thick blonde hair, not sure where he got that from. Hamilton's a bit pricey for me I'm afraid. if I want to see him, I just go down to the jetty and wait, it always embarrasses the little Lamington."

"Yes, I can imagine."

If they hadn't had their reunion day hijacked, Jan could have happily relaxed into her sister's bold and billowing personality. Drifting away towards the magical spell of the land down under where she too could be touched by the same beautiful paradise. A paradise that was part of Hayley and therefore part of her.

At the next picnic area, they passed a dusty black Mercedes van which caught Jan's eye.

"Look, there in the lay-by; it's them," she cried as her stomach filled with marshmallow jumping beans. "Foreign plates."

But, before Jan could create a useful action-plan with a detailed contingency for dealing with the van, the sound of 'I Don't Want to Talk About It' cut across her bow.

"That might be Clint; take the call," she said, unflinching from her command of the road.

"Hello yes, no this is Hays, Hayley. Jan is driving and wouldn't dream of taking the call, I don't know why, I mean everyone knows women can multitask."

At another time she might laugh, join in the banter but with jumbled insides, all Jan could manage was, "Hayley."

"Oh, no regrets? No of course not, we just got caught up in the cleaner's cupboard, don't feel bad, I know how you feel, I wouldn't have mentioned your body odour if...oh sorry, no, no just kidding, it must have been someone else."

Driving and listening to this tortured conversation by her loose cannon of a crewmate, Jan scanned ahead for a convenient place to stop.

"Oh, Edith Piaf 'No Regrets'," said Hayley, who sounded slightly disappointed with Clint's research.

"Yes, yes," said Jan, "we know that, her greatest hit."

"Did you hear that, Clint? she knows already. What? Virtual reality no regrets? You've lost me there, mate."

"Hang on I'm pulling over."

The P was in sight, Jan focused on the manoeuvre ahead; mirror check, indicate, speed. Within a short beat she'd entered the lay-by, switched off the engine and taken the phone.

"Clint, it's Jan, tell me that part again... Virtual reality no regrets what is that?... Is it a big thing?... The *latest* thing?... What sort of level?"

"I hope it doesn't involve frogs," said Hayley slightly too loud before she burst out laughing and then, through gasping breaths, managed, "oh, it already does."

"SSHHH, Hayley, I can't hear Clint. Well that certainly is a mystery, thanks mate, you're a star."

"Sounded a bit like me there, Sis," said Hayley, smiling and taking in the surroundings. With her earlier misdemeanour fading from memory, Hayley made herself comfortable and awaited lesson three.

"Well, this is certainly something different. Potentially, if Clint is right and the Edith Piaf connection to 'No Regrets' is correct, Mike may well be at the centre of something very big. Which would explain why the French boys are so keen to get hold of the know-how or technology or whatever this turns out to be."

"Jan!" shouted Hayley full to bursting. "Drive, drive!"

"Okay, yes but we have to stay calm, carefully consider the validity of this information."

"No, Jan, drive! He's walking towards the car!"

Jan glanced in the rear-view mirror annoyed that she'd been distracted by her phone *again* and had failed to notice the Mercedes pull in behind them. Instinctively she fired up the engine and left the lay-by before the smaller of the two men could reach her door. Driving seamlessly into the outside lane, she achieved nought to sixty in just over the published figure for her make and model which was hampered, in all probability, by the additional weight of a passenger and luggage.

"Wow, this is more like it," cried Hayley as she mouthed through the window. "Police, we're the police."

Is Clint right? thought Jan, could it be true? What *are* we dealing with? She gripped the wheel, trying to hold onto every sense that fought for her attention. At least she'd lost the Mercedes, that had to be a positive.

Hayley had entered another orbit, thrilled through space and time with every car they passed.

"Faster, faster; come on, Sis, we could bury them."

"This is the national speed limit, it's the law. I'm not about to exceed that and risk points on my licence."

"But we're the police, doing police work, just put your foot down."

"No, it is an offence and I'm not going there."

She speed-sifted through reams of documentation and options that had landed in the restricted space of her operational head. Her insides were back on the bubble and burn with an uncharacteristic scream only moments from her lips.

"So, what did he say about another level, what was all that?"

"He wasn't entirely sure, something he found on the dark web. Some breakthrough with virtual reality technology. I didn't fully understand it." Jan spoke carefully and pointedly as she struggled to suppress her internal combustion engine. "But apparently the next level is very important, whatever that means."

"Isn't that like putting on those big goggles that take you down a ski slope in Val-d'Isère and you nearly kill yourself in the living room trying to ski down the course?"

"No idea, passed me by that piece of fun. Although, now you mention it there are people, like your friend Stewart for example, who play all day on computer games. Maybe it's like him taking it to another level?"

"Stewart is *not* my friend, he called us a pair of old do-gooders, how rude. I am not old and past it, I'm vibrant, attractive and possibly wasted," said Hayley, her voice trailing.

The mental turmoil and external ache that a day of police work can bring was supposed to be a distant memory. These were feelings in history, not the future, not the life that Jan longed for.

"We have to get some food before we go any further, I can't think straight if I'm hungry. There's a garden centre coming up, they must do wholesome food." Jan scanned the mirror. "I can't see the van, but so long as we're in a public place, we should be okay I would have thought."

"Yeah, I could do with the dunny too."

Jan shook her head at the   toilet phobia that seemed determined to sail across her retirement horizon.

CHAPTER 11

"Strewth, Jan, you can put it away for a small bird. I've barely picked up me knife."

"Sorry, force of habit, one that I really need to get out of."

"Might do your insides some good, what other habits have you got to fix? How about that sleeping during the day one? Now, that's bad, unless you're on the beach of course, then it's right. Maybe you should relax a bit about all that honesty stuff too; I mean you are a free agent, who's bothered?"

"*I'm* bothered. Honesty is not a habit, it's in your core, it's a way of life, an *essential* way of life. Without truth and honesty where would we be? Life would be chaos, false. You have to be true to who you are; you only kid yourself if you lie and cheat."

"Slow down a bit, Sis. Jeez might have accidentally touched that nerve again."

"It's my guiding light, Hayley, my compass, why do some people not understand that?"

"Steady on, I *am* trying to understand your world."

With the conversation temporarily at a halt, Jan discretely puffed the air, like a smoker hoping the cloud of guilt would pass unnoticed. A sip of tea uncovered another habitual path, one that lead to the composted teabag mountain. She'd never questioned the importance of tea; it was a ritual, an element of basic training. It brought your team together especially after a challenging incident where a brew comforted and restored. As important as donuts, it was the order of things, a habit, she concluded, that must be preserved for times of madness and nonsense and definitely right now.

At 16:10, the clatter of cutlery and warm murmuring reflected the success of main course Monday with an extensive choice of mains for a fiver. Jan continued with her food but differently. Slowly and self-consciously, she chewed every mouthful of the rustic vegetable quiche and salad, it was painfully difficult, unnatural and surprisingly tasty.

"Why does it matter whether it's jam or cream first? It all goes down the same hole," said Hayley as she swirled the thick cream through the jam and suffocated the scone beneath.

"Look, I've been thinking, perhaps that's why virtual reality hasn't grabbed you, I mean it's not the real world is it?"

"No, and if I wanted to ski down the slopes in Val-d'Isère, I would just go out there, freeze to death and risk breaking my bones not an item of furniture that had got in the way. That's real life, that's truth."

"That's where we're different you see, living the other side of the world does have its problems you know. When your home is thousands of miles from a decent ski slope, what's a girl supposed to do? Dream a little, have a little fun, disappear into a different world."

Jan found herself dreaming in a strange twilight world somewhere between a job she knew and a place she hadn't a clue. How could she ever feel confident about tomorrow, if unscheduled events could just barge in without even the courtesy of a phone call?

Why had she entertained the desperate DS? Where was the briefing and contingency? This wasn't the Devon and Cornwall she'd left behind, this was winging it, big time.

At every turn, regret marched towards her, blowing raspberries and blocking the way with placards of doom. She longed for the positive, unmistakable identity of yesterday, her rank, her role, her uniform and a purpose. As she stumbled along that slippery conduit between serving officer and civilian, her hands clutched at a few delicate items from a box labelled 'Family'.

"Aargh," she said, "sorry, what I mean is, this day, this reunion, just doesn't seem to be getting any easier; the more I think about it, the more uncertain I am. I just don't know if we're doing the right thing."

"Now come on, my little fruit crumble, we're in your field, I'm relying on you to get us through this, strewth, I'm not much use on me own, am I?"

Jan dropped her head and focused on some quiche crumbs carelessly out of place as Hayley marched off into their shared memories.

"You know, Sis, just back there, you said that you thought I was the sensible one. I didn't know you felt like that. Well, I didn't know that maybe you had thought that back then when we were all together, I was pretty chuffed hearing that. What I remember from when we were kids is that you were always the sensitive one, took everything a bit seriously. Jeez, like I keep saying, you were so easy to wind up. Do you remember that Sunday afternoon when I said your form teacher was at the door and he wanted to give you extra homework? You fell for that like a nut from a tree. I laughed my head off long after you'd gone to bed."

"I know," said Jan, "it was difficult not to hear you, being only six feet away."

"So, you do remember? that's so funny. Look, we had a laugh, we had fun, lots of it. Even quiet Mikey joined in."

With her head beginning to thaw, Jan made a tentative chair shuffle across the icy lake to link arms and turn another page in their childhood story book.

"We were all cared for though. I'm grateful for that; aunt Ethel managed to guide me through." She tiptoed onwards through the emotion that squeezed like a flannel across her diaphragm. "You seem to have survived too," she said.

"Always a survivor me, can't stop an Elliot when they've made their mind up. Grab your chances, you don't get many. Sometimes you don't realise they're standing right in front of you. Eyes wide open, give it a go and make sure you bounce."

Hayley's irresistibly infectious attitude had sent Jan to the sunlit washing line where she could abandon her scrunched flannel and hang out in the queue for the carefree playground activities. She longed to bounce and play and learn from her sister, one of the normal go-getting exciting people that could make sense of a life without uniform.

Tales of happy distraction, this is what I've missed, thought Jan, I've missed my big sister, my lovely big sister showing me life, the jaunty version, where I can be normal.

Before she could learn the steps that would enable her to dance blithely into the sunset, there was still the Mike issue. Joy alone appeared unable to dissolve the mountain of angst that had landed in her playground and created an unseasonal winter shadow. She shivered and released Hayley then gripped her elbows and bowed her head as if the time had run out on a coin operated puppet in a seaside arcade.

Thoughts of his demise had churned into an unwelcome lump of lard that spread scorn on any future hopes of relaxed freedom. It's all my fault, he'll point to me for his corrupt and chaotic life and who could blame him?

"Do you think there's a connection between a law-abiding sister and a criminal brother?" said Jan without lifting her head.

"Course there flaming is," Hayley replied, "you're related."

Jan tried to curl herself into the smallest ball possible without falling off the chair until she realised that Hayley was snorting.

"Why are you laughing?"

"Got you again. That was funny, come on, Sis, who knows? Mum and dad died, we ruined an old lady's retirement plans, I left you to it. Could have been any number of reasons. Maybe he didn't like school, maybe he was bullied. You know we aren't qualified to know what life was like from his angle. We only truly know our own path and the decisions we've made and why. Whatever it is, it can't be changed, like I say grab your chances I'm not about to live me days with regret."

Jan pondered the sensible one and the wisdom contained therein. My one regret, she thought, is not being able to shake off the rejection, what was the point of that? I should have just kept in touch with them. That's what you're supposed to do.

As she fluffed herself back into the room, Jan checked the surroundings in case she had inadvertently caused a scene. It was then that she noticed them.

"Now, I don't want you to overreact or make anything of it but, I've just clocked the French twins sat at a table near the entrance. No, don't look Hayley please, we don't want to get into a situation."

But words alone weren't about to stop a king cobra preparing to strike. With lightning speed Hayley spun around and fixed her matronly eyes on the prey and there she remained, perfectly still and thoroughly menacing. The boys began to fidget and appeared to shrink inside their clothing until finally Hayley did what most snakes do, she stuck out her tongue and turned away.

"There, I think that did the trick. Anyway," she smiled "it's the wrong day for two for one."

Unnatural as it felt, Jan knew she had to take the lead, this was her operation, except familiar ground felt anything but. Why can't

Hays be in charge? She won't listen to me anyway. Well, she never used to. They were adults now although, with Hayley sporting a large swirl of cream across her bronzed chin like a child in training, Jan found herself wondering. In a revised attempt at leadership she sat up straight.

"Okay, let's forget the message you sent to Mike."

"Yeah, that was a bit mad, I realise that now, I'm just a bit out of me depth. Bit more difficult than you realise, all this police stuff."

"Right, well, we'll just have to work with what we've got. It was acknowledged at the start that you might be the liability." The quiet protest told Jan all she needed to know, she had to supervise, her inexperienced team were looking for encouragement and guidance.

"Let's start again, equal partners."

"Okay, so what do we do next?" whispered Hayley.

"What do *you* think we should do?"

"Well," she said clearly ruminating an important idea, "first things first, like I said at the beginning, I need the dunny."

"Oh, yes, well, not on your own, I'm not letting you out of my sight. You can have your own cubicle of course, I just don't want any more surprises bowling through my day and I suggest you clean that cream off of your face, so you can present yourself for duty."

Jan carefully balanced their debris onto the tray and slotted it onto the overcrowded stand, keeping half an eye on the boys as she raced to catch Hayley.

An old and long-standing toilet tradition precluded Jan from having a conversation from within her cubicle. She couldn't actually think of a succinct and pertinent reason why it wasn't her done thing. It just wasn't. These days conversation between toilet occupants had been eclipsed by the use of mobile phones; abhorrent on a whole different level. Unwashed, germ covered hands juggling the handset, loo roll and clothing, in a rush to buy goods online or deal with some urgent admin that had to be squeezed into this *me* time.

Jan was pleased to see that Hayley washed her hands thoroughly and said so.

"Yeah, getting rid of that sticky cream feels better too."

Jan opted for the quiet paper towel drying method and whispered her plan of action which would quite probably be subject to change.

"We're very close to the border, we really need to know where we're going. Can you check, see if you've heard from Mike? Otherwise we'll be going across the Tamar bridge and there we are, our destination – Cornwall." Still torn between top dog and second fiddle she added, "I'm sorry I didn't stay in touch, it was difficult," she faltered.

"Yeah well, I know, over half our lives apart, you're not easy to get a response out of, I have tried."

"I know you did, but it's hard when you decide to live the other side of the world."

"We do still have telephones, internet, a postal service."

"It was just difficult what with my job and life, I didn't know where to begin or how."

"That's a lot of time not sharing with your own sister. Oh yeah and Mikey of course, he could be an Olympic wrestler for all I know. The French boys probably know more about Mikey than we do and when he replies to me, they'll know that too, am I correct?"

"Undoubtedly, this is a bit above my skill set I have to say. Most of my patrol days were dealing with domestics, theft, drugs and sudden death. Anything that had a whiff of national importance didn't really come my way."

"Domestics, do you have a lot of trouble with domestics over here?"

"Yes why?"

"Well back home cleaners and home helps are usually quite good. What sort of things do they do?"

"No, domestics as in family arguments, violence that sort of thing."

"Wow, how interesting."

"No not really, loads of paperwork and risk assessments followed by the same again the next day. But there's potential for real harm within every family perhaps more so when they're dysfunctional."

"Like us you mean? And there was me beginning to think police work was quite interesting, but you're putting me off a bit."

"Good, because I think you're too old to join now. Come on let's get moving."

The sight of the French revolutionaries stirred anger and a determination that caused Jan to detour. She returned with her purchases and deposited two oversized croissants in front of them.

"Bon appetite, we're not there yet," she whispered.

Hayley moved forward. "Yeah we're watching you, cobber, you don't want to be messing with these girls."

Uncharacteristically quiet, the fox hounds remained in their kennel, possibly awestruck or more likely they were struggling with Hayley's version of English as a foreign language. Either way, she surged on a tide of excitement with clearly more to say until Jan grabbed her arm and dragged her towards the exit.

"What are you doing?"

"I was going to arrest them of course, put a stop to all this nonsense."

"Hayley, what are you thinking? We can't just arrest them; I mean what powers do you think we have?"

"Come on, Sis, we're the team, we're the police, we had them right there."

"No, not the police, we are just some mugs that have been roped into this apparently top-secret romp across the West Country. We have no powers, no evidence, we have nothing. What are they? What were they doing? They're just a couple of tourists drinking coffee miles away from the Arc de Triomphe."

"Yeah, but we know who they really are."

"No, we don't. We have been given a theory by a policeman who freely admitted to knowing very little about them."

"But they threatened us."

"Yes, I agree, they burst into Mrs Marshall's house, made threats and were a bit rude but we can't go around trying to arrest them. That's not our job, in fact we don't have jobs, we are just idiots to even get involved with this nonsense." Jan began to slide past second fiddle on the way to reserve triangle.

By the time they had reached the car, the black Mercedes was mobile.

"Come on, let's hope we get something from Mike soon, I think that pair could get a bit impatient."

"What happens when we finally do find Mikey and then they find us with Mikey and the police arrive after we're dead?"

"Well, it would be wrong to ignore that as a possibility. We have got to stay focused and not allow information to slip out, we have to stay ahead, buy ourselves some time, deliver the goods and slip out the back door."

"Do you think we can do all that? I mean I just came over for a holiday, little family reunion, pasties and cream tea. You just said this is a bit more than you're trained for and now I feel a bit up the creek in a canoe without a paddle."

"That's one way of putting it. Look, I don't know everything, but I do have my training, some discipline, a raft of underused combat skills, perhaps with a bit of common sense we can get this done. Mike can be arrested and I can start my peaceful new life."

"Yeah and I suppose cos I've brought up two strapping lads with Leonard, they shouldn't even think of messing with me, I'll knock their heads together."

This was the perfect time for the team leader to deliver a fortifying speech to motivate the troops and instil a confidence that would carry them to victory. But instead, Jan was still teetering between commitment and going AWOL. She longed to be at home, paddling around in comfy slippers, safe and in control and as far away from decision making as was humanly possible. It didn't help that her sister was complicating matters by running up and down the seesaw and tipping Jan in all directions.

As she touched down on the side of duty and commitment, a road sign declared that the crossing point was five miles away. Which, put another way, meant that Jan was rapidly running out of Devon. It was time to distract herself with a further chapter from 'the family'.

"How are things in Australia?"

"Well, Len is still just about running the air conditioning business – LA Cool jeez, he's been doing that since he was twenty-three, no wonder I fell for him all tanned and gorgeous and living by the sea. I wouldn't have minded if you'd followed me out there, I did think about the two of you, but a girl has a life to lead, got to see the world, make things happen, you know how it is."

"Well, I know how it was for me, carved out my police career, fight the good fight, do something positive and worthwhile with my life. Stop failing in the Mike department, I just wasn't as good as you at the looking after bit, I don't think I got that gene."

"No, I can't see you much as the mothering type, is that why you didn't have kids?"

"Well, it never really seemed like the right time. It was frowned upon too in my early career, certainly didn't make it easy for women to have a family."

"Jeez."

"I had to stand by what I believed in and I believed in the job. I would have liked the happy family route like you though, I mean look at Carl and Johnny."

"Yes, I do, on Facebook; like I said, they aren't in my life much at the moment."

"You've still got Leonard, even after all these years, is he aging well?"

"Erm, yes, he's changed a lot, but then who hasn't?"

"Do we change for the better or do we just make bigger mistakes? Or do we just not care anymore? I wish I didn't care, but I wouldn't know how to do that. Come on, Mike," said Jan trying hard to keep frustration out of her voice, "we really need some help here."

Hayley was strangely distracted as she stared through the countryside and verges that hugged the carriageway.

"Yeah, show me someone who doesn't need help."

The silence returned for a few miles until the sprawl of the grey urban landscape pushed the countryside to the back of the canvas.

"Len and I are having a few problems, if you must know."

"Oh, are you? Oh erm, like what?" Was her sister confiding? thought Jan, hastily searching for the hat she didn't have, in a day that wasn't really looking for any more uncharted territory.

"Well, we haven't been seeing eye to eye for a while and because of that he has taken control of the money and I'm a bit strapped to say the least. I didn't want to tell you, but you know this illusion of happy families you paint? It's not true. Your life seems far more exciting to me, freedom without the baggage or restrictions."

"Hayley, you should have said. No wonder you're so keen to throw yourself into this challenge with a carefree attitude not usually befitting a fifty-five-year-old mother and wife."

"Hey, you can keep your opinions in the cupboard thanks, there are plenty of go-getter Aussie women who'd be a bit upset at that."

"Yeah but you're my sister and I know, underneath all that, you're English."

Brunel's iconic rail bridge appeared ahead of them alongside the considerably younger toll bridge where, Jan discovered, they would not be charged to enter Cornwall.

"How do you do for money if you haven't got any control? Surely you have your own account and cash?"

Jan couldn't imagine losing her independence in that way, wouldn't let that happen. She controlled everything about her life well, apart from what was happening today. But aside from that, financial control wasn't something to relinquish.

"Well I have a savings account, but it was pretty empty, just a bit of money for girlie things like coffee, the odd cocktail."

"How did you get the air fare? I mean if he let you have that, then you must be able to discuss day to day finances surely?"

"Well, not really, I got here out of my benefits."

Like a boxer floored in the ring and struggling to stand Jan steadied herself on the ropes.

"Oh, I didn't know you had benefits, what's that for?"

"Well, it started on a little holiday I took down to Brisbane." Hayley dried up, as if searching for the appropriate tale.

Is my sister okay? Perhaps I've been asking too much of her, she thought as she squeezed the life out of the steering wheel.

"In a nut shell, I fell at the bus station, twisted my knee, pulled some ligaments and ended up on crutches for a few months."

"Oh, I see, how is it now?"

"Erm, okay."

"Yes, you look okay, bouncing around. So, you saved your benefit money to buy an air ticket?"

"Yeah, sort of."

There was something about this hesitant and vague delivery that allowed the furnace of fear to scorch all support from Jan's reply.

"What aren't you telling me?"

"Well the thing is, I know you'll go through the roof, storm out of the bedroom, slam the door get all serious. So, in order to limit that, I'm going to say 'sorry' up front."

Jan clung to the ropes, a bucket of anxiety splashed across her face and all reference to rational thinking was kicked aside as she spat out her response.

"Sorry for what?"

Hayley had somehow managed to shrink into her seat like a tiny, insecure sibling on the verge of a proper telling off. Even so, on one breath of monotone air she went for it.

"I still claim the benefits."

"What?!"

"Look, it isn't what it seems, I'm in England now, no one knows, although I thought that detective at the robbery had sussed me out, but they're not likely to follow me to England are they? So, I decided I'd be okay without me crutches."

"But you *are* okay without crutches, look at you, you've been skipping around confronting the enemy, what part of that needs crutches?"

"You have to use crutches if you want to be paid benefits, no good me surfing and fooling around on the beach back home, or the spies will stop me cash."

"I don't believe this." With knuckles of snow and ice Jan was consumed by a blizzard of polar proportions. Unable to accept or justify this statement of fact, or indeed drive safely under the circumstances, she took the correct evasive action and turned off the A38, following signs for Saltash.

Robbed of further speech, her mind began to riffle through scenario drawers in search of clues for the way forward. Clarification was often the best idea, be clear of the facts she thought, pulling into the largest space she could find.

"Where are your crutches?"

"Still going around the carousel at Heathrow for all I know. I didn't need them anymore. I had to take them on the plane, but once I got here that was different. I didn't want them to slow me down, make me self look weak."

"Exactly, you are not weak, you are not disabled, you are claiming benefits that other people need, genuine people, not liars, not fraudsters, not you."

It was an odd feeling for Jan to rise above her natural order and seethe at her sister from the moral high ground. No longer shoehorned into the middle child seat, this was stratospheric and who knew what tears lay fit to burst up here.

"I had to string it out for a bit longer, I couldn't have got here else."

"Well, then maybe it would have been better if you hadn't come. Cod ham it! It looks like I'm condoning a fraudster, I am complicit. Don't you understand? *I* am a witness; I'll have to stand up in court and give evidence of a benefit cheat – my own sister. This is unbelievable, why did you leave it until now to tell me? You could have told me at Tiverton, I could have just left you there. Whose day is this that I'm living? Because it *isn't* and *shouldn't* be mine. How is it that in the first twenty-four hours of my retirement, I not only find out that my brother is heavily involved in some crime of the century but also that my sister is committing fraud? Oh cod, I hope the spies that photograph you don't catch me too; I'll be tarnished with your dishonesty. My first day out of uniform and I'm a floundering criminal."

"Hey, don't get so mad, I'm here now, I can stop my claim, go home with the excuse that my English holiday produced a miracle cure and no one will be any the wiser."

"*I* am the wiser. *I* know. No, I'm sorry, this whole stupid idea is done with, you're on your own, it's your phone they're tracking, not my car, you can lead them to Mike and the pair of you can take your chances. You're two of a kind and welcome to each other."

"Don't be daft, Jan, I don't know where I am. I can't do this police work and besides it's dangerous and…"

"Look there's a station just down the road, you can hop on a train and go wherever you please. I am not carrying on like this, Hayley. To think I was nearly envious of your lifestyle, well, you've not quite made a fool out of me, that isn't going to happen."

With Hayley's case deposited on the pavement, Jan opened the passenger door.

"Please, just get out. I've got better things to do with my day."

CHAPTER 12

Covered by a protective blanket of numb nothingness, paralysed in the beady eye of a mental storm, Jan stared without focus or desire at the service area car park where she had come to rest. Winded, wounded and very definitely wound up, she was incapable of dealing with the demands of further disappointment and had no desire to move ever again. Or, at least until this very dark cloud had released its hulking, universal ache from the sky above her life.

This was her big day, moving on along the road to paradise. She tussled through the peaks and troughs of the worst day, ever. The more she tried to figure out what had gone wrong, what had just happened, no, what on earth had just happened, the more she wanted to cry. And now as she clutched the title – 'The new head of the family, the only honest and responsible child in the roost', she did indeed begin to leak. As the tears poured down, Jan deflated into an unfamiliar no-man's land without a rule book. Feeling sick from quiche and catastrophe, her face screwed up in ways that were inevitably going to create a lasting lived-in look.

"What am I supposed to do?" she asked. As if Howard, the most faithful of cars, was capable of offering guidance and support. "I am dragged, against my will, into some bonkers operation to bring down my estranged criminal brother with the help of my sister, my sister who I have revered all my life who turns out to be a common thief."

She sniffed loudly then took a clean tissue from the glovebox and blew loudly and concluded loudly.

"I mean these are people I need to drop like the hot potatoes they are. I need to head off into the sunset, find my special place and forget all about them. Close this sorry chapter and begin a new page in the morning, live happily, as I always have done, alone."

She'd been so close to feeling at home, the two of them, just like old times. Until her dance on the phone wire of 'family' was vandalised by her own relatives.

"Cod ham it, cod ham it," she shouted, banging the steering wheel, as is customary.

A young couple, holding hands across the car park, turned briefly to look at her crumpled form, then continued on towards the service building, with heads together in private discussion.

Jan scrutinised their body language, their entangled closeness. Jealousy began to crackle from a hot bed of discomfort as she imagined a life without secrets. They disappeared from view and like a well-established routine, she lapsed into the working banter of yesterday.

"They're probably having an affair; she's got two kids left at home with her husband who bores her to tears. She told him she was off to Asda. The guy is on his lunchbreak, met her on social media and here they are living the deceitful dream." She turned to her imaginary colleague sitting in the front seat and fell silent at the absence.

In her world of torment Jan played and replayed the ridiculous unplanned events that had led to this afternoon of nonsense. Now confident that even if she had turned up on time at the station, it was far too late to prevent her brother and sister from embarking on their individual paths of crime. The dreadful events of the day couldn't be hung at Jan's door which did offer comfort and a little strength.

I am strong, I am strong, the mantra for occasions such as this pulsed through her mind as she opened the door to survey the tired rest area into which she had landed.

Oh, this is ridiculous, a retired officer, my whole life ahead of me and I'm sitting in some dusty service area car park feeling like a mug. How could they betray everything I believe in, my own relatives?

"Get a grip, Jan!" she shouted.

The rooks seemed unfazed by her outburst as they squabbled raucously around the handful of cars. They waddled arthritically in baggy trousers with steps punctuated by a bounce or skip as they searched for any scrap of anything edible. Jan could see the similarity with her own 'crook' of a sister, the hobble that turned to a joyous bounce when the authorities turned a blind eye.

"Lucky cods – look at you," she said splashing around in another helping of hot soup, completely unaware of the three young lads who had come into view on her short horizon. But it was too late to project any of her preferred public qualities, their faces were made up, she had been labelled a 'mad woman'.

She returned to the world of birds to observe their carefree existence in secure family groups. Every day a song before breakfast, then foraging and games during the day before they settled down together to share stories at the top of the tree. They have no concept of death or retirement, no time for lies. They live an honest day-to-day existence and know their place in the flock.

Her unhappy place dripped in darkness inhabited by a world of rowdy rooks that flew in the face of her own lonely existence. But, before a highly trained therapist could triumphantly slap another label on her feelings, a squeaky fan belt somewhere nearby sent them back to their tree.

And with her body strung out like a long ribbon of sun-dried seaweed that the sea had accidentally left behind, Jan found herself abandoned all over again. Rejected by all she had clung to and angry that, for too many years, she had imagined people to be something they most definitely were not.

She wiped her face roughly; longed for her mother's hanky that could dab and reassure, put a childish world to rights and send her back out to play. But that wasn't about to happen so, she got out of the car and walked a short distance to the edge of the parking area where she sat on a cleanish kerb stone.

17:05, she wondered how many more retirement days would be wasted worrying about unimportant nonsense far away from her idyllic world.

I am in charge now, I have the power to take control, to walk away and find my own cloudless oasis. This insipid, poisonous manifestation will be vanquished, turned to a dried-up riverbed, devoid of life.

Then, with a death grip on the kerb she focused on breathing. This overused self-help therapy was supposed to be handed in with her uniform, a thing of the past gone and buried. But like an old flame turning up on the doorstep in her hour of need, she breathed slowly and deeply for old time's sake.

Now, positively exhausted, she stretched out her legs just as the young couple walked back across the car park. He was carrying a newspaper and a milkshake; she didn't seem to have purchased anything. Jan began to think maybe they were not having an affair, maybe they'd naturally stopped off for a comfort break and just happened to like each other. She drifted into an area of vain hope, where she imagined having her own special person, someone to share little jokes and reminisce. Someone who loved her.

This further ocean of emptiness stoked her anxiety like hot surf burning a wave to her deepest core. Her antiquated breathing apparatus was being pushed to capacity as she fought to retain control through every measured breath. The world pulled further away and her mind plummeted into a small insular protected place. Where, above the rhythmic noise of her own making, she became aware of a voice.

"Are you okay?"

She expelled a deep pant, then rushed up the staircase from her inner sanctum to look at the sunlit silhouette that had spoken.

"Yes, fine thank you, just breathing that's all, only breathing, perfectly natural." She pulled her knees in, leaning backwards to get a better view of this youthful being that eclipsed the sun.

"You're my first incident, but I am trained and competent in all areas of the car park." He delivered his piece to a good scenario standard but offered no more, just remained a few feet away on the grass holding a black bag and litter picker.

Her first attempt at self-sabotage had left Jan wondering why she couldn't just disappear into a hole in the ground without attracting a witness to hijack her train of thought. He'd done more than that, he'd called her an 'incident'. How many more hurtful labels would she attract before this doomed day was done with her? And, what now? It began to feel uncomfortably rude to ignore this trained and competent youth casting a shadow on her day.

"So, what happens next in this type of incident?" Jan was sufficiently curious to wonder what measures were in place should a lone female be found perched on the kerb breathing.

The litter picker swung gently from side to side as the young man compiled a collection of short stories, that he felt were appropriate for the circumstances.

"Well, if I think about my mum when she does this at home. Well, then I know it's all about to kick off." He hesitated as if he realised that his mum and her problems didn't transfer too well into the workplace.

"Go on," said Jan.

"Well, then she throws a slipper or ashtray at me, swears a lot and tells me to 'get out!', I thought that's what you were going to do but you haven't so…"

"No, that's not really me. Does your mum do that often? Is she taking any medication? Who lives at home with you? I'm sorry, I shouldn't ask." She knew she shouldn't ask, not now, not here. If he answered truthfully what then? Without the back-up or resources to intervene in the home life of this troubled youth, she was giving him false hope and although she felt a sense of duty once again, she could at least, for the moment, accept that her own needs would have to take priority. Her lack of 'casual conversation with a youth' skills were now evident as she clumsily plunged into a shallow pond of general chatter before, all too soon, they were both left high and dry with their own calamities.

Desperate to have another go and learn from this one-to-one tuition with a youth, she took a deep breath and tried again.

"Don't tell me, you haven't always been a litter collector, you were once the youngest Navy Seal in history and…Oh, I'm sorry, it's Jan by the way."

"Declan, well my mum calls me Dex or Dexy if she wants something. What's a Navy Seal?" enquired the semi-clean young man in his ironed service area uniform.

"Oh, a diver in the American navy, I was just being silly, well not silly of course, there's no reason why you shouldn't be whatever you want to be," she stumbled. "But I like their motto 'The Only Easy Day Was Yesterday', or at least I used to like their motto. Now I'd like to think that tomorrow will be the easy day."

This brief life affirming diversion was lost on Declan who still seemed stuck on the previous page.

"I don't like putting my head under the water," he offered, "but I like the navy. I can see the dockyard and the sailors and the submarines from our flat in Devonport.

"I didn't want to get a job, because I didn't know if I could. Mum said I had to bite the bullet, sounded funny Mum saying *bullet*, what would she know? Anyway, she meant I had to do something painful. Then she said that if I carried on staring at the dockyard and didn't get a job, she would paint over my window."

"That's a bit extreme, mate," she said allowing her own concerns to evaporate a little. "How are you getting along here?"

"I like it, I'm my own boss in the car park and I get free meals at Burger King – I can have whatever I like, as long as it's under £7, it's brilliant."

Declan had come into his own, the unemployed dreamer forced into the workplace, he had found more than a job. He had an extended family, where work and commitment filled him with pride and a belonging that he never knew he needed.

"I empty the bins and sort through the bags taking out the rubbish that can be recycled and put it in those bins over there. I have my own system and the area manager said I was doing a very good thing for the planet."

"Well, yes you are. You seem very efficient; it's nice to see such enthusiasm."

"Efficient, is that like fast?"

"Well, more like being productive with little waste."

"So, like recycling?"

Jan allowed herself a relaxed smile. "Yes, I think that may be true."

"Why did you look unwell just now?" he said playfully snapping at the air with the litter picker.

"It's too complicated, but thank you for asking and well, thank you for being brave enough to do that. I do actually feel a little bit better having spoken with you."

Leaking personal information to a strange boy in a car park was peculiar. Sharing inner most thoughts or feelings wasn't high on Jan's list of priorities. But on this occasion and for some reason of necessity, she felt safe talking to the car park spirit, concluding that he wasn't likely to take this information and turn it against her. That for a moment she could just be comforted with this brief encounter.

"Do you often give car park counselling? Chats I mean."

"I don't speak to many people, my boss looks out of the window and keeps an eye on me," he said. "I don't want him to give me the sack cos he said he would. I have to keep busy not idling as Mum calls it."

"Doesn't the boss trust you yet?"

"It's only my second week; he says I'm on trial. I don't mean like a scumbag in court." He held the picker in both hands straight across his body causing Jan to recoil from the prisoner that stood before her in the dock.

"Have you ever been in court?" Jan tried to steady her tone, but it had changed and she couldn't pull it back to the light.

"No, not me. Imagine, I think I would confess to everything. It would be very scary."

"Have you ever been in trouble with the police?" From the moment she had vocalised the words, it was too late to stop herself, it was an inappropriate line of questioning that could easily destroy their fragile relationship.

"You sound like the boss at my interview, he asked that. I told my mum and she thought it was very funny. We had scampi when I got this job; I think she was pleased with me."

Declan didn't appear concerned by Jan's emotional inconsistencies. He seemed immune, accustomed to this kind of behaviour from those around him. But she didn't want to be in that camp, she'd hoped to stand out as a guiding light as a person he could aspire to. Someone who was fair and non-judgemental, a human being who would believe in him for the kind soul he appeared to be. But she'd given him nothing better than he already knew; that people could doubt him, fail to understand what he stood for and leave him unsupported. They would shout, threaten his window on the world and sometimes, they might throw an ashtray.

"Listen, I don't want to get you into trouble talking to a silly woman sitting on the kerb but thank you for your help, I'm sorry."

"By the way," he said, starting to walk away, "I think the rooks have been looking into your car over there."

"Oh, oh thanks." She hurried back berating her absent-minded failure to close the window and secure Howard in the proper manner. The unhurried mob landed nearby and filled the air with raucous laughter as Jan surveyed the poop that slid down the door mirror. "Cod ham it."

As she cleaned the mess with tissues and a bottle of water, she reflected on a wasted encounter. The job had made her cynical in a way that only comes into focus when you move amongst the real people. There was nothing wrong with Declan, nothing that needed hanging out to dry under a cloud of stupid suspicion.

Look at him, happy as can be, making a contribution. Possibly not a bad bone in his body, nothing to trouble me at any rate. Why did I have to ask about his offending history? Why am I so stupid? He is just a nice lad doing his honest best.

She sunk into the driver's seat with the door wide open clutching a soggy heap of soiled tissues. Still hoping for a rule book to appear out of the darkness, she reflected on the 'Us' and 'Them' mentality of yesterday. It was easier when there were clearly defined rules, this was hard, she was going to have to make her own unregulated decisions regarding who is good and who is bad. Like the mythical all-knowing Santa that she wasn't.

Why can't people have a tick or a cross or a question mark pinned to their head? she wondered. Then I could comfortably move amongst all those displaying a tick and keep the cross people as far away as possible. The question marks could be thought about on a case-by-case basis during afternoon tea.

This futile hope would place her brother and sister in the cross corner. Although at a push Mike might make the question mark pile because the extent of his dishonesty had yet to be thoroughly clarified. But that was unlikely, Jan knew that honesty didn't have a grey side, it didn't come in shades despite how a desperate miscreant might try to argue the point.

The wasted beauty of the day magnified the sadness and regret that surrounded her as she stumbled into a familiar world of self-doubt and misery where she was always assured of an indifferent welcome. Her eyes fell from the window onto the vile sodden tissues cradled in her hand. A horrid heap of discomfort that propelled Jan, at considerable speed, to the nearest bin where she flung the sticky mess into the fresh black bag.

"Yuk, yuk," she wailed, brushing her hands with pointless despair.

Come on, come on, make a decision. Thirty years of public common sense doesn't just disappear overnight does it?

She seized the bin and began to crumble in full public view. Except, luckily the public were a bit thin on the ground. Declan on the other hand had just emptied the bin.

"Are you sure you're okay?"

Jan couldn't let go; she was stuck by the glue of remorse. She wanted to peel her hands away, she had to. This was Declan's bin that she'd just selfishly filled with rubbish.

"I'm so sorry, I really am sorry, Declan, please forgive me." Taking one hand away and steadying her weight through the other she made eye contact with her only friend in this all new uncomfortable world.

"It doesn't matter, someone has to be the first to put stuff in it. I mean, I'd rather they put stuff in the bin. You wouldn't believe some people, they can't even be bothered to walk over here, they just drop it by the car door. I keep all the registration numbers in my little book and when the police come in here, I tell them. They're very grateful for my help. They never said at my interview that I would be able to help the police. I'm very lucky, it is so varied what I do."

During the enlightening short story that Declan had a gift for, Jan was finally able to release the bin. Keeping her hands away from her clothes she began to reacquaint herself with the surroundings. Her car was twenty metres away, the door wide open, rooks currently occupied elsewhere and Declan one metre to her left. Her eyes felt puffy and irritated as they fed this vital information back to the nerve centre.

"What I mean, Declan, is, I'm sorry for being sharp with you back there, it was uncalled for and thoughtless. You appear to me to be a very kind person with a lot of depth. And I *am* sorry that I messed up your bin."

"It's my job. I like saying that, 'it's my job' or 'just doing my job'. Sometimes with old people when they're walking towards a bin, well because I know they'll be doing the right thing, I save them the bother and take it for them."

"That's going above and beyond your duties I'm sure but don't let that stop you."

He smiled and tapped his picker on the toe of his black trainers.

"When I'm at home and I don't quite feel right, a day that's upside down where my head's in a bucket, I think it's a good idea to make a cup of tea. You can sit quietly and let the tea work its magic. Mum told me that, she does have some good things to say, I like the good things."

"You're right, Declan, I think I need to get cleaned up and sit down with a nice drink."

"My head wasn't really in a bucket; it just feels like that doesn't it sometimes?"

"Yes, I suppose it does."

Jan wandered across to Howard to re-establish her security routine before dutifully making her way to the facilities; her head held low in reflective shame.

Not the first time today, Janet Elliot, that you have rushed to judge people and been woefully off the mark. Normal was complicated and new and came with unexpected feelings of responsibility and friendship.

Whatever happened next, Jan knew it would be foolish to pass a loo stop or a brew stop. That part of her previous life could stay.

It was difficult to ignore the clinical chemical smell of the liquid that served as hand wash but, nonetheless, Jan intended to be thorough, despite the lack of soapsuds. This repetitive motion allowed her mind to consider the two key issues that wouldn't go away; her sister and her brother. How could she sit with them, converse with them knowing everything she currently knew? There was no going back and more worryingly still, there was no going forward in any direction she could possibly imagine.

With hands restored to an acceptable standard, she selected a cubicle not too near the door and not too far away, just right. After final checks concerning cleanliness, toilet tissue and working lock, Jan closed the door. Several people were moving about, doors were opening here, clattering shut there, it was a brief moment of comfort. But, as Jan zipped her trousers, she was forced back against the toilet bowl by the sight of a hand waving under the partition.

"Ham, ham, ham, ham, ham," she whispered on a rapid intake of breath hoping the walls weren't as thin as she knew they were.

It thrust towards her, urgent and persistent, clutching a neatly folded sheet of paper.

Chapter 12

The restricted space within a public cubicle becomes overwhelmingly apparent when you are desperate to distance yourself from an unexpected violation.

Clamped to the toilet bowl in an undignified standoff, she was eerily drawn to the waggling hand that seemed hell-bent on communication. And like the spam email that you open at your peril, Jan was tempted by its contents, hooked into the foolish belief that it contained something she really needed to know.

The hairy knuckled, tanned fingers continued to implore the importance of the communique until she weakened and struck out. Careful to avoid flesh she seized the paper from the unknown messenger.

Cod, I haven't even washed my hands, this is a germ filled nightmare, she thought as her fingertips unfolded the note.

The content, scrawled in black biro was brief: 'What are doing here?'.

Yuk, disgusting, what a pick-up line, yuk, yuk she thought as the note bounced back under the partition, such was the force behind it. As the impatient hand snaffled the paper, she hoped its next move would be to open the door and leave the cubicle, but it did not. Unable to move she stared at her hands, the hands that had just participated in an exchange of the seediest order. Then, just as she'd recovered enough to make her exit, the hand reappeared with another paper offering.

Cod ham it, why aren't I still in the Job? I'd drag the pervert out of there, this must contravene the human rights act, cod knows most things do. With a deploring lack of manners, she snatched the note from the hand, hmphed with feeble superiority and read it. It was very scribbly, hurried and to the point: 'PC Kent Collins – Why aren't you with Hayley? Don't blow this operation!'.

All of a sudden, she found herself accepting without question that the author of this note and the occupant of the cubicle next door was a policeman. What she couldn't accept is why she hadn't been told on her final day of service, that you can retire any time you want to but you can never actually leave the organisation.

Jan exploded from the cubicle to the handbasin where she covered herself in incompetent soap; cleansed, rinsed and repeated. The mirror reflected a pink flustering mess that did not, on any level, personify 'relaxed retirement'. As she patted a damp paper towel across her face, a door creaked – the mystery male was about to reveal himself, so she ducked her head and hurried to the lobby.

Jan took her place at the back of a small queue of customers and immersed herself into a new world of disappointment and disbelief.

Who was Kent Collins? she thought as her eyes idled along the cake display. Has he been watching me? What possessed him to skulk into the ladies' toilets? And *why* is he bothered about Hayley?

As she shuffled along the counter, a hairy knuckled hand crept like a spider across the buns and settled onto a double chocolate muffin.

"Well, that might blow your diet," said Jan turning to snatch a glimpse of the animated hand operative.

"We can't afford to blow anything," came the quiet reply from a casually dressed slim male who maintained a forward stare towards the enormous menu board.

They moved along at a pace dictated by the magisterial coffee machine that was in no hurry to express. The plain clothed officer – whispering and aloof, invisible and yet, as far as Jan was concerned, as obvious as a man in a banana suit. But discretion was paramount, whoever he was, she couldn't compromise his safety so, she tiptoed carefully through the menu.

"It appears to be discontinued, the drink I usually have, taken out of service. Still, I guess it's for the best, too many calories, be honest with yourself I say. Take a new path, ditch the baggage, start afresh, leave the past behind…"

"What can I get you?" enquired the barrister as Jan liked to put it.

"Small latte with sprinkles please, just the one I'm travelling alone."

PC Collins hurriedly paid for his muffin and then studied the sandwich display keeping tabs on Jan as she waited for the freshly brewed milk. Then in a contrived but casual way he followed her to the cutlery stand and meticulously selected numerous items superfluous to his needs.

"The station is compromised," he whispered, to no one in particular. "They smell a rat, D for danger, do or die."

She flipped the lid from her latte and stirred it slowly and excessively as she thumbed through the serviettes.

"How has it come to this?" she whispered, forcefully maintaining a keen interest in the napkins.

"Desperate and impatient, need to get back on track."

Jan didn't feel able to monopolise the tissue dispenser any longer so, she headed for a quiet area of the restaurant. A space to process his words and hopefully let the coffee work its *magic*. She didn't doubt he was a policeman, not for a second, even with cutbacks and dwindling numbers, you could almost guarantee the presence of an officer moving quietly among us wherever we might find ourselves. Of course, they were more likely to be retired or off sick, on leave, rest days, career break, any number of guises that wouldn't normally bother the law abiding civilian. A few might break cover and declare their identity, should the need arise, but in the main you shouldn't be troubled. But on this occasion and in every way imaginable, Jan *was* troubled. D for danger, do or die, desperate and impatient, meaning the police operation surely? He couldn't be referring to Hayley, what does he know about Hayley; the fraudster, the relative, the complete disappointment?

She swirled the milk around the carton and couldn't ignore the possibility that she'd made a bad decision, that this was more like a flat white moment than anything you could lavish with frivolous froth. What if Hayley *was* in danger, what if she'd been fed to the lions by her cruel judgemental sister? She might be tortured and eaten; my nephews deprived of their mother. For cod's hake, Jan! As the words seethed around her mind, she grabbed the edge of the table in the midst of a fictional earthquake; frozen by fear and regret.

The words of Kent Collins penetrated again; do or die, before she realised, he had sat in the seat behind her and was trying to have a conversation.

"I'm trying to help you, Jan, if you won't do it for the operation, do it for Hayley, she needs you. I will do everything I can to protect you, everything."

Jan found herself at the edge of a floodlit circus ring, whip in hand, dampened by the breath of unruly lions as they defiantly roared in her face and scared her witless. She must crack the whip, gain order and see sense in the chaos of the pride – that's the word, pride it has got in the way, shoulder to shoulder with principles and ideals. Hayley was entitled to a fair trial surely? A detainee must be treated with respect and dignity, their health and wellbeing paramount. Innocent until proven guilty... but she *is* guilty; she confessed, thought Jan realising she had played judge, jury and jailer and had toyed with throwing away the key.

Ham, ham, ham, ham. She deserves her day in court and she mustn't come to any harm in the meantime. Jan was almost ashamed of her behaviour, her own behaviour towards her own sister Hayley. What had got into her?

The predictable fact that expensive coffee will quickly turn to tepid milk is on a par with the abject certainty that regret will always appear in the troubled mind. Regret on this occasion would haunt every waking hour, which was surely every hour because who could sleep if they had wilfully shown a careless disregard for the safety of their sister?

"Yes, yes," said Jan finally acknowledging the existence of PC Kent Collins. "Small latte eh? I thought that might have helped me live longer. I should have covered it in squirty cream, had a final blow out. Might as well start eating for two again, get myself right back on track. Do or diet I say." She carefully rocked the lid back onto the remains of the milky offering and stood by her table to fastidiously wipe a small spillage from the surface.

Her feet were stuck to the floor, not due to any housekeeping malfunction but because Jan craved the support of a colleague, a colleague like Kent Collins except he wasn't supposed to be there, he was supposed to be invisible. Even so, surely, he could make use of the most versatile, biodegradable, free item available in any cheap restaurant? In a moment of quality undercover acting Jan took two paces to her right and placed a serviette next to the muffin plate.

"Hello, I just wondered if you could make use of this? I seem to have too many, although you can never have too many in my opinion. Perhaps it's a security thing, you know, when you don't have any other *kit*. Anyway, I'm sorry that's all I have, I hope it's useful. Well, I've got a bit of a journey to do, places to be, people to meet so I'd better get going bye."

As her hand lingered on the serviette, unable to let it go and walk away, her eyes began to scrutinize the face of Kent Collins the un-caped crusader. Kent Collins who had just, very tenderly, rested his warm hairy knuckled hand over Jan's fingers in the briefest of encounters.

"Well, if you'll excuse me, I have a train to catch."

"Good luck," he whispered in a velvety warm tone.

On a glistening sea of serenity Jan floated back to her seat behind the steering wheel. A few final sips of cold milk took nothing away from the pleasing ambience that surrounded her in the comfort of this moment. Until her conscience rang like an over-excited egg timer desperate for attention.

"Come on, Jan, action, action," she said, securing the empty cup in the holder and decisively pulling out her phone. But what followed was a dithering stand-off where seconds felt like hours, hours felt days, which felt like...

Declan, what would Declan do? Declan would bite the bullet, push through the discomfort to please his mum and find his place in the world. His words chimed and churned until unsurprisingly, it was Jan who blinked first.

Hayley picked up immediately. "Strewth, what took you so long? We, I mean I or is it me? Well, just beginning to think you'd got lost. I mean, Sis, it was kind of you to let me wait here, stretch me legs, look for some coffee. I wouldn't have missed wasting time in a quaint little old town I have no desire to visit again whilst you fix that puncture, you know Howard, well, not Howard obviously. I mean we don't want Howard to confuse the continental drift."

She rambled, more than usual and the tangible fear that dripped from her words drenched every strand of Jan's existence since that day when Hayley left home. She began to wobble, monumentally which forced her mind to shut down for essential maintenance. All senses had closed early except for the hearing department of course who would remain on duty until the very last moment to relay important information from the war zone.

"Anyway," continued Hayley to the silent caller, "as you know we must be on our way, places to visit people to see. So, what time can I expect you?"

CHAPTER 13

It could be argued that driving whilst in the middle of an emotional crisis is on a par with the other major factors that contribute to the number of people killed or seriously injured on our roads. But that isn't usually the uppermost thought in your mind when you're in the grip of a self-made nightmare. Indeed, being totally honest, as Jan was – of course, it didn't enter her mind at all, in fact, in keeping with any number of journeys that we can all relate to, she could barely remember anything about the route she'd just taken to Saltash station.

But, the sight of a confidently dressed traffic warden, the ironically named civil enforcement officer, brought Jan to her senses. Torn between moving Howard from the double yellow lines and running the fifty metres towards Hayley, Jan opted for the latter and took off like a hotly pursued gazelle.

"Jeez, about time, never been so delighted by the sight of a traffic warden in all me life," breezed Hayley happy to high tail it out of the heated face-off with the French.

Jan turned her back on the enemy and retreated in a display of calm unity with her sister and the suitcase in tow.

"Look I'm really sorry, Sis, I know I've let you down, but I need you, I can't do this journey without you, I'm a bit scared to be honest and I can be honest when I put my mind to it."

With the cargo secured, Jan made a swift U-turn and left the station. Hayley seemed happy to fill the silence.

"It was all getting a bit difficult back there, you'd only just dropped me off and the croissant twins turned up. It's such a small place, they were soon breathing down me flippin' neck. So, I did what you said and put me self amongst the people at the shops but they clung to me, I was getting drenched in Eau Sauvage and garlic. Then, and who'd have thought I'd say a good thing about a traffic warden, Barney turns up, a proper have a go hero who seemed determined to look after me. You know you've still got it when three blokes can't leave you alone."

The informative summary rumbling from the front seat was about to be elbowed from the path of a pent-up runaway train.

"I looked up to you. You held the three of us together, all that was left. We were family, how could you just leave? Was it my fault? Mike's fault? You just took off all adult and confident and never looked back. The next we hear; you wind up in Australia married to Leonard."

Hayley shuffled and settled into the awkward corner against the door and turned her attention to Jan. Like a therapist who'd revised her subject thoroughly, she flicked to the appropriate chapter.

"It wasn't you or Mikey. I had to go, it was time to fly, find my life which ended up out in Oz with my new family. I would have come back to see you if I could, but it's a magical place thousands of dollars away and besides, I just loved what was happening."

Jan trundled back to the A38 still unsure where the road or her emotions were heading.

"You had everything, husband, family, excitement, I wanted that, I wanted all of that. But look, here I am; single, retired and now completely lost. How can one person mess up my head so much?"

"I'm truly sorry, kiddo, but like I said, my life isn't all it's cracked up to be. Show me a person who is happy and has everything. They're just stuff of films and fantasy if you must know."

By 17:35 the aimless drive through Cornwall had resumed, about the same time that an uninvited knitting workshop had popped up into Jan's head with too many loose ends to make sense of. So instead, she maintained a steady speed of forty and focused solely on the road ahead for both of them.

"So why did you decide to come back for me?"

Jan couldn't answer, wouldn't answer that particular question right now, although she did know the reason. It was made sparklingly clear when she'd been swept along by a carnival of loud hailers and banners proclaiming 'power to forgiveness and understanding'.

But the truth, the whole truth and nothing like the truth would have to be a form of 'damage limitation' that could, for the moment, accommodate Hayley's transgression. And that was only part of the story; Jan too was in the dock for her own shoddy behaviour and misdemeanours. Misdemeanours that had toppled her from the high seat of principles during the race to rescue Hayley. On more than one occasion she had exceeded the speed limit whilst balancing her mobile across her lap and then shamelessly parking on double yellow lines in front of an enforcement officer.

I did it for Hayley she would plead, realising that any attempt to express her feelings would be like pushing a feather into an inflated balloon. Even so, with ill-fitting blinkers and emotions riffling through her body like a venetian blind rattling in a warm summer breeze, she set off for the moral high ground. Where she was tasked with bringing order to an overflowing dam of lawlessness.

Like a swan with its legs tied together, Jan attempted a synopsis.

"If you must know, there was an incident in the toilets – another one. I was visited by a guiding spirit with hairy hands who spelt it out for me over a coffee. I realised that, for the moment, it would be better if we were to stick together. But that doesn't mean I condone your criminal behaviour; I can't forgive you for that."

"Harsh."

"This isn't what I want, but I don't want you coming to any harm on my account."

"Any harm? What do you mean?"

"Hays, I don't think there's any doubt that this is a pretty big police operation; let's not underestimate that. When the word 'terrorist' is used to describe persons or groups you have to put that word into context. It goes hand in hand with 'ruthless', 'violent' and any number of poor people skills you can dream of."

"Well that's just great," she said, "you left me right in it back there."

Her words fell like a house brick in the duck pond sending shock waves through everyone who felt them, or more accurately – Jan.

"I realise that now."

When a person is entrusted to your care and you are charged with looking after that person, you cannot, for a second, loosen the rope and allow them to drift from reach. For if, in that moment, they slip and come to harm whilst foolish pride and stupidity attempt to justify the position, there can only be one outcome: REGRET, scrawled in indelible ink on the shadow of pain that will accompany the rest of your miserable days.

This frank meander through the culpability cupboard had left a small gap in the conversation which allowed Hayley to paddle further along the creek.

"Look, I've said I'm sorry. You're my little sis, I'm sorry if I've shattered some images. But you know, I needed that benefit cash. How do you think I could have got to England without it? That's only partly dishonest isn't it?"

"Benefits, Hayley, are for people who have a pressing need, who're unable to lead a normal life without assistance or some support."

"Well, I can't. My life isn't normal, I *do* need support. Look at Brian from the cleaning cupboard, who would have thought he was a courageous army guy?"

"Your point being?"

"You don't always know what's going on in a person's life, do you? I was just trying to take control, find some freedom. I was very lucky as it happened when I broke my leg. Benefits were the way to go, it's natural. You know it *is* allowed in OZ when you're a bit crook."

"Yes, exactly – a bit crook."

"You know what I mean. Anyway, it was paid into my own account and Leonard and the slightly failing business couldn't touch it. I just had to limp about a bit longer than necessary to get some spending money too."

"Hays, this is not endearing me to your crime. You had a choice, everyone has choices, there's the honest road and the dishonest road and we can all see which route you've taken."

"Look, you might not believe me when I say this but, I'm proud of you and your little police job. There was a time when I thought differently, I thought that if my little sis has joined the best police force in the world, it can't be that good."

"Wow, thanks. Have you got anywhere else you'd like to go with your enormous shovel?"

"No, look what I mean is, what I've seen today, it's been awesome. You rescued us all with some dog you found. You spoke to Mrs Marshall in that amazing way, found out who she used to be, sorted her out, stepped between me and Stewart the walrus. Challenged the French boys with your buttered croissants and resisted the urge to arrest them."

"I told you we couldn't do that; we didn't have the power."

"Exactly, you know all this stuff, Sis, you've got morals and standards, things you believe in; you're good at your job."

"Was good you mean, as I keep telling everyone I am *retired*. Left it all behind yesterday except it all seems to be tangled up in my ankles and is dragging me through Cornwall without a practical plan and that is not a good place to be."

In receipt of this further delivery from a dishonest mind, Jan consulted the knitters who were still plying their trade in her head, and asked if they were able to unravel the latest loose end to join the group: 'partly dishonest'. Two words that surely couldn't stand next to each other no matter how relaxed they might look. Hearing Hayley's explanation only served to highlight her criminal intent, it was calculated, pre-meditated, it might as well be murder.

"Maybe I regret leaving you two behind or maybe that is just life and growing up. But I do regret that I had to gather money together for my trip in the way that I did. You asked me to come, you wanted me to come. That isn't some kind of guilt trip, I'm just saying. You've never asked me for anything before, not ever. So, when I found your airmail letter in the box I was jumping for joy, you needed me and I desperately needed a break too. It was perfect except that I couldn't afford it but I just had to, somehow, I couldn't let you down."

If Hayley needed the air fare, she could have asked me, thought Jan, why didn't she do that instead? I would have helped her if I'd known.

Even viewed down a dark rabbit hole, it was impossible to ignore the sincerity of this latest revelation. And, although the burden of guilt had not been intended, Jan caught that ball squarely in the outfield. If she hadn't asked Hayley to come, she wouldn't have committed the crime, assuming that this was her only crime of course.

As the investigation continued into the family offences, it was now only right that Jan had to include herself on the crime sheet. She may not have been caught, although you could never be certain with a speeding offence, but that didn't mean she was innocent.

It was entirely regrettable, as always when you step away from the situation and realise that your excuses are unlikely to stand up in court. But, at the time, in the heat of the moment, she had thrown caution to the wind, been whipped along by a storm of passion and desire, of guilt topped with anger. And as each firm step began to crumble like crushed meringue, Jan could no longer ignore the eccentric wobble that rumbled through her moral mountain.

This ping pong of private debate could carry on for the rest of the day or even forever. So, Jan decided to file it in a box marked 'unresolved cases' or similar and return to the more immediate matter of surviving the day.

"I need to know where I'm going, you'll have to rattle Mike again or we'll be working on this in the dark."

"Yeah okay, I'll get onto it but can we please put all the other stuff aside? I'm ten thousand miles away from home you know, it was pretty darned scary having you leave me like that. I didn't come all this way for a liaison with two French blokes."

Putting stuff aside of course wasn't that simple when your sister had just skipped across your sandcastle. There would be sanctions and strict conditions attached to the crew if they decide to continue and Jan couldn't see that they had a choice.

"Okay, these are the rules. We work together, we find Mike before the French do, we hand him over to the police, we say hello and goodbye and I take you to the nearest train station for your return journey to Heathrow and beyond."

"That's hardly fair, Sis; why can't you understand how I feel? I did this for you, for us, for the family. That's what you do for people that you love, like you did, coming back for me."

The most important thing for Jan to do right now was to breathe, breathe deeply and slowly and then repeat quite a lot. Hayley danced with ease across the ebb and flow of normal life fearless in her exploration of the colour wheel. But Jan's pallet of family emotion still struggled in black and white from years spent in the frozen tundra of her isolation.

Cod in Devon! This is what happens when you lose your parents at an early age. She huddled towards her window where excess water from her eyes could drain unnoticed. Five miles of tootling along at forty had allowed Jan to brain-storm the stupidity of her harsh stance given all that she'd been told.

You wouldn't do that on a scenario sheet would you, Janet Elliot? No, you'd modify and learn with each page turned, until you arrived at your informed actions which should be proportionate, lawful, accountable and necessary.

"Okay, look, we should get this job done and then maybe talk and see if there's a way to resolve our differences."

"That's a bit better, but how come you get to make all the rules?"

"Because *I* can be trusted."

At times, the A38 felt like the motorway of Cornwall. Caravans, trucks and trailers hurtled towards their destination in a 'holiday or bust' game of dare. By contrast, over in lane one still travelling at a sedate forty, were the competitors for the 'guess our destination?' game. The team, trying to work together, could only be certain at this stage of one thing and that was the presence of the black baguette firmly on their tail.

"So, you want me to be straight; just ask Mike where he is?"

"Yes, but the problem is your phone is being monitored and we still don't know to what extent. Will you please try to be discrete this time?" Jan caught a glimpse of mischief so added a footnote. "Mike is also in danger, don't forget that and he mustn't go to ground else we're all done for."

"I know, I know, I won't mention that we're bringing the French fanatics to visit; oh, and that the police might just turn up to see how we're all getting along."

Responding to another sideways glance from the driver she added, "Only fooling with you, I can do coded messages. Got a way with words – all that practice with me benefit form filling.

Jan moved uneasily in her seat but didn't bite.

"Come on, Sis, I'm trying to make light of this exciting but obviously dangerous situation. You said we had to work together, good cop bad cop eh? Well, I'm just bringing my skills to the party, surely that's a good thing. Hey, I've got an even better idea. Why don't I use your phone? They're not tracking you; we can say what we like and not have to be quite so cagey."

It was a good idea; except, Jan had a non-negotiable view on that topic as well.

"I am not having social media activated on my phone. I have principals."

"Principals? You know everyone who is anyone uses social media."

"So you keep telling me but like I said, I don't. Since the invention of all this public look at me nonsense I have not and will not entertain it on my phone. It'll be infected and I'll end up with odds and cods from all over the world trying to nudge into my private space."

With the message delivered at 17:55 from Hayley's phone, Jan concerned herself with the issue of his late replies.

"What could a person be doing that they don't reply to messages very quickly? I thought the whole idea of social stuff was to feel connected and involved, to get the latest on whatever it was that you might be interested in."

"Maybe he's no good with IT and social media. Maybe he can't type very fast."

"Perhaps we are not a priority, perhaps it wasn't the top of his wish list that we all meet up. Perhaps he's trying to put us off. And what about these guys following us? What do they want? What's the connection with Mike? Why are the police so interested?" Thoughts spilled from Jan's mind like coloured Smarties cascading across the floor.

"Well, why don't you phone a few of your mates, pull a few strings ask them to do some digging, surely someone owes you, we could get to the bottom of this. It's important, I need to know what dress to wear at the press release party; this is definitely going on Facebook."

"You know you can't do that. Lives are at risk you can't just broadcast to all the world willy-nilly. And no one owes me, okay? No, I am just an ordinary member of the public – like you, but not like you of course."

"More like me than you think, Sis, and don't forget where you heard it first. When you're an ordinary member of the public, you have to think on your feet, use the resources at hand and get a grip on life."

They journeyed on, slowly. The French escort had relaxed their grip on Howard's bumper and dropped back, which allowed Jan to snatch a moment with Rod Stewart. At the tap of a button she'd been transported to her comfortable place with the simple sentiment of 'Some Guys Have All the Luck'.

"I didn't know you liked Rod Stewart, Sis? had you down as more of a Donny Osmond fan."

"Maybe it had something to do with the fact that my formative years were drenched in all things Rod. Tarnished by the choices of an oppressive older sister who drummed my ears for hours on end. Sound familiar?"

"Too right, if you've got the tapes, play them. Still, you didn't have to stick with my choice when I'd gone did you?"

Before Jan could reply, bad cop burst in with her news.

"He's replied, Mikey has replied in under five minutes."

"What does he say? Please say you've got the location," said Jan turning the music down to a drift of background comfort.

"Well, I don't really understand it. He says EVA M MMC. What is he going on about? I told you he wasn't very good at the IT stuff, he probably hit all the wrong keys, didn't bother checking it and posted it before he could fix his fat fingers."

"Maybe," said Jan tapping the steering wheel lightly, "Okay, let's assume he did hit the wrong keys; what does that give us?"

"Oh, this is fun, hang on, let me see, right so if he meant to hit the key on the left... that would be a 'D' then 'U' then... 'Ansa phone' that can't be right. Let me go the other way that is 'F' then 'W'... do you know, I'm losing interest in this idea. Perhaps he's dyslexic?"

With the miss hit key theory dismissed, Jan headed off in another direction which included the possibility that Mike had intentionally sent the message in a code that he believed they could crack.

"What about Roman numerals? What if that's the clue? Or what if EVA is accurate and she is talking in code?" Jan emptied her ideas into Hayley's lap with urgent stamped across the file.

"Okay, Sis, can't quite remember me numerals but I'm not sure there's an 'E' in the Roman numbers, I'll have to Google it."

"No, wait; we mustn't offer any help to the French boys, they've probably got the message too and for all we know, have an expert team working it out. We can't risk them finding Mike before we do."

"So, I scratch my head and try and remember me school day Roman lesson, do I?"

"No, we haven't got time to scratch our heads, we need some help. If only I had a number for Mrs Marshall, she'd have this sorted I'm certain of it."

"Yes, but there are a few problems with that idea. Like you say, you don't have her number for starters and secondly, she won't remember who you are."

The idea was flawed, frustratingly Jan could see that, but she wasn't done yet with thinking, there had to be a way.

"You're right, there's only one thing for it."

With the arrogance of a big sister who is always right Hayley sighed with relief.

"At last she sees sense, time to call in those policey favours, tap into your mates in the intelligent squad or whatever they're called, get some answers."

"No, we call Clint."

"What? You think me little mate is up to this?"

"Yes, Clint is our secret weapon, call him, tell him exactly what we've got, every space, every letter *exactly*."

"Alright, Marple, but are you sure? He'd better come up trumps before anyone else, I mean you're relying on an unknown kid to save our necks now."

"Well, as you haven't managed anything better, I suggest that before this day takes any more wrong turns, you just make the call."

"Jeez, you're certainly a bossy little thing at times. I bet the criminals were glad when you went off duty."

CHAPTER 14

The compact Cornish convoy journeyed onwards under a considerable amount of flak from a stream of irate motorists as they overtook the, obviously incompetent, middle-aged slow coach. It forced Jan to question her assumption that staying mobile would be a safe option.

"I'm determined, Hays, determined to get our man, if I'm going to waste my first day of freedom rounding up a criminal, another one, then we are definitely going to get there first, secure Mike at the earliest opportunity."

"Steady on a bit, he is our brother you know and I *am* still your sister."

Jan was skating over the facts, which were woefully thin and the evidence, which was little more than mere speculation until she arrived at an important realisation.

"What does he look like these days?"

"Well there's a good question, Sis, I don't have any recent photos in fact I don't have any photos since we went digital, got a few Kodak prints at home that he sent but they would be from the last century. That's a long time ago when you say it out loud isn't it? Don't you have anything? I mean haven't you seen him since I left?"

It had been easy for Jan to put Mike aside. Shift work had that knack of speeding up time, months then years pass by marked only by the Christmas duty sheet to remind you that *yes*, you would be working for the whole of the festive season and that the chief wishes you a happy New Year. The unimpressive truth was that since she'd left aunt Ethel's to join up, her face to face contact with Mike had been sparse. She'd spent her probation living in digs and studied to the exclusion of all else. Visits home would only be entertained in an emergency and as there weren't any, she didn't go home for two years. By that time, Mike had gone off to college to apply himself, no doubt, in a similar way.

They were both at home briefly, for a small get-together to mark aunt Ethel's sixtieth where a select few had been made very welcome. But, with a head full of law, process and her new life, Jan felt socially awkward and unnaturally suspicious of every last person. Mike was still being his usual quiet and studious self and so, their conversation had pretty much stopped at 'hello' and 'goodbye'. With only a handful of phone calls since then, all she could remember was his mellifluous, light West Country accent. It was an attractive tone but he was young then, a lot of growing could have changed everything, which left Jan with very little that might help to identify the suspect.

"Surely he's got a picture on Facebook?"

"Erm no, my little detective Sister, he's playing hard to find don't forget. He's unlikely to put up a photo of himself standing outside his country pile with the address tagged to Google Maps or whatever it does."

"Well, let's try and work this out." Gathering a blank piece of paper in her mind, Jan began her important new list.

"This will be interesting," said Hayley settling down in her seat with a sardonic smile.

"He's forty-five years old, he was a bit chubby in his late teens. White male of course, a bit taller than me at that time. Mousy hair, short and thick with an understated wave. Quiet, bit intense, deep brown eyes and he was wearing a cuddly jumper at the sixtieth."

"Well, Sis, we shouldn't have any problem recognising him in a crowd, should we? And since when was 'cuddly jumper' a formal term in the police line up?"

"You know, Hays, I feel a bit ashamed that I wouldn't necessarily recognise him in the street. Flesh and blood, we three and yet what have we done for each other these past three decades? Focused on our own lives and worries and closed the family hatch firmly shut."

"True enough and I've felt that hatch close in me face again, not more than an hour ago."

Deep in her own pool of dark inadequacy, Jan offered nothing in reply, she was too busy surveying the regret counter with its abundance of tempting dilemmas vying for her attention and withering her resolve.

"Hey, for all we know Mikey might be in the van behind us, he might be French, this might be a double bluff. We might be the real victims lured to our death by our own brother and some phoney policemen. It's revenge, that's what it is, all these years he's held it against us and now, now, it's payback time."

It was improbable but not of course impossible that Hayley's mental explosion might hold some truth. So, the idea was quickly forced through Jan's sieve of reason into the pan of all things painfully pertinent where it could fester on the back burner.

"Hays, you really have gone off on one."

They travelled silently on into the depths of Cornwall. Jan contemplated the real possibility that they may have already come too far, not only along the A38 but also in terms of their capability. What were their options if they needed to escape? If they could escape? An impromptu breathing exercise was gathering pace so, she leaned forward and turned the CD to karaoke volume. A teenager once more, she was at a private Rod Stewart concert in the village hall before the innocence and angst of youth had been firmly trampled under the shiny boots of Jan's determination to keep law and order. Where her ideals had bumped into the immovable truth of a brick wall as she realised that things could only ever be partly right in a game where criminals and justice have an equal throw of the dice.

"You still look the same." Hayley raised her voice slightly to compete with the village hall surround sound. "I knew it was you the minute I clapped eyes on you at Tiverton. Strewth that's my sister, I thought. Still athletic, still the practical clothing, the short hair, although the brown is going a bit grey. Do you ever think of touching that up?"

"No, thank you. What's wrong with growing old naturally?"

"Everything of course!"

"Well, you were easy to recognise too now I think about it. Although I was heavily influenced by the hat with the corks hanging from it and the fact that you were the only lone female looking wildly out of place."

"Well, strewth, hold me up, my perfectionist sister made a joke at last and with a criminal at that."

"Don't think that has slipped my mind, Hays, but I do have a duty to keep you safe during your short stay in the United Kingdom."

"I'll take that as a slight thaw around the ice maiden, it's better than nothing."

Let's get back to the matter in hand. Thinking practically, if you take us, we are still fundamentally the same in appearance, we have the same button nose, similar height, straight fingers, square hands. We both walk with lightness on our heels…"

"Yes, and that's about it, exactly what else do we have in common? Not much, we are a slightly different weight I think, different hair colour and length. How does that help us recognise Mikey?"

"The more I look at you, the more I think we would know. Surely, we would know him and besides your hair colour is no guide, it came out of a bottle I believe and has been abused by hours of sun."

"Too right, that's the wonderful price you pay for sunshine. But what if Mikey is in a wheelchair say, what then? We just have to hope he has our hands and the male version of a button nose or something."

"Why doesn't Mike stay in touch? It bothers me a lot, I really wanted to find out today but with all that's going on, I don't think I'll ever know, he is the man he is and no one regrets that more than me."

"You need to take that big old police head off now, Jan, my little Pavlova, it works both ways you know. We are all just as guilty; careless, that's what we are, losing our little brother, leaving him to fend for himself in the big world without a mother figure."

There are times in life's ocean of complexity, when the appearance of a polar opposite swimming towards you should be shooed away with a big stick. But if, in the form of a polar bear, it was prepared to swim your tiny ice floe back to safety, you would sensibly have to abandon some of your preconceptions and be humbled. Such was this surprise confession from Hayley. Her acknowledgment of guilt regarding Mike's neglect had served to shoulder some of Jan's burden which, whilst heartening, didn't mean she should trust a polar bear.

"Don't, Hays, please, I feel bad enough as it is." With her breathing back to tolerable, it was time to turn off Rod and prepare herself.

"Right, come on let's not get side-tracked. We need to work out what's happening, get Mike detained and put this whole sorry tale to bed."

Hayley shaded her eyes from the sun and appeared to be either geographically, mentally or emotionally lost, it wasn't easy to tell.

"You know, Sis, I think I need a coffee, not one of your flask efforts, you know a proper stop, get out of the car. Stretch, walk about, get used to my legs. After twenty-four hours on a plane and fourteen hours sleeping at the Ibis, I'm ready for some Waltzing – Matilda."

What harm could another break in this endless journey do? Anywhere public should be fine. Besides, Jan was growing tired of waiting for clues in the great Cornish treasure hunt.

At the counter, waiting to be served, Jan felt her confidence ebb like the drag from a retreating storm wave. She was at the mercy of the elements where supervisors played no part in these uncharted waters as she paddled in the deep, far out of her comfort zone.

"What can I get for you?" came a cheery voice from the other side of the continent.

Two small lattes, one with sprinkles, wouldn't trouble the credit limit of most people, nevertheless, Jan insisted she would pay. Partly as a kindness to her sister but also as a crime reduction strategy to prevent Hayley spending cash to which she was not entitled.

The McDonald's was crowded but they managed to squeeze into a small corner table with a window on both sides. Challenged by a lack of space, Jan slid the tray behind the table before stirring her latte for no particular reason.

"Thanks, my little jam sandwich," said Hayley. "I guess, now you've retired, you must be loaded; pension, pay off, golden handshake." She leaned across the table and looked Jan closely in the eyes. Which caused something similar to a negative magnetic force to push Jan back into her seat. She balanced the stirring stick across the plastic lid and crossed her arms with a loose elbow grip.

"We don't get a pay off or golden handshake. I have a pension and I commuted part of that – which is still my pension money by the way, so we don't get any extra, just what we paid in."

"So, what you commuted, that's a chunk of money?"

Jan disliked the conversation, this was personal, not something she discussed not in public and certainly not with someone who she knew to be dishonest.

"Yes, I have a small amount." She closed the conversation using the unequivocal tone of a no comment interviewee which unfortunately had little effect on this interrogator.

"Really? And what are you going to spend all that on? A holiday, facelift, camper van?"

Jan had not envisaged discussing this matter with anyone any time soon but, was compelled to tell the truth.

"I bought a flannel if you must know."

"What? Flaming expensive flannel. What's it made of? eyelashes from a bush kangaroo?"

"I wanted one and so I bought one, there's really very little else to say about that."

"Oh, there's plenty to say about that, but I don't suppose you're about to let me."

"No, because its 18:45, the clock hasn't stopped ticking and we are still swamped by a predicament that isn't going away. Our plan is vague at best and that is not how I work. My day has been hijacked, it was my idea to locate Mike and finalise things, just a small private matter that has now been blown out of all proportion by the demands of an organisation I thought I'd left behind. Oh, let's not forget the disagreeable twins who have just entered the drive thru by the way."

Jan followed their vehicle as best she could as it traced around the building and stopped as required at the attended windows. Until today, she had not really considered that a terrorist might need to eat on the way to their objective. She could not have imagined that these single-minded individuals, fuelled by a farewell breakfast, would queue patiently in line for unscheduled food. The fact that they were able to make provision for a meal break here and there on the way to their destructive destination didn't really fit into her terrorist stereotype.

With Jan on the observation deck, Hayley seemed more interested in the contents of her cup and a question that had surfaced.

"I know you'll shoot me down in flames but don't you think it's a bit mean setting Mikey up like this? I feel I want to let him know, tell him to pack his bags and run for the hills." Hayley curled her arms as high as they would stretch, like an expressive child gripped by fantasy.

"Hays, I admit that my resolve is also a bit wobbly at times and that's about the best I can come up with. But no matter what our own feelings are, we are obliged to assist the police in this investigation. You are the key to this, it's your phone and your relationship with Mike that could bring this mystery, if you like, to a meeting point and positive outcome."

"Positive for the police you mean, what about Mikey? Why don't I just reply something like 'the cavalry girls are coming'. That doesn't tell him anything about the police posse or the French fries. Just a bit of banter and if he works it out, well, good for him."

"We have to work within the rules, Hays, professional common sense might just keep us all alive so please don't do anything foolish."

Hayley drank some coffee and looked out at the dusty Mercedes as it squeezed into a very tiny space over in the retail park.

"I was quite excited at first, I mean there can't be many visitors to this country that experience a bungled burglary…"

"Robbery, an armed robbery."

"Well, okay fine, a robbery… with arms, happy? Anyway, there was all that flippin' excitement, all those big hairy armed policemen. The visit to an old lady with a few issues, then being shouted at by a couple of French galahs and then told we have to round up our brother and hand him in. I mean, it isn't your usual 'welcome to England don't forget to visit Buckingham Palace and the London Eye' is it? Maybe I'm still a bit jet lagged but this isn't how I imagined my trip to be. I don't want to say I'm disappointed, but it's kind of spoilt it a bit. I never came here with the intention of *capturing* Mikey, I was hoping more for a cuddle and a catch up."

Jan stirred the remains of her coffee seeking reassurance or something, anything that could remove the doubt that danced in her way. Without colleagues or communication, the call to arms grew faint and muffled giving Jan space to ramble away on a fragile limb.

"It's all a bit strange for me being in here during the day. On the night shift we often went to McDonald's, the atmosphere at three in the morning was strangely comforting. Helped by the fact that they very kindly gave us coffee, looked after us, it was very much appreciated."

"Free coffee?"

"Yes, it was a bit odd really but the franchisee for the area would give us coffee during the night shift as a kind of goodwill gesture I suppose. In the policy book it is termed 'A payment in kind', which isn't something officers are permitted to take advantage of. So, I would always pay the equivalent cost of the coffee into a tin at home, it seemed right, a sort of karma."

Leaning forward Hayley had taken an interest in this developing confession.

"What did you do with it? Your tin of coins?"

Jan noticed the offensive glow pulsing from Hayley's cash antenna again but, believed it was safe to continue.

"Well, usually something for the garden, I had enough for a bench once."

"Strewth that's a lot of free coffee! Why didn't you give the cash to charity? I mean, to my mind, you're still having that payment in kind as you put it, still taking something that ordinary folks can't get. If you were serious about pay back, why didn't you put your money in the charity bucket right under your nose at the counter? That would be an honest, above board officer with a full and clear conscience in my opinion. That sounds a whole lot easier than taking it home and then having the time-consuming effort of deciding what to buy for yourself."

Hayley sat upright and began to address an imaginary audience with her best gloating English accent.

"Do come and look at my garden bench, everyone, it was given freely to the tired police no questions asked."

Instinctively, Jan grabbed Hayley by the wrists and hissed.

"SSHHH! Please, you've made your point, you're just being embarrassing now."

"Me embarrassing? You should take a look at your hypocritical self, Sis."

"It wasn't like that."

Hayley wriggled her wrists from the short arms of the ex-police and moved cosily across the table where her words could quietly hit the target.

"Yeah but what's the difference between getting a free flight for me crook leg or you lot having something for nothing and acquiring a garden bench? I don't see anyone paying for anything."

The scales of justice were beginning to align, the lush meadow on the moral mountain was icing over, forcing the inhabitant to lower ground.

Living alone, Jan had taken unquestionable decisions in the pursuit of an orderly home life. Guided by her internal moral compass and frugal nature, she had built an efficient world. Her life seriously lacked the useful observations offered by a close friend or sibling, the friendly third eye that can call you a chump without fear of a meltdown.

"Look, maybe I should have dealt with it differently, but it was acceptable, it was sort of a blanket gift, we all had the same."

She was digging deep, hoping for comfort but instead, landed on the cold concrete of the naughty step.

"We'd better get going," she said, not feeling at all refreshed by the bitter coffee.

But Hayley sat firm as though the exciting gloss of the day had dried in the tin.

"I'm not sure I want to. There are too many questions, too many secrets and too much talk about policy, about rules and how the police can tell you what to do, even if they don't do it themselves. It's not how I live, Jan, sure I did something wrong, but I didn't do it for me, not like your bench. Like I said from the start, police are corrupt, I don't want any part of it."

"But we have to, we have to locate Mike. The shadow puppets out there are hardly likely to sit tight and do nothing. If you don't go, I guarantee they'll make a move and cod knows what they'll do if they get a hint of resistance or non cooperation."

"It's not just them galahs. Why can't we just wait for this whole thing to blow over? You're chasing our Mikey like he was a big time criminal; you've got your police hat on and you are a million miles away from the fact that he is a human being, our brother. How is he feeling? Are you even thinking about him?"

"This isn't personal, it's a duty and besides, he can't run forever. At some point he'll have to face up to what he's done and then maybe we can all start getting over this mess."

"I don't need a lecture from me little sister who dwells in some twilight area of truth, I think it's time we gave your police mates what we have, what we know, that message from Mikey for a start. Let them get on with it and deal with their issues, then we can visit our Mikey in prison. This is deception or something, we're playing happy families but all the while leading the police and some mad guys to his door – wherever that is. It's unfair, Sis, and when it's all done, we'll have that guilt to carry about. We'll be cut adrift because I bet in your heart you know there'll be no reward in this, no benefit or gain, not even expenses. We, my loyal duty-bound muppet, will be hung out to dry, a broken family who had an unfortunate brush with the law."

The restaurant heaved, if it were possible to heave any more. Tables were wiped by the speedy damp cloths of uniformed operatives who punctuated the hubbub with a discord of Americanisms delivered in a West Country accent.

Increasingly, the option to stay seated within the feasting wing of the after-school club was being squeezed. Parents shoehorned children two to a stool into improvised spaces where they could sit and play with their evening meal. The greasy fingers that danced between salty fries and mobile phones had no requirement for utensils. It was sad to imagine that their skills in the cutlery department would probably begin and end with a plastic McFlurry spoon.

There was a degree of awkwardness that accompanied the act of occupying a fast food table when you appeared to be fasting. Polite society dictates that if you have no further requirement for your table, such that you are no longer consuming food or beverage, you should give it up for those approaching with a burgeoning tray. An unspoken code with a clear indicator: buy more food or vacate the table. Only the morally uncouth seem immune to these social manners.

The corner table clung to their empty cups in brave defiance of the circling operatives. Until that is, an unwelcome maritime flare called 'morally uncouth' demanded a response from anxiety central. Jan began to pant like a steam train creaking under pressure. Her desperate desire to stare blankly into space was thwarted by the sea of bodies and searching eyes that hovered and hmphed at the crowded tables.

Despite the discomfort, Jan was thankful that she knew these social graces and behaviours, grateful for her early grounding. Qualities that seemed alien and absent from large swathes of the current world.

"You alright there?" enquired Hayley noticing, not for the first time, the noisy breathing and a searching attempt at the middle-distance stare.

Jan tugged on the loose reins that had allowed her lungs to gallop free.

"This isn't my life, it can't be. If I could rewind this day, I wouldn't hesitate. In fact, whilst I'm about it, why don't I just rewind to a place before stuff happened and then I wouldn't have to fix it."

Jan's ears shone through her short hair like radioactive goo in a B movie as she tried to keep it together.

"Well, that's going to put you somewhere in the womb I would suggest. What is all this, getting saddle sore up there on your high horse? Come on, Sis, you're a great person, done some great things I'm sure. You don't need to sound so hard on yourself, we've all got a history and as we've discovered only today, some things we're not too proud about but we don't need to rush out and book a week with the exorcist. Look, you don't have to fight them tears, but you might set me off in a bit if you don't dry up."

Jan rattled like a clapped-out banger uncertain of how much longer she could keep going. With a restart off the cards, she had to come up with something that would carry them through, the ultimate plan, the one she must stick to until the end, do or die and the latter wouldn't, under any circumstances, be entertained. Like now, as she caught sight of one of the French boys pushing through the crowd. With a hasty refocus, she leapt from the comfort of her confidential waste bin of discarded action plans.

"Hays, quick, grab the tray."

"What?"

"Grab the tray, quickly."

Hayley reached under the table with a faultless flourish and slammed it onto the table just as the taller of the French duo arrived.

"What iz ze hold up? Why are you not in ze car driving to ze ouse?"

"Lighten up, fella," said Hayley. "Can't a girl stop for the dunny and get herself some coffee?"

"Dunny? What is zis dunny?"

"The toilet you great galah."

"What is zis galah?"

"You don't want to know, mate. But what I can tell you is this, these tables don't clear themselves, so here we are," she said putting their empty cups on the tray, "just go and put them in the bin over there on your way out."

She pushed the tray into his hands sending the cartons tumbling across the surface.

"*Sacré bleu!* If you not getting ze moving, you will move no more." He gave them a continental look, then barged through the crowd to the bin.

"That was good work, Hays, not quite what I had in mind but brilliant."

With nothing but an unadorned table between them, Jan felt exposed as she tried to make sense of this latest assault on European relations.

"They are clearly getting restless and agitated and that is not good. It's funny to think that our brother, who is probably unaware of this pursuit, is capable of causing so much anxiety to so many people."

"Yeah, you wait 'til I get me hands on him, won't know whether to hug him or thump the little blighter. As for our little French friend there, he is, in many ways, much like my Carl. Moody little nipper at times, bit spoilt, I think. He was always on the edge of throwing his toys out. I'd sort him out with a mundane task, it would infuriate the life out of him so he'd go and try and moan at his father but Len would just take it in and let it out, he was more of a sounding board I suppose. When you're that laid back, kids hollering and shouting don't have much effect, it's only the other end of the scale where the issues lie, is that what you've got, that anxiety?"

On an outward breath of relief, Jan released the air from her balloon.

"Yes, if you must know. Thirty years of service squashed into one little head isn't very comfortable. Today hasn't helped much either."

"Yeah, I guess you must have dealt with some nasty criminals, not me obviously," she smiled.

"It's not just the criminals, nasty or otherwise, it's the dead people, the cliff jumpers, the accidents, the elderly. Every size, shape and age. Some you knew, most you didn't but they belonged to someone and it was part of our job to find and tell that someone."

Jan snatched a breath and clasped her hands together, each thumb rubbed in turn across the other until Hayley smothered them with her soothing hands.

"Look, Sis, we haven't got off to the best of starts, all this flippin' excitement, it's got me not knowing if I'm coming or going."

"I love you."

"Ah that's nice," she said squeezing gently before Jan pulled her hands away.

"No," said Jan. "Rod Stewart, it sounded like the lyrics to 'This Old Heart of Mine', it's one of my favourite songs."

"Oh, silly old drongo me, thought for a minute we were making progress."

"Sorry, you're right, we don't know which way to turn, there's so much to deal with and I, for one, don't have the skills to rewind a day, start again forget or..."

"Forgive?"

"Well, let's be sensible for a moment, we still have to get through this day in one piece and I'm concerned by the *galahs* as you call them. By the way what is a galah?"

"Not flaming you as well? A galah is a bird with not much common sense. Thought everyone knew that." Pausing for dramatic effect Hayley laughed, "you galah!"

Jan smiled. "Yes, okay but this isn't solving the issue, I still don't see any other option but to carry on. I really think we ought to move."

"Now, I can go for moving on to a shopping centre or finding a nice hotel with a comfy bed all day long but carrying on? Come on Jan, it's not just the deception, putting our own brother in a trap, it's everything. The risk that seems to be involved. What if we don't come out of it? What if we don't get chance to start over? You know more than anything, I just want to go to your little paradise with you, see how long I last before I get bored stupid. But at least then we'll have time to catch up and put ourselves straight. What chance is there if we keep getting deeper and deeper into the slime?"

"But I can't see how we get off this merry-go-round, if we don't move soon, I can imagine the shadow puppets taking us out of the game; going to their plan B."

"You mean like, liquidise their assets?" said Hayley with alarm.

"Well, I would hardly describe us as assets, but yes, apart from your phone and your way with words on Facebook, I'm sure they don't have much need or regard for two clueless females."

"Why would it be so bad to give them my phone? It would be flaming upsetting, I love my phone, I've had it a few years now, in fact it was a gift from Len on our anniversary, but I shouldn't think the laid-back lump would mind if I traded it for my life."

The basic cobbled plan that had just hatched over a bare, highly sort after, bistro table was hastily examined by the team leader.

"So, we just stroll over to their van, knock on the window and hand it over, do you really think that would work?" For a moment Jan dared to believe there was a chink of light peeping through the angry clouds of anxiety but then the rain came to dampen all hope. "No, it wouldn't work. Think about it, we apparently know too much, we are witnesses to their behaviour, their desire to find Mike and whatever it is he's up to. We know their location, vehicle, we can describe them, we're doomed."

"The drongo and the galah, that describes them well enough," said Hayley adding colour to their corner.

"I suppose we could sit here for the rest of the day, what could they do? But what of Mike? If they get to him first, they might kill him, not give him a chance of a fair trial. We would have allowed him to die when we had the opportunity to save him. Hayley, that would be the worst possible outcome, surely we owe him that?"

With a growing number of unanswered questions, Jan wondered how it was that life in uniform actually did seem like the better option.

"Why isn't there a supervisor to ask? A colleague to consult with? Even a sensible older sister would be useful."

"I *am* listening you know. Anyway, I am trying to help. All these vibes are a bit difficult, I'm a bit out of me depth. I'm not used to the uptight Britishness and the compulsion to do things by the letter. We do rather chill out in Oz, this has been a bit of a shock on all fronts. But I *am* available, should you wish to engage my services."

She then closed the hatch and picked up the phone filled with private memories and flicked through the pages in preparation for the final goodbye.

This sacrifice that Hayley was prepared to make for the team hadn't been lost on Jan. The sensible older sister had made a bold decision without a risk assessment. Jan was about to point this out until 'I Don't Want to Talk About It' drifted up from beneath the table. In her desperation for some good news from Clint, she answered without her usual scrutiny of the incoming call display.

"What is the hold up?" said the vaguely familiar voice of PC Kent Collins in a business-like manner.

"Hello to you too, Mr Collins, yes, it is a lovely day and yes, we are having a nice time, thank you for asking." Jan could feel herself slipping into a small melt down and hoped the caller would pick up on her frailty and charge in to rescue them.

"What?" he said.

He obviously hadn't done his negotiating course or had any Trauma Risk Incident Management input. Because he seemed oblivious to the unspoken communication that had just occurred.

"We have stopped," said Jan looking again at Hayley who quickly dropped the phone into her bag.

"Why?" said this man of few wasted words.

As her brittle makeshift shelter came under fire, Jan's hand wobbled towards the big red button. It was time to do the right thing, get hold of the day with no regrets. She fixed her eyes on Hayley and then spoke.

"PC Collins, you need to know that we have decided not to carry on."

She expected him to come straight back at her, smooth the doubts and reinvigorate the troops but he just listened which instilled Jan with the strength to elaborate.

"We are just two people who appear to be out of our depth and just want to stop. So, if you could sort that out please, Kent Collins, we could all start getting somewhere."

Hayley offered a big sister smile and squeezed the free hand that had slapped the table with every word.

"Jan," he said in a slightly more human tone, "what's happened?"

"This is just too big, we have no protection, no idea what we're dealing with and the guys that are tailing us are getting jumpy, they've just about threatened us."

"What? A threat to kill?"

"No not exactly, it was a bit veiled. He said; 'If you don't get moving, you will move no more'. Well, as you know that might just mean he's going to let my tyres down."

"Yes, clever but still concerning. Did he say anything else?"

"Well yes, a bit of a sentence in French, but my French isn't up to much although he did have a look about him when he said it, like it was a bit nasty."

"Where's the phone?"

"By my ear," said Jan as though it were the last day of term. "Sorry, you caught me off balance there, Kent Collins, you mean Hayley's phone?"

"Yes, and Kent is just fine."

"I'm sure it's a lovely place." Jan clamped her hand to the mouthpiece, her face scrunched in silent stupidity as she wavered between laughter and speech.

"It's here with us, Hayley is just having a moment to say goodbye to it."

"Why?"

"Oh, just a mad idea we had, you know, give them the phone and let them drive off into the sunset."

"I see, but you haven't told them that?"

"No, we've just been looking at our options."

"Okay I understand but please, don't do anything rash and don't move from your location, I just need some time."

CHAPTER 15

A polar wind swirled around a small table in Cornwall occupied by two sisters waiting for the thaw. It was 19:15 but felt more like midnight in a land where the sun doesn't set.

"Changed your mind then?" said Hayley looking at the turncoat who had retreated so far away, she might struggle to hear.

Jan was adrift in a barren wilderness somewhere near the end of the world where a large mirror covered the horizon. A mirror that exposed her deluded version of saintliness and the abject stupidity surrounding *Benchgate*. Stupidity that had failed to realise that these actions amounted to a 'personal gain', key words that thread throughout the Fraud Act 2006.

"Do you reckon your Kent friend will get back to us before there's a bun fight with the baguettes?"

Jan had sunk into a chasm of catastrophe where her career lay in tatters. Dishonesty and a lack of moral fibre roared like hot dragon breath across her burning soul as she pleaded for a second chance. A chance to redeem herself, to do things better and to not buy a bench.

"We've still got each other, Sis. You know you'll always have me; I'm going to make things right I really am. We'll laugh I know we will one day but at this moment, this very moment, we are in a fix. But we're in it together." Hayley slid her hands across the table as the sound of 'I Don't Want to Talk About It' rang through the air.

Jan dragged herself from the murky depths and checked her display, it was Kent.

"Jan," he said more hurried than usual, "we have a plan, it isn't without risk, but if we all go with it, we can get you out of this situation and on your way. Are you up for it?"

She looked at Hayley. "They have a plan; are you okay with this?"

"Too right."

"Okay, Kent, what is it?"

"The basics are that we need to get the phone without being detected and we need to leave in your car."

"Who's we?"

"I have some officers in plain clothes on their way to your location. You give them Hayley's phone and your car keys and we take you out of the picture like you asked."

"No way," said Jan. "A phone is one thing, my car? no, I just had it valeted all trace of police removed. Not a chance, no one drives my car." The moody dragon from Jan's dark world had escaped and was skipping in the general direction of a complete melt-down.

"We'll take good care of it."

"You clearly didn't hear me, Kent. The answer is *no*. Is the gold commander having a laugh? Is that someone else I might have piked-off during my not so illustrious career? Is this payback time or something? This is going too far. I have left the police force do you understand me? If this is your way of saving the pension fund by sending me over the edge then congratulations, you're near the winning line." She slumped, red faced and exhausted.

Hayley swooped onto Jan's arm. "Might want to keep your voice down a bit," she said nodding sideways towards the audience like a seasoned pantomime dame.

As twenty-two pairs of eyes came into focus, Jan scrunched into the window, her whispered curse puffing vapour across the glass.

"Basking shark! Basking shark."

Kent raised his voice above the molten mess, "Jan, Jan are you still with me?"

"Looks like I can't get away from you."

"Jan, we don't have much time. They'll be getting restless, they might use force to take the phone, cause you harm; the commander won't risk that." There was a pause in his delivery before he lit the blue touch paper. "If you don't volunteer your car, he will have it commandeered. This is too big an operation to allow a possessive, emotional female to stand in the way."

"Kent. Kent, I thought you were trying to help me? I thought you were a mate?"

"Not my words, the commander said that, I know how you feel, but he's going to take it anyway. Hear me out, Jan, if you want to walk away, then this is the plan. We have two female officers; they will arrive at your location in separate vehicles one of which will be a hire car. They will make their way to the toilets. I need you, without drawing attention to yourselves, to follow, not exactly together, but you get the idea, just a natural minute or so. The officers will be dressed as cabin crew, you should be able to spot them in the crowd."

"Truly bonkers, are we anywhere near an airport? Is the commander out of his mind?" Jan hesitated; a tidal wave of insolence had pushed her to these words. Did her respect for rank evaporate the moment she'd handed back her warrant card? Under a crumbling sky, she bundled her attitude into a reinforced loft marked private where later, she would lock herself in and scream.

Hayley leant across the table desperate to hear what Kent had to say about the get-out clause.

"Look, they have to be distinctive in some way and it'll be easier for you to recognise them, it's best all round. They will each carry a vanity case containing a change of clothing."

"If you are expecting us to dress up as…"

"No," said Kent, "that won't be necessary, although once they've gone, you can do what you like. Sorry, no that isn't part of the plan. No, they will leave their kit in the cases, you just need to make sure no evidence is left behind. When the coast is clear, you'll be free to leave and get on with your lives. We know your build and what each of you is wearing and with a couple of wigs to try, you don't need to worry. It's important that you hand over your keys and Hayley's phone, they'll take care of the rest. In return they'll give you keys to the hire car with unlimited use until we get the all clear."

"When's this likely to happen?" said Jan still trying to comprehend this branch of policing that had eluded her for the past three decades. She knew from experience and her treasured portfolio of attachments, that undercover work could be exciting. Even so, she had no inkling at all that there was a department capable of sourcing suitable lookalikes at such short notice.

"They should be with you within a couple of minutes."

"What? How did you manage that so quickly?"

"Well, not *that* quickly, they've been on standby since you left Hayley at the station."

"Really?"

"Yes, I told you we were here, here to support you, we weren't about to let you down, Jan, I gave you my word."

Kent had lowered the reassurance rope into the dark depths of her despair. He was a man of honour, an officer who could play chess and outwit this novice civilian with humble grace.

"Barney was a bit more of a rush but, all things considered I think we got the balance right; you know officious and aloof all wrapped up in one uniform."

"You mean he wasn't a *real* traffic warden?"

"Who wasn't a real traffic warden?" asked Hayley still craning her neck.

"Barney. Barney at Saltash, he was keeping an eye on you."

Like a time-lapse nature sequence, Jan had thawed and melted under the hot breath of Kent Collins. The reassuringly amazing Kent who, with one miraculous brush, had made the sun shine and her eyes water.

"Jan, like I said this isn't without risk, it would be better if we still had you on board, but I do understand. At least this way we're keeping it all in house with experienced officers who should be able to pull it off."

Kent had come to the end of the road, where their brief connection would terminate but not before he'd delivered a warm parting statement.

"Good luck, Jan, and enjoy the rest of your life."

An unexpected feeling of loss descended across her shoulders at the prospect of her newly found crewmate ebbing into obscurity. But, like most officers do, she managed to muster the go-to farewell.

"It was nice working with you, Kent. Bye, mate."

"Flaming barbeques, did I hear him right?"

"SSHHH, Hays; keep your voice down."

For the first time today, Hayley obeyed orders, but only for a second. Even with a hand clasped to her mouth, she couldn't stop the words from exploding across the table.

"Strewth, there's one; they're coming."

Jan didn't need to turn around, she needed to prepare, calmly and discretely.

"Okay, Hays, I think you should go first and I'll follow in a minute or two, keep my eye out for trouble."

"I think it's too late for that."

A familiar male with an air of style and confidence, swerved and sidestepped across to their table. He was the shorter accomplice, the one who grasped English a little better, or so Jan thought.

"You are pulling my chains you are messing with the wrong boys and you will do now as I sez to you. Get up, go to car. Running will be shooting me, don't think I can't. My gun iz loaded. Try no games, I have you crowded."

Hayley didn't appear to be at all concerned by this misguided young man, she was far more interested in the immaculate air hostess that had just walked behind him towards the toilet area. So, in an act of defiance, she stood up and spoke in the unmistakable voice of a not to be messed with mother.

"I, young man, am not going anywhere until I have visited the dunny, you know, the toilet over there?"

He turned in the direction she had indicated just as the second air hostess pushed the door and entered the small lobby.

"Aw will you look at that?" said Hayley causing panic to cross Jan's face. "Look at that posh Sheila, you might have to wait your turn."

She looked at Jan with a level of acting that could have won an Oscar, a Tony or a Sheila if there was such a thing. And with that, she had pushed past the startled young villain and headed for the conveniences before he could mount a challenge in a language of his choosing.

With the operation moving forward, Jan's clothing was under attack from within by a heart too nervous to adlib. However, she reasoned that this boy couldn't be the brains of the outfit; his face was full of discomfort, colour and kindness. Perhaps, following his partner's humiliation in the cup collecting event, he had been pushed forward as spokesman to try and make sense of the English.

"Why don't you sit down, you stick out like a sore thumb," she said pointing to Hayley's vacant seat.

He hesitated.

"*Asseyez-vous,*" she said, "I'm sorry I don't know how you say sore thumb?"

"What is thumb?" he said shuffling his eyes and bottom in equal measure.

Jan gave him the thumbs up as she looked towards the glass panelled door that led to her destiny. Somehow, she had to leave him, hope he stayed where he was or, better still, left the building. With her heart bounding headlong to oblivion, she stood up and waved her pointy finger towards the toilets.

"*Asseyez-vous!*" commanded the minder as his soft young hand implored her to sit.

But she mustn't. Spurred on by Hayley's no-nonsense treatment of this bewildered soul, Jan summoned the last lonely token from her closet of courage and began to improvise.

"They'll be handwashing now," she explained, wringing her hands and pointing towards the toilets.

Pensive and perplexed he looked set to stumble into the rescue plan with Jan about to fail in a room full of sauce and French fries. But she couldn't allow this weakness, she *mustn't* be the team member that messed up and blew the operation. No, it was showtime, her life was about to reach a whole new level of embarrassment. So, in the middle of a crowded room, in the hope that he would guess the charade, she began to dance. An uncomfortable cross-legged display of desperation behind a face of burning beetroot.

"*D'accord, d'accord, aller, aller.*" He waved his hands, shooing her from his sight in that way that young adults do when parents cause a public spectacle.

She wobbled away in a forced display towards the panelled door with her outstretched hands grabbing at the handle. The door, with its unnervingly loose swing, struck her right knee and caused her to buckle and stumble into the passageway. She peered through the glass panel, relieved that her new French bodyguard was still exactly where she'd left him.

Phew and ouch blended into a new nonsensical phrase as she hobbled along to the door for the ladies. There was a time when such attention from an attractive Frenchman would have induced a less fearful reaction. But for now, in this uncharted moment, she was quite terrified. Terror turned to panic with a capital pee when the toilet door she pushed so urgently against offered unwelcome resistance. Would he twig what was going on if she loitered at the door? Perhaps, but for the moment and reassuringly, the predator remained in his seat.

She tried again and this time it opened, just enough to reveal an unknown face framed by an ill-fitting wig on the smiling head of a mischievous fawn.

"Quick," said the woman in a warm West Country tone as she pulled Jan through the slender gap.

Like four oversized children, they were crammed into a giant dressing up box. In reality of course, it was a tiny efficient space of three undersized cubicles with little spare room for four grown-ups practising to deceive.

PC Mandy Miller introduced herself in the reflection of the tiny mirror.

"You won't be able to tell us apart when we've finished."

Her bouncy delivery offered reassurances that were at odds with her emerging appearance. Without the luxury of space, she could only partially extend a hand towards Jan who grasped it willingly and, in that moment, was absorbed into the comfort of this new team. She was certain they could be trusted; the plan might be hugely flawed but at least with these two in their corner, they outnumbered the French. And with that encouraging thought, Jan offered to help with the dubious creation of an honest version of Hayley.

"Just in case you're wondering, I'm PC Shaunna Jackson, mistress of disguise and graduate of the Royal Academy of Dramatic Art. Well not that last bit although I think with all the jobs we've done, I could easily pass the audition. 'Jacks and Mills' as the boss likes to call us." She pulled a pair of cargo pants from the case and discarded the court shoes of her previous incarnation.

"Well, you're as skinny as me sister but do you really think you can get away with this?" said Hayley holding a pair of socks in readiness.

"Bit rude," said Shaunna breaking into a playful grin. "You two really need to relax and put some trust elsewhere, the boss said you were having a pretty hard time of it. Well, worry no more, Mand and me are the girlies for the job, we've been in tighter spots than this."

"This is pretty tight though for a dressing room," said Mandy inching herself away from the jumpy hand dryer. "I saw you had company out there, how did you leave him?"

"Sat at the table, eyes trained on this door, told him I was desperate."

Jan *was* still desperate, desperate to know how on earth this ill-conceived idea was going to work or indeed *help* their situation in any way at all. Because as PC Shaunna Jackson began to morph into a third-rate pirate copy of Janet Elliot, the potential flaws began to plume like pollen on a summer wind.

"It'll screw the whole thing up, the minute you walk out of here, he'll know straight away. I'm sure he's not stupid and he's quite fit and he might have a gun or a weapon or something else that could take us all out."

"What, like words? I think gun or weapon covers most things you know, Jan. Try and remain in your seat until the aircraft has landed." Mandy Miller's calm observation should have reassured the passengers but it had not.

"Basking shark."

"Don't take any notice of me sister, she swears like a fishwife although sadly she isn't a wife to anyone."

"Why did I agree to this? Why did you agree to this? Dab it, it's risky for you two as well. There's still time to back out; look, we'll carry on as we were, forget the plan, it's got failure written all over it."

Jan's downward spiral was interrupted by a force against the door that rendered her silent. With feet glued to her piece of the flooring, she hoped against everything that the person on the other side hadn't heard a single word of this nonsense.

Mandy shook Jan's arm and nodded towards the potential intruder. This automatic promotion to steward couldn't be rebuffed, after all Jan was the nearest person to the door who still looked like themselves. Seared by the heat that burned through the bonfire of this deception, Jan struggled to speak; her sticky tongue had been struck by delirium and fatigue and lay like a sun-baked turtle in the sand. Her eyes screwed tightly in one final hope that she would wake up somewhere else, but she didn't so, the door was opened – slightly.

On the other side stood an impatient teenager in quiet protest with one hand flat against the door.

"Big queue in here," said Jan delivering a version of the truth, "I'd use the disabled one over there if I were you."

The teenager didn't reply but gave a look that could condemn you down a dark hole. Her hand dropped with attitude as she swivelled on her sandals and squeaked off across the floor.

With the door closed, Jan turned to the beaming crowd; her heart now ringing triumphantly through her ears and eyes and everywhere that a nightmare allows your heart to sound.

"Calm yourself," said Mandy giving her a reassuring hug. "Shaunna and I are almost ready. We are very experienced; despite your misgivings, we can pull this off. Now, have you got the car keys?"

Jan held them tightly in the depths of her pocket as she surveyed the two would-be doppelgangers who had a cavalier attitude towards accuracy.

"Please, please take care of him, it'll worry me, it's not personal you understand, it's just not what we do. We look out for each other, a team, a bond, things no one understands."

"I think we're getting the idea," said Shaunna, "you live on your own."

"Well, yes, but…"

"I'll have to hurry you with those keys, it's a necessity, Jan, that's all." Mandy held out her hand and took custody of the car, Jan's place of safety, her only constant in this difficult day. "Now, who has the phone?"

"Jeez, I was hoping you'd forgotten," said Hayley clinging like a limpet to her worldly goods.

Mandy seemed unfazed by this game and carefully prized each clammy finger from the surface of the phone as Hayley whispered her emotional farewell.

"Take care of yourself, you beauty, have a nice life."

"You two crack me up," said Mandy stowing the items securely about her person. "You ready, Jacks?"

Shaunna nodded as she packed up the final pieces of her discarded ensemble into the case. "If you could take these with you when you go and leave them in the hire car out of sight that would be excellent," she handed Jan a key fob. "I'd give it five minutes after we leave, should be good to go then and look, don't be so hard on yourselves, it's just another day in the office. One step at a time, things are rarely as bad as they seem, but I don't need to lecture to you pair, do I? Chill, you might find that your clouds are gone before you know it."

With one carefully executed shuffle, Mandy was next to the door with Shaunna squeezed into second position, only inches from the excitable dryer. And, even though they looked nothing like anyone who had ever visited this McDonald's since the day it was built, they seemed fearless, confident and ever so slightly mad.

"Ready?" asked Mandy.

"Definitely," said Shaunna, the epitome of calm.

"Okay and…action."

CHAPTER 16

In the silent safety of the police cockpit drill, Jan familiarized herself with the silver saloon. It was important, methodical and, in its own way, vaguely relaxing.

"What if we *could* just swap ourselves for someone else, get off this awkward stony path and be free from all this nonsense?"

"Well, I'm surprised you haven't noticed, but we kind of have, Sis."

"Well, yes, but not exactly, I mean it does make you think, it *has* just got us out of a situation. What if I could swap and meet up with the version of you that isn't a criminal, a sister who had the same morals and standards as me."

"Steady on, you're hardly *Miss Perfect* yourself."

"I am *not* a criminal," said Jan still privately debating that point.

"Neither am I really; it was one flippin' white lie."

"It's fraud."

"It was a means to an end, a bit like those coppers, strewth, who else would have thought of that? Set off the flaming fire alarm, awesome. Everyone including the froglet is swept out to the assembly point, they make use of the distraction, take your car and off they go."

"Yes, that's inspired I'd say, there's a lot of improvisation going on today and most of it has one thing in common."

"Me," said Hayley with a flourish.

"No, toilets."

Jan blew a short, exasperated breath and returned to her meticulous check of their unfamiliar ride. The standard of cleanliness was impressive, the carpets vacuumed to such a degree that they looked new. Life sucked out of the scuffs and stains that accompanied not many miles of hard use. How many grubby hands had mauled the key fob? And who previously had rocked around on the dark fabric of this seat? She tried to float above it, but instead had slipped into a whirling pool of panic.

"My car has disappeared, I handed keys to a woman in a wig that I met for the first time in some tiny toilets. Cod ham it! What if we've been conned? What if my car has just been stolen and the French twins and the air hostesses are working together? What if they do this all the time? I'll have to call the police, the earlier they know, the sooner they'll find Howard."

"Not if they've changed the number plates." Hayley playfully joined in with this crazy notion.

"It's possible isn't it?" said Jan taking the bait into her watery vortex.

"Now look here, my little neurotic neck scarf, you need to just take a moment and step back." Hayley took hold of the hand stuck firmly to the gear stick. "If they have stolen your car why would they leave you another one which looks quite nice and tidy?"

Jan gazed through the steering wheel at the instrument dials. "What was that?"

"I said thieves don't usually leave you a quality part-exchange, do they? Seems like a bargain to me, shame it didn't come with a mobile phone and then we're almost quits," she said opening the glovebox.

The life was being squeezed out of the bottom rung of a ladder that had descended into Jan's soggy world. She processed the rational offering from her sister and slowly began to climb.

"Yes, I suppose that does make sense and it was Kent Collins who arranged it all." As the words tumbled from her mouth, she slipped back to the bottom rung. "Kent, who I met in another toilet. What an idiot!"

"Don't beat yourself up, Sis."

"No, I *am* an idiot, who is Kent Collins? Some pervert I met in the ladies who has taken me for a mug. I didn't see ID, I'm too trusting, what a fool. Cod in Devon! first day out of uniform and already I'm being preyed on. No protection, no mates to consult with. Just little me, myself, and I'm screwing it up already."

"Well, let me just see if I can help your poor little tormented head, you are not screwing it up because look what I've got here." Holding a green folded document, Hayley continued. "It's a hire agreement 'Phoenix Car Rental', dated today and checked out of the Plymouth depot this afternoon. Is that far from here?"

"No, not really." Jan sat shoulders bowed staring into the footwell through an unexpected brain fog. Single-minded clarity seemed not to feature in the real world. Travel plans disrupted, real life on hold and those that can be trusted don't appear to wear a uniform or a badge.

"You're feeling a bit lost aren't you, Sis? Let me just sort out what's going on in that little head of yours. What I see," continued Hayley without waiting for the green light, "is a child that's just left school. There are no rules anymore, nothing to get out of bed for and no one to notice if you don't turn up. You're in limbo, you don't know who you really are although yesterday you imagined that as soon as you woke up it would be easy, you would have your new label and some handy notes to guide you. And then you meet up with your long-lost overseas sister and discover she's a criminal, and now you just want to get back into bed or better still go backwards to a time when you were living in the cosy police bubble surrounded by support and protection such like most of us will never have the privilege to find in our back pocket."

Thumbs turned over and over in the silence of Jan's lap until a warm torrent spilled from her eyes and splashed onto her tired hands. She wiped her face haphazardly and turned to the driver's window.

With nothing further to say, Hayley rummaged in her bag and produced a small pack of tissues. "Here you go."

"Thanks," mumbled Jan feeling more exposed and vulnerable than she could ever remember. Sorting out the leakage, she looked in the mirror at her reddened reflection, saddened by the distress she had caused it. "First day of the rest of my nightmare."

With Operation Mike out of the window, Hayley focused on the mess sat next to her. "You are such a funny person, I don't think you realised that when we were kids, maybe I didn't appreciate it at the time either. You would always be putting things straight, organising our stuff, keeping your half of our room tidy. I had hours of fun hiding your adventure socks as you liked to call them. So many times, when you were off on one of your outdoor romps, you'd be going mad turning the room upside down to find them. Then, when you did, you would spend ages getting everything straight again before you could go out and enjoy whatever it was you did out there."

"You were pretty horrible to me."

"It was only a bit of fun. Soon ended though, that day you took so long to find the darned socks and get tidy that a flippin' monsoon rain stopped you going out. When I had to suffer you moping around the house and more importantly, our room, I decided to knock it on the head. Change of tack after that, I made sure they were all ready to go, laid out on your bed, just so I could get you out of me sight a bit quicker."

"It's no wonder I'm unbalanced," said Jan quietly.

"Yeah but in a good way, I toughened you up. Don't forget we did play some tricks ourselves on aunt Eth. That time – you remember, that time we left a window open with two sheets tied together and we hid for ages under our beds knowing she couldn't bend down and see us."

"Our tea went cold."

"Yes, that's true but you still ate yours I remember."

"I couldn't waste it; she'd gone to all that trouble. She did look after us very well you know."

"I do know and it can't have been easy. You realise these things when you have your own kids. My boys were little sods at times but they've come good in their own way. They're mine too and that's a bond you can never explain to anyone else. I could bore you all day long and you still wouldn't get it. Not being a mother yourself and all."

"I was just starting to feel a bit better until you said that. I could bore you too on life from my viewpoint but I can't be bothered. I think, at the moment, it's more important to consider poor Mike. I mean I know he was quite lucky having his own room but then again, he didn't really have the same banter like us, did he? He didn't get toughened up; he was just our little Mike."

"What's all this poor Mike malarkey? thought you'd posted him into a starring role as an international criminal."

"Well, yes but, we could have left our door open a bit more. Maybe taken an interest in his brackets and screws, I don't know. Maybe we, well I, should have put aside a construction hour once a week or something."

"Jeez, here you go again. You were a kid, Jan; you weren't expected to schedule inclusive meetings with your brother to talk about his aspirations and career options."

Hindsight, the most overused word in the history of the British police force, thought Jan as she scanned the car park for a black Mercedes van – but it was nowhere to be seen. Oh, good cod! She screamed at her inner voice of reason, what if they were all in it together? What if Kent *was* impersonating a police officer and that soft-soaped reassuring flannel was all part of the con? Hire car documents weren't proof, just pieces of paper that have stalled contact with the real police.

It was time to move, carry out a hasty search of the area and be clear of the facts before she reported the crime. If only they could move but, they couldn't. They were boxed in by a fleet of highly polished fire trucks glinting with importance and serving hot food and drinks to relaxed personnel. No matter that this was a false alarm and that no water had been spilt, this was the fire service, where pumps and pies had equal billing.

By contrast, a police officer could stand on a cordon for an entire shift with little more than a bottle of water. There would be public outcry if an officer in uniform was 'caught' eating in the open air, whilst on duty and funded by an extortionate percentage of the council tax. But, if they were lucky enough to assist Trumpton at an incident, a warm arm of welfare would protect them from public scrutiny and starvation.

As the evening sun began its descent over the tanned muscle mountain, Jan pummelled the steering wheel. A vacuous crater of separation and stupidity bulged in her stomach and pushed her lungs aside as if they were no more than delicate chintzy curtains. Every motionless minute that passed meant Howard was further away, caught in a web of lies and abuse. What untold damage might he suffer and could she ever forgive herself? It was time for action.

"I'm going to ask them to move so we can get out of here and sort out this floundering mess."

"Hey, why should you have all the fun?" said Hayley getting out of the car. "I need to get a bit closer and spoil me self."

In the rear-view mirror, Jan watched as her sister worked the smiling crowd.

"Come on, Hayley… hurry." Jan patted her forehead in a growing frenzy until she'd peaked at boiling point and grabbed the door handle. But, before she could do something else that she might regret, 'I Don't Want to Talk About It' broke the spell. She gabbled into the phone as her mouth exploded in a burst of relief.

"Hello, Clint, how are you?… Wait, wait, wait, you've done what?… Are you sure?… Blenny, you really are a genius, I'd never have got that. And you think that's what it means, really?… I know, I know, I'm sorry I'm not doubting you, it's just a bit cryptic isn't it?… Well, okay, thank you… yeah, speak soon, take care, mate."

She terminated the call – abruptly, it was rude but, she was drenched in adrenalin, there was no time to lose, they'd just had a code zero.

CHAPTER 17

"I hope you haven't told them that we may have had something to do with their false alarm?"

"Don't be daft, it was just fun listening to their side of things, anyway, I've managed to snaffle some chocolate, so I think I did alright and they did help you back out."

"I was perfectly capable thank you."

"Sorry, I forgot, you don't do charity. Anyway, what a fab bunch of blokes. Oh, and there was a Sheila too, she had some muscles I can tell you and the most beautiful long dark hair, quite stunning."

"What are you saying?" Jan enquired, "that beautiful women can't be firemen?"

"Hit the nail on the head, Sis – can't be fire *men*. Do you see what I said there?"

"Yes okay, fire people, personnel, whatever their term might be. Actually, it's firefighters. Yes, that's right covers everything."

"Unless, like just now, there isn't a fire? Must say though, she did look a tiny bit blokey, the fire woman."

"Well we are multi-cultural, gender diverse and all embracing. Who cares who comes to the fire, as long as they rescue you?"

"Fair point, but what's happened to you in my absence? You're sat there grinning like a Space hopper," said Hayley stuffing chocolate into the glove box.

"Clint got back to me."

"Clint? you mean my boy wonder?"

"Yes, and he really has put us into a dilemma."

It was 20:10 Jan's concerns about double dealing and car theft had taken a back seat, she was, to all intents and purposes, in a job car responding to an urgent call.

"A dilemma? you mean like a curved ball or something? What did he say?"

"He worked out the code, you know; EVA M MMC?"

"You beauty."

"Yes, if he's right and we can find Mike, what do you think we should do?"

"Oh, I see what you mean, with us two being off the case as it were. Lost touch with the brioche boys, free as a couple of birds, that kind of thing."

"Yes, Hays, but it has given us a bit of a conundrum all the same."

Jan headed slowly south-west shading her eyes from the sinking sun with each twist and turn in the road. An excitement was brewing like a bale of bubble wrap waiting to burst open. It felt real, every expanded thought every possibility awaited them and yet, they were still blind to Mike's crime and naïve as to the danger. She shuddered, trying to find strength in her own abilities now that she had cut loose for the second time in twenty-four hours from what she still hoped had been the real police force.

"Let me have a little think about this, a lot has happened since I got off the train this morning. And it's criminal to use one of your favourite words, that it's come to this. But we've travelled all this way and I would still like to meet him. What about you?"

"Yes, that's how I feel too."

"You're not going to embarrass us all and arrest the poor fella when we get there are you?"

"No, as I keep pointing out, I can't just arrest anyone, that was yesterday. No, it's probably best to meet Mike, try and understand what has gone on and then leave the authorities to do whatever they deem appropriate."

"It'll put you in a flat spin if we get there and find he's an evil mastermind."

Speculation was running out of road on the way to redemption, whatever was done couldn't be undone no matter how much anxiety she poured over it.

"Maybe, but I'll just have to deal with it when we get there."

"You mean *we* will have to deal with it, I may have limped about for a bit too long and got paid for me acting skills, but I'm still your partner in crime so to speak."

As they passed a large scrap yard on the nearside, Jan was already starting to falter.

"What if Howard has been abandoned on a tangle of wasteland, balanced on bricks where his wheels should be?"

"Come on, Jan, rise above it, everything is probably okay."

Hayley was right, they had a plan, a certainty well, a Clint certainty and Jan could take comfort from that, something positive to sweep away the Howard nightmare.

"Yes, we can't stop now," she said panting like a Pekingese at the parlour. "I've already put Mevagissey into the satnav; we're about twenty-five minutes away."

"Mevagissey?"

"According to Clint, after he'd looked at possible towns and villages in Cornwall, he determined that EVA M was probably an anagram of MEVA – short for the little fishing port and the MMC was likely to be the Mevagissey Male Choir," explained Jan finally able to speak his theory out loud.

"I'd never have got that, not in a million years. Male choir? that sounds promising although a bit odd, do you think Mikey is one of the singers?"

"Perhaps, although I can't see there's much of a crime in that." Jan held up her hand before Hayley could state the obvious and interrupt her train of thought.

"Look," she said rubbing a sweaty hand on her trousers. "We need to let Mike know we've worked it out, so he can be reassured, or perhaps not, that we're still heading his way."

"Well, that's going to be a little difficult isn't it?" said Hayley in an exaggerated whingey voice, "I haven't got a flaming phone."

"Okay, yes of course, you can use my phone." Jan pointed to the centre consol.

"I see you've already made yourself at home in this car, my little creature of habit, you won't want to give it back."

"Yes, I will," said Jan at pains to keep Howard and the look-a-likes out of the conversation.

"If you say so Sis, now, what's your pass code?"

"My collar number; 3485."

"Jeez, you're priceless, did you miss the lesson on security? Not your brightest idea, if you don't mind me saying."

"Maybe not, but it was one less thing to remember and listen, don't you go putting any social media nonsense on my phone. I've told you before, I don't want to find my inbox or whatever you call it, overflowing with people claiming to be long-lost friends."

"No worries, I know my way round the system like a true blue professional, let me just get me self in here and... what shall I say to him?"

"I don't know, we still have to be discrete. What about... alleluia?"

"Brilliant, Mikey's bound to get the drift."

As the light began to weaken through the trees, an unforeseen possibility hit Jan square in the solar plexus; what if the sun went down on unfinished business? It was plain to see that they hadn't met a single deadline since the shoddy ten minutes late incident and that she must brace herself for further consequences. To believe with any certainty that today would be the day she could finally shake the creases and skeletons out of the family airing cupboard and move forward was foolish.

"You know, the other thing we have to consider is that it might all be over. Mike could have been detained by now and we might not see him," offered Jan still working overtime through her catalogue of concern.

"Or worse, what if the French twins got there and they've disposed of him? Flaming Nora, that won't be the case will it? You know how these things work; we're not going to be too late are we?"

Jan glanced at Hayley and detected a small chink in the laid-back confident persona that had been dancing up in the clouds for most of the day.

"Look," she said cheerfully but not convincingly, "the police or whoever, may now have cracked the code on your phone but, realistically they're probably still scratching their heads over that and haven't a clue where to direct their officers or people."

"Do you think so?"

"Yes, unless of course the French twins have disposed of the women in my car. But, if the code wasn't known at that point, I'd be surprised if the French, with an interesting grasp of the English language, could crack it on their own. I still think there's a good chance that we'll find Mike first."

Jan's skin, now hot and clammy, began to prickle beneath her clothing. Her bold supposition was underpinned by the disappointing probability that they were closing in on a criminal mastermind whose veins ran with Elliot blood.

"Yeah that'd be right. Great, well, let's find the young rascal. Well, forty-five years of rascal. I just always think of him as my little kid brother. I wonder if he does have the Elliot looks? You know, handsome, attractive?"

In an effort to restore internal order, Jan turned to Rod and began to sing, quietly.

"You do know that Rod Stewart is a criminal, don't you?" Hayley looked pleased that she'd found another example to chip away at Jan's perfect world notion.

"Is he?"

"Fair dinkum, back in the seventies he was banned from some hotel chain because of all the damage he caused. Wreaked havoc he did and threw a television out of the window too."

With less than fifteen minutes to their destination Jan refused to be drawn into battle and decided to play down the accusation.

"Oh that."

"So, you knew and you still like him? The man's a criminal, I bet he never did a day behind bars. That's the thing when you're rich and famous, you can buy yourself out of trouble, it doesn't mean it didn't happen though."

"Things were different then, it was normal to a point and totally fuelled by headlines and publicity, he is not a bad person."

"How do you know that? Besides, surely what he did was just criminal? You can't pick and choose who, in your life, can commit crimes and who can't. I thought as my self-confessed little honesty and integrity queen sister you might see that. The law is the law you said. Well here I am sat with you singing 'I Was Only Joking My Dear' with a common criminal."

"Who are you referring to now?" asked Jan with a hint of irony.

"Now, listen here, I haven't risked my flippin' neck and got myself into this mess just for a bit of fun. Like I've already told you, I didn't have a choice." Hayley's voice whipped like the tail on an angry cat.

Note to self: jokes aren't your forte, thought Jan.

"You're right in many ways. According to the media, he does have a criminal history and qualities that I wouldn't wholeheartedly agree with. But to me, in a strange kind of way, he isn't real, he's just a musician that I'm unlikely to meet and I don't, therefore, have to be definitive about his behaviour."

Although Jan was pleased with a point that she considered interesting, in reality it had only served to add a question mark in pink highlighter over the rules for being *normal*. Already she appeared comfortable to gloss over offences and make up her own guidelines. Even at a fingerpost in the middle of nowhere she seemed happy to consider another direction.

Surely this wasn't the way forward? Is it not possible for a civilian to lead an honest life with scrupulously honest friends and acquaintances including every member in a social gathering and anyone at all that they might ever have to walk past?

The clock and the car moved forward. In contrast, the travellers each with their own expectations of this day, were held in silent breath. Hayley was quiet, too quiet, and their rafts seemed to be drifting apart.

At first, Jan couldn't decide whether her attempt at reconciliation had been effective. The badly timed joke, her social ineptitude and lack of judgement had created an atmosphere but, even so she decided to continue.

"He's a big fan of model trains and train sets. He has created amazing scenes and structures that depict life in miniature along the railway line. I find that quite fascinating," she said.

There was still nothing, so she limped along a bit further.

"These days apparently, when he's touring, he'll book extra rooms in the hotel for his train things. It's hard to imagine a greater contrast between the man on stage singing: 'Do Ya Think I'm Sexy' and the quiet modeller who patiently makes a rusty dustbin or telegraph pole for the shunting yard."

It was the first time that Jan could ever remember voicing this trivia in an effort to justify her liking for the artist. An artist she had clung to from the moment she found her sister's discarded cassette tapes. He brought Hayley to life but, the man and the musician would be forever two dimensional. Jan's love for Rod was taken at face value, a concept that her career found hard to accept.

The B3273 pointed them towards the sea, and closer to the end of the line. Jan had been counting breaths so methodically she'd almost fallen asleep in the silence that surrounded them. The sun sparked through ancient trees like it had done for hundreds of years and would continue to do so, until the powers that be decided they must come down for health and safety reasons.

"Look, if you must know," said Hayley from a quiet place in front of the glovebox. "I've sort of left Len, that's why I'm in this flaming mess."

New in tone, Hayley's voice and statement, clearly screamed of a darkness that demanded attention. Curious and concerned had shown up in equal measure. Jan needed to listen to her passenger, her crime fighting partner and, of course, her only sister and hope she wasn't about to disintegrate at this rather unsuitable moment.

"It's a toughie, not an area I'm familiar with. It's alright for you, you must have seen most things in your illustrious career I shouldn't wonder."

Well, maybe she should wonder, thought Jan whose relationship advice had previously been compared to the gaping holes of Emmental cheese.

As the satnav declared they were nine minutes from their destination, the enormous balloon of anxiety inflated in Jan's stomach and pushed her to the edge of information overload. But, no matter how inconvenient this might be, Jan knew she had a duty to make provision for Hayley's apparent crisis.

"Well, I didn't notice at first, the boys had left home and Len spent quite long days at the unit. I think it must have started years before because suddenly the business just seemed to be standing still, which was curious because he had managed to grow it. Well only by a tiny bit every year, but that's some going for a bit of a bludger."

Hayley scrunched her hair with fidgety fingers and continued.

"Anyway, then he always seemed to be in our bedroom. I would often come in from shopping or an afternoon on the beach and he would be at home already which was odd in itself. Sometimes he'd look a bit flustered too, before making some excuse that he had a stack of stuff to do back at work."

She paused and sniffed along her trail of decay.

"Jeez, here's me thinking he's having an affair and I start looking around for clues – who is this woman? How has my Len met anyone? I mean he was a looker in his younger days, but you know how it is; one or two too many snags on the barbie and we all spread out a little bit. Don't get me wrong, he's not a heap or anything."

"So, what was the problem?" asked Jan who had managed to find her gentle care in the community voice.

"Strewth I feel stupid telling yer it's pathetic."

Offering no encouragement Jan tried to give her sister all the room she needed.

"Well, one afternoon he was in our bedroom with the door wedged shut. I nearly hit the flaming roof, what the hell was he doing in there? I yelled through the door, 'You get out here now, Len Allblack!'."

Jan noticed the familiar signs of mild anxiety puffing from her sister, now totally convinced that their looming deadline and this painful confession were on a collision course.

"Slowly the door creaked, and he opened it to its full extent and there in the doorway was...was, oh, I just can't describe what I thought I'd seen and what I flaming knew I had seen. He was wearing women's clothing and a long brunette wig and blue eyeshadow. He had a hand on his hip and looked at me kind of sheepish. 'Flaming Nora, Len!' I shouted, I was rooted to the spot, shocked to me very core and lost as to what the hell I'm supposed to do next."

"That is a shock," said Jan genuinely not expecting any of this.

"Tell me about it. I was flaming staggered. I wanted to slam the door on it – whatever it was. Why is my Len doing this? I couldn't, in that shock of a few seconds, quite comprehend what all this meant. Jeez, to think for one moment, I thought he might be having a clear out in the drawers but in a way I was right. It fair knocked me sideways. I wondered why we were struggling a bit financially. I mean not only had he lost enthusiasm for the business but, it turns out he was spending cash on all that gear. I hadn't a clue because throughout our marriage he's always controlled the money."

"I'm really sorry," said Jan offering very little. "It can't be easy coming to terms with that."

"What am I coming to terms with though? The fact that my Len likes dressing up? Or the fact that he actually wants to be a woman? I mean come on, I don't have any experience of all this, Jan."

"No, you're not expected to prepare yourself for this day somewhere down the line in a happy marriage."

"But was it happy though, am *I* the problem? Am I *not* woman enough so he's decided to take on both parts? Jeez, I've become redundant in me own marriage!"

"I doubt that's the case, it isn't that simple." Jan desperately tried to find some concrete experience to work with. But it seemed that this particular area of expertise in her corner of policing was a bit sparse.

"What happened after you saw him?"

"Well, I wanted to have a flaming stand up row with the lazy lummox, but I refused to confuse me self by tangling with this creation, I told him to go and put his strides back on and have it out with me proper."

"And did you?"

"Well, honestly, he took more time than I do when I'm taking off me face paint. I'd had time to think and the more unanswered questions I'd lined up for me self, the more flippin' irate I was getting. In the end I drove off down to the beach café and sat outside with a cool one staring out across the ocean. I don't know how long I'd been there, I just floated far away in me mind across to the Whitsundays trying to erase that image that had burned forever onto the back of me eyeballs."

"That's really tough, Hays, why didn't you tell me?"

"Tell you what exactly? I mean it would be easier to say he was having an affair, not try and explain I was suddenly living with another woman."

"Did you manage to speak to him?"

"Well, he did eventually show up at the café in his shorts and singlet, I could still see eyeliner on him which didn't help matters. We sat in the Ute and I all but screamed at him except we were in public and I didn't want the whole town knowing the ins and outs before I'd had chance to digest what was going on."

"Did he ever do that again?"

"Jeez, all the flaming time, when he isn't at work he's living like Linda and it won't be a surprise to learn, I'm in the spare room. I don't want to see him taking off his bra and wig with the care and attention to girlie things I certainly haven't been used to for a long time."

At the end of a bright day in June, you could be excused for feeling mellow satisfaction as the warm summer's day faded to a close and those who had been there took strength from such beauty. Unless you were Jan, who felt like a child in oversized wellingtons who'd been sploshing around in puddles and then fallen over. She felt small and uncomfortable and above all else, she wanted to cry.

Her life felt like a board game and she really didn't understand the rules, didn't know what winning should look like and wasn't sure she wanted to play anymore. Challenges had sprung up in every direction from strangers and family who had problems of their own and needed an arm or a leg or whatever the game entailed. Freedom should never be this complicated, how can so much happen in one throw of the dice? And, why wasn't there a 'Return Home and Start Again' square?

Hayley had just unloaded a fairly weighty sack of malted mitigation which should influence Jan and her justice system except; with her partner about to call in sick and their destination coming in to view, she was rather consumed by the weighty issue of breathing.

"How long has it been like this?" she said trying not to rush the words.

"Linda moved in about six months ago. I haven't told a soul until now and as you don't do social media, I feel quite safe that you won't blab."

"Well, of course not," was about all Jan could offer, she couldn't imagine the level of confusion that Hayley was going through. Without the comfort of an action plan for such a scenario, she chose, instead, to role-play a supportive sister.

"So, what about the boys, do you think they suspect?"

"No, like I say they rarely come home at the moment; although, it worries the heck out of me that they wouldn't bother to call if they were coming, they'd just show up. It's a constant dread that they'll find their dad lounging around as Linda."

"How are things really with Len? I mean did you get any understanding from him about what has happened?"

"No, not really. We seem to live separately in the same house, I wait until the door opens and see who I've got today. I can determine my attitude by who emerges from that seedy boudoir that used to be our marital bedroom."

"You must talk though, surely?"

"Yeah, not about Linda. But, I mean, if he's wearing shorts and going off to work then yes, we have a yak and he'll still come and kiss me before he goes. I wanted to reject him, but I do still love the old sod. I just don't want him coming near me when he's dressed like Linda and I was doing alright with that plan until I broke my flippin' leg. Then, I became reliant on him for a while and sometimes he would help lift me up or fix me some lunch as Linda. I could hardly refuse, could I? Over time I guess I just got used to her as an addition to our family. It is indescribable to anyone else, but Linda seems to live with us and in a way, I do get on with her."

"Hays, I don't know how you're managing, what a shock," said Jan thankful for her own straightforward single status that seemed light compared to the weight of her sister's odd basket of emotions.

"Couldn't you somehow continue your relationship, fall in love all over again, with Linda?"

"That would be too weird, can you imagine that? I mean am I straight or am I not straight? What about Len? Is he straight? What is going through his head?"

"Is it the man in the dress or the dress in the man that you have the problem with?" Jan felt quietly smug that she'd thought of something useful to say.

But Hayley didn't reply, she turned to the window where she stared out at the Cornish countryside that had given way to a small scattering of houses.

A few notes from Rod Stewart marked an incoming text as they continued down the hill into the settlement.

"I had to make a break for it so, as you know, I used me welfare dough to get over here. I needed to catch up with me past and try and work out the future. I know you're cranky with me and who can blame you?"

Jan pulled into the large car park on the edge of town and selected a generous, neatly lined bay that she believed would show respect to the hire car.

"We're here," she said. "I can't believe we've finally arrived after all that we've been through." Hayley was silent as Jan read her text.

"It's Clint, he's just brilliant, isn't he? He's found out that the male choir rehearse this evening; seven thirty to nine thirty at St Andrew's Church. Amazing, I guess that's our starting point, cod I'm so nervous." She clasped her hands, waiting in the wings of anticipation for a dose of her sister's courage.

"Jeez, so many emotions just bombarded me then," said Hayley re-entering the conversation. "I was thinking of Len, Linda, and how all that might work before realising I'm ten thousand miles away from me life. Instead, I'm parked up in a little Cornish village with me sister who's been a bit fractious with me, looking for me little brother who we might not recognise, for a reunion where any one of us could end up in jail. That's that Karma for you right there. I arrive by criminal means and then my whole life with its secrets and lies slaps me right across the face."

"Hays, I've been thinking…"

"Is that a good idea, my little jumping bean?"

"Not always…" she hesitated and then thought better of whatever it was that had pressed her to speak. "I think you're getting a bit tired."

The long inward breath that followed caught Hayley's eye, she smiled and joined in, like warriors preparing for battle. A ritual to galvanise and set them on their way and what harm could it do?

"It's 20:45 now," said Jan having located the church on her phone, "only a couple of minutes away, we'll be in time for some of the rehearsal."

"What do we do, just gate-crash? Just sit ourselves down and hope Mikey's there and recognisable?"

"I think that's all we can do, it's a start anyway; one step at a time," said Jan taking herself off to the ticket machine in this little town called Mevagissey. Now was the perfect time to complete a risk assessment to guide them; what was known, what they didn't know, what they didn't need to know and how to extract themselves from all of it should things go horribly wrong. But, with the sea so tantalisingly close, she drifted ahead of herself to the soft sand and sunshine of her happy, peaceful place.

A seagull squawked his authority across the tarmac and jolted her back to the moment as it begged for whatever it was that she fed into the machine. Mike could be close by, he might be hostile, cause them physical harm before he gets taken off to the gallows. This final journey could be the biggest mistake of the day, but they were here now what else should they do? And besides, there was still that niggling call of duty, the civilian version that came with a whole sack of things you weren't now allowed to do to another member of the public, but even so, she had to see him.

They were about to enter a fire pit, a cave of crime with no plan, no back-up and little effective power to intervene. It took all of Jan's strength to walk back, her breathing in perfect harmony with her laboured steps. Hayley had been watching.

"Jeez, how much was that ticket? A hundred dollars? It really seems to have upset your little face. I thought you were rising to our new challenge; I'm relying on you to take the lead on this one."

"I know, I was just thinking."

"Well stop it, it makes you look old."

"Look, Hays, I just wanted to say that… I appreciate the fact that you came here because I asked you to. That *actually* does mean quite a lot. I just wanted you to know before we… well, before we go any further and…"

"And come out smiling, that's what we're going to do, I have every faith in me fearless little sister; now come on else we'll miss the sing song."

CHAPTER 18

Looking for a stranger in a strange building in a strange town had overtones of a major operation supported, naturally, by armed officers perched on rooftops as far as the eye wasn't supposed to see. But a major operation this most certainly was not, this was major hypertension on a scale that wasn't long enough.

With the aluminium door handle two degrees from being bent like a teaspoon, Jan released her grip and shuffled across the threshold. The foyer was dull with a faded mosaic floor, further muted by a sheen of street dust that didn't exactly make 'All (feel) Welcome' as the board outside had suggested.

In fact, there was a distinct lack of excitement about the place as they looked for signs of life in the lower hall. With the chairs stacked neatly around the room, and not a whisper of a tune, Jan began to doubt the hi-tech skills of Clint, the telephone consultant.

"We might as well wander upstairs," said Hayley heading for the wide steps to the upper floor.

Jan, like a mule cast in concrete strapped into an uncomfortable girth, had no desire to move away from the escape route and clamped herself to the very beginning of the claggy varnished bannister rail.

"Is this the big deal? is this the something *big* that Mike's involved with?"

"Well they are quite big," said Hayley pointing to a display stand. "They've got all these CDs and appear to be fully booked for most of the summer according to that calendar over there."

With the curious enthusiasm of a travel blanket Hayley headed up to the next level followed by Jan who dragged two steps off the pace with an agitated eye on the entrance door.

The stairs opened to a wide landing bathed by a happy babble that percolated through a set of double doors. Hayley peered through the glass panel, flapping her hand like an overused duster in Jan's direction.

"There's not much singing going on, looks more like a lads' dry drinking den."

The large, richly carpeted church hall with rows of red velvet chairs, was alive with the enthusiastic jollity of men standing shoulder to shoulder in comfortable camaraderie. They were camped along the front five rows at the far end of the oversized man shed.

Sitting on a raised platform in quiet contemplation was the round bearded face of their conductor. Behind the main event a small gathering of assorted individuals waited in quiet anticipation.

The absence of music and song rang Jan's internal alarm and set off the sprinkler system that drenched her with adrenalin and an overwhelming desire to run down the stairs and out to the getaway car. This crowd, this unknown threat, lured them, the predator relying on the curiosity of the human mind to open the doors and enter.

Well, not me, thought Jan turning for the stairwell, you'll have to come up with something better than that.

But before she could descend to freedom, Hayley had taken the bait.

"Come on, Sis, we can plonk ourselves at the back." As she pushed against the door, the warm resonant sound poured onto the landing and pulled the stragglers on a sea of caramel into its beating heart.

Jan swallowed hard and pushed up to her full height, shadowing Hayley to a seat three rows behind the choir.

"You said the back row," seethed Jan wobbling with one cheek on the soft padded chair nearest to the aisle.

"We'll be right," said Hayley scanning the assorted knitwear and T-shirts that dressed the back of the choir. "Can you see him anywhere?" she whispered loudly.

Jan viewed the rear of the athletic male that stood in front of her, dismissing him as too old. In the next seat was a shorter, slender male with glasses and bright ginger hair and next to him a male in an Asda fleece who appeared too young to be Mike. As a jumbo drum of liquid anxiety pulsed across her eyes, she realised the absolute folly of giving her consent to this futile rear-end identity parade. Voices drifted further away as she slid into a swamp of stupidity at the very idea of being in this room. Fortunately, before she totally disappeared down the vortex of doom, her thoughts were interrupted by the sonorous voice of the conductor as he addressed the choir and assembled audience alike.

"Ladies and gentlemen, who have kindly come to hear our rehearsal and share in the joy that our choir brings, you are all welcome. Unfortunately, our very talented and skilled musical director has just heard that his wife has gone into labour and has felt it necessary to turn his attentions elsewhere. We wish them well of course and look forward to raising a glass and our voices to what we hope will be the latest addition to our choir. Now, that means that the second half of our rehearsal tonight cannot be of the same entertaining standard. Nonetheless, we are blessed to have such a fine collection of male voices and I have little doubt that they will unequivocally meet with your approval. So, unless anyone from our esteemed audience would be able to step in and play the piano, we will continue with the simple pure beauty of the voice."

Gentle chit-chat washed across the hall as the men prepared themselves and the audience settled. Then, before Jan could stop the mighty voice, Hayley was on her feet.

"My sister is a brilliant piano player, mate; do you want her to give it a go for yer?"

Jan rocked forward but before she could cradle her head in the comforting darkness of her lap, all the men on the back row had turned around. They smiled warmly at her as though mesmerised by this curiosity of the gentle kind.

The conductor spoke again. "Well, it would be an honour to have a lady play for our choir," he said, not quite able to see the guest virtuoso. "Perhaps, if you would care to come to the front, I can run through the planned pieces with you before we make a start."

The mind can play such tricks, especially as regards time for, in only a nanosecond, Jan had successfully imagined the following: the classic – floor opening up and swallowing her; standing at the bottom of the stairs with Hayley and deciding not to bother exploring the upper floor; forgetting to collect Hayley from Tiverton Parkway and best of all, sitting on a beautiful clean bench gazing dreamily out to sea.

After the events of that nanosecond and with her sister pushing at her arm, Jan was compelled to stand. Immediately the men began to applaud loudly and heartily, two of the back-row boys held out their arms to guide her through to the spotlight of the lonely keyboard. Hayley walked behind like a close protection officer guarding her woman. If we get out of this alive, thought Jan, I'm going to kill her, disown her, buy her a plane ticket home and push her into the cabin myself.

The conductor was wearing long shorts in much the same serviceable way as the character Lofty from *It Ain't Half Hot Mum*. He held her hand in an appropriate firm grasp, his jolly physique clothed comfortably in a navy fisherman's jumper.

"Andrew."

His mahogany eyes of rich maturity wrapped her in an unseasonably warm blanket that seemed able to dispel fear on an industrial scale.

Enthralled by this ethereal presence, Jan sat spellbound onto the carpeted, well-trodden steps of the platform without a care for her trousers. A temporary shelter of calm confidence cloaked them together in mutual respect as Andrew carefully ran through his breadth of musical knowledge.

She had been transported to a different world with every sense tuned to the trusted stranger, in a room with a keyboard that she knew she could play; knew she could enjoy.

Hayley seemed unaware of the transcendent growth that had just blossomed on the altar steps as she plonked herself on the empty seat near the keyboard. With an excitement rarely seen in a grown woman, she scanned the faces of the front row for signs of Elliot life.

Jan took her place and ran through the pre performance checks; lightly pressing keys and adjusting her seat before arranging the manuscripts in her favoured way. As she turned towards the conductor, Jan carried out a hasty search of the immediate faces in the barren hope that she'd see Mike beaming with the same uncomplicated warmth as Andrew.

Then, with a nod from the rostrum they began. Hearts and heads combined to create the purity of 'Ave Maria' and after only a few beautiful bars, the curtain of billowing peace descended. The turmoil of just a few moments ago sank into the warm velvety scarf of gentle voice and harmony; the innocence of choir boys held within a giant form.

Jan ebbed and flowed on the warm tide that trickled gently up the white sandy beach of her happy place. Where music had soothed her disorderly day into one so agreeable, she was in no hurry to leave.

This could be an unexpected home, the three siblings in a warm secure environment, sharing a passion and forgiving the past. Although, it had to be said, Mike was still to show his head above the parapet.

'Alleluia' came next on the programme; a profoundly moving rendition. It uplifted and energised and carried Jan on a soul filled flight to a place only music can find.

Expression and passion flowed through the keys as the choir tackled the popular 'Angels' which moved most of the audience to tears of joyful appreciation.

At the end of each piece, Andrew gave quiet underplayed direction, an emphasis here, more power there, a different colour perhaps, whatever was needed, he knew exactly where to look. With a gentle, constructive ear he listened to the tenors and the baritones, each in isolation. Then, he dug deep into an area that most men won't acknowledge and drew out the prized layer of expression that would make all the difference. It was perfection from a respected genius with a soul full of song and an ear to the beautiful.

In this bubble of bliss, it was a surprise and enormous relief to Jan that, so far, Hayley had made no attempt whatsoever to join in. Convinced it was Andrew's hypnotic aura that had suppressed any urge she may have had to introduce her palette of vocal shades.

They sang as one, comrades and vocal superstars pulling in diaphragms, stretching faces and necks in order to reach that note so crucial to their beautiful rendition. It was men in sheds, Old Guys ruling and some younger faces along for the powerful fraternal bond that this choir oozed, it was men-ship, a special connection. They shared emotion through music, it was love they couldn't find anywhere else. Different and inexplicable to their wives and partners, this mattered and they embraced it and you could hear it.

Caught up in the overwhelming kind energy that floated all around her, Jan turned the pages and began 'Bring Him Home'. Men singing of love and devotion, of feelings and tenderness, men who were in touch with this deeply emotional assembled energy. As she looked up into the crowd, standing in row three amongst the tenors she saw her brother, the unmistakable Mike. He held her gaze and as he sang, his mouth breathed into a beaming smile.

How could she ever have imagined that she wouldn't know him? He looked like an older version of that boy sat on the carpet with his train set. Naturally, he was taller, a middle-aged man, the cuddly side of slim. His light brown hair, waved in that understated way as a healthy complexion glowed above his neat brown beard.

With her fingers keeping time, her heart started to gallop. Mike was in the crowd, he didn't look hostile, but then she realised that nothing in this moment was hostile or difficult or wrong. This was a special moment and a special place and for the first time today, she really didn't mind that an unscheduled event had barged across her plans. They made music like long lost relatives could. A harmony of all they were, the glue and the purity that could, for just a while longer, draw a curtain over the uncomfortable past.

The sixties medley saw the older guys step it up a gear as they crooned like times gone by to 'Silence Is Golden' before belting out 'Da Doo Ron Ron'. Finally, floating on their crescendo of compassion, they captured every eye-watering beat of 'Tears in Heaven' until a stunned silence enveloped the room.

As Jan fumbled in her pocket for a much-needed tissue, the silence was broken by hands that rippled and clapped in appreciation of the men from Mars that spoke the language of their hearts.

She wobbled onto legs that were no longer load-bearing but, needed to join in, she needed to applaud, this was a moment that mattered.

Andrew knew his moments too, and extended his arm towards Jan, prompting a reinvigorated show of thanks that pulped Jan's tissue into a useless soggy mess.

All too soon, the experience was at an end, her bubble of heavenly happiness deflated and the choir began to disperse in pockets of satisfied merriment. The crest of Jan's wave flattened with the ebbing tide and reminded her of one important fact; she was still clueless as to the magnitude of Mike's crime. All she could say with any certainty was that he'd been identified as a tenor. But, would she ever be able to accept Mike, turn a blind eye in much the same way as she had done with Rod Stewart? The same eye that in all probability didn't want to scrutinise Hayley, given the circumstances.

A tangle of indescribable gunk was still clogging up the stale plughole in Jan's day. It was time, for all concerned, to face up to the Mike issue so they could all be free – well, maybe not Mike.

She gathered the sheet music, checking through the papers for folded corners and double creasing, then clutched the neat pile across her chest. The tide had turned, she had to let go, face the unbearable truth that Andrew would soon say farewell and expect them to leave. They had finally reached their destination and Jan knew she had to take it from here, get things straight and start again. These thoughts were swiftly brushed aside by Hayley who had just risen from her catatonic state.

"I've seen him, I've seen Mikey. He's been singing his little heart out, just over there…"

But Mike had gone.

CHAPTER 19

"Come on, Sis, you'll have to get a move on soon, or we'll be locked in for the night."

"Would that be so bad?"

The mask of this dusty entrance had taken Jan to the protected world within, where friendship and harmony meet once a week. As her anchor dragged across the mosaic floor, the comfortable port in the storm was about to close and heave her onto the darkened street.

"What did your new best friend say?"

"Apart from thank you and it would be an honour to have you on our standby list? He didn't say anything, oh, unless you count 'quite simple' when he gave me this."

"Jeez, this is worse than trying to get info out of me flaming kids, what does the note say?"

"I could live here forever, I feel a genuine passionate connection to those men," said Jan sounding just a touch overtired.

"Well, I know it doesn't say that, my little jelly cheesecake. Still, you certainly seem like a nicer person after your little play with the boys. See, I know what's good for you."

"Yes, thanks, Hays, it has certainly made me think and possibly re-evaluate a few things," she said shaking her head to block up the hole that was leaking thoughts from her inner sanctum.

22:05, time for another clue in the frustrating game of hide and seek devised by and starring her elusive smiling brother.

"Do you think they're all in on it?" said Hayley. "You know, this crime or whatever Mikey is wrapped up in. Do you think the choir boys are involved too?"

"I don't know what to believe. They obviously know where Mike is hanging out and they seem a bit secretive about that. Does that make them involved? Maybe they just protect their own and respect that not everyone goes to the pub after a rehearsal."

"Yeah but don't that sound like a plan? a nice cold one," said Hayley as a contented dreamy look wafted across her sun kissed complexion.

"These directions do appear to be simple," said Jan, finally able to step outside into the narrow street. Her eyes danced around the landmarks and then, having turned around several times, she stepped forward. "Come on, I think if we walk down here, we might get to Fore Street and then we turn up a street by the pub."

"Could we just stop at that pub?" pleaded Hayley.

"No, Mike is obviously expecting us, I think we should just get there then hopefully, just for a few minutes or maybe just a moment we can all be together before we have to confront whatever the grim reality turns out to be."

In silent haste, they trotted along the lanes of the quaint fishing port with every street sign and paved passage coming under intense scrutiny. And, short of wearing a labelled fluorescent vest, they couldn't have made it any more obvious that they were *grockles*.

Eventually, a street leading through a small residential complex guided them up the gentle incline to a small car park and a building signed 'Mevagissey Model Railway'.

"This must be it. Although, there's no mention of a model rail on this note, that's interesting."

"Do you think this is the right place?" asked Hayley.

"Well, it is a big shed; like the note says, we just need to find the open fire door."

Still buoyed by her transformative musical experience, Jan approached the building brimming with her old confidence. And, with Hayley reassuringly glued to her shoulder, Jan chose to ignore the fact that they didn't have authority or any useful back-up to safely enter an open door onto private premises.

After a short choreographed soft shoe programme of movement and mime, Jan located the door in a dark recess secluded from view. It was here that she bounced on frozen toes as the deep rumbling freight train of common sense ploughed across her chest and caused her to speak in a pinched raspy breath. She turned to her inexperienced colleague and whispered as best she could.

"This could be a trap, we don't know how many are inside, we don't know what's inside and we don't know the level of threat. It's important that if we go in, we remember where this egress point is, just in case we have to make a run for it."

Hayley, who had been attentive in the extreme, waited for the moment that she could whisper an observation of her own. "Flaming Frosties, I don't normally get briefed like this in order to visit me flippin' family."

"SSHHH," said Jan keeping half an eye on the door. They exchanged glances but neither moved they just huddled under the inevitable spotlight of a community that had clocked this foolish pair meandering up a dead end to the model railway when it is quite obviously closed.

Jan's head was now earnestly occupied with the yes or no game until Hayley interrupted play to chatter about cool beer and life before Linda.

"SSHHH," said Jan landing on yes and forcing herself towards the door.

Hayley shrugged and shuffled up behind until a voice caused them both to freeze. With her head perfectly still, Jan's eyes darted from side to side for no useful reason, Hayley's hot breath roared down the back of her neck serving no useful purpose either. But the voice, soft in tone repeated the message which did seem able to characterise purpose and reason.

"Come inside it's perfectly safe."

With another glance and another dithering dance of indecision on Jan's part, Hayley decided to take the lead. She pulled at the door, grabbed Jan's arm and marched into the room just a few feet across the threshold. And there, in front of a bench on a high stool less than ten feet away, sat Mike.

Jan surveyed the small workshop from the security of the open door, looking for anything that might prove relevant before she would make her move.

The decades of absence, regret and apathy concerning her family had welded Jan to yet another floor where she stood, condemned. The words in her head tumbled and tangled, she wanted his forgiveness, wanted to be absolved, desperate to unhitch the burden and move on. Her body prickled under the weight of this burning embarrassment as she wished it were over and had never begun.

Mike sat comfortably in long blue shorts and scruffy brown deck shoes, his arms folded and held at the elbows across his black and white rugby shirt. He observed them as a teacher might observe two naughty children trying to explain themselves, except they were silent, still rooted where the light had found them.

So, it was Mike who finally broke the deadlock and took the lead, he leant forward and made a word.

"Hello."

Hayley, who seemed relieved to start talking, immediately replied. "G'day."

But for Jan, things didn't feel right, with her stomach tingling and her lungs still on their rest break, all she could do was swallow hard in a desperate bid to lubricate her sticky mouth. A timid "hello," was the best she could manage.

"It's been a while," he said softly.

Hayley, gaining in confidence, responded. "Jeez, been a while? You were just a little boy in shorts last time I clapped eyes on yah."

"Well, I'm a big boy in shorts now." He smiled at the two specimens that had recently arrived on the platform of his world.

Jan stared straight ahead with a cardboard expression, as her mind cartwheeled down some distant hillside in the midst of this minor meltdown.

How am I supposed to react? What do I say? I can't let my guard down, something is going on, this place is full of weapons, hammers, saws, electrical soldering stuff, batteries and bits.

The shelves were indeed crammed with small component parts, engine wheels, carriages, paint pots and numerous essential fiddly bits for the dedicated modeller.

On the end wall to the left of the bench were two large clocks that once ticked in time with punctual trains before modernisation and questionable timekeeping had made them redundant. Now, they hung retired and neglected, no longer concerned with accuracy. Each told a different time which caused Jan to despair at anyone who could entertain such eye-catching items when they didn't perform their intended function.

Shoddy, this whole place is shoddy, what is that telling me? Come on, Jan, think.

First impressions from this windowless room had drenched her with unbridled concerns in this foreboding, unfamiliar world of the criminal modeller.

She cursed her own timekeeping, her lateness into a morning that had promised simple hope and release. A day now clogged with pointless baggage dragged by some station porter along the creaking platform of life. On the brink and sick to her stomach she urged the nightmare of torture to pass her by.

"How are you, Jan?" said Mike interrupting her private crumble.

She had to speak, she had to reply, it would look worse, worse than this must already look if she didn't. Her voice fell apart as she squeaked again the basic response.

"Hello, Mike."

In the billowing of a silk parachute, Hayley came to the rescue. "Well," she said with a convincing upbeat tone. "I haven't come all this way to stand on ceremony." She moved towards Mike who slipped from the stool to welcome her, they embraced warmly and she kissed his beardy cheek.

"Look at you, you old scoundrel, what are you doing down here in a miniature railway shed?" she said looking a little more relaxed than Jan feared she would ever be.

"Living my dream. I repair and upgrade the lines and displays, create new attractions, source rare engines and carriages from all over the world. You'd be amazed at what's out there and of course, what's here in my collection."

"So, not a lot has changed then since we left you on the lounge floor?" She laughed and looked at Jan as if to offer reassurance.

"No, everything has just gone up a few sizes," he said visibly warming to his big sister.

"And who would have thought you were a choir boy as well? That was a beauty of a concert this evening. All those men singing about love with such feeling, fair made me want to cry and take you all home with me."

"It wasn't a concert, just a rehearsal." Mike oozed with pride for the choir and the recognition it had attained from his sister. He turned to Jan who had not moved since the light had caught her. "You play the piano beautifully, Jan, thank you for stepping in. The last time I heard you play was at Ethel's and, I have to say, that for my young ears, it was pretty awful!"

Jan wanted to smile, she wanted to trust him but she was wearing an inflexible suit of armour, and struggling to be human.

"Only joking," he said. "Good skills take time to learn, but you've taken piano playing to a whole new level."

Hayley was relaxing into the workshop atmosphere and began to fiddle with some of the modelling equipment and supplies on the bench.

"Look at these tiny trees and bushes," she said holding up a small item of greenery.

But Jan didn't want to look or get distracted by the little things, she wasn't about to play happy families or any other games, it was time to clear the air ready or not.

"What exactly are you involved in, Mike?" she said in a ridiculously deep voice.

Hayley, still rummaging on the bench held up a tiny model station master and declared: "little people of course!"

Mike smiled and perched back on the stool breaking away from Jan's challenging eyes.

"How did you find out?" he asked calmly.

"Well," said Jan, her voice simmering. "If I wasn't suspicious before, you have kind of put the clues out there. I mean that code on Facebook. Did you expect us to crack it or not?"

"You did very well there."

"I'm not sure about how the musical interlude fits into your plan. Why the secretive note? Why couldn't you just put *Model Railway* instead of all that turn left and right and up by the pub nonsense?"

"Maybe I'm just a private person."

Jan didn't believe a word of it. He could so easily have waited for them; where was the harm in walking here together and having a nice relaxed conversation? Perhaps, as Hayley had suggested, they could have popped into the Kings Arms too. She willed herself to stay calm, think clearly, but her family ties were unravelling and she wanted to cut loose.

"Tell him about the French boys, Jan," said Hayley over her shoulder as she fiddled with short lengths of track.

"French boys?" asked Mike in a curious tone.

"Okay, if you must know, we have been pursued, threatened and abused by two young Frenchmen who somehow put a tracker on Hayley's phone and followed us across Devon and part of Cornwall."

"Well, probably from Heathrow and even from my flaming home address too," said Hayley looking quite at home with her bench activities.

"Yes, they were pretty keen to find out where you were, Mike." Jan stood quietly fermenting that Hayley had introduced the French foxes into the chicken shed.

"So, they must be nearby, they will have followed you." Mike left his stool and looked at the inner door to his left. "We might not have much time," he said, his calm demeanour now lashed to a professional air.

"I'm guessing it's not your model railway they are interested in?" probed Jan still desperate for information.

"No, it's bigger than that."

"You mean a full-sized railway?" Hayley laughed, pleased with her connection. "Don't panic, Mikey, I don't have my phone anymore, so the croissant twins are hopefully wherever my phone is, if they haven't lost interest."

"Why don't you have your phone, where is it?" he asked.

"Is this like a signal box?" said Hayley fiddling with a small wooden looking building.

"We don't know, about Hayley's phone," dismissed Jan refusing to get side tracked. "Look, just be straight with us; what are you involved in? Because I think it might be the right time to introduce an important point that you may not already be aware of; I am *not* the sort of person who will tolerate lies, deceit and danger, I am done with all that, Mike, and do not intend to rub shoulders with the criminal fraternity. I make an exception, at the moment, for my sister over there."

Mike followed her eyes but did not pursue this secret between sisters, instead he moved towards Jan in a short flourish and raised his hand, she flinched as his arm shot past her and pressed against the fire door. As he retracted his arm, he stopped short of touching her.

"You may want to harm us, you may want to embroil us in some nonsense but if you just open the door and let us walk away, that would be for the best." Jan felt her recent upsurge in confidence ebb with some speed on a tide of foolishness that shone like an old cine film across the workshop walls.

With her body crumbling, Jan struggled to remain on her feet as sweat poured out in a clammy torrent of hopelessness. Mike had pushed into her personal space; all she could do was look at his comfortable old deck shoes and wait for the pain.

How proud our father might have been, she thought, to see this handsome grown man capable of such evocative beauty in music. Why couldn't she just hug him, show him that she was sorry he got left out? How she deeply regretted not having made time for him?

But, the shadow of his underworld had cast that idea from her mind. She stood in readiness for the physical harm, the dejected brother eager to exact revenge on a pathetic, selfish sister.

Trembling and detached, she was overtaken with Stockholm and the unsettling syndrome associated with the capital. Already she had entertained thoughts of hugging him, what else might be necessary in order to survive?

But, thoughts of Stockholm and absurd behaviour would have to wait, for she had just been struck by an enormous eddy of adrenalin that pushed her headlong into something more useful. With one deep breath and everything clenched, she hauled herself from under Mike's shadow and roared with commanding verve.

"Back away! Step back, step back!" Her voice getting ever louder.

Mike grabbed for her arms but she flayed and wind-milled like a wildcat until she felt the solid door press against her. In a desperate need for space, she pushed her hands against his chest and stared into his eyes, they were warm, dark and mystifying.

What is going on? she shouted to herself before catching sight of Hayley creeping towards them with a hammer held aloft.

"NOOO!" shouted Jan.

Mike turned to face the threat – Hayley in possession of a small modelling hammer barely six inches long.

He skirted around her and resumed his position on the stool where he could survey his two siblings from a relatively safe distance.

"We have to keep your French entourage out, it's for our own protection, that's all."

Despite knowing that she could open the fire door herself, Jan was reluctant to take the risk. Hayley seemed more confident in their predicament and might not follow which would leave Jan potentially locked out of this mess. She took a moment, revisited her fragmented decision model and then commanded her diaphragm to deliver enough air to speak with modest authority.

"Right, if you must know, the police are following," she bluffed, knowing all too well that they would have lost interest the moment Jan pulled the plug at McDonald's. "If you cause us any harm, they will storm the building, the place will be surrounded by now. You might as well give yourself up."

Jan had launched these words into the public domain with immediate regret. She'd intended to keep the police involvement quiet, in case Mike ran to ground.

"Yeah," said Hayley enthusiastically joining in on the act. "We've been hired as Cagney and Lacey and we're on a mission to find you."

Mike leant back with a curious smile as he held a hand to his chin and slowly scratched his beard.

"Now," said Jan still trying to organise a way out to the night sky with her sister in tow. "It would be to your credit if you allowed me to open that door and let the two of us get back to our lives."

"Well," he said after more beard scratching. "I finally get my two sisters in the same room and they want to run away. That's so like when we were young, it was you two and all that girlie giggling from your pink room with little old me sat outside wondering why I wasn't able to understand the point of a sister."

"Pink was Hayley's idea," said Jan quick to distance herself from any historical inaccuracy.

"Look, mate," said Hayley speaking from her platform of maternal authority. "You had your own little ways too. What about the Lego bricks in the bath? That was a right pain in the bum, and that traction engine thing that puffed out fumes all down the hallway,

258

I'm sure that's what caused me bad cough. But don't forget, we did let you have first dibs on stuff we'd got from the larder."

"And we watched your back when you were having a mad half hour. You know, things like running across the furniture, getting in the shed, hiding aunt Ethel's glasses. And our battle cry, you were in on that too don't forget," implored Jan trying to dilute her remorse.

"Tinker tailor soldier spy, getting caught will make you cry, count on me to keep you dry, keep the circle don't ask why," began Mike who was soon swamped by the rousing childhood duet of the Elliot sisters.

There was a momentary amnesty in the room, they each looked one to the other lost in a world long ago when the glue of tinker tailor bound them faithfully together. It filled Jan with sadness, her childhood had been archived as *done and necessary* where she hoped the painful bits would never again see the light of day. Yet here they were, three grown siblings who could remember and feel the importance of their unique solidarity. It seemed as important in this moment as it had been forty odd years ago.

It was Mike who spoke first in the adult world, to sum up the situation from his view point.

"So, from what I understand, there are some French guys looking for me, you have the building surrounded by police and you," he said looking at Hayley, "no longer have your mobile phone?"

"Yeah, that'd be right."

"Oh, and I don't have my car either," offered Jan caught out by Mike's charm offensive.

"Why would that be?" he asked looking genuinely surprised.

Inside, away from public gaze, Jan was incandescent with rage about the enormous sacrifice she had made in their bid for freedom. Still concerned that she'd been taken for a mug, it was far too soon to conduct a balanced conversation on the subject so, instead, she presented the cold facts.

"In order to stop the French suspects from following us, we arranged for a couple of female officers to masquerade in our place. They took Hayley's phone and my car in order to complete the operation. That left Hayley and me free to go our own way safe in the knowledge that we were no longer being pursued."

"But you still continued even with your belief that I was involved in something and that there may be danger attached?"

"Yes of course," said Hayley. "I wanted to see me little brother before he went off to prison."

Mike laughed in a matey kind of way without a hint of malice. Jan grew concerned, perhaps they had shown their hand too early. Perhaps he thought he had the better of these inept women bumbling half-heartedly into a police operation without back-up or knowing where all the exits were. She felt cold and yet confused by the warmth he remembered in their games and childish ways. He appeared to have just got on with his life whilst his sisters lived in their own make-believe world along the hallway where boys were excluded.

He was probably scared on the inside and acting on the outside, she thought. But, why was he not showing himself as a cold-hearted criminal? Why did he possess nice qualities? Why did he wear deck shoes? Criminals don't wear deck shoes, do they?

"So, the place won't be surrounded by police then?" enquired Mike stating the blatantly obvious.

Jan's blood ran with liquid ice, she had moved from volcanic lava flow to the great ice melt and any minute now, her boiler was going to pack up.

Think, Jan, think! What is the plan? Where's the contingency? Desperately trying not to pant she threw a futile spanner of hope at the problem.

"We may be slightly ahead of the operation that's all but they'll be here soon enough. Just didn't crack the code as quickly as we did," she said clutching at very bendy straws.

"And you think the police will crack it today, do you?"

Hayley started to giggle. "That's what you said didn't you, Jan?"

In this final gutsy attempt to save their position amid the rattle and splutter of the engine room, it had all back-fired. She had nothing left, no fact or piece of intrigue, nothing that might help or mitigate their hopeless situation. Inadvertently and with a laudable attention to detail, they had played all their cards and it was Mike who held the aces.

CHAPTER 20

Mike was five nine or ten, younger, possibly fitter, surrounded by a large selection of tools – all potential weapons. Although miniature, it would be unwise to show a cavalier attitude to such potential danger. When she factored in the door on her right that had so far remained closed, it became clear that they were well and truly on the back foot which, in itself, was a wildly unhelpful statement.

As Hayley continued to idle along the bench and rejoice in the discovery of all things fun-sized, Jan tried to deal with the very foolish disclosure at 22:41 regarding their level of back-up.

"Well, what a fine start to the family reunion. I didn't expect you both to be so clever and so funny. Oh, and a little jumpy if you don't mind me saying."

Mike waited for the audience to settle before continuing. "Now, before you two blow any more fuses and try to take me out with my bench tools, let me try to explain. This is my place of work; I've been a modeller most of my life. I love all this, repairing, creating, working on the tiny detail, it's like an escape I suppose and it's very rewarding when the visitors make nice comments about the realistic displays."

Jan watched as Mike spoke with affection about his workshop domain, breathing passion and warmth into this tiny empire.

"So, what do the French twins want you for? Don't tell me, you've got a rare French train set and they're coming to take it by force," said Hayley with juvenile sarcasm.

"There's still way too much that you aren't telling us," said Jan tired and a tad irritable. Time was slipping away; they were rapidly running out of platform and she needed answers.

"Yes," he said quite openly. "I am involved in something else. Something at the highest level of national security."

Stunned by what she thought Mike had said in those last few sentences, Jan whipped straight back.

"So, what is this amazing project that you're involved with? What is so special about this place in a tiny town in Cornwall that has sparked a major operation?"

"Well, let me just rewind a few minutes so I can get things into context for you. After a short spell at college, I studied quantum physics at uni and came out with a first and a head full of theories and excitement. That took me to Sheffield where I worked on a programme looking at the work of Einstein; wormholes, relativity that sort of thing."

"Whoa, hang on a minute," interrupted Jan in full flight. "You went to uni? You've got degrees and all sorts?"

"That's right, an intensive course that needed a distraction so I started collecting trains and memorabilia. It was a great escape and as you know, a passion of mine. I had boxes of stuff I'd either made or found during my years up there in the industrial north. At the end of my research, I just wanted to come home and chill out. It was lucky finding this place, I could unwrap my collection, put down some foundations."

"Rod Stewart has a model railway, ask Jan," said Hayley trying to join the conversation.

Unfazed, Mike continued. "I looked at several companies that could offer me a position, but nothing really excited me. Until I made a useful contact at a jobs fair, although I didn't know at the time just how important that would turn out to be."

"So, you're a real clever koala are yah?" Hayley glowed at the prospect of a proper brainy person being a member of the family.

"Well, it's not clever to know what you know, I just do the things I enjoy, what's the point otherwise?" he said. "So, when this contact invited me on to the programme many years later, it was too exciting to turn down."

This dubious information was getting mixed reviews in Jan's kitchen where a tangle of sticky spaghetti had accumulated on the wall and messed up her straightforward version of the world. He had told them something and nothing which didn't in any way explain why British and overseas forces were showing so much interest in Mike's modelling career.

No, thought Jan, he's talking in riddles, we are getting precisely nowhere and it's time to sort out this mess, time to be clear about a few things. And with that she launched into action.

"What programme? What contact? What do you mean?"

"Time travel," he said in much the same casual tone that he might have said *signal box*.

She nearly stumbled in the face of his unflustered reply but rallied to sweep aside this oddity and trample onwards.

"Is that it? I mean, you work on some computer game or something?"

"You're right about computers, but it's not a game. I've been working on a specialised concept using virtual reality. Well, it's more than that but the science bit might lose you somewhere."

"Try me," said Hayley who looked excited but wasn't quite sure why.

He playfully accepted the challenge to deliver a simplified version of his important breakthrough.

"It's testing our relationship with dimensions using quantum physics and other scientific theory. There was a widely held hypothesis that life could exist in multiple dimensions which supported a corresponding theory that individuals could, through a *Timestep*, access a different version of themselves. Not to be confused with the common theory of time travel, where you might assume a trip back or forward in your life. In that theory, the physical paths on which we travel would remain the same; time travel in a single dimension that runs the risk of interfering with history as illustrated by the grandad paradox. Which as you know, is the problem of returning to a world where we no longer have a place in that dimension of time."

Jan rubbed her eyes and Hayley admitted defeat.

"You've lost me there, Mikey, whose grandad is this?"

"Okay," he said, "that was the science bit, let me try and summarise. Everyone has their own unique path of existence shadowed if you like by multiple emotional copies of themselves. We have discovered how to access those copies. A discovery that can allow an individual to select a different emotional version of themselves from any moment in their history."

"So, like therapy?" said Jan trying to flick to the end of Mike's science fiction annual.

"No, not exactly but it's a good starting point for you. If you would just indulge me for a few more minutes, you might begin to understand. A widely publicised programme of research has been carried out in America, Russia and Israel to name just a few. They are engaged with a 'No Regrets Virtual Reality' you might imagine it as virtual psychotherapy. Like a sort of immersive brain training where you are able to give your mind a better memory of an event which then allows you to take a positive step forward."

"No regrets!" cried Hayley. "It's the French twins, Edith Piaf, and all that."

"SSHHH, let him finish, Hays," said Jan longing for an end to this preamble.

"What we have developed is access to an entirely separate aspect of yourself. It doesn't fix your mind; it extracts a small component of emotion and replaces it with a version that you prefer. You then continue your life with no reference to the previous version because that now exists somewhere else. It isn't a fixed or repaired emotion but an altogether different one. So, the chance of lapsing or leaking back to old ways is totally eliminated. It may be easier to understand if I use a computer to illustrate the point; If I take a microchip out of a computer and replace it with another, the computer can no longer reference the qualities of the old microchip because that was sent back out into the warehouse to exist elsewhere. There is no longer a connected pathway to that element of memory. In our brain, the *Timestep* is the portal to that change, it's permanent, you ditch your old self and hop onto a new strand.

"Psychotherapy uses methods to help an individual change their behaviours in order to overcome problems or traumas from their past. Its success rests with the individual working on these methods and committing to change. Our breakthrough actually takes that individual back to the moment in time that has traumatised them and allows them to select a version of themselves that dealt with it the way they would have preferred."

"It all sounds a bit geeky, Mikey," said Hayley adjusting her hair in a small wall mirror, with eyes about to glaze. "I'm not sure how those French boys are going to get on with this mumbo jumbo – they barely understand plain English."

Mike, in full informal flow, appeared more concerned with the task of finding the right words for his English audience.

"Just consider this. For every single decision we make, there are countless other options that are available. We usually make subconscious split-second decisions driven by our character and behaviours that enable us to move forward without too much debate. We either live with or live to regret those decisions. That is until now, now we can access all the other options open to your mind, through the *Timestep*."

Jan folded her arms and began to sway unsteadily, her head nodded more from fatigue than agreement. But she couldn't deny that elements of this condensed science course did sound plausible in a dreamy end of the day sort of way.

"I know," he said picking up a large mirror from beside the bench and holding it towards Hayley. "If you look at your reflection in that mirror and pick it up in this one, we can demonstrate the infinite number of images that exist in a multi-verse."

Hayley took advantage of this two-mirror opportunity to check out her rear view before making her own observation. "Yeah but that's just me, the same Hayley." She said twirling her hair and getting full use out of the styling assistant.

"Exactly, but the images demonstrate the proximity theory of the parallel strands. How we are all here at exactly the same moment, whilst living side by side with countless other emotional options."

"Does it?" said Jan starting to get very lost.

"Yes, my job was to develop the gateway that enables that connection with our other selves at any chosen moment in time. To create a pathway that allows an individual to change their relationship with events by selecting a different degree of emotion. The barrier through to this dimension is unimaginably thin, you only have to consider how the brain deals with all the issues you experience in a day. Through this miniscule membrane, in dreams and daydreams, you are constantly processed in another realm if you did but realise that."

"Mikey the mad scientist, who would have thought?" Hayley's eyes softened with fatigue and affection as she tried desperately to stay awake during the remainder of Mr Elliot's science class.

"Every emotion creates a tiny fusion of matter and energy in another plane, a multi-verse, a sort of wardrobe if you like, with an infinite collection of mood costumes. How you deal with the future is entirely dependent on your relationship with the past. We have discovered a real and measurable engagement with these dimensions. It is a wholly repeatable process that will have an immediate effect for the future."

Jan shuffled her mental course notes and still couldn't remember having enrolled onto this fantasy module so late in the day. Like an atom in chaos, bouncing off the virtual walls, she was unable to work out whether Mike was telling the truth or just emptying the contents of some fictional comic series over the heads of his naïve sisters.

Is this tosh and nonsense? Is he taking us for fools? shouted Jan to the internal body that governed her life. They responded by making her dance one foot to the other, hands falling loosely to her sides. She was, for the whole world to see, agitated.

Mike slid from his stool and held out an upturned palm.

"I'm not sure that we've connected yet, have we?" he said.

Jan stared out through inhospitable eyes searching for the conflict in his but finding only kindness. She stumbled forwards, unable to defend the emotional storm that swirled through her sails. Tossed between compass points, she raged at the incompetent internal committee that were supposed to oversee this type of crisis.

Powerless to monitor the threat or defend her position, she turned away with eyes blurred and dripping. It was then, with disarming warmth that Mike made contact and clasped her hand as though he had gently caught a butterfly in his large square shovels.

He turned to Hayley but she was having none of this subtlety, she just barged into him broadside.

"Come here, you great lummox," she said, trying to hug the life out of him.

Jan wriggled free under the pretence that she needed a tissue, more importantly she needed to think. As she dabbed her eyes with the sorry pocket specimen her voice, dismissive and detached, spoke to no one in particular.

"So, you've invented some marvellous hi-tech contraption to provide therapy so what's the big deal?"

"Well," said Mike picking up the campaign trail once again. "It can be whatever it wants to be. There are huge potential cost savings across the board, which is why the government are involved. Some codenamed, fictional boffin buried deep within the basement of the security services is heading up the project, I'm just a small cog in a workshop. They're literally throwing billions into this whole concept in order to secure the intelligence and knowhow before it's discovered by any other group or superpower.

"It can help an individual or couples for example. Imagine using this concept for relationship counselling, being able to improve stability in the home with more tolerance and understanding. It would create a better environment to produce well balanced kids. It could reduce demand on social services and the police, improve education, get more people into work and so it goes on and on. A taskforce for every area of our lives, an endless circle of improvement throughout the whole of society with a massive billion-pound side order of savings.

Approaching the end of her concentration threshold, Jan's face had embarked on a series of unflattering contortions, blinking and stretching in a bid to stay connected with the lack of action.

"So, couples who have had a row could go back and fix things? You know, if they both went back and identified an issue, sorted things out between them, that kind of thing?" At some point along the explanation highway, Hayley had seen the potential.

"Yes, and will almost certainly be an application that falls under some minister charged with improving the fabric of society."

"I don't buy that, none of it, it's bull squit," said Jan, "Why would anyone develop this technology just for marriage counselling? Doesn't make any sense."

"Flaming Nora looks like the fish is off. She's getting a bit cross now, see what you've done, Mikey? I'd buy it though, for Leonard and me, go back to our happy place, remember what's important. Maybe I could get him to turn right instead of left into Linda."

Pushing aside her sister's personal needs Jan continued on her weary crusade.

"What aren't you telling us, Mike? What is this really all about? What exactly are you involved in? Because at the moment, it doesn't explain why a couple of French terrorists, as the police called them, would be chasing you across Europe just to fix their relationship."

"Perhaps they're emotionally unstable and need some therapy," Hayley offered.

"Okay," he said, "perhaps that's a better example.

"You're right to say that they're emotionally unstable, they are both the prize and the problem. There are certain groups that will see this model as a way to develop evil intent. Where, instead of trading emotional experiences for a better self, they could use it to train terrorists.

"Imagine a group of people who go back to their moment of perceived weakness, where they had shown consideration or empathy for example. If they could ditch these softer emotions for callous, hostile and ruthless in a few easy steps. Well, you can see why the government and security services need to get involved."

"You mean you can create a whole load of flippin' zombies and destroy the world?"

"Ultimately yes. Instead of terrorists physically going out to camps to be trained and brainwashed for a few months, it could happen in the time it takes to make a cup of tea. Organised hardened superhumans forming platoons while we're fast asleep. The devastation to life on earth as we know it cannot be underestimated."

The icy declaration delivered by her barmy bearded brother ran coldly the length of Jan's spine. She shuddered at his big ideas and this apocalyptic prophecy that was too far removed from reality to fully register and yet, somewhere in her satchel of manuscripts, he'd struck a chord.

"I suppose, when you look at the levels of hatred and anger some people are capable of even now, you have to wonder whether this has been around for ages. I can tell you that there are people out there; I've seen them, dealt with them, they're cold and cruel and hateful. What if the threat on the streets is already influenced by this technology? I mean how long has it been a possibility?"

A penny, or more likely a pound coin, had just dropped into a cognitive corner of Jan's head, giving credence to the idea of a mind swapping concept. The possibility that some people she had dealt with were perhaps a product of some big experiment instead of just being a mindless thug or 'hard-working citizen' as their solicitor might describe them.

"This version has been live and viable for about six weeks, we believe we are the first organisation in Europe to have a full working model but, we could be wrong. The world is an enormous place and there are plenty of labs hidden in remote locations that you won't find on any map. We can't rule out the possibility that another agency has already created the worst kind of human being, like Bond's Blofeld if you like.

"There is a good reason why the contingency plans that cover every incident, accident and conceivable threat known to the UK are kept well away from the public gaze. For, if they were privy to every shred of intelligence, glimmer of doom and catalogue of catastrophes that bubbled around their community, there would be mass hysteria, a run on the banks, civil unrest and anarchy."

Which is pretty much how Jan felt, a normal member of the community who should be protected from this deeply distressing information. Instead her throat had been constricted by the invisible hand of an over confident balloon modeller. Stress-free retirement had just been wiped off the happy board of options, she crumbled, frazzled and frayed in the grip of her own civil unrest as her battle with the enemy, whoever that turned out to be, looked set to continue indefinitely.

Mike, who seemed to be in tune with the elements of Jan's meltdown, offered reassurance.

"We're safely locked in, why don't I show you my creation?"

He turned to the bench and collected keys and a USB stick from a jumbled pile of clutter. Jan noted his actions with marked despair, how could anyone, particularly a person who was supposed to have a brilliant mind, work or more to the point, *find* anything of importance on this surface of neglect?

Hayley grabbed Mike's arm as he opened the inner door to lead the way. But Jan had managed to settle, she'd declared this area to be a relatively safe place and didn't feel ready to move away from the escape route.

Mike and Hayley watched and waited for the broody child to get on and make a decision or risk being left behind.

Jan's eyes flickered like exhausted candles at the end of their wick. And as the fire door flashed into view, she was caught by a draught of regret that forced her to move.

CHAPTER 21

Strange and incommodious might best describe Jan's current location, the smallest room of the house or the workshop or wherever it was that she'd managed to secure herself. Where, with the pleated face of a child chewing a gooseberry, she inspected the objects necessary to her confinement.

A shabby male influenced shelter that, in addition to its usual function, would have to make do as the emergency planning office. But fatigue jumbled all connection she once had to common sense and danced across her mind in a mist of playfulness. With a laboured squeeze, she pinched her cheeks, her eyes watered but nothing had changed, she was still a grown woman who spent a disproportionate amount of time creeping about in toilets.

How should she react to Mike after what he had just told them, was it the truth? Surely my little brother has not been the architect of some incredible monster mould? It's a complete outrage that my own personal Mike issue has been swept aside in favour of what appears to be, a pressing threat to humanity.

Jan moved to dry her hands on the once fluffy towel but instead, wiped them across her shirt in a hopeless clutch at cleanliness.

How can we exist elsewhere? How can there be another version in fact hundreds, thousands of me? She stared at the tiny mirror above the sink. I am here looking at you as you copy my every move. What if *you* are thinking something else? What if *you* are the version with all the confidence? The one who could deal with horrific incidents with cool indifference instead of disabling concern and mental wounding? What if *I* could be more like you?

Jan longed for the answer but had to give way to the person on the other side of the door who also had a question.

"What are you doing, Sis?" bellowed Hayley. "There's a queue forming out here, you're not the only one who needs the dunny."

Jan patted her clothing, slightly reassured that she was the real and only version of herself. Then, with a slide of the door bolt, she presented herself to Hayley.

"Sorry."

"Are you okay now?" enquired Mike tenderly.

"Yes, yes thanks," came the practised response as she followed him along a narrow, dimly lit corridor towards a solid door. Her eyes swept the passageway for anything suspicious, other than Mike of course. He was still an unknown, the science lecture didn't in any way prove his honesty or integrity, he was still a real and credible threat. And why, if this was such a top-secret operation, was it openly discussed with herself and Hayley but especially with Hayley?

The probability that this was a trap had just been raised to the brink of 'beyond reasonable doubt', knowing too much had made them infinitely dispensable.

"This is my other workshop," he said pushing the door into the self-illuminating room.

Jan immediately sensed movement within and flung herself into a defensive stance to face the threat. Trying to see around Mike, her legs began to shake with adrenalin overload.

"Look out," cried Mike as the large ground predator bounded forwards and pushed past him to barge sideways into Jan.

"Sorry," he said bursting into gentle laughter. "Skipper, here, Skipper, come on, you big soft lump. Put her down, you don't know where she's been."

"I know where she's been," said Hayley rubbing her hands together as she joined the introductions. "Don't often see a bar of soap these days, have you had that one festering since the 70s?"

"Is it that bad?" he said keeping tabs on Jan who was mumbling at the dog.

"This is Skipper, she's a guard dog of sorts but she's too soft for words, wouldn't hurt a soul. Not that I broadcast that fact. She's an Italian Spinone – intelligent, loyal, gentle, will bark if she feels the need, makes up for my shortcomings."

"Why are all the dogs I've met today from Italy?" asked Hayley.

"Sabre wasn't from Italy, he was German," said Jan who had already managed to offload four boxes of emotional baggage in the presence of the soft angel.

"Aren't they almost the same place? Oh, come on, when you live as far away as Australia, countries just blur into one like brown Plasticine mush. So anyway, what's this stuff all about, Mikey?" Hayley's eyes fell upon a laptop on the small desk that faced a large metal structure that housed a circle of fixed seating.

Jan, still gently ruffling Skipper's coat, finally turned into the room to note the contents. It was well lit and at least four times the size of the first workshop. Sparse almost tidy, it felt organised and clinical as though an altogether different person worked from this space. She watched Mike as he gathered a couple of stools around the leather desk chair before he beckoned them over.

"Well, this doesn't look like model trains," said Hayley as she swivelled around on the amazing hi-tech stool.

"No, this is the other part of my work. That over there," he said pointing towards the structure, "is the Proximity Centrifuge, the *Timestep* where the magic happens." He looked at his sisters through excited playful eyes.

Jan, still distracted by the large affectionate hound that leant against her leg, realised that her investigative attack had been forced through a bed of marshmallow and had consequently lost the desired edge. But nonetheless, she tried to make a few important points.

"How can group therapy work when no two people are identical?"

"Good question," said Mike beaming like a not quite mad scientist. "Now, undeniably, each mind is unique with deep personal experiences, a journey like no other. But the approach that can bring about the greatest change is the one where we harness the enormous power and benefit found within group ego. Where there is that determination to succeed through a united endeavour, here the end result can be mind-blowing – literally. This vastly underrated energy is a measurable force that opens the door to the Proximity Highway where real change can begin."

"Yeah well, what happens if everyone says they're going into the time travelling contraption to deal with anger for example – I'm only randomly choosing that one. And then one person in the group has a different idea and instead of dealing with some anger from way back, they start thinking about, I don't know, being more grateful or something?" Hayley had lowered herself so far to the ground on the gas-lift stool of extremes, that she looked like a newly born giraffe struggling with leg coordination.

"Brilliant question, Hayley. It matters, is the simple answer. Collective determination will create the necessary energy required to slip out onto the Proximity Highway but, with conflicting desires, the chances of reaching the vast options available in your personal strand library is considerably reduced. Research so far indicates that, in this scenario, the strongest mind will still have the ability to access a small change for themselves leaving the hapless changelings with little more than a headache.

"The Proximity Centrifuge – well I call it my bandstand," he said with casual pride. "It's a six-seater model – the lowest perfect number. If we imagine that our six people are all solidly determined to exchange places with their evil incarnation, they could all potentially jump hundreds of strands to reach unbelievable depths of depravity."

Jan sat on the vacant stool, lowering it sufficiently to accommodate a dog. Skipper didn't hesitate, she placed her head across Jan's lap and dripped gently with polite drool. Torn between the temperament of her new best friend and her overwhelming cynicism at the structure before them, Jan had a question.

"So, what happens when you come back?"

"You always return to exactly the same place, after all that's where you left the physical you, but it will be approximately twenty seconds later."

"Now surely the average person is going to be highly confused by that. I mean, what if you tiptoe into the bandstand thingy as a timid mouse and come back roaring like a flaming lion?" Hayley raised her stool to the highest height to illustrate her point.

Mike, with the excitement of a young boy who had discovered a Roman hoard at the bottom of the garden, beamed with all the warmth that Jan hoped he possessed. He knew his stuff and seemed keen to convey this knowledge to his captive audience.

"It doesn't alter anything that has already happened. The history of the three people sat here for example would be identical. All events, much like the photo album, would remain the same."

"If we had a photo album. I don't have anything but me own memories from when we were kids. It's a shame that." Hayley looked at Mike who nodded before continuing.

"Let me illustrate what I mean," he said turning to Jan. You would access the Proximity Highway and travel back to a traumatic moment in your own history. You'd find the version of you, that you believe dealt with the situation more favourably and take the *Timestep* to bring that emotional strength back to this moment. And, by doing so, you make it part of your new reality. A slightly different butterfly would emerge. Nothing in history has changed apart from your attitude towards it. In selecting the depth of emotion that you prefer, you create a history looking through different eyes at the same events. A stronger character with no regrets. Going forward, you write the future using the inner strength that was swapped. You won't notice a thing because you haven't *entirely* changed, you just traded a strand of emotion for a different model and this model with these attitudes is all you will know.

Exposed by this example, Jan folded her arms, which allowed Skipper to settle on the checker plate floor. Any further questions would pander to this fantasy and yet, she was compelled to seek clarity.

"People would notice though surely and then what?"

"Well, using the terrorist example, the group should come back on a similar strand and therefore with a similar degree of evil intent. The collective change will feel totally normal. But, undeniably, when that person is tested emotionally in a situation where their new tolerance or intolerance drives the response then, I would expect family and friends to notice a degree of change. Of course, they could attribute this to any number of things including a breakdown, illness or drugs perhaps. They may express happiness or concern at the way you seem able to deal with something that once caused a different reaction. We all naturally change and evolve remember, that's life. We never entirely know how someone else thinks or feels.

If the change is reasonably subtle it will, on the face of it, be hard to quantify.

"Look," he said turning to Hayley, "perhaps it's like plastic surgery where you have a subtle surgical change. Your friends and family know something is different but can't put their finger on it."

"Cheeky blighter, don't think for a minute that you're too big to clip round the ears, Mikey."

"Proximity strands are difficult to comprehend because most people believe that this moment is the only version of themselves that could possibly exist. But, from conception to death, this isn't the case. For every baby clenching its fists demanding more milk there is a calm laid-back version created at the other extreme."

Jan tried to pull her own strands together, at least what she could remember of this tiredly confusing and frankly quite unbelievable day. 23:29, the final chapter of retirement day one. With so many unresolved issues and only thirty-one minutes left to unravel them, she felt increasingly that these events were destined to crash into day two.

Hayley and her revelation of international fraud seemed minor against the backdrop of Mike's claim to have invented a mind-bending bandstand, his gateway to global self-destruction. Perhaps now would be a good time to call for some back-up.

"Do you get a signal in here?" she asked bending down to Skipper for reassurance.

"No, Jan, this entire place is invisible as regards mobile phones, great little device from the agency. They've provided a lot of nice Gucci kit, like those stools, as a matter of fact."

"So that's why you're a bit slow with replies. Jan thought you were dyslexic."

"I did not," protested Jan as a short storm of middle child dissent breezed through.

"Don't mind her," said Hayley nodding pointedly, "she's been a bit bristly all day, you'll get used to it."

"You two," smiled Mike. "This is so like our childhood, the number of times I would hear the pair of you argue, desperate to put your own spin on things before you'd stomp off in opposite directions. The self-assured and the cautious, nothing has changed really, it's fantastic to see that you're just how I remember."

"Steady on, mate, I haven't always been cautious." said Hayley in their playful exchange.

Jan took off with the autopilot and dropped into line with Mike and Hayley where she could see the world with the unblemished innocence of a child.

She was transported to a time long before this workshop and long before her career, to that time before the nonsensical events that would later translate into decades of separation. Before the mortifying teenage years of stupidity and headstrong pride; wretched years where many a campaign is fought and lost on the strength of not very much at all.

Jan didn't want this *no regrets* nonsense, Jan wanted to travel back in time good and proper, she wanted to pull the plug on all things teenage, well, most of them. Moreover, she wanted to erase any decision or outspoken word that had anything to do with hormones or growing pains. But it appears, from what Mike was saying, that there would be some paradoxical problem with grandad.

Despite the lack of reaffirming contact over the years, the order remained unchanged. Hayley was still self-assured and funny. Then it was indeed cautious Jan followed by Mike – always thoughtful, mechanical and occupied. Mike and the imagination. Except now he created real things, important believable discoveries. Things Jan wanted to know but knew she shouldn't know. More confused than she had ever felt about the integrity of a suspected criminal, she was trapped in an invisible hi-tech dungeon. Her stool sunk to the basement for an emergency counselling session with Skipper.

"No regrets eh?" said Jan combing through the comforting fur. A clean page had been selected from an untroubled part of her mind and she began to scribble, out loud.

"So, you say it's possible to go and fix a few things that might be causing concern? That I… I mean the person, would still be themselves and life would carry on in a more desirable way?"

"Yes," confirmed Mike.

"Sorry," said Jan raising herself up from the floor, "that was hypothetical, you know, not a wish list or anything. Has anyone actually been through this and come out alive?"

"Yes, of course. So far, all of my guinea pigs have been agents on a field skills improvement programme. They believe they're here to take part in mental resilience therapy with light and sound cues, which is true up to a point. The reality of course is that they've stepped out onto the Proximity Highway and made a *real* change, a permanent swap. They won't remember the *Timestep* experience, only being seated on my elaborate bandstand so the security risk is zero.

"Jeez, you brain wash the poor sods. Leaving yourself wide open to decades of insurance claims if you ask me," said Hayley idly pulling at areas of her chin as if to dispel the facelift comment.

"Being a top-flight agent in the security services involves being virtually owned by the organisation, it's part of the risk and reward package enjoyed at that level. Besides, they will have signed numerous disclaimers before they make the journey down here. With the successful six looking to improve the same strand to varying degrees, they should all leave here singing from the same song book eh, Jan?"

"Right, yes I see. So, in terms of the security risk who *does* know about this?"

"Apart from the DAMEN? Which is a silly acronym for 'Don't Ask Men' open to irresistible abuse don't you think? There's supposed to be a comma after 'Ask' but why bother? Anyway, it was the DAMEN that gave me the brief and arranged a fee from the darkest recess of the organisation."

"Yes, apart from the DAMEN." Jan had already received the chilling predictive text message into anxiety central but wanted Mike to confirm the reality.

"Me of course and now... you two."

"Yes, but why? Mike, why?"

Where is the bubble wrap when you need it? thought Jan as a heavy lump of sinking doom plummeted towards her tortured depths. Cod what danger we are in, why has he put us at risk? We have been betrayed by an assassin grinning and reminding us of childhood innocence. Did he really hate us that much that it has come to this, a revengeful stitch up?

At her full stool height, Hayley assumed her position as head of the family. Possessed by a largely unstable soul that breathed fire through red mist.

"You flaming drongo! You've shoved us into your scandalous threat to national security. Now, I really am going to get into trouble, my passport taken and I'll never see me homeland again."

"This is your homeland," said Jan sifting through the hysteria for relevant points.

With the stool sufficiently lowered, Hayley leapt to her feet.

"Are you stitching us up, mate? cos Jan and I, we've got some moves you know; don't think for a minute that we won't deck you and shoot through."

"Whoa, whoa calm down, Sis," he said folding his arms in the Elliot way.

"Hey," sparked Hayley still considering a left hook. "What's with you doing the elbow thing again? Jan does that you know, holds onto them, I reckon it's cos she's scared of herself or something."

"I'm not surprised," smiled Mike holding tight as he twisted playfully from side to side. "We all did it, as I remember. Our secret code, holding the circle, a sign of unity."

The intimate revelation from long ago caught Jan unawares. The man before her represented a symbol of denial and angst, an open wound that had burdened her entire adult life. He was not a man who should be permitted to romanticise their childhood with tales of solidarity. This had been Jan's crusade, the chance to clear her conscience and bury the remains for ever. But now, he truly had the upper hand, playing her for a fool with his carefully selected infantile references as he lured her towards some wretched end.

Hayley emerged from her mist cloud and bounced excitedly with thoughts from long ago.

"Yes, I remember now, Mikey. Poor aunt Eth, we stuck to our stories and woe betide the person who let those arms slip. She got to realise that we would just stick together no matter how unbelievably bonkers our explanations were. Jeez, just remembered that one where we'd taken apples off the tree next door. Mr Aitch must have seen us but we stuck together, totally in denial. It was only when she suggested a search of our rooms that you started blinking like a loony, you blinking loony. Nearly let them arms go, boy that was a close one. Lucky she was only bluffing I say."

Transported by the comforting wave of the Antipodean storyteller, Jan could remember all too well those wonderful moments of unbreakable unity. Huddling together, protecting each other no matter what, solid in their silliness until the abrupt end when Hayley chose to abandon them and everything changed.

We *were* like that once, she thought, connected and trusting, learning to work together and care for each other when life had left us exposed and vulnerable.

They made their own rules, moved forward and were happy, well most of the time. But as quickly as this warm wave had scooped her up, it dropped her harshly onto a shingle beach in a moment of blinding guilt, the memory now swathed by a curtain of crime.

Theft, she declared to the internal jury. Scrumping apples is *theft*. Did you not grasp the gravity of these acts? More skeletons, more crime littering my life, what kind of child was I?

"Not too man to say I missed our little ways," said Mike wandering over to a collection of sparkly black units along the far wall. An intense beam of blue light outlined his frame as he bumped around with the cupboard doors.

Jan kept vigil as best she could with fading eyes and tattered senses. She needed to stay a step ahead but this was his domain, he was familiar with these cupboards and drawers, he knew how this bandstand apparatus worked and he knew *exactly* how far Jan would have to run to reach freedom.

A repetitive chant was reverberating through the confines of her frazzled mind. Carried by an army that marched through her head, the rallying cry grew louder and burst across the battlefield.

'Stockholm, Stockholm, Stockholm'.

It mustn't be ignored; she must yield to common sense. This might be the only way to get out of this alive, she checked through what she could remember of the criteria.

First, you experience something terrifying. Well, that's true, I'm locked in with a mad man: Tick. I had to ask to go to the loo and he was outside waiting in the corridor – he has control: Tick. Mike is the only person who can save us; we have to believe in his contraption, like we really *do* believe. Oh cod, I'll have to remember some of that technical stuff, but I've already been humouring him, he must have noticed, if only there was a small act of kindness from him, then I'd be sure he wants us to live.

"Cup of tea?" asked Mike placing a small police box on the desk.

Oh, cod in Devon! I told you so: Tick.

"Bonza, and here was me wondering whether the depressing future would still serve tea. Milk with one sugar thanks, Mikey."

"Jan? you look miles away, what can I brew for you?"

"Tea please, no sugar, just milk, however it comes really, I don't want to be a nuisance or awkward or put you to any trouble."

In an effort to stop the tidal wave of emotion leaking out across the checker plate floor, she gripped the edge of her stool with white knuckled determination. The Gucci equipment, possessing either humour or intelligence, responded to her needs by swiftly launching her towards the ceiling where, legs dangling, she looked down on Mike.

No, no, you mustn't get the upper hand, you must be subservient and agreeable, get down, get down. Jan wrestled with her face, trying desperately to keep private concerns away from her captor.

"If you'd shared a room with her, you'd know that she gets like this when she's tired – a right grumpy gecko."

"Sorry, yes, not used to the equipment, but I can work on that, I'm definitely on-board with the project, count me in." She screwed up her face again. Shut up, Jan, shut up you muppet.

Mike returned to the small tea station allowing Jan the privacy she desired for a quiet descent to the lower ground floor of subservience. Red faced and unattractively tortured, she hopped off the stool and knelt beside Skipper.

Surely this was just a replay of childhood, where you jostle for position, shout, sulk and celebrate until the soft bedtime bell calls time. Issues would magically evaporate and set the scene for a happy tomorrow. But Jan knew that at five minutes to midnight it was unlikely. Even a child could see they weren't even close to any sort of resolution, fluffy pillows or peace.

The rekindled sense of duty to save Hayley and hand Mike over to the police still knocked loudly on her back door. While at the front of her mind, survival had set off in a different direction altogether, a path that was neither familiar nor comfortable.

Mike served the drinks and quickly took the lid off the police box, shaking the contents gently in front of his sisters.

"This is a first," said Hayley relaxing almost too far back, "Mike making us tea."

"Well," said Jan standing up, "the last time we were all together, he wasn't allowed to operate the kettle, too young to be exposed to dangerous domestic appliances." She selected a chocolate biscuit and resumed her position on the stool.

Sharing those few restorative moments with Skipper had injected new hope. The panic on the Stockholm exchange had eased, order was restored and Jan could focus her attention on their immediate predicament.

The copper coloured bandstand, that reminded Jan of a vintage birdcage, seemed little more than a benign lump of metalwork that dominated the room except, it was a secret. A secret that Mike had casually introduced as he reminisced with affection about their early life. Was he playing a well-rehearsed mind game, preparing for the final showdown?

She dunked and deliberated, allowing herself a moment of work place reflection. These, she thought, were good biscuits; they didn't just splosh into the mug at the first sign of dunking. It was only a fraction of a second later that half the biscuit disappeared into the depths of the tea and caused an equal and opposite reaction as hot liquid sloshed onto the floor.

Skipper mobilised and shuffled her head close enough to reach the droplets with one glide of her tongue before she flopped, eyes closed, into an approximation of sleep.

Hayley and Mike watched, then dared to laugh at the minor catastrophe enveloping their semi-perfectionist sister. Much to her own surprise, Jan didn't react. Instead she allowed herself to be seen as fallible which, under the circumstances, was quite a step.

She smiled into the middle distance as their voices faded into that muffled sound you experience when sinking underwater. All connection to time and place swirled in a vortex of thick paper glue. She was wrapped and restricted, unable to engage or scream, not that Jan screamed ordinarily, but the idea of not having free will had garnered her spirit. The grip on her mug tightened as she pulled herself from the slippery edge of her flat world on a makeshift raft of hope.

"You still didn't answer my question," she gasped. "Why have you let us in on your secret; why have you put us in such a dangerous position?"

Her eyes cleared and locked so firmly onto Mike that she felt in command of his soul. Truth or dare? Good guy bad guy? Stockholm or, or Skegness? If time was so important, then *now* was the time, she *needed* to know. But she wouldn't know.

A hail of hammering propelled Skipper into action. Charged with dog adrenalin, she switched from sleep state to full on security barking as she challenged the noise with her loud throaty woof.

Jan shuddered like a horse shaking every bone in its body down to the hoof clattering crescendo. Instinctively she turned to the threat, the unrelenting discordant din that punched deep into her diaphragm. Hayley closed ranks; a welcome distraction and comfort at her shoulder.

"I think we've got company," said Mike moving towards them.

One day of retirement, that's all she could manage, a day of half-truths and mystery, deception and dishonesty and above all, disappointment. She'd been thrust into the light, centre stage at midnight in Mike's futuristic pantomime where she could be certain of only one thing; this late-night intruder wasn't Cinderella.

CHAPTER 22

An insipid vapour of silent apprehension filtered through the building and smothered all that dared to breathe. The fortress had been breached; the enemy were within – somewhere.

Jan's back was against the wall near the sink, propped up by her brother and sister in a loose embrace. A princess amongst thieves might have described them yesterday but today, lines were blurred after mitigation had shown up and brought doubt into the mix. Whatever the truth or integrity of her siblings, right now she stood, not quite solidly but clearly, on the side of family.

Sounds of a scuffle and raised voices in the corridor sent Skipper bouncing towards the door. Barely able to contain herself she barked and jumped and gave it her all.

Then, with a grandeur beyond its frame, the door flung open and there, peacocking on the threshold, stood the long-lost French boys who were obviously not quite so lost.

Skipper's bark surrendered to the enthusiasm of her tail as she nuzzled the nearest French hand; greeting the intruders as every good guard dog shouldn't.

"I think she needs more training," said Mike to his sisters.

"Ah ha!" said the taller of the two as he brandished what appeared to be a handgun. "You sink you can give uz zer slippers, eh? Vee ver not flued by your dressing games."

"What took you so long then, bright boy?" offered Hayley moving slightly forward.

"Stop, stop, stop! We will not be made your monkeys. *Garçon* the regrets will be mine. Stop us we kill you."

With an impatient prod to the arm, the speaker shouted at his smaller accomplice, *"maintenant imbécile!"*

Hurriedly the *imbécile* took a folded sheet of foolscap from his trouser pocket and stepped towards the crowd.

Mike unfolded the paper with a theatrical flourish, cleared his throat and voiced the request written in short English sentences.

"This is the demanding. You demonstrate regret machine. I take regret machine. I kill you. If resistance you die. If police you die. If take me the fool you die. Signed *Voleur Payé*."

"*Voleur Payé?* how's your French, Sis?" he asked, turning to Jan.

"*Voleur Payé* or Paid Thief is the anagram of Edith Piaf and no regrets, that's all we know."

"Yes, got it now thanks, so much for top-secret, I thought it might be them."

"Silence! I will be speaking, *moi parle moi!*"

"Jeez Mike, what now?" asked Hayley as she pressed into the wall, her eyes fixed on the tall one.

"Silence!"

"Alright mate, keep yer toupee on," she continued.

The room swirled with movement as the Edith Piaf boys dashed between the bandstand and the laptop in a hopeless effort to determine if they themselves could operate the gateway to world domination. The workshop felt crowded, dangerous and stuffy as cold tea and sweet biscuits blended disagreeably with panting dog and garlic breath.

The cabaret, worthy of star billing at the *Folies-Bergère*, made lavish use of the space as they chest slapped and toe stamped to a chorus of little-known expletives.

During this self-absorbed chaos, Mike managed to whisper some useful guidance to his sisters.

"Just follow my lead, I'll need you to trust me but just go with it."

"Jan isn't big with the old trust thing at the moment, had a few of her high hopes dashed already today," said Hayley.

"That was yesterday actually, it's now 00:13 although, the way things are going, today isn't looking much better."

Jan's hand fell onto the soft comforting head of her rescue dog, the only creature capable of saving this drowning fool. She was caught in a maelstrom of complicated family crime while the French seemed to be paddling off to victory. But there was no time for reflection or complacency, they were all destined to be killed or arrested for their part in cod knows what. With the turn for the worse languishing on the road behind, the time for action was now. But how exactly? Jan felt so far away from her familiar operating circle that she might as well have been on the moon.

"Poor old Jan," whispered Hayley a bit too loudly, "are you still crawling about under the weight of all this dishonesty?"

"There's no dishonesty here, Jan," said Mike his voice gentle and reassuring.

But that wasn't true, it couldn't be, thought Jan. The workshop was awash with a sophisticated selection of law benders and breakers.

"Silence, silence," barked the French foreign leader as he watched his imbecile bounce from seat to seat in the bandstand. After a failed but entertainingly good effort to make it work, the leader changed direction.

"Garçon, garçon ici, ici," he said beckoning with the gun.

"Well, looks like I'm the only *garçon* in the room," said Mike looking at Jan before adding, "that does mean boy doesn't it?"

"Silence!" shouted the spokesman who had called time on the seat bouncing activity. He manhandled his colleague from the bandstand and redeployed him to the task of translator.

"Switch it on *s'il vous plaît*, please," he said

"Simple," said Mike responding warmly to this first sign of manners.

The activated laptop promptly lit up the bandstand. Each seat illuminated by a bank of miniscule green lights from above. An intense white light formed a circle on the floor beneath whilst a bead of red glowed with bloodshot intensity through the loosely draped lap straps.

The eyes of the spokesman beamed as brightly as the bandstand beads as he rushed up the steps to twirl upon its stage.

"Oui, oui, c'est magnifique!"

With all eyes on the entertainment, Mike discretely inserted the USB stick into a hidden port under the desk. This sleight of hand could easily have gone unnoticed, but Jan was all over it.

"Plus rapide!" shouted the spokesman with childlike effervescence as he rushed over to Mike. He pointed frantically at the desk and shoved his colleague in the arm – again.

With excitement mounting, Mike looked to be next in line for the poking and prodding treatment. But, with masterful serenity he engaged the attention of the docile one and began to fill his head with instructions – the simple version.

"Take a seat, any one will do and belt up," said Mike waiting for the translation to filter through in the manner intended.

The dutiful translator walked up the steps and surveyed the area like a passenger without allocated seating, he seemed to agonise over this unexpected choice. Eventually, with the leader dancing around behind him, a seat was selected on the left of the bandstand. Where, as instructed, he clicked the lap strap together which caused the red lights to turn blue.

Far from obediently following instructions, the leader seemed too full of beans to consider taking a seat. The man so close to his dream seemed lost in a final savouring moment at the dawn of rebirth. With narrowed eyes he scanned the room and all that stood within, before it became abundantly clear that his final moment was about to go on a bit.

"*Ici, ici,*" he demanded waving the gun recklessly in the direction of Jan and Hayley. Any childlike cheerfulness was cast aside possibly forever, as the evil alter ego grabbed hold of his senses. But he couldn't grab hold of the prisoners because Skipper had benignly blocked the way.

"*Ici, ici,*" he repeated wildly as he pointed towards the five remaining seats.

"Flaming Nora," said Hayley grabbing Jan's hand.

"No, no more," she cried shaking free from her sister as dignity and self-control swirled off down some polluted sink drain. Like a thoroughbred refusing to enter the starting gate, Jan was determined to hold her ground against the trembling anticipation of a heart that had every intention of racing in the three thirty at Aintree.

Why did I retire? This is worse than the worst shift I've ever endured, the normal world is hell in hooves. Monsters at every turn and no time to sleep. What does this contraption do? Where are the guinea pigs? Is this where I die? The fuse had been lit and glowed in a final fizzle before its spectacular explosion. With a desperate gasping breath, Jan launched into her dying declaration.

"NOOO!" she screamed, not only to the surprise of Mike and Hayley but also the, up to now, confident conductor of this swansong. Water splashed from her eyes with messy indifference as she began to bounce to the tune of a shameful adrenalin dance, with Skipper faithfully trying to keep pace.

"Stop!" he shouted. *"Toi ou le chien?"* He spoke with the cool detachment of a madman and lowered the gun towards Skipper.

Her legs buckled as though he had already pulled the trigger. She fell to the unreceptive floor and wrapped her arms around the neck of this most faithful of hounds. Her own spikey fear now smothered by a thick compassionate custard of lemon affection.

"Don't shoot, don't shoot," she sobbed into the warm woolly shoulder of her charge. "I'll sit down, I'll sit down, whatever you want."

With the message translated, the leader looked set to make a declaration. Like a gladiatorial grouse he swished pointedly across the bandstand stage searching for the words to convey his victory.

"Je suis triomphant, le pouvoir est à moi."

"What's the jumped up drongo saying now, mate?" said Hayley, with her eyes drilled into the translator.

"I am triumphant, power is mine."

"Silence!" said the strutting leader as he slammed the gun into his long-suffering colleague then hopped off down the steps.

Jan was as certain as she could be that the gun had lost interest in Skipper so she whispered reassurances and planted a kiss behind her ear before pushing up to grab Hayley's hand. In a slow show of unity, they took the steps of the bandstand as if walking across the Bridge of Sighs where life, as they had just come to know it, would end.

Skipper seemed unwilling to walk the same way and trotted off behind the desk to be with her dad.

The leader pointed the gun at the seats opposite the translator.

"Asseyez-vous, asseyez-vous," he yelled like an unstable being on the edge of a despotic destiny.

"Hey, Sis, you seem to be getting clucky over a dog, there's hope for you yet," said Hayley as she casually clipped her lap strap and stared at the beautiful bead of blue that held her in position.

Jan's futile effort to immediately unclip the lap strap had summoned demons from every phobia that had ever been labelled. She was trapped, her freedom curtailed and health and safety had been drop kicked into history. And, as her mind began to ferment at the vision of their burning bodies strapped in this human microwave, a trickle of religion popped up on the horizon.

"We got to stick together no matter what; do you hear me?" whispered Hayley clutching Jan's hand.

"Continue, continue," said the translator directing his words at Mike under the orders of his leader, who had now taken a seat.

The secured players turned their eyes to Mike who appeared by design to have taken control by stealth. Free to leave and turn out the lights he could chuckle in the face of their predicament, disappear into the darkness, never having to account for his actions. But he took the opportunity to milk his part by reading from an arguably made up safety brief. He spoke slowly, allowing the subservient comrade time to translate – assuming he himself had fully understood the instructions. Then, either scripted or improvised, Mike added some conditions.

"Now, each of you must share your pivotal scenario and your desired emotional change. The power of these combined emotions will determine the success of the journey along the Proximity Highway and must be declared in order to successfully complete your passage through the *Timestep*."

Mike looked at the gun-toting tiny tot of a terrorist, figuratively speaking, and asked for name and aim of transformation then scratched his beard and waited for the cogs of the interpreter to respond.

"I am the great Pierre. I will dominate the world. I will revisit a time when my mother made me cry because I was sorry for breaking her glasses. Well, I will not be sorry. This time I will laugh in the face of this stupid woman and I will take a hardened stand and never feel regret ever again. My mind is strong and I will find the path of the heartless and evil, the path I should have taken, I will abandon this weak version of me and come back with the mind I should have chosen at that moment. I am a Frenchman with the stupid sensitive mind of a girl. But not anymore, the power will be mine."

"Thank you," said Mike looking a little surprised. "That was comprehensive and very informed. But I digress, I'm sure we can make this a pleasant and successful journey for you."

Mutterings were exchanged in the French arc and in the English arc, Jan made a quiet observation.

"It doesn't feel very scientific all this."

"Just the modern way I expect, Sis; science isn't like it was when we went to school."

"Silence!" shouted Pierre, now positively alight at the prospect of entering this exchange programme for the troubled mind.

Mike, having tapped enough characters on the laptop, turned his attention to the translator.

"Name and journey plan," he said blandly as though he were behind the glass at a British Rail ticket office.

"Jean Paul. I will be helping Pierre when he is ruling the world and I will be thinking very hard of the time when my father died. But I will not have the pain. I will find the me and become the person who feels nothing; pain will not touch me; I will be blank."

"Might be easier than you think," said Mike quietly as his fingers tapped across the keyboard.

"Hayley, what emotional journey are you undertaking and what incident will see your transformation?"

"Jeez Mikey, I didn't even know I was going to be doing this, you think I've had time to think about how to make my life better and which parallel me I'd rather be? I mean how long have you got? There's a lot of fixing to be done in this seat."

Pierre began to fidget. Probably because, on his pig-headed road to redemption, he had failed to take into consideration the baggage allowance of his captives.

As they sat, each in their own world, in the lounge for delayed departures, Jan was consumed by her failings. Why didn't I keep Hayley away from harm? Family should always come first and I *have* a family, *I* have a family. A transitory tropical storm forced her to fumble in the pocket that contained the disintegrated tissue. A fool's errand like my stupid attitude towards my sister. She looked at Hayley's damp blue hands as they sulked in her lap drenched with schoolgirl sweat as she struggled to remember what she'd done with her homework.

The room had disappeared behind several millimetres of salty water. Jan's breath became laboured her voice barely audible.

"I love my family," she sobbed, whilst offering a prayer, not to the gods but to any armed response unit that was listening and could attend.

Of course, Mike was family too; only it didn't appear that he'd received the epiphany email. He still seemed hell-bent on destroying the minds of those he's supposed to love and yet, why *should* he love her after he had been shown such blatant indifference and a woeful level of care?

Her day with Hayley now flashed before her, re-tinted with the breath-taking, colourful fragments of fun that she'd failed to see. They had lived, learned and survived in some style. The first day of the rest of her retirement. These words she'd grown fond of repeating, were now confined to history. History with highlights and a day she wouldn't have missed for the world.

Unfortunately, the early hours of Tuesday morning didn't look as promising, Mike had curtailed their fun. A blue strap, a tiny lap trap had control of the rest of her life, a prisoner on the highway to oblivion with the deluded duo.

Hayley's prolonged bout of hand-wringing had collided with Pierre's lack of patience. The gun, now wide awake and animated, began pointing around the room forcing Hayley to respond with a hasty summary of her complicated world.

"Look mate," she said catching Pierre's contorting face, "I don't necessarily need to fix my messed-up life; I am, as it happens, pretty happy with my lot. But I might just have to look at tolerance and see if I can find the me who manages to put up with the crazy people like you without wanting to knock your flaming block off!" Hayley tried to stand but was held firmly. "Jeez, I suppose if I had the chance I'd go back to a time before Linda, look for me happy tolerant head."

"The mysterious Linda," said Mike. "Would you like to elaborate?"

"Not now, life's too short."

Pierre seemed equally frustrated by the seat clamp that curtailed his expressive desires. So, like an indecisive squirrel, he pointed the gun one to the other and then back again as though he might be considering how to hit them both with one bullet.

"Femmes stupides!"

"I might not have finished yet, mate. I'm thinking that if this is the final journey, I might want to record a few words for me kids."

"Silence!"

Jan despised him; he mined some acrid angst from deep within her soul and scorched her with an unfamiliar hate fuelled acid. How dare he dismiss my sister's turn? she seethed.

Like a baby in a high chair, Pierre seemed determined to squirm free of his trappings but publicly failed. Instead, he unleashed his pent-up frustration on Jean Paul. He rattled loudly in his native tongue, using the butt to emphasise the important bits, forcing the distressed Jean Paul to quickly translate the message.

"You will hate me, I will make you hate me and I will succeed, the power will be mine."

His words pushed Jan to the edge of a disused mine shaft that echoed to the sound of a crow bar clanging to the bottom. She would not help him by hating him, she must not slip. Concentrate, breathe, concentrate, breathe, find the sea, find the peaceful, find the calm, don't you dare help another Cod ham criminal.

"Okay," said Mike. "Finally, it's you Jan. What do you hope to achieve from this emotionally transformational journey?"

"Erm."

Pierre's unsupportive behaviour within the group, forced Jan into her dimly lit library of discomfort where every volume was a tribute to public humiliation. She wanted to disappear, disengage from the session, admit defeat and die – well, not exactly, not yet. But these group introductions were always the worst part of training or therapy. This requirement to state your name and your role in a clear and concise manner was fundamentally debilitating. Voices tumble towards you like a row of dominos, vocal cords dissolve and you struggle to remember your name. Then, compelled to speak, you mess it up, it's all over. You switch off from the class to take shelter and a vow of silence as you watch the clock until the session is over.

"Erm," she repeated in case, perhaps, there was any doubt that she was already a hideous pulp of emotions.

"Plus rapide!" shouted Pierre.

"Faster!" shouted Jean Paul.

Too tired to care and now, too far removed from the audience, she decided to go for it.

"I'm Jan, I have trouble with anxiety, it started when I realised my world is not perfect and I could not ever hope to be good enough to fix the lives of victims I have met through unjust and unfair circumstances. I have failed my family, because the burden of responsibility was too great. I must restore the wrongs in areas where I don't even know what is supposed to be right. I am not free; I am shackled to a life of repentance and I don't even have religion to guide me."

"Plus rapide, plus rapide," shouted Pierre.

"You're not even supposed to interrupt when someone in the group is talking, it knocks their confidence and is disrespectful," snuffled Jan from a small animal bed somewhere in a large draughty kitchen. Tears flowed again and her speech was about to require interpretation. "I, I," she stumbled, "need to have no regrets, I need to find acceptance and understanding, I need to forgive myself."

Hayley took hold of Jan's hand as her tough little sister fell to pieces in a group of select participants.

"Assez, assez!"

"Enough," said Jean Paul actively leaning away from Pierre and the gun.

"Okay," said Mike, taking control of the situation. "The combined power of quantum consciousness will determine the spectrum of strands that can be accessed within the parallel multiverse. The scores, if you like, are two for evil and broadly, two for tolerance which are conflicting emotions. However, we should be able to generate a level of power to fulfil your wishes." Mike addressed the audience generally and routinely with only a slight nod towards the significance of the fifty-fifty score card.

He dimmed the house lights and viewed his illuminated creation through eyes washed with pride. This atmospheric light would allow the travellers to prepare mentally as they waved a fond farewell to the old and journeyed to the new. But Pierre and Jean Paul *weren't* preparing mentally, they were translating.

The fifty-fifty penny had finally dropped with heft into Pierre's lap with his dream of world domination now looking a bit wishy washy thanks to Jan and Hayley. As his feet began to beat like a bare footed sprinter on a grape press it wasn't unreasonable to assume that he was about to explode.

With a face of grated scarlet, he screamed like a banshee *"Merde, merde!"* Then, raising the gun, he took aim at the desk where Skipper lay and shouted *"Tu détesteras!"* and pulled the trigger.

Jan screamed, letting out a lifetime of emotion. "You bustard! You bustard!" she sobbed, no longer caring for how this might end, she just wanted this day to stop.

"You will hate," added Jean Paul totally surplus to requirements.

"You flaming drongo." Hayley looked close to ripping his head off only, she couldn't reach.

Pierre slumped, exhausted from his deed, eyes on fire like the megalomaniac he hoped to become.

Mike had control, icily composed in his mysterious domain. Their destiny held in the hands that tapped their final taps. And then it was done, he leant back and smiled through his beardy face and folded his Elliot arms.

Hayley clocked him and copied, then passed the message along, only Jan wasn't paying attention, she'd pulled up the drawbridge to grieve in the darkness. So, like a deranged woodpecker desperate to make a hole in the fortress, Hayley prodded her rib cage until a crack appeared and forced Jan to turn. Wearily, she stared towards Hayley and then noticed Mike in the background.

Held in the tightest cameo, the significance of his posture screamed at the child within. The circle was closing but who the halibut could she trust? With only seconds to spare, Jan gripped her elbows as the bandstand lights turned to orange.

CHAPTER 23

In a few seconds time Mike would head up the homecoming, evaluate the success of his endeavours and deal with the aftermath. But, before all that, his priority lay under the desk.

Bent almost double, he ducked down to find an ugly crease in the metal panel. Proof, if ever it were needed, that expensive furniture was worth every penny.

Held silently in the activated material, the bullet had done no harm to man nor beast. Skipper was stretched out across his right deck shoe, as comfortable in these surroundings as her dad.

The journey was over, pottery people flashed briefly in the kiln, soon to awake resplendent into the dawn of the rest of their lives. Bathed by a short period of exhaustion, they should emerge from a different volume of the same tale, coaxed by Mike into the here and now, the only now that should be remembered.

As Pierre swayed a little and dropped the gun, Mike took his cue and recovered it to the bottom drawer of the lifesaving desk.

Jean Paul wrestled with his shoulders pulling them up from imaginary bed clothes like a man disturbed in the middle of the night which, as things go, was quite correct.

Mike returned the workshop to house light order, prompting further sluggish motion from the party.

With Jean Paul reacting as though a figure was moving about in his bedroom.

"Excusez-moi," he asked.

"Ah, hello," said Mike perching on the corner of the battle worn desk.

"Je suis français."

"I thought so."

Pierre looked at Jean Paul through half lidded eyes before his weighty head fell upon his chest. A further galvanized effort thrust his chin forward as he squinted in the general direction of Jan and Hayley.

"Qu'est-ce que c'est?"

"Je ne sais pas," replied Jean Paul softly raising his hands to the bandstand as though connecting with a deity.

"First test complete," said Mike privately as he swivelled towards the laptop and tapped out the lap strap code changing blue to red.

Jean Paul fiddled with the clasp and managed to free himself. At first Pierre did nothing, he was far away, shallow breathing like a person who felt very sick. He appeared to stabilise then grappled with the simple clasp, pushing the strap aside. He made no further attempt to move and remained in his seat as though he had been instructed to do so by some absent pilot.

Mike hopped up onto his magnificent creation again and placed a hand on Hayley's shoulder and squeezed gently.

"Are you okay?" he asked.

"Sure, never better, must have fallen asleep in this comfy chair. Is this your hospitality level?"

He smiled as though pleased with the results from this latest crop of troubled minds. Just one more to check and she looked spark out.

Hayley unclipped her strap and looked across at the French boys.

"Are we safe?"

"It's going well so far," said Mike putting his hand on Jan's shoulder.

As her cheek brushed the back of his warm hand, dreams slipped away and her eyes popped out through their reddened puffy containers.

"Are you still in there?" he asked as she tried to organise her face.

"I'm a bit hungry," she said softly.

"Don't talk about food do you know how long it's been since Macca D's? I could eat a yard full of kangaroos." Hayley stretched out her legs, shifted her weight about but remained seated.

"*Monsieur,* Pierre and Jean Paul do not wish to stay in nightie club. Attend to our coats *s'il vous plaît.*"

"Wee, of course, I'll see what I can do."

But, before his foot could touch the checker plate, the workshop door crashed open to release a long line of bellowing, booming personnel crammed into the corridor. With lateness marked all over their report, it was safe to assume that the sweeping line of black spilling into the workshop was an armed police unit.

"Police, get down. On the floor where I can see your hands! Get down now!"

Dressed in an enormous amount of black, their pockets bulged with armoury and other items useful to shouty officers like food and throat lozenges. And every head sported a black canvas cap neatly embroidered with the word 'Police', to avoid any doubt.

Still groggy from their recent experience, the four bandstand turns slid from their seats onto all fours then collapsed. Any thoughts of sleep were soon stamped out by a nervous bunch of armadillos who methodically searched for anything they deemed relevant.

With no weapons of mass description or anything more exciting than a soggy tissue in Jan's pocket, she was allowed to return to her seat; Hayley soon followed. Names and details were taken above the noise of twitchy officers still spouting important nonsense to each other.

Through the black forest of formidable legs Jan caught sight of Skipper weaving her way through the excitement. She slipped from her chair but this time, like a child eager to greet a new puppy.

"Hello, old friend," she said scooping up the adorable face. Still fragile and puffy, her eyes filled as she touched Skipper's wet nose with her own. "I thought I'd lost you."

"Jeez, how many more guys, oh and girls, can you get in here?" said Hayley having spotted two female officers near the door. "Not sure where Mike has got to though."

Jan floated on the gentle swell of a waterbed, feeling more rational than she had been for the past twenty-four hours or so.

"What just happened?"

"Well," said Hayley, beneath the hubbub of activity, "I'm not entirely certain but have you noticed a change in the garlic twins?"

"They do seem subdued and definitely less aggressive. I don't know about you but I feel like I'm still getting over a rather long and emotional dream, I keep getting little flashbacks but I can't really remember what went on oh, except you were in it."

"Yeah kind of the same for me, Sis."

Jan returned to the vexing question of resources and where all these officers had come from, the last time she could remember seeing this many was in the canteen on a training day. But that thought was soon swept aside by a different colour in the crowd, a familiar face or rather some familiar hairy knuckled fingers. Stifling a yawn and blinking him into reality, she formally recognised PC Kent Collins, her toilet companion.

"Hi Jan, how are you holding up?"

"Oh hi," she said feeling strangely comforted. Whether this rested with the fact that he was indeed the police officer he had claimed to be or whether it was more to do with feeling like warm bubbly custard from the moment he came into view.

"I've been worried about you, going off on your own like that. Didn't want it to get messy, that's why we kept a tail on you after the switch."

"Is that a police expression, *messy?*" asked Hayley.

Jan interrupted. "Sorry, Kent, this is Hayley, my sister."

"Yes, we know all about Hayley but it's nice to finally be introduced."

Hayley hesitated. "You know all about me?"

"Well, yes without your connection we wouldn't have collared the French pair with Mike. Or more appropriately, it wouldn't have been as interesting," he smiled a warm, soothing steamed pudding sort of smile.

"I mean, you know *everything?*"

He scrutinised her face like the police often do. "Everything we need to know," he added slowly.

"Are you going to arrest me?"

Jan pulled in tight, leaning across Hayley to shield her from further inquisition.

"I hardly think that's called for; we can barely remember what's just happened. So, why did you eventually decide to turn up?" she diverted.

"Yes, *eventually* that is, I mean you police never flaming get here on time I've noticed."

"Well, I can't give everything away, but like I said, we had a small follow team with you the whole time. Most of our units were with the decoy, keeping an eye on the subject vehicle. We had to keep *Voleur Payé* out of the picture until we were certain you'd found Mike. Having all our resources in one town ran too great a risk. But, with the decoy vehicle near to running out of fuel…"

"What?" said Jan sufficiently awake to understand whose car he was referring to.

"Yeah but we were in the *right* town, this is where you and your police buddies should have been. I mean how difficult is this police work?"

"Well, even when we do finally arrive, procedures have to be followed, we have to act on the most up to date intelligence. What I'm trying to say is – sorry we were late but quick decisions aren't us."

"Well, hoorah for British intelligence," said Jan adding her own slice of sarcasm.

"Look, you're safe and those guys look a lot calmer than they have been all day so hopefully without any harm or injury, we can get this tidied up."

"Hang on a second, mate, we *were* nearly injured. Pierre took a shot at the desk over there."

Discovering how close a rescue team had been in their moment of need seemed inflammatory to Hayley at this hour of the morning.

"Yeah, we heard the shot when we were positioned outside," said Kent who appeared to be retreating into the need to know corner.

"You heard a shot and it still takes you half a day to get your butts in here?" said Hayley with eyebrows dancing off towards her hairline.

"Risk assessments and orders, you know. I mean, what if entering in a blaze of glory put more lives at risk? Besides, we didn't hear anyone scream," he added playfully.

"You can't scream if you're dead, mate."

Jan shuddered on the side-lines of his familiar coy authority, the secret police, the language and play of her old career. While here, in her new life, the recent near-death experience was being shown with cringeworthy highlights in the theatre of her mind.

"Did you hear me shout the B word?" she asked as her eyes idled through the sea of black.

"I couldn't possibly say," replied Kent raising an eyebrow. "Anyway, do you know where the gun is now?"

"I don't," said Jan blandly.

The tired French party-goers were taken from the room in handcuffs prompting a lyrical, barely recognisable, response. It was a modern-day marvel for Jan to witness forward thinking officers using a mobile phone to record this dialogue after caution in case, it may indeed, be given in evidence.

Her mind wandered into the future of policing where the hi-tech world would necessitate a different kind of officer to the recruit of thirty years ago. She had joined a force that resented the complicated ways of women and their desire to wear trousers. But, over the years, as the handbag disappeared into the closet, a positive transformation took place that allowed women to be equal among men but still two steps behind society.

Eventually the gun was located and made safe, under the watchful lens of a forensic officer who, equipped with a complicated flashy camera, captured the desk in the appropriate evidential way. A further SD card brimmed with pictures of the embedded bullet prior to its extraction. This was swiftly followed by an indulgent number of snaps of the desk itself. So many in fact that Jan felt certain it would appear in a glossy magazine anytime soon flaunting a shameless price tag.

It was now 01:10 on day two of retirement she noted, acutely aware that she was still heavily involved with police work. Her concern faded to soft focus over the specialised officers as they searched, sifted, bagged and tagged their way across the workshop. Will I ever experience an ordinary life? she thought as her hand fell lightly onto the ever-present Skipper.

"You girls still with us?" said Kent parting the sea of darkness with his comparatively colourful casual attire. "Now, the news is, you can leave the scene, I've found a quiet area for you where... well you know the drill, we just need statements before you go."

"Not two statements in one day?" said Hayley flapping her arms like a petulant penguin.

"Well, it is *actually* Tuesday now," he offered.

"Are you always this smart? Well, I don't think you can be, because it's common knowledge, Kent, that I am in fact on holiday. 'Welcome to the United Kingdom where you can spend half of your day writing statements and the other half being pursued by men in black'. Not sure what time will be left to see the sights and catch up with my long-lost family."

As life continued around her, Jan's liberation had been overshadowed by the elephant not in the room. The topic of conversation that had slipped out the back door without explanation. But she needed an explanation, there were still loose ends, boxes to tick and words to be spoken.

"Where's Mike?" she asked.

"He's been taken away for questioning," came the closed reply.

"Is he in a lot of trouble?" It was pointless to ask, almost foolish, she'd turned into a cul-de-sac and could go no further.

"I'm sure he'll be in touch as soon as he is able," offered Kent as if sensing her predicament.

"Looks like you might be right, Sis," said Hayley, "you know, surrounded by criminals and all that."

"I'm trying to be too tired to care," she said following Kent's lead as they left the inner workshop and found themselves in a large hall with a huge model railway running around the centre.

"Will you look at this? Do you think this is Mike's big train set? Wow, bonza." With eyes overburdened with delight, Hayley shook in that way that a dog often does just before they're released, unbridled, into an open space.

"We're safe in here, it's already been checked and cleared. A couple of officers will be along shortly to separate you up and take your statements. I must say, I just wanted to say…I'm glad you're safe." Looking as bushed as his witnesses, Kent remained professional, pushing on as Jan used to, until that final moment when units were stood down and released back to their own life cycle.

Even if her next question wasn't fully answered, Jan needed his opinion.

"Do you think there was ever a possibility that we wouldn't be? Safe I mean."

"You know how things are? It's been a long day for the team, lots of leads and loose ends. We weren't aware of the gun until about an hour ago, although it was always a consideration. Terrorists don't normally wing it and hope their posturing will do, do they?"

"Well, they did a lot of posturing especially that Pierre. I was ready to flatten him," said Hayley with a short burst of twilight energy.

"If it helps, we had your back and if it really helps, I wasn't about to let any physical harm come to you. Now, to prove a point or perhaps just distract you, I'll see if I can find some coffee. Although I think I may prove a disappointment on that front, I mean what are the chances of finding latte and sprinkles in this establishment?"

"You won't disappoint me, it's just such a special feeling to be part of the team, I'll be happy with whatever you can find."

"Me too," said Hayley. "And what about that rumour that you police people are always eating donuts? Wouldn't mind if you can find us some tucker whilst you're at it."

Kent smiled and set off on his quest to satisfy their needs.

"You like him don't you, Sis? Don't try and lie to me now, not that I think you would of course, I realise that you wouldn't do that sort of thing, you know, lying and stuff." Hayley pushed playfully into Jan's personal space.

For most of her adulthood as a single entity Jan had wandered through life with relative contentment. Unrestrained by a family umbilical cord that could pull her back to the nest for routine scrutiny and all-round ribbing. Her life had found protection under a thick sheen of turtle wax where the peaks and troughs of social high flying were viewed from the safety of her paddling pool. She could float in the shallow waters of excitement, on gentle ripples that bobbed her about without fear of being drowned. But now, a connecting cord had been hurled from the deep end and firmly snagged across Jan's orderly bows. Sailing under the flag of 'derring-do', Hayley had dropped anchor nearby, bearing the unexpected but most welcome treasures of kinship and belonging. All of which may have contributed to Jan's unguarded response.

"I can't even say it's the uniform, can I?"

"You know, I think we might be cracking the egg, whatever next?"

Jan rested her elbows on the barrier that surrounded the display, her eyes drawn to a miniature hedge maze and the plastic people that were standing in a shrub cul-de-sac.

If only my brain was this straightforward, thought Jan, who had easily found her way through the maze. She urged the plastic people to turn around and take the second left and the next right; to benefit from her vantage point. And how simple it all was, this puzzle without ambiguity where you could step back from a dead end without consequence or disaster, where you could have another go without guilt or regret.

It was at this point that she bounced off the barrier with a head full of words and a mouth full of sand.

"Hays, Hays," she spluttered, "am I remembering this correctly? I mean *did* something just happen?"

"What?" said Hayley pulling her nostalgic gaze from an expansive open-air car park filled with the retro vehicles of her youth.

"Hays, don't you remember Mike asked us to say what we wanted in the bandstand? Some experiment or other, like an embarrassing therapy session, we had to think about our emotions."

"Yeah, that's right, you blubbed everywhere and shouted at Pierre whilst you were about it."

"Okay yes, yes but, he said we could go and collect a different emotional path out of a situation, we could fix who we were by finding a strand or string or something.

"Put us on the spot there a bit, I wasn't prepared, hadn't done me homework. You know, if I'd had the time to think about it, I would have gone back before Leonard discovered dresses and enrol him on an outback survival weekend with a loin cloth and machete in the hope he'd come back as the man I loved."

"I don't think that's quite what Mike had in mind."

"Yeah, I know but it has made me think a bit. I mean I can't just go shopping with Linda. I can't help him in that way. I can't even be close; I mean am I loving Len or Linda? What goes through his or her head? No, it's too weird for me, I'm of that generation between the liberal sixties and the orange and brown of the seventies. Somewhere in there lie my morals and beliefs. I can't just adapt to the new ways of living, these new life styles. I can't be expected to be comfortable with all the rules and emotions that come out of the wardrobe."

As her mind rummaged along the costume rails looking for a suitable outfit for the occasion, Jan concluded that not knowing about a topic didn't mean she knew nothing.

"Well, perhaps, if you could just put that aside for the moment and ask yourself this; do you still love him?"

"Course I do, the stupid lummox. I love my Len; I just wish he hadn't flippin' found flaming frocks. It's Linda, flaming Linda. I mean, who agreed that she could move in anyway?"

Jan had no further questions, she was too tired to deal with the unfamiliar answers that this subject would bring. Her eyes faded across the miniature platforms and shunting yards as sleep lured her towards another mystifying dream. But the dream was shattered by an incessant cry.

"Fire, fire, fire!" shouted Hayley.

"What?" said Jan jumping like an all-round, ready for anything action hero. "Where?"

"Look, there on the little building. There's a fire engine and all the little guys are putting it out. Isn't that amazing?" she turned to Jan, eager to share the tableau. "You alright there? You don't have to get involved Sis, you've retired remember?"

Hayley, now robbed of the power of speech, turned her head and fell heavily onto the barrier. All further attempts to shout *Fire, Fire*, were lost in a snorting, wheezing mess. She grabbed Jan in a tussled embrace and then fell about laughing.

She surrendered, unable to resist the giant marshmallow that hugged her heart like nothing her adult world had ever provided. Shining cheeks touched and squigged as their bodies jiggled in foolish displays of shared humour.

"Come here, my little retired copper," said Hayley smoothing Jan's arms as she tried to pull away. "You're not getting all soggy on me, are you? This is happy, Sis, we don't need to cry at happy."

Jan stared at the carpet and the four shoes upon it, melting into a place where little else mattered except this. She became acutely aware of every part of her body as it brushed and hugged against her sister in simple childlike submission. A feeling so foolishly rejected and yet so badly relevant and required. A place to rest your heart when the playground has battered you, where crumpled minds are comforted and protected by the absolute love of a family.

Kent stepped into the moment with two mugs of coffee and a brown paper bag, the latter gripped between his teeth. And as the coffee changed hands, he rescued the bag.

"Not interrupting anything am I?"

"No, but well…"

"What she means is *yes,* Kent mate, the sisters are having a little reunion but it's okay to barge in if you're bearing gifts."

"Well, you'll be pleased with me then," he said smiling. "Shaunna and Mandy had these left over from their extended excursion through the Cornish countryside. You know how it is, we have to have car food on these long operations and stake outs."

"They were *eating* in my car?" said Jan with a mild hint towards stridency.

"Stand by for a flaming row," added Hayley winking playfully in Kent's direction.

"Come on, Jan, this has been successful, the team are sorting things out next door, we'll soon be free to leave, get you out of here and tumble into bed."

"Now that's what I call a bit forward, Kent," said Hayley continuing to tease.

He beamed an unflustered policeman's smile and looked at Jan.

"I promise, we will have your car valeted and refuelled and delivered back to you. You're welcome to hold on to the hire car until then and you even have my permission to use it for a careless three course dinner with gravy, if it will make you happy."

Jan acquiesced to no one in particular then took a bite of the slightly crispy, but welcome, donut.

"I've remembered what I said," blurted Hayley through a mouthful of the sweet claggy food. "I was thinking about tolerance; I mean I wanted to think about a lot of things but as it goes, tolerance was rattling around me head."

"That's funny," said Jan swallowing the contents of her mouth. "I was all over the place but the last thing I can really remember is you saying that. Tolerance was in my head too, I'm sure it was."

"Don't forget," said Kent, "put as much into your statement as you can, the officers will be here soon. I've got to get myself back to base, get booked off before the overtime budget gets blown on me being a tea boy. But I'll ring you later tomorrow, make sure you're okay and get the cars swapped over if you're ready." He hesitated with relaxed eyes glancing towards Jan.

"Take care of each other," he nodded respectfully and closed the door.

"You beauty!" said Hayley raising her donut hand to the ceiling.

CHAPTER 24

"I can't imagine retiring or even leaving," said PC Adam Lewinski. "This is the best job in the world and how can you ever stop being a police officer? It's ingrained, we're a family."

His words had gently nudged Jan into an emergent reality.

"I don't think you ever really say goodbye, you just get out of the river and walk along the bank instead. I think that's how it is."

Jan praised herself for the analogy of this special multifaceted family that swirled through the river of other people's lives. Assorted strokes and styles that pulled in the same direction under the watchful eye of the commander in a canoe shouting encouragement or having a quiet word.

As she struggled under the weight of her oak eyelids, she pushed up from the chair and shook hands with PC Lewinski.

"Good luck with the rest of your retirement," he said, "and remember – I'm paying your pension." He held her hand warmly and smiled. "Your sister shouldn't be too much longer."

As he disappeared in the direction of the bandstand, Skipper nudged through and trotted across for some unbridled attention.

Jan's hitherto, orderly way of life and associated peculiarities couldn't accommodate, on any level, the mess from dog feet and dander. Such thoughts had always been dismissed with cold indifference until, yesterday. Now she couldn't quite understand how anyone could ever consider living without a dog; this dog; Skipper.

"You know what's going on don't you, girl? I bet you know where your dad is and what this is all about."

She drifted to the bandstand, that brief moment when her face snuggled against Mike's reassuring hand. He hadn't caused her harm when he had the opportunity, at least not physically, but what revenge had he exacted on her mind? What destructive alchemy had been used to reshuffle her senses?

The total radio silence regarding his whereabouts was no surprise, Jan was well aware of how the system worked. Better to say nothing than to mislead, misinform or inadvertently raise hopes. There would be news when there was news and at least then it was more likely to be accurate.

So, with her questions unanswered, fear and concern strolled casually into view; harbingers of gathering doom – usually. But, on this occasion they had rearranged themselves into a small potpourri basket where they flopped onto a deep bed of fragrant rose petals.

And yet, the nature of Mike's crime still lingered. Was he a persistent offender? Why does he have such an honest and loyal dog and what about those deck shoes? Criminals wore branded trainers, knocked off chavvy clothing, this was the stereotypical streetwise criminal attire she was familiar with. They were confident and cheeky and could spout all the legal jargon learnt during state funded private lessons with their 'Brief'. Could this really be the world of Mike?

She couldn't decide right at this moment, even if she had all the facts to hand because Skipper was pacing side to side with increased intensity.

"Now, old friend, am I right in guessing that no one has considered your needs in all of this? Do you need to go outside?" she asked politely. Skipper pushed against Jan's leg and wagged her tail with meaningful thrusts.

"Okay, I'd better find you a lead or something, can't have you running off and adding to my woes."

Deciding that the small workshop may be the best place to look, Jan retraced her steps towards the fire exit. On the threshold to the large workshop she paused, concerned that fatigue had disrupted her navigation system. PC Lewinski and two plain clothed men, presumably officers, stood in front of another door across the room. She blinked as her neck flopped forward and her jaw slackened like a camel at the watering hole.

"Are you okay, ma'am?" enquired one of the officers.

"Yes, yes, I am looking for a lead," she stuttered.

"Yes, we've had a few of those here this evening," he joked flatly.

"The bandstand, the desk; it's gone," her words inviting confirmation and explanation in equal measure.

"Ah, yes," said the jokey officer, "evidence gathering."

"But seizing the whole room?" continued Jan with her mouth and eyes stretched wide.

"Yes, bit odd perhaps but we follow orders and get things done. Are you looking for the way out?"

"Yes, we came in through there," she said nodding at the door behind them. "I just need to walk the dog."

"Sorry, ma'am, yes of course, on you go." PC Lewinski opened the door as the officers stood aside.

Skipper showed little outward concern at the large empty space where her life was almost taken. She had been consumed by the immediate requirement for a large outdoor space and bounced off down the corridor. Jan flagged along on leaden legs weighed down by disbelief at the astonishing speed of the removal team.

The small workshop, the chaotic bench and the stopped clocks brought comfort and a sense of the familiar. Jan noted the time, 02:32, as Skipper weaved and whined at the fire door.

"This blue rope will have to do, Skip, nearest thing to a lead I can find."

The quickly fashioned noose slipped easily over her head as desperation grew and she danced on hind legs at the door bar. Then, in a moment of sheer joy, Jan and her new companion pushed out into the stillness where the desperate hound generously watered a tuft of grass at the top of the sloping car park.

A small block of flats and some aged cottages appeared indifferent to the early morning activity of their largest neighbour. An operation of stealth and secrecy, a higher order than any late-night, noisy warrant Jan had experienced.

A marked car and a badly parked silver Skoda hugged the main entrance doors from where PC Lewinski and another uniformed officer emerged.

"Your sister has just popped to the loo, hopefully she'll find her way out. Nice to meet you, goodnight, sleep well," he said as the clunky central locking mechanism breached the motionless morning.

Her attention returned in earnest to Skipper who, having fulfilled her call of nature and scent assessment, sat pointedly at the top of the service road, quiet in all but breath. The pattering, rattling job car that had percolated every window of every home in the village, faded away over the distant hill. And Jan perched on the cool kerbstone brushing her dusty hands with relaxed resignation.

Skipper, preoccupied and tethered, spun her shaggy head from front to back, as she absorbed every fragrant sound. Occasionally she stalled nose to nose to offload her findings directly into Jan's eyes. Each troubled in their own world, Jan had issues with the bandstand or rather, the lack thereof. She sifted between fact and reality, but her assumptions were flawed. There *had* been a bandstand, of that she was certain. She recalled Mike giving specific instructions regarding its apparent capabilities and their imminent journey towards change and improvement.

Did I go back and change into a street urchin with no regard for the cleanliness of my hands or my half decent trousers? Happy to perch on the public pavement without a sit mat? Cuddling a dog – of all things, when I don't know where it's been?

Her resignation at the point of no return was veiled with regret. Change forced against a lifetime of better judgement, her very being and values altered. Where have I gone to? Why has this happened? Who am I?

She turned to Skipper and was forced to acknowledge that her breathing was easier than her mind usually allowed in these circumstances. The unhurried uptake and release of the processed night air felt positively profound.

"Quite a lot has happened since we first met eh, girl?"

Skipper tilted her head, like dogs do when they are called upon to listen, and fixed her eyes attentively upon the speaker. Jan felt pressed to turn away and check the time but stopped herself.

"I don't know why I'm so concerned about the time; it's an old habit I suppose." She still had Skipper's undivided attention and didn't quite know how to switch it off.

"Are we surprised that Hayley is still in the building?" Jan shook her head and agreed with herself in that exaggerated manner often reserved for small child communication.

With the absent bandstand still high on the agenda, Jan began to wonder how Hayley's mind might have been affected.

"What change has she noticed, is she angry? If there's one thing I know about my sister she won't sit quietly whilst an opinion passes her by. No, rest assured, Skip," whispered Jan, "Hayley will be pushing for a refund but how? Without the bandstand, how can we go back?"

Jan's musing was interrupted by a resentful Robin that sat perkily on a green industrial wheelie bin and chirruped at the top of its little voice. This irritation of feathers was furious with the morning whisperer who had invaded his territory. A blackbird joined the rally for natural order and roused the seagulls. Silent rooftops became a stage for squabbling sea birds dreaming of chips and ice cream.

The beauty and optimism that pour into the gap between night and day tunes the rhythm of your heart, if you get up early enough. When nature sets the agenda and all you have to do is allow your soul to follow the plan. But invariably the agenda is pushed aside, swamped by commitments and worry; where the working week is largely at odds with the natural world.

As retirement spluttered up the dusty track of day two, it dawned on Jan that she was free from work, not that they'd been too much evidence of that so far. But nevertheless, this early morning moment held promise and potential. The bubbles in her stomach began to move with anticipation, excitement and hope.

"Skipper, my lovely thing, look how easy it is to breathe." She indulged herself with further calm and exaggerated breaths as if to prove to them both that recent events had not entirely frayed her nerves; anxiety having stepped out for a while.

Overhead the electric blue night would soon be infiltrated by the pale burning orange that nudged ever westward. Enjoying the moment, for the first time she could remember out of uniform and for the first time *ever* with a dog, Jan rested against Skipper. But it wasn't to last, the ever-vigilant watchdog was back on high alert, her eyes fixed on the far corner of the service road. Jan sensed the faint sound and rhythm of distant steps and scrambled to her feet. And with her heart at a gentle canter she tried to reverse towards the fire door. But, Skipper danced onto her hind legs and pulled the slippery rope from Jan's grasp and set off at a gallop towards the approaching male.

Mike was soon bowled over by the weight of his favourite fluff ball and rolled exuberantly across the gritty tarmac.

"Hello, Skip, how's my girl? Have you been keeping an eye on the place for me?"

"Mike? Mike, what happened?" exclaimed Jan trying to keep her voice down.

"Is that a friendly note of concern from my sister?" he said, brushing dust and gravel from his shorts. "Well, the day is getting better by the minute. How are you two doing, have they been treating you well?"

With Skipper bounding and bouncing at his heels Mike sauntered towards Jan. "Is there a name for that little jig, Sis, or are you just cold?"

"No, I'm fine," she said unconvincingly even to herself. His demeanour didn't fit her expectations. The criminal out on bail with that undeniable air of resentment was absent. His face, once again, radiated warmth and kindness with every step towards her. But, how could she trust this crackpot hobbyist and how dare he mess with her head and force her to change?

Mike wrapped his arm around her shoulder, guiding her back to the workshop as Skipper and the rope lead pranced along at his side.

If it hadn't been for the gripping paralysis caused by elbows clamped either side of her rib cage, Jan would have been out of the blocks and away, or at least that's what she imagined she might do.

"I'd better have a look at the damage eh?" he said with casual indifference.

The two plain clothed officers pushed through the fire door carrying the last of their exhibits.

"Hi Mike, are you all done?" enquired the jokey officer.

"Yeah, thanks for all your hard work, it's been a good job, hope you haven't left me a mess to clear up," he said flashing a boyish smile.

"It's not too bad, although I can't account for your sister, she's been in there a while unguarded. Anyway," he said extending his free hand, "we've got a long drive and a sack full of exhibits to catalogue." He shook Mike's hand with the warmth of a valued colleague, "stay out of trouble." He then turned to Jan once again, "Ma'am," he nodded.

The fear that had gripped her the first time she'd entered this building was notably absent, which gave her the confidence to close the fire door. Mike unleashed Skipper and after a short programme of fun and obedience, she settled with a chewy stick onto a scruffy picnic rug under the bench.

What if this was just fun and obedience? thought Jan, half resigned to the fate she knew she deserved. Mike had caught them and neutralised the cold indifference of the sisters that had left him to play in a world of his own. It was out of her hands; she knew that control of this situation had been snatched in her moment of weakness. Desperately she had wanted to say her piece and run for the hills, unhitch the baggage of life and regret. But in this elaborate ambush, Mike had engineered his own coup and successfully dealt with these two birds in a single orchestrated *Timestep*.

The billowing ripples of line-dried sheets that flapped through her mind seemed reluctant to throw caution at this wind. Even so, whilst she may have accepted passenger status in her own therapy, she wasn't about to throw in the towel completely so, staring at his shoes, she went for it.

"Mike, what have you done?"

He didn't get a chance to reply because the inner door was almost pushed from its hinges as Hayley entered with a flourish.

"Oh, hey Mikey, how's it going? Didn't expect to see you standing there. What's been happening and where has all your stuff gone?"

"These are good questions; you'll have to give me a minute though, I'd better have a quick check to see what they've done in the workshop, I'll be right back." He sauntered off in a Cornish kind of way.

"So, what's the story with Mike?" asked Hayley entwining Jan's arm in an affectionate gossip.

"I still don't know; I don't know what to think and he hasn't exactly been forthcoming. The minute I get to ask, you breeze in and Mike disappears again."

"Well, he's definitely had one of his toys confiscated *and* in the middle of the night. That doesn't just happen. Jeez, it's all very exciting to me, although I suppose you've seen it all before?"

"No, not on this scale, this is a whole new high budget blockbuster, which makes my career seem a bit tame. But I suppose it's all in the interpretation, talking of which, I need to ask you something."

"Fire away, Sis."

"The flight by fraud, is that your only crime?"

"Strewth, I didn't see that coming, I thought you'd let it go. But, seeing as you've asked, yes of course it flaming is what do you think I am? You know Sis, when you take a good look at all the so-called normal people around you, you'll start to see that some of the good people have had a past and maybe even a present. It's normal and okay for a bit of – 'oops, did I really just do that?' You don't want someone feeling your collar every five minutes whilst you're trying to get the hang of life."

Jan couldn't disagree it was a point well made; not all transgressions are punished, very few are witnessed and often, she hoped, those that knew better would cling to integrity, learn a lesson and thank their lucky stars. She held onto Hayley's arm and drifted introspectively to a parade ground where regrettable misdemeanours stood rank and file with medals and medallions for long service and special events. Even during her career as a sworn officer, she knew she could have done better.

"Have you fallen asleep, Sis? Or are you getting the hang of life on the outside?"

"I'm thinking." she said turning to the incident inside the missing bandstand where her final wish had been for tolerance.

Was it possible that the anguish of the past could simply be filed away in a place where it could happily exist without the need for a caretaker manager?

"They tidied up quite well," sighed Mike as he re-entered the room. "Still, that's a nice big space to build something else or extend the railway, or create another experience, who knows? Hey, look at you two almost dead on your feet I shouldn't wonder. Come on, we're all locked up here, it's time for a change of scenery."

As the harbour came into view the horizon split like a giant crisp packet spilling light across the dark glutinous sea. Thick protective walls, wide enough for vehicles and port machinery, curled around an assortment of colourful boats as they bobbed cosily to the rhythm of the dawn from their tranquil inner pond.

"How could you not love this place?" said Mike. "It fills me with supercharged energy and enthusiasm. Workshop days peppered with glorious walks and relaxation out here, such simple things, eh girls?"

"I'm on your wave length there, Mikey," said Hayley snuggling up to his arm. "I could stroll along here for hours with me little kid brother and the bristle hound. No, I'm not talking about you either, Skipper."

On his port side, comfortably separated by a trotting dog, Jan remained at arm's length. Too preoccupied in the shade of her mind to fully embrace a new beginning while her in-tray bulged with unanswered correspondence.

"You didn't answer my question, Mike, what have you done?" She shaded her eyes and held court with feet that were bathed in the burnt orange of a new day.

The pitted concrete path flowed molten as the sun intensified to show her hand. At the end of the quay wall on the outer harbour, Mike stopped near the small lighthouse. He checked around the blind side whilst the sea lapped in a gentle rise and fall along the upright stone.

"It's safe to talk out here," he said. "I would often reply to you from this point. On most maps, it looks like I'm in the sea which adds another element of confusion."

"Not a bad phone booth," said Hayley clearly enthralled by the beauty of her surroundings.

"I had to make a decision and take a risk. All that safety brief nonsense and journey planning was just to get your French friends to talk, everything is recorded too, but it helped me understand their motive and how best to deal with them."

With her nose tilted away from the sun, Skipper was upright and alert, scanning the endless horizon, her fur fluttering in the gentle on shore breeze.

"She loves it down here, it's as if she's picking up clues from distant lives and listening for sounds of distress. Who knows what goes on in the mind of a dog? Still, that's not quite as important as knowing what was going on in the mind of my bandstand subjects."

"So, everything I said, my intimate fears and private thoughts have been recorded?" choked Jan as quietly as she could manage. "How could you do that?"

"Necessity, a means to an end."

"That's what I said, *necessity,* sometimes you have to do things which means you break the law and become a criminal. So, don't be too harsh on Mikey," said Hayley in defence.

Mike smiled himself into a friendly nasal snorty laugh. "I'm not a criminal."

"You're not a *criminal?"* quipped Jan, unintentionally messing up the emphasis.

"Of course not, I did tell you what I was doing."

"So why were you taken away? Why were so many officers involved? Why has everything been seized?" Rambled Jan, tired and evidently quite delirious. In her heart, she knew the answers but at this milestone, she wanted it spelt out.

"Well, I'm a victim and a witness. That should take care of part one. The *Timestep* is a highly sensitive project commissioned and funded from within the security services, again, my little detective, I did mention that. Finally, if you really need total reassurance, it's too dangerous to leave a fully functioning working model out in the community. I mean you know what the crime rate is like."

Before he could finish, Jan had buried her head against Mike's square chest, where a small patch of his rugby shirt mopped up the rainstorm of relief.

"Jeez, we're making progress here, Mikey, the long arm of the law is finally loosening up."

Mike hugged his sisters tightly and gently jostled Jan. "Come on, Sis, don't cry; everything's sorted, look at this beautiful day, we need to be happy."

Jan sniffed and turned away scrabbling for the overused tissue in her pocket.

"I *am* happy," she wailed.

"Listen, Mikey, if that stuff is all so top secret, how come we know all about it? Surely your secret people will be wanting a word with us?"

"Know all about what?" he said attempting a serious face.

"Come on Mikey, you know, the *Timestep* thing. You told us how it all worked, gave us a ride in it."

"Timestep? is that a dance move? What do you think, Jan?"

She snuffled, hoping she'd done enough with the soaked tissue to stay on the right side of embarrassing.

"No evidence, who would believe us? But it *did* exist, we've been affected by it."

"Well, if you say so," said Mike, looking every bit the sun-drenched cormorant.

"You know, Mikey, something *has* happened, Jan's become almost human. You should have seen her yesterday a right spikey stone fish."

Optimism bubbled from the hot treacle sponge that bounced across the water like a warm wave of contentment. Areas once sealed and sensitive were being breached before Jan's eyes. If this is supposed to be normal, she thought, I could give it a go.

A small working boat chugged towards them and filled the air with soft music. The unmistakable and breathtakingly brilliant sound of 'We Are Sailing' drifted from the deck speaker of MV *In Dreams*.

"Hey that's Rod Stewart," smiled Jan.

"No, that's Dan," teased Mike. "Dan is a proper character, walked away from a well-paid job in Nottingham and followed his dream to live off the sea. If you speak to him, you'll realise it has definitely lived up to his expectations. He's one very happy fisherman and says the music puts his mind in the right place."

"That's brilliant, even awesome," said Jan continuing to smile as she waved at the tanned figure in shorts that swayed south to an unwritten destiny.

In her own dreams, part of Jan's heart had opened a tea room full of welcoming hot scones, she visualised washed wood floorboards and driftwood seats filled with nice people who would pay compliments and their bill. But in the kitchen, somewhere near the clotted cream fridge, a cold front had developed. It swirled through the narrow gap under the door and snapped with resentment around her ankles. Was Mike's revenge a step too far and unforgiveable? What would this moment have been like if their reunion had followed the plan brewed in some historical recess of Jan's mind, instead of this unforeseen enemy incursion? Before she could address the dilemma, there appeared to be a customer.

"It's been the strangest get-together, but what a full-on blast. Will you just look at us? Nearly forty years apart but you're still my lovely family. There aren't words, we just connect, don't we? This has got to be up there with the greatest of days. No, actually, it *is* the greatest day, you can only really be great in the moment, nothing else counts for much, least not in Straya. Makes you a bit sad though, all them years we've missed." Hayley pulled away from Mike and twirled with her arms loosely stretched.

"Ah, the wisdom of the eldest sister, everything you say sounds about right which is why we needn't start dwelling on the past, this feels good to me – you two being in my world. I don't know much about where all that time went, but let's just enjoy the now." Mike joined Hayley in a dreamy sort of twirl. "I hope my mates aren't watching this," he said, laughing himself breathless at a failed attempt to scoop Hayley off the ground.

Jan stepped out from behind the stripy blind that covered the tea room door, it opened to the tinkle of a little bell that commanded her to speak.

"Mike, I'm getting used to it but, did you have to change me, could we not have talked about it first? I could have said sorry and explained why I didn't play with you like I should have. I could have flogged myself publicly before you, to convey my message of regret and remorse. Why couldn't we have done it that way?"

"Stand by, take cover, she's had too much sun already, you'll get used to her one-woman crusades, Mikey."

"It's important, Mike, this is such a lovely moment, I just wish it could have been me standing here, instead of whoever this is. Why couldn't it just have been me?"

Mike straightened himself up, taking a moment to study the illuminated outline of his terracotta sister.

"The power we can harness is undisputed. We function on many levels, there's a lot of stuff out there being worked on, because the potential for change and travel is infinite."

"Are you seriously saying we *really* did visit another universe and pick up another one of us?" said Hayley landing in front of him.

"Well interestingly, what happened was, I used my trump card – my USB which activates the safety override. Need a contingency for unwanted visitors you understand, present company excepted. With the seats isolated, I could send the French boys travelling a short distance towards a bunch of strands in the happy spectrum – that's a simplified account of course. My sisters, on the other hand, had a short, deep power nap in their own world. The result of all this subterfuge meant that Pierre had mellowed, like a dog castrated, having toned down his evil intent to somewhere between accommodating and slightly opinionated. That's why he was subdued, he will brighten after a sleep, but he should be a lot less hard hearted than he once desired. Jean Paul took the same journey, but didn't have to go far to find his happy space. I think he was already on the fence about Pierre's dream to rule the world. Who knows? But, with the right intervention and a set of new friends on the continent, he may well do something useful with his life. The point is, they will have no memory of the experience because they went through the Proximity Centrifuge. And, like I said, the new you won't notice the difference or remember my wonderful contraption."

"But I *do* remember it, Mike." Jan held her hands to her chest as if waiting for the results at an award ceremony.

"Exactly!" chimed Mike with Hayley doubling over as she realised the significance.

"Jeez Jan, look how much good that power nap did you, this *is* you. The thawed-out version with a heart and some flaming feelings and dirt under your fingernails."

"You're not kidding me, are you?" Had Jan heard correctly was it her name they had called out? Could she dare to breathe?

"You are the same people, the same sisters I strapped into the seats, thankfully. Why wouldn't you be?"

"Mike, Mike, Mike, Mike..." her voice trailed into the stripes on his shirt as she attempted to hug the life out of him. This connection between siblings had grown in strength and purpose in spite of itself.

"I just need to say sorry, Mike; I'm really sorry." Jan spoke from the sheltered platform she occupied near his armpit. "I wish I'd done more to help you and include you when we were kids, it makes me very sad to think of you all alone. Playing and thinking all by yourself." Without interruption she rambled on. "I regret that, I know what it's like, I've seen the detrimental effect it has on kids that aren't helped and encouraged."

Mike started up with his snorty laugh pulling Jan from under his wing. "Now listen here, Sis, are you trying to tell me I'm not a wonderful person?"

"No but..."

"But nothing; if the me standing here is all *your* fault then thank you, you have made me a rather nice chap if you don't mind me saying. I certainly don't have any regrets. Maybe it was the sight of you two getting on with life that pushed me on, or maybe I just *liked* being on my own. Gave me time to build and imagine and create. Whatever it was that brought us to this day, I can't fault it and you certainly don't need to be sorry, not on my watch."

With a whimper and too many sniffs to ignore, Jan was firmly crying into the soggy fabric of the kindest man she had ever met, who happened to be related, in fact it was her clever little brother of whom she was extremely proud.

Having launched with a fanfare of flames and glory the sun had now settled into her journey across the sky, she was pale and yellow and lovely.

Jan scraped a shoe across the loose grit and mumbled to be heard. "You two, I don't know, look at us our little family."

"Oh, don't be normal, Jan, I couldn't cope; we're all a bit bonkers you know," said Hayley as she organised Mike's free arm and fashioned it snuggly across her shoulder. "You know, even if I could have changed, I wouldn't have bothered. I mean you can't top this can you? Yeah and before you go on about it, I know I have rather blotted the old copy book, but look what it's given us; you can't deny the prize."

Jan let the message travel to her brain and settle in an appropriate corner before she felt able to respond.

"If you ever repeat this, I may have to flatten you both, but I *do* accept that you had good intent, so let's just leave it like that," said Jan trying hard not to smile. It was retirement day two, the heavy drapes of duty and restraint were lifting into the gods, the stage now set for her to improvise and enjoy whatever this live show had to offer.

"We're just people, people with a history and some mystery, it's who we are. I wouldn't trade this moment for anything. In fact, I reckon I should join the Edith Piaf fan club because, *I Regret Nothing,*" laughed Hayley.

Jan bounced on marshmallow shoes as an easy-going, slightly scruffy woman began to emerge. She didn't much care to know the time either which set her off in a cross-legged fit of the giggles with hands fanning pointlessly in front of her face.

"Now what's the flippin' matter?" Hayley stepped aside, to get the full picture. "Did you tickle her, Mikey?"

"Not yet," he said. "What an amazing discovery you two are. Of course, I am taller than the pair of you now and I can see me having a lot of fun from up here."

As Mevagissey tinkled into life with the rich symphony of a harbour town, the Elliot family were ready to sleep.

"Right girls, lovely as this is, we all need to rest and then later, I can give you the grand tour of my backyard. How does that sound?" The response was positive, if not a little muted so Mike guided his sleepy sisters back along the quay as Skipper snuffled in the piles of netting and fish boxes along her familiar route.

"I live just up there," he said pointing an abstract finger towards the hillside where assorted cottages clung together to admire the view. "You can both crash at mine, Helen won't mind."

"Helen?" cried Jan and Hayley more together than expected.

"Yes, my wife. Boy, there's a lot of catching up to do isn't there?"

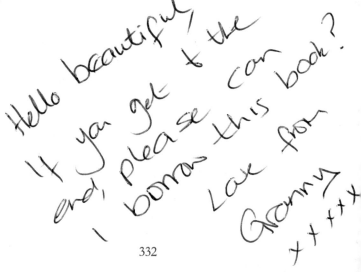

Hello beautiful, If you get to the end, please can I borrow this book? Lox from Granny x x x x x

About the Author

Sandy Fish lives in the West Country with her important people and a few cats who believe they are important too.

She has worked in local radio, circus, stage and very small screen before heading off to the private sector for a chapter of stability. Most recently she retired from Devon and Cornwall Police, the finest police force in the land… and by the sea.

When she can sit still long enough, she writes. When she can't sit still, she walks.

You can find her on Twitter @SandyFishWrites.

Blue Poppy Publishing

We hope you enjoyed this book. If you did, we know that Sandy would love to know your views. You can add a review to our website, www.bluepoppypublishing.co.uk or on sites like Goodreads and social media. Authors also love getting personal messages via social media, or you can email us at info@bluepoppypublishing.co.uk and we can pass it on.

Blue Poppy Publishing is a North Devon based publisher assisting local authors to self-publish their books and we have a range of other titles for everyone from children to adults in many genres. With more titles being added to our range every year there's bound to be something to suit your taste.